THE GRAY PALADIN

GARET DAVIDSON

BESET BY THE ABYSS PUBLISHING
GARETDAVIDSON.COM

U.S. City of Publication: Portland, Tennessee
Originally published in American English

ISBNs:
978-1-962495-00-4 - paperback, First Edition 2024
978-1-962495-01-1 - collector's edition hardback, 2024
978-1-962495-02-8 - eBook, First Edition 2024
978-1-962495-03-5 - audiobook, First Edition 2024

Library of Congress Control Number: 2024900411

Map by Garet Davidson
Cover art concept by Garet Davidson
Cover designs and interior formatting/layout by Miblart
Collector's Edition printed in China. Paperback printed in USA.

Beset by the Abyss Publishing, LLC
705 South Broadway
#1002
Portland, TN 37148
United States

Other books by Garet Davidson in the works but not yet available at the time of this publication:

PALADIN SERIES

Book Two: Chronicles of the Faithful
Book Three: The Dread One
Book Four: Rending the Heavens
Aberrations of the Abyss

FATE WEAVER SAGA

The Men Who Move Mountains
The Brothers Who Break Bonds
The Women Who Went to War
The Kraken and the Siren

THE PLANES WARS

Necromantic
The Second War for the Last Gate Key

STAND-ALONE WORKS

A Candle for the Darkness
Songs from the Suffering
A Collection of Short Stories and Poems

See the "Other Works" section at the end of this book for a primer on these forthcoming works.

TABLE OF CONTENTS

AUTHOR'S FOREWORD

As is my habit, I daydream and ask random questions requiring answers of a creative nature. Such was the origin of this story. Some notion took hold of me, which caused me to ask, what is a gray paladin? Thus began an exercise in answering that very question. I was not concerned with whether such an answer might exist already or whether one should exist. I had no idea at the time that it would birth this story.

I suppose that some seasons bring storms and others a renewed sense of life; others yet wistfulness—which I find autumn to bring in heaves. There is a magic that infuses certain moments of our lives yet is painfully absent in others.

Nostalgia resurrects portions of it, but it is a sorrow that the burdens of modern life often strip that modicum of joy so that it is less potent. Our hope and eagerness for the morrow wane amid such troubles as come our way until, finally, even the best among us is overwhelmed.

It is often in such dark places amid stillness and solitude that one's mind and spirit may find their wings or have them torn asunder, though sufficient grace might restore that which has been taken and thereby grant access to new heights. Such is the peculiar struggle of those seeking purpose in a world full of fellow aimless and wounded souls starving for the succor of seemingly unattainable satisfaction.

We hurry up to get to places we don't want to be, linger where we don't have any business, stare down as the world passes over and around us, and look everywhere but within to find ourselves. I do heartily wish that should you find yourself in such misery, make the most of it and spare no prayer in finding a way out—expend no tear in vain. You only have so many.

Myriad struggles and events assail us throughout our lives, and we may find ourselves beset by innumerable things outside our control. We soon find ourselves staring into the abyss. In response, we are tempted to lock ourselves away in towers, some of our own making, but if we are going to do so, they should at least become magical places that equip us for the journeys ahead.

May you reap a harvest in even the most difficult of times; may blessings, even if in disguise, be heaped upon you; may you kindle warmth from the fire within you in this cold, dark world; and may you remain true to who you are, no matter what threatens to pull you below. When you are beset by the Abyss, no matter the odds, keep the faith.

I want to give my special thanks to my wife and kids, who have endured the unintended consequences of the creative process. Many hours have been spent away from them to make this possible, and it would certainly not be possible without their encouragement, love, and understanding.

My deepest gratitude to those who endured my first draft and provided encouragement and meritorious feedback to guide the necessary touch-ups to finish this story stronger than it began. In no particular order, these kind souls are Samuel Tetterton, Brittany McElwee, Micah Wright, Atif Williams, Luke Bridgeman, Joel Bontrager, Corey Davidson, Rhonda Pepper, and James Murphy.

Sincerely,
Garet Davidson

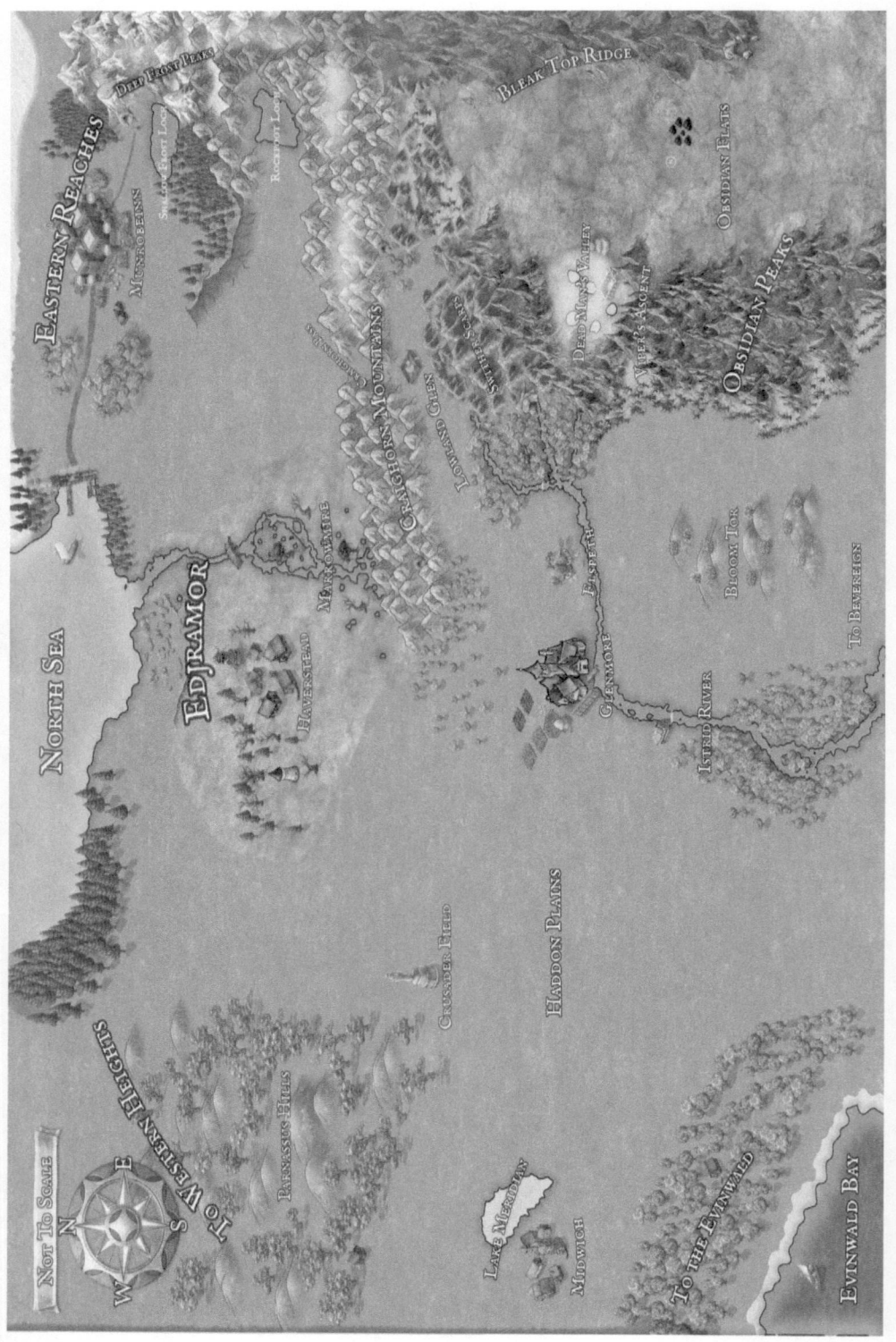

Men of conviction seldom survive the turning of the ages.

CHAPTER ONE

AN OUTSTRETCHED HAND

It came to pass that the Old Ones betrayed the celestial treaty, and the Abyss trespassed upon the world. Man was driven to madness and despair, except for the first man to pray to the Divines for help. They answered and sent him courage, so he became the first paladin. To this day, there has always been a paladin to seek the will of the Divines and bolster the will of man.

1

His cloaked figure darkened the doorway of the windmill's ruins. Three windmill blades, partially burnt and wholly forgotten, lay where they had fallen over thirty years ago; the fourth still hung, pointing toward the ground like an omen and guide for the living, for those in Edjramor are said to be destined for the dirt. The windmill's stonework was charred in places, and moss grew in others, and the inside was a maze filled in by the upper portions that had collapsed on that fateful day.

The rain poured, making the ground muddier by the moment, and its muck ascended skyward against the low-hanging, deep, dark clouds pouring out their wet wrath. The morning sun shone somewhere but not upon these blighted lands. A damp chill permeated everything, like death's touch, and in the center of the town below, last night's blood was being washed away.

She had been huddled against a broken beam and pile of stones, too afraid to move, shivering, crying, and praying all night in this unfamiliar, dangerous land. Her family's small caravan had been attacked by a lone fiend the night before as they passed through the abandoned town of Haverstead in Edjramor. She was sure she was the sole survivor, and she was sure that the fiend still wandered nearby.

He extended his hand, and she took it without hesitation.

"We must move quickly, child. Do not speak, and do not leave my side. Understand?" His voice was demanding but mellow.

She nodded, and they moved out from the windmill. Rather than descend the hill to the town where her family and horses lay slaughtered, they moved straight toward the closest stand of trees, which formed a more extensive, sparse wood line on the town's northern edge.

Their feet pattering among the puddles was the only sound that filled her world. Each step threatened to summon the fiend. The man, with eyes darting to and fro, led her through the thin stands of trees and eventually to the far side of the town, and they continued for a while before arriving at a lone stone tower in a clearing. Scanning around before daring to move further into the open, the man quietly studied their surroundings.

Whether the man's eyes tracked unseen dangers or fearful hesitation gripped him, she could not tell, neither could she tell how long they had walked; it was a blur. However long it was, they waited equally as long before moving into the open. The rain intensified, obscuring their surroundings behind its torrential wall.

He tugged her hand and began running toward the tower.

The tower itself was not impressive, at least not as towers are often thought to be. It was several stories tall but had relatively simple stonework, and the roof tiles looked decrepit. Neither torches nor candles illuminated its door or windows, but it offered sanctuary. A single large iron-reinforced wooden door stood as the portal to the tower's promise of safety.

The man placed a hand on the door and muttered quickly before throwing it open and pushing her inside. He slammed it closed and breathed a sigh of relief. She stood still while looking up at him. She had no idea where she was, and her family was gone. Nevertheless, a sliver of hope remained despite the grim events. She had been rescued, after all.

He looked into her eyes with his hooded cloak still drawn tight. His eyes focused upon hers, but he soon leaned back and looked away. He brought a hand to his mouth and took a quick, raspy breath followed by a slow sigh. Like a ghost from his past, something in that young girl's face demanded more of him.

He lifted the hood from his head and removed his cloak, hanging it on a nearby hook. The room was dark, but this would soon be remedied. He walked over, stoked the embers in the fireplace, and threw some twigs and a small log inside.

"Come, sit near the fire, little one. You must be chilled." He motioned to a small wooden stool near the hearth as he sat in a wooden chair. His voice was inviting, and she quickly did as he suggested. She walked over, sat, and wrapped her arms tightly around herself.

The sound of crackling wood, the fire's warmth, and its light began filling the room, but disquietude accompanied the comfort of the fire. She mainly sat still, aside from occasionally rubbing her hands together and fighting off the shivers. She regularly took a deep breath, followed by several small ones, to suppress crying in front of the stranger. The screams and sounds of the night before repeatedly played in her mind. She stared into the fire and shuddered, but when it seemed safe to steal a look at the man's face, she did so.

The man's hair was more gray than black, and his face was covered in stubble. He had tired but kind eyes set in a worn countenance. His lips were chapped; his hands looked capable, and his frame hinted at a constitution now gone.

After some time, she became bothered by the silence and felt compelled to say something. She desperately wanted to be distracted from her thoughts.

"Thank you for coming," she whispered, afraid to break the silence with words too loud.

"Yes." He nodded while staring into the flames.

"I wasn't sure you would . . . but I prayed all night, and you did," she added.

His eyes cut over to her with a snap. He rubbed his chin with a hand and shook his head. "Prayed all night?" he asked. "What exactly did you pray for?"

"That the Gray Paladin of Edjramor would come save me," she replied.

"I'm afraid the paladins are gone," he replied matter-of-factly.

"No," she responded with furrowed eyebrows. "It is known that the Gray Paladin still lives in Edjramor. I prayed for him to save me, and you came. You are the Gray Paladin of Edjramor."

"Child, do I look like a paladin to you?"

She shivered. "I don't know. I have never met one. I have heard stories, though."

"That's because they are nothing more than stories now. Do I look like what they say?" he asked.

"I have heard they shine, in or out of armor. Their presence inspires faith, hope, and love. A person need not be afraid when a paladin is nearby. And I am not so afraid now." Though weak and weary, the girl spoke with a precious certitude.

The man took several deep breaths while shaking his head and staring into the fire. He then brought his eyes to lock onto hers. "I am glad that you are not so afraid. I don't think you understand what others mean when speaking of the Gray Paladin. The name is an insult. Paladins are said to be pure and devoted, in stark contrast to the mire of this world. They stand out from it and radiate like you suggested. Do I seem anything of that sort?"

She studied his features and their surroundings more. The inside of the tower had little to look upon. There was nothing ornate or decorative. It was austere and had the fire not been going, everything and everyone would have looked like muted extensions of their surroundings. Even her fair skin melded into the room and blended into his dark skin.

"I think everything, including you, looks a bit gray. Seems fitting for the Gray Paladin, and I don't say that to give offense. And I prayed, and you came. Paladins are champions of the faithful who—"

"You don't know what paladins are," he interjected. He jabbed at the fire with a snap of his arm and tossed a dried peat brick inside.

"Then who are they?" she shot back with a faltering voice.

He shook his head in exasperation. "There are those who fight with flesh and blood . . ." He paused. "Then there are the paladins." He opened his mouth as if to add more, stopped, and shook his head again. "Maybe next time you should pray for safe travels, girl. Me coming was nothing but a coincidence. I wanted to take a walk, is all."

She stared at the floor, hurt by his remark. Her family had prayed for safe travels. Each day they set out, they prayed together. She reasoned that this was not a failure of the prayers; sometimes, bad things happened for reasons. "Maybe my prayer led to you wanting to go for a walk. Maybe that is why—"

"I doubt that is why I wanted to go out for a bit of a walk. I really doubt it," he stammered with a grimace.

"Why else would you go walking in such awful weather?" she quickly reasoned back.

He opened his mouth, raised a finger as he was prepared to make another sharp remark, and then said nothing. He looked back into the fire and stirred the embers. He tossed in another brick of peat.

"Doesn't mean I'm the Gray Paladin. It doesn't. Just means I wanted a walk, and when I discovered what had happened, I felt obligated to help."

She pulled her folded arms tighter to her body and looked away from him. Despite what he was saying, she was confident in what she believed. "How did you know I was in the windmill?" she asked.

"I checked to see if anyone had survived the attack. I saw your shoeprints leading between buildings and up the hill to it."

She looked at the fire, bit her lip, shuddered, and bent over her arms. She began rocking back and forth. "Did you see it?"

"See what?" he asked.

"That thing that attacked us?" she asked.

"The fiend? No. I think it is still nearby. We are safe here, though."

A noticeable shiver shook her body with a slight jump. "It was awful. It looked like a person but hunched over. On all fours. Long hair on its head and claws on its hands and feet. So many sharp teeth, rows of them—and it, I think it laughed—" She could not finish her sentence as she began to sob.

"Shh, shh, child. You are safe now. You are safe." He leaned forward and brought the palm of his hand to rest against his forehead. Her youthful face was ensconced by long, dark chestnut hair. If she was older than eleven, it was not by much. She was beautiful; she was innocent; she was sharp. If her fate had befallen anyone, it would not be fair, but it did happen to her. All its horror, purpose, and calamity had heaped itself upon her.

He cleared his throat and made an effort to speak kindly. "It was a pox fiend, a grotesque aberration of the Abyss. Given the tracks I found and your description, I'm sure of it. Did it ever touch you?"

She shook her head.

"Good, good." He paused and took a deep breath. "Their flesh develops sores and wounds which fester orange-looking pox-carrying pustules. If you catch the pox contagion, no one will be able to cure you. Apothecaries would not even so much as touch you. That contagion will always spread with contact, and that foul disease is alive. It can wait weeks or months for the opportune time to reveal itself."

"Why would it attack us?" she asked. She stared into the fire and soon found the aromas of the burning peat pleasant.

"Well, the fiend, or any abyssian for that matter, does not need reasons." He looked back into the fire and shifted in his chair. He stirred the embers once more.

"Did you see another man out there?" she asked.

"Another man?" He frowned briefly and shook his head.

"I am sure I saw another man at some point. Was a local man killed in the attack, too?"

"I doubt it. The town has been abandoned for many years. Thirty or more. Too dangerous. No one lives in these parts for fear of such things. If there was another man, he is likely dead along with everyone else."

She nodded slowly. "And what about my family? They need to be buried."

"Your family will have to wait. It is not safe now, and you need rest." He looked into her eyes for a moment before continuing. "We can consider that tomorrow. I have a bit of venison left, which I will warm, along with a few vegetables."

She nodded. He handed her a water bladder and went upstairs to prepare their food. The rest of the day was spent without exchanging many words. The girl would often doze off and wake with a startle. She was hesitant to truly lay down and rest despite her fatigue. She was emotionally drained, and her waking moments passed that day in a stupor. As the evening dragged on, she had repeated moments of disbelief.

Perhaps what happened last night did not happen? This is just a bad dream, she thought.

The man made a very simple pallet for her by laying a deerskin on the floor, and he gave her a small wool blanket. It was more than sufficient to keep her warm near the fire. After checking to ensure the door was secured, the man bluntly reassured her that he would be upstairs. She nodded and lay on the pallet. While staring into the fire, she eventually lost her fight against sleep, but she never slept deeply.

¶¶

The morning came with a languishing silence. The man sat about, mostly brooding or finding things to keep himself busy. He most preferred to whittle a piece of wood near the hearth idly, and once he had amassed a small pile of shavings, he would toss them inside. Occasionally, he would toss a small chunk of dried peat inside, and its aromatic, earthy smokiness would fill the air anew.

The girl brought up her family's burial more than once, and he reassured her he knew. She eventually understood that he had no interest in doing what she wanted, but she was not in a position to press the issue. She did not know what her future held, but she —at least for the moment— preferred the uncertainty over what *might* happen if she attempted to bury her family by herself. And she had to be honest with herself. She could not do that alone anyway.

She had espied every feature in the lowest room of the tower. She had heard stories of the paladins' towers. While she imagined such a place in her dreams as wonderfully decorated inside, she was disappointed with its reality. Nevertheless, she was optimistic that it held secrets. She wanted to venture beyond the lowest room and its two closets, one of which was the latrine.

As she wondered about the tower, she also realized that she did not know the man's actual name. She was still confident that he was the Gray Paladin of Edjramor, and that was name enough for her, but she knew he would not accept her referring to him as such. She looked over at him as he sat in his chair whittling, and she decided to introduce herself formally.

9

"By the way, sir. My name is Lilium. I am pleased to make your acquaintance."

His dagger stopped mid-whittle, leaving a long, thin strand of wood hanging. He turned, but his eyes stared beyond her.

"I am . . . I am Braeanor. Yes. I apologize for not introducing myself earlier, and I am pleased to make your acquaintance as well, though I wish it had been under better circumstances."

She nodded and smiled politely back.

"May I take a walk? Maybe just upstairs to stretch my legs?" she asked.

He looked at his hands and then nodded. "I suppose you have been cooped up, and it could be nice to do so. I'll tell you what. I will show you around a bit on the condition you don't ask about tending to your family again today."

Lilium bit her lip. "Okay," she muttered while trying hard to hide her disappointment.

"Ever been in a tower like this?" Braeanor asked with genuine curiosity in his voice.

"No," she softly smiled. "But my father was on the city council in Munrobeinn. I lived in the keep before we fled, but that old place was boring." Her curiosity was greater than she realized, and she felt a delightful rush of excitement.

"Oh, you lived in the keep? Were you tutored?" he asked.

"Yes, daily." She smiled politely. At the time, she didn't care about her parents' insistence on education. There were games to play and dreams to dream. Additionally, her lessons had always felt easy, and she knew her time could be better spent elsewhere. Now, she wished more than anything to spend hours bored to death under the expensive tutelage that once plagued her life.

"It shows. It is good to be educated in a world of fools," he said bluntly. "Well, I bet you hadn't seen a place like this, even if you had lived in the keep. And nowhere has this tower beat. Nowhere," he declared while lifting his hands to gesture around. He placed the piece of wood and dagger on the hearth and motioned her to follow him.

Lilium thought she saw a smile cross his face, and she was glad to see that Braeanor could be something other than grumpy. She noticed that the dagger looked unlike any she had ever seen, not that she had seen many. Its bright metal flowed and swirled.

They ascended the spiral stone staircase to the next floor. The tower was constructed so the staircase wrapped each subsequent floor, and a single door on their left would lead into a single room. Two people might fit side by side on the stairs or, in Lilium's mind, one paladin in armor.

Braeanor opened the second floor's door, and they stepped inside. It was a kitchen. There was a fire pit with roasting pans, pots, and a large skewer that could be rotated. There was a metal rack across the top for the pans. A table against the wall had knives and spoons of all shapes and sizes. There was a small, empty, square ꝏꝏꝏꝏꝏꝏꝏ above a shelf which held vegetables. No other food was in sight.

Lilium walked over to another door within the room and opened it, and she observed a small pantry with empty shelves. She closed the door back and looked at Braeanor with expectation, signaling she was content to move along. Her eyes scanned the room again as she exited.

They went up to the next floor. "This is the library," he spoke with a tone hinting at disappointment.

There were four simple wooden chairs along the room's perimeter facing inward, each accompanied by a small stand that held a candle and bookrest. There were no shelves, and the ceiling appeared higher than she would have guessed before entering the room. A large round candelabra hung from the center of the ceiling; its lit candles burnt gently, but no wax dripped.

Up against the farthest wall from the door, a dark blue velvet curtain with faded gold embroidery hung forlornly over yet another fireplace. She walked up and pushed the curtain aside, expecting to see a tower window; instead, she saw a dark, empty cavity about an arm's length in depth. There were no books in sight, which was very different from what she expected from a library.

"What's this for?" she inquired.

Braeanor stood staring at a section of wall between two chairs, and he did not acknowledge her. His hands were brought to his mouth, and his fingers covered his lips. His mouth was moving, but she could not hear him saying anything.

"Braeanor?" she asked.

He coughed to clear his throat. "Hmm?" He turned towards her, realizing he had missed something.

"What's this for?" she asked again.

"Well, books," he replied. He spoke as though it should have been apparent.

"Seems odd to put them behind curtains. And where are all the books?" She walked over to the only interior door and opened it, but this too, similar to the kitchen's below, only opened to reveal a small empty closet.

"Yes. The books." He lifted a hand toward the curtained alcove and hesitated with it outstretched. He then let it drop back to his side. "Well, seems I have none presently."

"I see that, but I guess what I'm really asking is how can you call this a library. A library without books. It can't really be called a library, can it? And why four chairs and stands if only you live here?"

He bit his tongue and cut his eyes away from her while grimacing. "Maybe more people used to come to this tower? Maybe it once had books? Maybe we should be done with this little tour then?"

"No, no, I'm sorry. It's nice and all, just not what I think of when I think of a library. Didn't mean anything by it." She turned while looking over the room to ensure she had not missed something.

"Right, well. Shall we?" Again, he motioned out the door and upward.

The next room, the fourth floor, contained racks for weapons and armor, as well as two large locked chests. A stone forge, anvil, whetstone wheel, and other implements occupied about half the room. A larger window with a wooden shutter was right over the forge. Spotting another door on this floor, she walked over and opened it. To her disappointment, it was yet again another empty closet.

"This is the last floor, as you can plainly see. I know it isn't much without weapons, armor, and such. Obviously, in a bit of disuse." Braeanor was disinterested in the room, and Lilium could see that he was becoming bothered by something.

As Lilium spoke, she made a concerted effort to sound impressed. "Yes, but it is nice. I can imagine the hard work and the heat from the forge. This was the center of much grand toil before your adventures, I imagine." Her eyes were wide as thoughts of what might have happened in that room flew about her mind.

"If you say so," he replied bluntly. "Tour is over. Let's head back down."

"What's that ladder go to?" she inquired while pointing up to the hatch in the ceiling above a wooden ladder against the wall.

"It's access to the roof for repairs. Come along now," he motioned. They went back to the first floor.

As she reentered that room, she felt its coziness. Perhaps it was merely its strange familiarity. She had not been in the tower for more than one day, and most of it was spent in that room. It *had* become familiar, and it *was* cozy. As she stepped across the room, she felt a creak in the floor beneath the rug in the center. She had not noticed this before.

She knelt and began to lift the corner of the rug. As she began to pull it back, one of Braeanor's feet emerged into view and onto the rug.

"What do you think you are doing?" he boomed. His tone was harsh and unapologetic; his furrowed eyes revealed that he was not asking a question but was making a point that what she was doing was unacceptable.

"I just—I just thought I heard the creaking of wood, and the floor is made of stone and—"

"And what? Just gonna have a look? Just do what you want inside my home, then? No consideration of whether you should ask first?" His eyes pierced Lilium's, and she was quick to look away.

She stood without a word and returned to the stool where she had been accustomed to staying. Her world had gotten a little bigger for a much-needed moment, and now she was back to reality. She was in her corner of the world again, a place without the loving help of family and enveloped by the irritable trappings of the man who saved her.

The day finished much like the evening before. She ate a little and then once again fought sleep. She was not as dreadfully tired, and her mind felt more relaxed. Perhaps because Braeanor did not want her snooping under the rug, he made himself a pallet downstairs for the evening.

CHAPTER TWO

CAUGHT IN THE GRAY

. . . And the light dawned upon the face of man, and there was no sickness or death for a time. The Godhead made themselves known unto man as the Divines, and so they communed by faith. But the Dread One set his face against mankind, and the age of peace gave way to one of sorrow, despair, and horror. Mankind cried out, and the Divines heard and took pity upon them . . .

1

The sun was not far from lifting its eyes over the horizon and gracing the rest of the world with its light when Lilium struggled in her sleep. Words, some half-spoken and others stammering out whole rose from her pallet.

"Mother! Father! No!"

She was seeing it all over again. Her mind had been trying to sort it all out since she had been in the tower. It was now coming back to her, all too vividly.

The unknown man stood in their path, obscured in darkness and just beyond the reach of their torches and lanterns. Traveling at night was unsafe, but her family had hoped to make good time and reach the Western Heights. Most of all, they did not want to spend another moment in Edjramor. As her father called out to the man, a shadow moved to their right, and the man was gone when they looked back.

The fiend launched itself upon them. The stable keeper's throat was ripped out, spewing blood upon her mother before anyone could make sense of what was happening. Her mother was pulled off the wagon and dragged out of the torchlight and into the darkness screaming; by the time her father was off the wagon with his sword, the creature was upon him. It had knocked him down and was over him, trying its hardest to bite his face. Her father tried to push it off and struggled, twisting, turning, and cursing in vain before shouting, "Run! Get help!"

The horses reared, squealed, and jerked at the wagon while her eyes remained fixed upon that fiend and all its horror. She was dazed, unable to look away until her cousin pushed her off the wagon and shouted, "Go!"

She ran until she found the windmill, not looking back despite the screams and haunting cackling that filled the air. Again and again, this played in her dream. Again and again, she sought a different ending. Again and again to no avail. Again, and again and again—

"Girl! Wake up now, wake!" Braeanor yelled.

Startled, disoriented, and with wet eyes, clammy hands, and profuse sweating, she found herself leaned up from her pallet and cradled in his arms. She looked upward in confusion between the dream world and haunting reality.

"Shh, it was a dream. Was a dream. You are safe now," he reassured her.

"It was real. It really happened. Everyone is gone. I am alone," she began sobbing.

He held her but said nothing more.

Some words may mend the broken, but even the right words spoken at the wrong time can wound. Braeanor remained there, holding her gently as she cried back to sleep.

Later that morning, after she had eaten breakfast, Braeanor let Lilium know that it had stopped raining for once. In those days, it always rained. She was pleased to know he was intending to give her family a proper burial. She expressed her intent to accompany him, but he was unwilling for her to undertake such a grim enterprise.

She persisted and assured him she would stay back so she could not see all that had happened. He relented with significant reservations. Strong emotions can strike without notice, and emotions run roughshod over all judgment.

He laid out preconditions and made it known that she must retreat to the tower should they encounter the fiend. Under no circumstance was she to remain or intervene should it come after them. He would deal with it as best he could while she made haste to the tower.

With arrangements made and a simple spade in hand, they made their way out of the tower. He left the door slightly ajar to ensure she could enter the tower, and he then traced a similar path through the woods back toward the windmill. Once there, he surveyed the town from the edge of the woods rather than ascend the hill for fear of being too easily spotted from afar.

He was tense and uneasy about the matter but understood how this might provide some closure and comfort for Lilium. It had not been on his list of priorities. Despite this, he was trying to empathize.

She needed this. Surely, after two days, the creature has moved on to somewhere else, he reasoned.

With a measured gait and gaze, he made his way out of the woods with her following behind. They eased to the outer buildings of the town and scanned around corners until they worked their way to the town center. The carnage lay before them. Both horse-drawn wagons used by Lilium's family remained, but one was pulled farther ahead of the other; one horse had made a little distance as it tried to flee before being killed. Braeanor realized that only portions of Lilium's family remained.

As he surveyed the scene from his position of concealment, he observed a man standing at the back of another wagon pulled between two huts on the far side of the town square. The man was pushing something through what appeared to be a covered cage, and slobbering and snarling could be heard in the distance. A mahogany bay horse with a white patch above its eyes was tethered to the cart and shifted about anxiously.

He immediately recognized what was happening, who the man was, and what had befallen her family. Before he could plan his next steps, Lilium was already out in the open, speaking excitedly.

Averting her eyes from the carnage, she called out to the man, "Sir, sir! Did you trap the beast?" Shouting back at Braeanor, she continued, "It's the man. The one I saw that night. Look! He captured the fiend!"

Lilium was well out of Braeanor's reach. He could not seize her back to forcibly silence her, and her words were as the first volley of arrows loosed in battle. It was too late to stop what was in motion.

The man turned slowly in her direction while Braeanor commanded her to stop and get behind him. The man reached over and unlocked the cage, and he unbolted the iron door. Shouting something and pointing in their direction, the man stepped away from the cage. The very fiend from two nights before emerged.

Braeanor said, "Now you done it, girl! He's no trapper. Damn man is of the Abyss cult and has bound that fiend to himself!" He stepped into full view and waved toward the man. "Girl meant nothing! We were just heading back and will let you tend to your business."

"Ah, if it isn't the cowardly—what do they call you these days? Gray Paladin? I didn't think you would step out of that tower. What a pleasant surprise. The Abyss would raise an army to destroy you, and here I have the chance to claim you as my prize, single-handedly."

The man's pallid face and squalid clothing reeked an affinity for otherworldly things; despite this, the crimson robe did lend him a rakish quality. The fiend lurked up to the man's side.

The hair on its human-like head was long but matted and clumpy from smatterings of blood. Its wide gaping mouth reached ear to ear and revealed several rows of teeth, and viscous, red saliva slowly stretched and, after hanging for a moment, dripped to the ground. Wretched, twisted flesh covered its sinewy frame, though its stomach was full and distended. Long claws extended from each grasping hand and foot. It was hunched over, and its body twitched and trembled excitedly as it rested on its haunches. There were several clusters of orange pustules on its shoulders and back.

Braeanor said, "See, the thing is, we really weren't looking to interfere with whatever you are up to. We never saw you and are just going to walk on our way and let you be. Right girl?"

Lilium was petrified and did not speak. She looked straight ahead with eyes wide open at the nightmare opposite her and Braeanor. Her expression was pale, frozen terror.

"Well, this is too good of an opportunity to pass up Gray Paladin," he said mockingly. "You are so rarely out of that tower, and I'd much prefer being the one to kill the last paladin."

The man uttered something unpleasant and unnatural in a strange tongue, which caused the fiend to bristle and bellow a hideous, gurgling laugh. The cultist and the pox fiend walked across the square toward Braeanor and Lilium. Then the fiend began sprinting on all fours.

"Right then. Lilium, run to the tower and don't look back. Close the door behind you!"

Braeanor had already unfastened his cloak and threw it in the path of the charging fiend while simultaneously drawing his dagger from his waist. The fiend could not avoid the cloak as it had already begun its leap into Braeanor. He sidestepped the creature's outstretched, clawed hands and drove the dagger home into its right side with his left hand, setting it with a firm twist of his hips and the handle.

The creature screeched and hissed as it fell to the ground with the cloak around its head, writhing in pain as it clawed to free itself. Braeanor had two equal gut-wrenching realizations in the next moment; his dagger had been pulled from his grasp and remained embedded in the fiend, and Lilium was kneeling nearby praying.

"Divines, strike down this creature. May it be so," she repeated feverishly.

"Girl, go—get back to the tower!" Braeanor shouted.

The fiend was back on its feet and furious. Braeanor realized he would have to be on point with every step and move over the next few moments. He needed that dagger back to have a fighting chance; nothing else nearby looked close to being a suitable weapon.

Braeanor stepped back and anticipated its next jump. He rolled onto his back as he brought his arms up to shield his face and chest, and he placed his feet squarely in the fiend's chest mid-air. The creature was launched through the air toward the cultist, who had to dodge the soaring beast.

Braeanor used his momentum to roll backward into a standing position, and he turned to face his foes with a twist and hands up at the ready. He glanced over his left shoulder, and Lilium was still there praying, hands together and knees on the muddy ground.

"Lilium! I said—" he shouted before having to focus on his survival again.

The fiend was momentarily dazed, but the cultist was upon him. With his twisted dagger, the cultist stabbed repeatedly at Braeanor. As Braeanor blocked and parried the cultist's attacks, he answered with several punches and a solid knee strike. Braeanor briefly controlled the fight. He then realized the fiend was circling him—not for an opportunity to pounce him but to get Lilium without interference. The fiend cackled as it bound toward her.

Braeanor pushed the cultist hard enough so that he tumbled backward to the ground, and he then sprinted to Lilium and intercepted the pox fiend with a front kick to its unwounded left side. Its path was narrowly diverted to Lilium's left side by no more than an inch, but she did not flinch. Its momentum carried it forward, and it rolled several times. Braeanor rushed forward and kicked the creature's stomach before it was back on its feet. It retched and quickly vomited most of an undigested hand, but this did not slow it.

This time, the creature ascended effortlessly into Braeanor, sinking its hands onto his shoulders to hold its victim's head in place so it could bite his face or neck. Braeanor exclaimed and struggled under the claws digging into his shoulders. He pressed his forearms into the fiend's throat to keep its maw back. Noxious, warm smells and bits of flesh flung from its slobbering rows of snapping teeth.

With careful timing, Braeanor placed his right hand against the fiend's throat while using his right elbow to drive the creature's left arm upward. At this exact moment, he shifted his weight, stepped back, and, pulling the fiend off-balance while twisting with his hips, threw it off him. Braeanor winced as its claws tore free with it.

He then saw the cultist nearing out of the corner of his eye.

Braeanor faced the fiend and quickly repositioned himself between it and the cultist, ensuring his gaze appeared so focused on it that the cultist would believe he had the element of surprise. Braeanor counted on the creature jumping to bite and slash him without delay, and he was not disappointed.

With impeccable timing, Braeanor sidestepped while dropping to the ground and rolled away from the cultist's downward stab and the creature's leaping attack. The cultist's blow struck the air, but the pox fiend latched onto the cultist's throat while tearing at his chest. The cultist fell backward with the fiend still clinging to him.

From the ground, the cultist looked at the pox fiend and Braeanor with his remaining moments. He did not have enough throat left to mutter a final word, and he was gurgling blood. The pox fiend looked at its master with what might pass for regret. It then collapsed dead, having lost its master and source of binding to the world.

Braeanor felt his shoulders and grimaced. There was less blood than expected, but he must treat those wounds thoroughly. He then checked himself for signs of the orange pus, which would infect him with the pox contagion. He seemed to have avoided that. He was fine.

Lilium! he suddenly remembered with anger.

He spun around to face her, and she was still kneeling, repeating her prayer over and over. He shouted at her. "What you doing? You knew what you were supposed to be doing! You just going to kneel there and pray while all this fighting is going on around you!" His eyes began to lose their focus. Motioning around with his hands and pointing at her and in other directions, he continued. "You just gonna keep praying when your brothers are dying! They need you! This is not the time for prayer, get up and help! Fight! Get up and fight!"

Braeanor spun around and reached out with both hands. He then let his hands fall and dropped to his knees. He looked left and right and then raised his shaking right hand outward as if reaching for someone.

"Meliador . . ." He looked to his left and reached out, his voice now trembling. "Vesuvimorian, Tresiun!" He looked to his right. "Cresinor!" He began rocking back and forth. "No!" His speech then became quiet and mumbled as he spoke through tears. "I'm sorry, brothers. I'm sorry. If I had known. Forgive me. Wherever you are . . . forgive me."

Braeanor continued in this manner for some time. During this, Lilium approached his side and wrapped her arms around him as much as her stature would allow. His body trembled and occasionally would jolt with a renewed heave of crying. She remained there with him, her tears joining his.

After Braeanor regained his senses and composure, he approached the cultist's horse. From a distance, Lilium watched as he held a hand out and seemed to inspect the horse while talking. He then cut it free. The horse snorted and took a step towards Braeanor.

"No," Braeanor shouted at the horse. "Go west, just go west!"

The horse neighed and ran westerly.

He then tended to Lilium's family. He dug a single large grave and buried what remained. Braeanor found it difficult to explain the circumstances in a way that lessened the awful reality of it all, but there is no easy way to tell a girl that most of her family had been consumed by a pox fiend over the course of the last two days.

Braeanor tried his best to say words appropriate for the situation, but he struggled. He was ill-prepared emotionally, and he was spiritually bereft for the task of conducting something resembling a funeral for Lilium's family. Of course, he knew this before ever leaving the tower to do that very thing; he had just hoped that maybe it would all come back to him in the moment. He did make an effort to tell her he was sorry.

Lilium spoke quietly and gently once Braeanor had finished. Amid tears, she mostly expressed that she was sorry and missed them but was glad they were resting in the light of the Divines in Bright Haven.

They walked back to the tower. This time, Braeanor did not move along the outskirts of the town. Once inside the tower, Braeanor tended his wounds and prepared food for them, but neither felt particularly hungry. They were both drained, and they turned in early for the evening.

ⅢⅢⅢ

Braeanor tossed and turned in his sleep.

A shadowy figure emerged and stood before him; the dim light of the surroundings did not illuminate any distinguishing features.

Braeanor addressed the figure. "I brought your cloak and some clothes. Come back with me, brother."

The figure, hoarse and lacking any semblance of vitality, said,

"Has it ever bothered you . . . how many orphans there are? And that not even the Sisters who care for them are kept safe by the Divines?"

Braeanor said, "This is why we—"

"They whisper to me. They call me by name," the figure interrupted.

Braeanor replied, "Do not listen. Come, we will get through this together."

"Malcreus, they say. And they say you will forsake your name. Have you?" the figure asked.

Braeanor hesitated. "That is not your name."

"We were always outsiders, you and I. When you stop and think about it. One foot in other realms. We were just fighting the war on the losing side."

"No, we can still overcome. It is not over yet. We can rebuild. Come back with me, brother. We must not lose hope," Braeanor pleaded.

"Hope? That is the last and greatest evil gift of the Divines. They created us and blessed us . . . but what do they give us in our hour of need? We reach out, and they fill our hands with it. We eagerly look down with gratitude but . . . but they are empty." The figure looked at his own upturned hands and studied them. "They are empty. Join me. Stay here with me. We could do this together."

"Hope is something. This darkness will pass. Do not give in. Come back to Haverstead." Braeanor held his hand out for the figure to take.

"No. You can't take me alive anyway. The apostate must perish, remember?"

Disembodied voices, like a wind sneaking around the darkness, began chanting mockingly, "Kill, kill, kill the apostate."

Braeanor looked around for the source, but it was still just the two of them. "It's not too late. Come back with me. You are not beyond redemption. Please. I beg of you."

"He is already here. He has always been here. He calls out to me," the figure said.

"Who?" Braeanor asked.

"He who slumbers until the dark choir sings his praises. In a place of ice, but his house is not yet ready."

Braeanor awoke with a startle. He sat up and looked around the dark room. He then heard the latch of the tower door being jostled. It opened, and light flooded the room. A figure entered, but the light was too bright to see who it was.

"Do you remember me?" the man's voice boomed.

"Who are you!" Braeanor shouted back in surprise.

"I mend the broken. I heal the hurting. I give hope to the downtrodden. I encourage the brother. I am the true sword of the Divines!"

"No, no, no—" Braeanor repeated.

"I am Ildradath! Remember!" the light-cloaked figure commanded.

Sweating profusely, Braeanor awoke and shot to his feet. He put his back against a wall and felt the stonework. He dug his fingernails into the stone and scraped them against it until they hurt. He glanced around the room while his heart beat out of his chest. The room was dark, and the door was shut. After several minutes, he became convinced that he was awake this time and began to relax. He walked over to the hearth and stoked the embers.

Later that day, Lilium held the wooden bowl containing her meal in her lap. It was fuller than she expected. Even though she had not eaten much in the last two days, she had no appetite. Braeanor's insistence that she must eat something prevailed. She was too exhausted to say no, and her mind was numb. The twice-reheated stew waited patiently inside her bowl. She had long since stopped trying to understand how he could return from that barren kitchen with food.

Some have been known to experience a peculiar malady, a melancholy of the spirit and digestion. So, she was. Her heart was lost in a sea of dark thoughts, and her mind was straining for some glimmer of hope, some vessel that might draw near and rescue her. The rescue she sought was life restored to those she loved and to return to the way things were before, but this was impossible. Her thoughts listed between such futile longings and accepting things as they were.

In abject misery, she swirled the wooden spoon in the bowl and stirred its contents to see what things hid beneath.

The first thing to catch her eye was the potatoes. They were somewhat small and generally square. Some had peel stuck to them still, others partially so, and others yet none. The potato peels were a rich tan with brown spots all over. Their outside looked rough, but those pieces that had come off exposed a slippery, smooth underside.

Once in a while, she found a round potato. These were unusual, she thought. Why was this round unlike the others? It wasn't cut that way. Perhaps the stirring rubbed them so. Maybe these were the most abused potatoes, the ones most often smacked by the spoon and tossed against the inside of the pot when stirred.

The carrots were larger than she would have liked. Rather than pleasant, even, thinly sliced ones, they were chunky. She discovered more than one piece with a firm center, and she detested those. After all the time spent being heated and reheated, they still resisted. She liked the ones she could squish beneath her spoon.

The celery was thankfully diced small. She did not know what to do with celery. Sometimes, she loved it. Sometimes, she hated it. She was always told to eat it because it was good for her. She wasn't so sure of this, but it was a vegetable. She found celery quite a proud and arrogant vegetable, often too bold and unpleasant for what it actually offered.

The onions were a nice touch. The quartered petals of the onions were perhaps too large, but they had a great texture, neither too firm nor too soft. She enjoyed pressing them and seeing if their translucent form would float up and reemerge.

The chunks of venison were a saving grace. Although they were not seared in any way, they cooked up nicely. They were remarkably tender and greedy, too. Lilium could press and smoosh off a piece with her spoon and found that it had indeed held onto as much of the stew's seasonings and flavor as it could within itself. She dared a nibble, and it tasted remarkable. Therefore, she did not resent venison for its greediness; perhaps if celery had dared add to its flavor, she would appreciate it more.

The broth was quite rich. Its dark brown waters hid more than vegetables and meat. She was curious why she was not more perturbed by the broth. Had it been anywhere but her bowl, it would likely look disgusting. However, it was a marriage bed of the ordinary and the profound in her hand. Occasionally, a tear would fall in, and she found the small ripples a pleasant distraction.

In the stew's murky waters, herbs and seasoning floated and sunk like flotsam and jetsam. She wasn't sure which, in any case. She could never remember the difference. Had Braeanor intended to use as much as he did? Was everything cast out intentionally? Anything unintentionally? In her bowl alone, she had a bay leaf, a small sprig of rosemary and thyme, and other blessed seasonings that moved about in the wake of her spoon's swirling and twirling.

The soup was hot, and she appreciated the aroma wafting to her nose. The steaminess was encouraging, but she had been tricked many times before. It was meant to entice and fool one into eating too soon before adequately cooled. Many a meal had been ruined by an over-eager tongue being scalded by a meal biting back.

The bowl was hot in her hands. Its warmth radiated into her arms. The bowl felt well-made and had a nice wood grain. It was wonderfully polished, and the spoon was the bowl's equal. Her hands held the bowl with an occasional tremor, originating not from being chilled but rather a shiver of the soul.

She continued swirling her spoon around, straining to believe that some light might soon dawn upon her and provide some insight or comfort to her present distress. She listened to the spoon scrape against the inside of the bowl like it was trying to tell her something. She was not playing with her food. She was delaying as if it might keep the anxiety, sorrow, and terror at bay, but these ancient feelings were adept at clawing their way to the surface. They possess the power of inevitability in a world facing endless horror.

Perhaps in that bowl was a hidden morsel of comfort and hope if only she persisted in searching long enough. Her emptiness was not from hunger, and she worried that if she ate all of the stew, she would return to where she started. She would not even have the pleasant warmth of the bowl and its possibilities in her hands, but she would still be lost in her sea of despair, something from hidden depths waiting to pull her below.

Begrudgingly, she resigned herself and finished the stew, wiping tears that had not fallen into her bowl, and she stared into its emptied chasm. As her trembling hands clutched the bowl, the spoon rattled inside. What is hope in the face of the Abyss?

IV

Braeanor awoke the following day to see Lilium stoking the fire. She was entranced with the glow of the embers and the soft, small billows of smoke that occasionally arose as she moved them around.

"Good morning," Braeanor said as he left his pallet and moved to the chair near her.

"Hi," she responded. Her eyes did not leave the glow of the embers. She continued poking around while Braeanor sat silently. He realized that they were both fine with the silence, and he soon felt bothered by this fact. He began cycling through possible things to talk about, but each one seemed forced and awkward.

"I was wondering," she said with a long pause, during which Braeanor felt relief that she was breaking the silence. "I was wondering, why do such things exist? Why do such bad things happen?"

"Hmm," Braeanor grunted. He was surprised by the question, but it was one he might be able to answer. "Well, I can explain some of it, but I'm not sure there is a satisfying answer. You've read the *Oracles of Faith*?"

She nodded and turned toward him more.

"I know you have heard plenty of stories, and I can see you've been led in the worship of the Divines. You have shown you have faith. Unfortunately, over the ages, the true story of our world, of our existence, of our struggle, has been told and retold with inaccuracies—most are unintentional and arise through ignorance, while others are intentional and for gain or to empower the machinations of the Abyss cult.

"It has been easy to take the *Oracles of Faith* out of context, and because of that, I cannot assume that what you have been taught is correct. Moreover, there are some things which have simply not been recorded.

"Now consider for a moment the many stories of monsters you've heard. For example, flying serpents that breathe fire or men who can become wolves or bats and drink blood are based on certain truths. They are efforts to comprehend the actual monsters that lie beyond comprehension. The real story—the truth—is much more than things that go bump in the night.

"Nevertheless, from kings to commoners, all like stories of knights in shining armor slaying such things and rescuing the helpless. But these are mostly good political stories that inspire the lowly to trust in their rulers and warriors to protect them. Some stories are told to perpetuate a belief in a system of power designed to protect the weakest of them, and it inspires boys to grow up and become real fighting men even though they will most often die with little glory or reward.

"Such stories also ease the frailties of a ruler's pride and actual power, for they know that men are rarely capable of doing what needs to be done when the real shadows step into the light. Even bad rulers understand that the shadows of this world are great. Regrettably, many have a callous ambition to wield the true power of faith for their own gain.

"Many years ago, warriors arose who discovered the power of faith in fighting back the forces of the Abyss. Some of these warriors, or paladins, began as simple religious advisers to rulers. But paladins are not bought and sold and do not fight for kingdoms of men, even if they were to serve in their courts. They do not fight for land and tithe, nor title and hold. They fight for what is right and true and good for all people in service to the Divines. Their treasure is valor and honor through a life lived by faith. Their tools are not weapons and armor but their faith. They learn to wield their faith with purity, not Kadathian dynasty building.

"How I wish paladins were only pawns in the realms of men. That would be a much safer truth for all of us, but they are the mortals who dare wage war against the dark gods, the Old Ones, on behalf of the Divines. It is this purpose which united the Paladin Order."

"Is it still true," Lilium interjected, "that the Divines cannot fight the Old Ones themselves due to the Celestial Treaty? So, they use paladins?"

"Yes," Braeanor responded. "But to explain that, we must go further back. It is said that before time, there were countless ages of nothingness. A primordial confluence arose, which birthed the ancient gods—celestial beings not bound by time or any such limitation as we can conceive. Gradually, personalities and identities arose among them.

"Eventually, division erupted. Those given to the desire to create and unify became the Godhead, or as we call them now, the Divines. Those who were independent and driven by their whims became the Old Ones. There was turmoil, and it was clear there would be a war among them. But what happens when a god is struck down?

"Thus, two sides formed. The Divines held creation and harmony as the self-evident good, and this was the ideal nature of all existence—after all, they each had arisen, and that was good, was it not? They could use their power and essence to perpetuate this. They were truly one in purpose, favoring compassion and love and creation.

"The Old Ones held unfettered will and power as the self-evident good and only valid foundation of existence. They favored power and control and would not permit themselves to willingly submit to any other or even be considered equals. Eventually, one rose to prominence. Like the others, he has been called different names, but Dread One suffices. He acts as regent among those he has forcefully bowed to his will.

"A celestial treaty was made between the Divines and the Old Ones. They each arranged separate realms so that they remain eternally separate. They were never to enter the others' realm under any circumstance, but it was also devised that a middle realm, Kadath, should be created in which each could indirectly exert their influence through man to demonstrate the superiority of their respective being.

"But," Lilium once again interjected. "Shouldn't the Old Ones be punished for violating this? Is there not some reason the Divines do not simply destroy them?"

Braeanor nodded. "Yes. The Divines' nature is such that they will not and cannot violate their word. To do so would be to invalidate the very nature of their being. They could not be trusted. It would change everything. And, if they lost a direct fight with the Old Ones . . . it would be unimaginable for mankind. Once the treaty was agreed upon, this bound them. The Old Ones are not burdened with a violation of their word. It is in their nature to always do as it pleases them.

"So, Kadath was originally born as a battleground for celestial vindications in which neither side could take direct action. With the Old Ones' betrayal, our world and souls have been forced into a perpetual cycle of creation and destruction, life and death."

"But what of the gifts given to man?" Lilium inquired.

Braeanor slowly rubbed his palms together and stared into the fire before answering her. "You are learned, are you not? Tell me what you remember, beginning from the laying of the foundations."

"Okay," she replied. "It is said, in the beginning, the foundations were laid. The great mountain, Kadath, was placed in the sea of the cosmos by the Divines. In the unending darkness of its expanse, lights were placed to shine upon its glory. The Divines caused the mountain to be shaped, and their laborers formed its peaks and valleys and flat places. The Divines then wept for Kadath. They foresaw great tribulations, and the rivers, seas, and oceans were born.

"They gave pieces of themselves. Their hair became the grass and trees and crops. Their flesh and blood become all the living things, but their heart was used to fashion man. They placed their eyes within our hearts, for we needed to be able to see with our hearts. The Divines gave their ears to become our brains so we would act in accordance with their voice. Their tongue became our tongue so that we could speak with them. The Divines gave of their brain to be our eyes and soul so we could recognize what is right and to value the virtues and to seek their will. So, to this day, the Divines are without a body."

"May it be so," Braeanor added. "Though we were formed completely by the Divines, the Old Ones gifted man with a desire for power and authority. That is all. Giving is not within their nature, so much so, it has been said such an act weakens or drains them. They gave nothing of themselves to mankind, save these inclinations.

"The Divines' gifts were many and intended so man could live a good life and resist and fight the Old Ones' future treachery. The Old Ones' gift was to make man exploitable.

"They both agreed to make us mortal, for this would catalyze our choices. It is thought that the Old Ones believed it would compel man to accrue as much power and control over others in his lifetime as possible, no matter the cost, turning us against each other and away from the Divines and into their hands. The Divines believed it would create a sense of priority in which man would value the preciousness of fleeting life and live compassionately toward one another, our hearts longing to return to the Divines and abide with them in Bright Haven.

"And as has been said, the Divines and Old Ones both had agreed to take no direct action in the world and waited to see what would become of mankind. The Old Ones waited for thousands of years before breaking their word and setting their plans into motion. The Divines, as painful as it has been at times, have kept true to their word.

"This is why paladins and the prayers of the faithful are so important. Paladins endeavor to fulfill the will of Divines through their actions, and prayers are like invitations or even commands that permit the Divines to take action through the faithful. But the Divines are not required to act simply because we pray.

"The Old Ones had set about making their realm, the Abyss, and they made it ready for war against ours—to raise their abyssian army to assault us and drive our focus toward desperately exercising authority and power in selfish ways to survive. The Dread One orchestrated those dark acts of creation. Following the betrayal of the treaty and this trespass upon our world, he disappeared and entered a great slumber to recover the power he spent in readying for war, awaiting a great surge of dark power to awaken him to finish his plan of dominating our world by force and madness.

"In the meantime, the other Old Ones—in their own twisted way—nurture the Abyss and maintain its disorder and the assaults against us until that day arrives. It is said they do not even know where the Dread One slumbers, and even they fear rebelling against it.

"Paladins once appeared to be winning this war. In hubris, a paladin named Ildradath believed he could turn the tide once and for all and perhaps even end it. With the support of the paladin order, he dared enter the Abyss and led paladins on a crusade into the Old Ones' lands."

His face contorted through a mix of disgust and sadness.

"Unfortunately, the paladins were not prepared. Now, make no mistake. A mighty blow was dealt. A horrific artifact needed to awaken the Dread One from his slumber was taken. Yet, we learned other darker truths. In the end, only one other paladin and I emerged from the Abyss. The abyssians were on our heels, and we could not shut the portal before they emerged.

"The remaining paladins were summoned to fight and close the portal. For weeks straight, we fought there in that field. We struggled to push the abyssians back to close the portal device that Pythaganor had created.

"Once we finally managed to do so, Pythaganor was consumed in its closure. He was drawn into the Abyss, his final act of sacrifice for the Paladin Order. I was one of the few remaining paladins, and only myself and one other—the same one who survived and exited the Abyss with me—survived our wounds. But he stripped naked and walked off into the horizon. Madness had taken him.

"I am the last paladin, and the threat of the Dread One persists. He still slumbers, only to awaken one day." As Braeanor finished speaking, his head hung low.

Lilium stared into the embers, and she poked them idly. "You destroyed the artifact, though, right? It cannot be used anymore?"

"We tried. Much time was lost in the Abyss attempting it. It appears to be indestructible. The one time we believed we had, it reappeared on its dark podium. We then realized that we must take it with us and hide it away forever. It is hidden now, where only a paladin could find it. I will never divulge its location nor retrieve it."

"What became of the paladin who went mad?" Lilium asked.

"Him?" Braeanor questioned back. "I prefer to think of who he was. He was a good man. He was bright, the best swordsman, and had all the proper makings of a paladin. A tad too much pride, but his faith was an encouragement. Nevertheless, the Abyss can consume all, and whatever is left of him is no longer my brother. It was too much for him. He now resides deep in the southeast among the mountains. He lives there now, somewhere between madness and anger, an apostate."

"So, what are we going to do?" Lilium asked.

Braeanor looked at her incredulously. "What do you mean?"

"If it is as you say, then the war is not over. We must find a way to do more."

"Girl, I wish I could see things the way you do. I did at one time. I am not the same as I once was. I've seen the danger of pride. I am but one man, a single paladin. I cannot do this alone."

"I will help. I will go with you. I will do whatever I can," she insisted.

Braeanor smiled politely at her. "Sometimes, among even the most devout of paladins, it can be difficult to distinguish between meritorious faith and naivete."

She crossed her arms and turned her head away from him. "So, you plan to stay here and do nothing."

Braeanor said nothing and looked into the fire. "I don't know what else there is to do."

"What did the paladins of old do to find such answers? Surely, they prayed, and the Divines provided guidance?" she asked.

"Yes," he replied glumly.

"Have you tried?" she asked.

"I've said more prayers than you can imagine, and here I am." He leaned forward onto his knees, covering his face with his hands.

"Did you get answers?" she asked.

Braeanor exhaled sharply. He was getting frustrated by her incessant questioning. He envied the simplicity of how she looked at the situation, but she did not understand all that he had been through, all the prayers and tears spent over the years.

She persisted. "Is it possible that you got an answer but didn't like it? My father used to say that the thing you least want to do is the very thing you need to do most. Where you don't want to go is where you need to."

Braeanor felt anger welling up within himself. He quietly cautioned himself against any outburst. He was just frustrated that such a simple mind could discern the truth of the situation so plainly, but he was not ready for it even after all these years.

"Paladins can pray and receive special quests from the Divines. We have a room for such things. The Divines may provide an answer in the form of a quest the paladin is to undertake." Braeanor's stomach turned in knots, and he felt the urge to thwart her line of questioning and prodding. He decided he would tell her the most bitter of truths he learned during the crusade.

"There is a terrible truth you must know. When people, paladins or not, are killed by abyssians, their souls do not ascend to the light of the Divines. The Old Ones claim them, and their souls are imprisoned within the realm of the Abyss, where they fuel their ruinous powers. They are mere husks of their former selves, and they are the wells of energy intended to supply the dark artifact its power. I have seen these cages, innumerable and stretching as far into the distance of the Abyss as one can see."

Lilium's eyes had grown wide, and her eyebrows were raised. She was trying to understand the implications.

"I long to return to the Abyss to free as many as possible so that they may ascend and deprive the Old Ones of power, but I would not be able to find my way to them. I am sure of it. The Abyss is unlike anything you can imagine. And again, I remind you that I am but one paladin. There was a large force of us when we entered the Abyss all those years ago."

Her eyes were filled with tears. "Does this mean my family is—" She strained to keep from sobbing, but the tears flowed freely.

Braeanor only briefly looked at her before looking back at the fire. "I'm sorry. If I thought I could do something, if I had a way, I would return to the Abyss one final time, even knowing that my death there would seal my fate to be locked away there for all eternity, too. I would do it gladly for my brethren, for all the faithful."

They sat there, each trying to sort out their feelings. Braeanor looked at Lilium and recognized the despair within her soul, for it was his. He began to regret dashing her hope against the rocks. He had just created one more reason to hate himself. After some time, and with no further words exchanged, Braeanor ascended the stairs, leaving Lilium to cry alone.

Lilium mourned alone for much of the day until she eventually decided she did not want to be alone any longer, so she ascended the stairs until she made her way to the library. She noticed the door was slightly cracked. She placed her ear to the door and listened carefully. Braeanor's voice could be heard from within. He was talking, but there was no other voice. Cautiously, she nudged the door open by just a sliver more. She peered through the gap.

Braeanor was looking at the section of wall between the two chairs again. He stared at it and seemed to be peering at different stones on the wall. He was speaking things under his breath. She strained to hear what he was saying. She made out sounds like names, and then she heard a common phrase after each:

Doldatherin, I remember and honor you, for you were faithful to the end.

Cruxeorian, I remember and honor you, for you were faithful to the end.

Haptistrian, I remember and honor you, for you were faithful to the end.

Lintarrian, I remember and honor you, for you were faithful to the end.

Pendemarian, I remember and honor you, for you were faithful to the end.

Meliador, I remember and honor you, for you were faithful to the end.

Trinmach, I remember and honor you, for you were faithful to the end.

Grendalough, I remember and honor you, for you were faithful to the end.

Jochorian, I remember and honor you, for you were faithful to the end.

Athanasor, I remember and honor you, for you were faithful to the end.

Braeanor continued like this for another half hour. He worked his way from one part of a wall to another as though seeing something she could not. His voice wavered, and he stopped more than once to collect himself.

Lilium was curious but knew it was best for her not to disturb him. Whatever it was that he was doing, she would let him do so without her further intruding upon his privacy. She sat outside the door, her back against the cold stone. She leaned her head against the wall and began to remember her family.

Lilium began to cry as she remembered years gone by. She thought of special times playing with her father, like how they would hide from each other in the keep. They would take turns searching for and trying to catch the other. She remembered how she sometimes felt so scared playing with him—that he might suddenly jump out and catch her—even though nothing bad would happen when he did. She would only be snatched off her feet, tickled, maybe playfully tossed around. She wondered if the stairs upon which she sat had ever known laughter or the happy sprinting of feet up and down its length.

She thought of her mother and brushing each other's hair while talking about many things, of times cooking, or gathering around the dinner table. She recalled playing in the stable with her cousin and them getting into trouble for misbehaving at the dinner table. Her aunt and uncle were fun in ways it seemed her parents could not be. She missed all of her family. It was so unfair. She would give anything to see them again, to hear their laughs, to feel their embrace.

However, as she sat outside the library, she struggled to comprehend how her family was actually gone. She could not even take comfort in seeing them again in Bright Haven one day.

Was there no prayer that could change it? If she screamed to the Divines, would they hear? Would they pluck her loved ones out of the Abyss? Did they not know how cold this world of hers was, of the great suffering, of the misery straining each beat of her heart and clenched fist? She tapped the back of her head against the stone repeatedly with increasing force, hoping the physical pain might lessen what she felt inside.

Braeanor knelt in prayer inside the library but soon became prone. His left cheek pressed against the cold stone floor. He scraped the fingernails of his right hand against the stone as if clawing through them for an answer. He then slammed his fist. He began sobbing.

"Can you not feel my heart? How many years must I suffer? All I hear is silence. Won't you take me? End this. Do you not fix the broken? I am of no use. Is there no help for the hopeless? I'm sorry, brothers, I'm sorry. And what do you do, send a girl to tend to? Would you mock me, and to what end? I failed them all. I have failed everyone, and I will fail her too. Do you hear my prayers? Will you not answer me? All I see is darkness. Or is this your answer? Am I the mad one, still praying, crying out? Is Bright Haven too far for you to hear me? I have nothing left. Do not be cruel. Take me."

He moved a hand to cover his face. He wanted to sink into the floor, to disappear, to have never existed. That would have been best.

That would have been best for everyone. Instead, he had come to exist in two alternating states: melancholy and utter despair.

"What have I become?" he whispered out between sobbing breaths.

A champion of the faithful, a steward of the souls of men, lay on the floor as though his soul had been torn from him by the Divines out of spite and denied any hope of ascending to Bright Haven. He wondered whether he genuinely believed anymore and, given all that had transpired, whether his faith all those years ago had ever been real.

Hours later, Lilium carefully eased away from the door, returned downstairs, and took her place on the stool near the fireplace. She then grabbed the fire poker and began a new past-time of poking at embers and trying not to cry. She held her head in one of her hands upon a knee while her other hand played in the fireplace.

Together but apart, Lilium and Braeanor wept. This was but one of many days of abject sorrow, and each day promised the curse of another such day. They felt no reason to rise each morning and longed not to see the end of the day. They felt it would have been better had they never been born at all, and their prayers were sometimes pleas that the Divines might somehow change the past and make this true.

Despondency had joined Lilium and Braeanor in the tower to ensure that neither felt a moment of comfort, in or out of the other's presence. The seasons passed, spring giving way to summer, and summer ran its course unnoticed. The months passed with neither leaving the tower. With the passage of time, words were exchanged in equal measure to hope, and it was a most unpleasant time—one not to be recounted in detail by anyone lest it break them too. The awfulness of those days did reach a terminus, from which point this tale shall resume.

Lilium reclined against the stone hearth of the fireplace. The flames and the heat radiating from the stones warmed the right side of her body to the point of discomfort, but she rested there motionless, save for her eyes. At some point, her eyes traced shadows that danced upon the farthest wall.

As the hours passed, their forms changed quickly and then lingered, then fled again. Some shadows concerned her, however. They slowly crept across the ceiling and partially descended the wall where they perched, watching her. Slinking in and out of where the wall and ceiling intersected, they prowled under her watchful eyes. She knew that they knew she watched, yet they moved still.

They were not fearful of her, but she was increasingly alarmed by their presence. The longer she gazed at their movement and wanderings, the more she realized they would eventually descend the entirety of the wall and creep across the floor to take her away. She denied this at first as some figment of her imagination. It was preposterous to believe in the first, but as time passed, she came to believe that they were indeed conspiring against her.

She realized this presented a series of problems. For one, she could call out for Braeanor, but he was upstairs. She was not sure he would hear her. Additionally, there was no guarantee that he would get to her in time. She was confident the shadows would waste no time in descending upon her.

A second problem for her was whether she could outrun the shadows if she suddenly jumped up to flee. She felt that she might have some element of surprise in that the shadows may not know she was actually planning her escape. Perhaps they did not know she was aware of their intentions. Perhaps she could outrun them; if not, all would be lost.

The final problem was that of whether she should even try to escape them. Perhaps it was best to remain there and let what might happen come to pass. While it might not be pleasant, all her other pains would disappear.

Or would they? she wondered.

Perhaps the shadows would pull her into the Abyss for an eternity of additional torment. She would languish there, even worse than in life. No prospect of escape or hope of a new tomorrow. She would just become fuel for the Old Ones.

Just like my parents. Like all of my family, she thought.

But she would be with them again in some manner. They would be together for whatever happened next. Perhaps that was worth it. She was not sure. Her mind bounced back and forth between her options.

Shout for Braeanor. Flee the tower. Acquiesce to the shadows.

Her mind flashed across the options and cycled through them repeatedly. If she survived this encounter, could she ever learn to look forward to another day without those she loved? Could she dream of Bright Haven like she once had? Was Braeanor even alive further in the tower, wherever he was? Did it matter?

The shadows began moving faster. They swirled and danced, moving with delight at the thought of their soon-to-be prey. They would strike any moment now. Spontaneously, she decided to flee, her choice made unconsciously out of fear.

I can't move! she realized in dismay.

Her legs would not move. She could not lean forward to sit up. She was frozen in place! Instinctively, she called out for help, but no sound was made.

I can't talk! she realized in shock.

Her voice was gone. Only a lump of fear sat notched in her throat. Her tongue, jaw, and lungs could not coordinate to shout or utter a sound.

I can't breathe! she then realized as she spiraled towards doom.

Imprisoned in panic, she lay against the hearth. Her mind raced through the innumerable thoughts of the horror that awaited her and the desperate pleas she might offer to be saved from each one. With every passing moment, she made an effort to do something: speak, cry out, breathe, stand. There was nothing. She was just a wretch leaning against what would soon be her headstone, already in the grip of death, its shadows coming to claim her soul for the Abyss.

Divines, help! her soul cried out, uttering a final plea to Bright Haven that, somehow, she might be rescued from her predicament. Without further thought, she gave one more effort to call for help.

"Braeanor!" she audibly cried out. Her voice, loud though with a stilted crack, rose through the tower.

Braeanor heard the fear in her voice, and he did not delay coming to her. She remained motionless and watched the movement of the shadows while hoping Braeanor was coming.

"Lilium! What's wrong?" he called out.

"I'm here. By the fire!"

Braeanor hurried off the steps and into the center of the room while scanning all around for the danger. He saw nothing.

"The shadows, Braeanor. There! Look, they are coming for me!"

He turned to where her eyes were focused. There was nothing. Only the darkness of an unlit room. He stared for a while to ensure that he was not discounting the source of her fear, but he was soon assured there was nothing.

"I see nothing," he stated bluntly.

"They were there—the shadows. I have been watching them. They were moving, and I knew they were going to come after me if I hadn't called for you." Her eyes were fixed upon where the shadows had been.

Braeanor followed her eyes and stared intently where she was, but still, he saw nothing. He took a deep breath and tried to sound like he believed her. "Do you see them now, anywhere in this room?"

Lilium looked around. She could no longer find them. "No, they are gone." She began to realize how she might appear in Braeanor's eyes. She suddenly felt embarrassed. "It must have been the light of the fireplace playing with my eyes and a lack of sleep."

"Maybe so, Lilium. But the fire died out hours ago before I had even gone upstairs. Though unlikely in this tower, it could have been an apparition sent by Orph the Acedious, or . . ." His voice trailed off.

She leaned forward and looked to her right. There were only the faintest of embers left. The hearth was cold to the touch. She stared blankly at the scene before her.

"Or I've lost my mind," she softly answered back to Braeanor. Her eyes scanned the hearth and the floor and then Braeanor. Braeanor averted his eyes.

She was trying hard to understand what was happening. She realized she had been in the tower too long. She was trapped there. She needed to get out of it. To go somewhere. To do something, for to stay would be death by madness.

"I'm leaving." Lilium stood and walked towards the door.

"What? No, where would you go?" He crossed his arms tight against his chest.

"Anywhere but here." Lilium walked past him, and he turned. He was taken aback by her episode with the shadows. Now, she was bent on walking off on her own. Surely, she had gone mad.

Braeanor shook his head and then pointed at her. "Alone? You won't make it. Stay and–"

"I am alone! I'd rather die out there than slowly die here. Do you want me to stay so someone can be miserable with you?" Lilium opened the door and marched outside into a cold rain falling from dark clouds; Braeanor followed.

"Just stop and listen. I'll take you somewhere safe." Braeanor motioned towards the tower, but Lilium's back was turned to him. "Give me time to get my things together."

She turned and lifted her hands into the air before letting them fall back to her sides in exasperation. "Maybe it's not safety I'm worried about! I lost my family! It—it doesn't seem real. But it is. And I've seen those things. I know the creatures of the Abyss are real. They are out there. And what are we doing? Locked inside a tower. You don't want to do anything about it. I have no life here. So, I'll go try somewhere else, and if I die, so be it."

His stern face cracked a grin at the thought of how ridiculous her sudden plan was. "That's a right lovely plan. Go where? And to die? That's a certainty. You wouldn't last a second against any abyssian."

"The man who could won't. He's too busy crying and doing nothing, and I won't last another second here—with a paladin."

Braeanor's eyes grew wide with surprise at her comment and then narrowed into a squint as he strained to comprehend why she was being this way. "That's some tongue on you, girl! The Divines no longer answer my prayers. Do you think I haven't tried? And you don't understand all I've lost, what I've been through! They were family to me and much more than that, too. We—"

"I lost family too!" Lilium shouted.

Braeanor raised a hand and pointed a finger while stepping closer. "It's not the same. My brothers were—"

"Not the same? You can stay and continue to wait for death like a coward but I'm leaving." Lilium waved one of her hands as if to dismiss Braeanor as she turned and began to walk away.

Braeanor stepped forward and grabbed her right arm. Lilium yanked and twisted in response, but he squeezed tighter, unwilling for her to go off on her own.

"Let go of me!" she yelled.

"No! Come back inside," he demanded.

She tried to jerk away again. "Let go of me!"

He squeezed tighter. "Come back–"

Lilium turned towards him and smacked him in the face with her left hand. Braeanor let go and looked into her eyes in a daze. She stared right back at him defiantly. "I told you to let go."

He stared back at her momentarily in silence before walking over to the tower, where he sat on the grass with his back to the stone. He cradled his forehead with his hands. Lilium rubbed her arm where he had grabbed her.

"I'm too far gone . . . I have been ensnared by the Abyss. It will pull me below. I will be fed into its maw soon enough . . . an apostate . . . too lost to be saved." He looked up but stared blankly through Lilium as if she was not standing across from him.

Lilium looked at the ground and shifted uneasily. "We should pray, Braeanor." Her voice was soft and carried desperation. She did not like what just happened, and she wanted things to be better.

"Do not waste your prayers on me." He shook his head. "I am unworthy of redemption."

Lilium stood rubbing her arm while pursing her lips, trying to decide whether she should share a story or just break down. The rain pouring off the top of the tower fell into puddles, bringing back memories of when Braeanor rescued her and how loud and dangerous the splashing puddles sounded. She took a breath and began without further thought.

"I once heard my mother and father. I was supposed to be in bed, but they had been arguing louder than ever. I snuck to their door. I then heard my father apologizing. He said, 'if we can't embody the love of the Divines in our marriage, we are unworthy of Bright Haven.' Mother said, 'Redemption is for the unworthy.' She always had a way of saying things that made you feel like they were the truest words in all the world.

"She then said, 'We will right this. We will do better. Not just for us, but for her.' And all the fear I had just felt, all the worry about what might happen . . . just went away. I snuck back to bed. And even though I didn't know what the next day would be like—I knew it would be fine because—because . . ." Tears began to stream as she struggled to finish, but the rain was quick to wash them away. "Because they would be there with me."

Braeanor looked at her crying, and he brought a hand to cover his face as he, too, began to weep. "It is hard without those we love, isn't it?"

She nodded without making eye contact.

"Would you come sit next to me?" He patted the ground beside himself. Without a word spoken, she walked over and sat. Sitting against the tower, they were just out of reach of the falling rain.

After collecting himself, Braeanor spoke. "I'm sorry, and you are right. I should be doing more, but it's not like I haven't been praying all these years. I've asked them to send me an answer. To guide me. They do not answer or send for me. What am I to do? So, I have stayed here, hoping they would just take me to Bright Haven or let me die. Just as you say."

Lilium wiped her eyes with her wet sleeve, but it did not do much to help. "What would you do? If the choice was yours."

"Without a doubt, I'd reenter the Abyss and free as many of my brethren as possible before I am killed. I would rather they ascend to Bright Haven, and I stay below for eternity than to know for all eternity what they endure and have been deprived of by the Old Ones."

Lilium shifted uncomfortably with her back against the stone tower while she continued to hold her right arm. She was growing increasingly cold. "Would you free others too?"

"Of course. Everyone I could."

"What is stopping you from just doing it?" she asked.

"I need a paladin to quickly shut the portal behind me. Regardless, I would not be able to find anyone easily once I was inside the Abyss. It is unimaginably difficult to navigate. I might die before finding them."

Lilium bit her lip, unsure that she really wanted to know the answer to what she was about to ask. "What's it like? The Abyss?"

Braeanor shuddered, and Lilium noticed.

"The Abyss?" he asked rhetorically to buy himself a moment to wrap his mind around where to begin. "There are dark nebulous clouds set against a deep, blood-orange sky. The black edges of the clouds break the sky into devious portions, like separate domains at war. There is no sun, but a gibbous moon-like thing hangs and illuminates without motion. It emits a faint purple light, dissipating not far from its source. I'd call the place dark, but there was enough light to see, as when the sun has become eclipsed.

"The clouds belch thunder of a sort, but it is akin to the rumblings of a beast driven mad from hunger. Its anger shoots forth occasionally as fiery flashes; the lightning cascades outward where it pleases. We never saw the lightning strike the ground, but if we could help it, neither would we.

"It was occasionally firm but had the character of flesh. The ground had a slight give to it and a dark pink and pustulent color and texture, which made one loath to walk upon it. Putrescent, gooey strings of some primordial ooze would cling to our boots with each step. A smell wafted around us–the smell of carrion and rot, but occasionally, a strong whiff of something good would shoot through our senses—like the Abyss wanted to keep us from growing accustomed to its malodorous vapors.

"There was a presence which stalked us, yet we never laid eyes on the exact source. Feeling spying eyes gazing upon us, we'd occasionally turn and look around, expecting to see *it* standing there—whatever *it* was. We'd see fiends and horrors on occasion, but the paranoia was ever present no matter how many things we slew. It would make the hair stand on the back of your neck. You felt that every shadow hid slithering, skittering, skulking things. All these things looked upon us as strange, unwelcome visitors.

"As if such things were not enough to dismay and disorient, the Abyss sometimes makes no sense. Least not as we can comprehend. We soon learned that our perspectives were unique and local, so those who split off or became separated entered some other 'side' of where we were. I recall running through a gorge or canyon and seeing what appeared to be brothers running in the same direction, but they were running on the cliff face. I was alarmed but could tell they were not falling. After a sharp turn, we lost sight of them, and when we made it to the other side, they were running straight toward us.

"They were now on the ground with us, but they recounted their alarm at seeing us running on the cliff face. Each of us had the same account of the others, the same general location, but very different perspectives and places with respect to the others. It was enough to test one's wits and resolve.

"All these years later, I still wonder whether the Abyss is so maddening and nonsensical to those fiends who dwell there. Does it seem normal to them, and can they comprehend it? Can they find their way around easily? Do they call it home? Surely, they must. But if so, does our world seem disordered and frenzied to them? Or do they covet its simplicity and safety. Do they long for its sounds of ordered nature and beauty? No, no, surely not.

"I know that they do not share what we call 'love', ' purity', 'charity' or 'peace'. They are only driven by selfish ambitions or fear of the Dread One. They cooperate with fellow abyssians for personal gain and pleasure while in submission to the Old Ones' schemes. They enjoy the toll they exact upon us and each other, but it is known that abyssians will fight and even kill fellow abyssians. But I suppose that is no different than our kind. We are not so dissimilar in our impure and corrupted natures."

He paused and looked at Lilium's face, and she looked back at him. Lilium was intrigued by the account. It was beyond her imagination and terrifying. No matter how much she grasped the idea of the Abyss, it did not make sense.

Braeanor could see her eyes alight with fascination. "Child, do not think so long about it that you become obsessed. It consumes all. We have lost good paladins who were given to divination and the study of the workings of the Abyss. Such men were able to peer into it, but the secrets of its nature are elusive and costly. Staring too long at the Abyss is costly, and most of those good men lost their sanity. Madness consumed them, and most took their own lives.

"Only one paladin, Pythaganor, seemed to endure its nature. He was a brilliant man whose giftedness in the sciences and his great faith allowed him to reason out certain facets of the Abyss. He argued the Abyss could just as well be called 'the Tesseractian realm.' He argued there was an order, but it was ordered differently. He had begun working out a theory on understanding it and describing a method of how we might effectively traverse that wicked place. He is the one who created the portal device so that we could enter the Abyss.

"He is also the one who designed and built these towers, the paladinariums, and ways to store many things within—well, within things in a way that should not be possible. These towers are protected by great workings of faith, or as some might call it, faith magics. This tower holds secrets accessible only to paladins. It is like a safe house for traveling paladins on their quests."

"I was sure there was something special about this tower, though it does not seem so grand or magical," Lilium replied.

"Yes, well, that is a big part of the magic which protects it. You must be a paladin to get the intended use out of these towers. The towers know us by name. They remember us. A paladin must simply place their hands on the door; recite their name; then enter. The tower then makes itself available for their service. Others cannot.

"We, emboldened by faith but under the influence of pride, entered the Abyss without having truly solved the issue of navigating it. We presumed that it would be like taking a stroll with nearly a hundred paladins, and we would have all the time we needed. We were wrong and paid for it. Our prayers often could not reach the Divines, and our powers were greatly limited. Rather than turn back, we pressed on. We were fortunate to free some souls and escape with the artifact."

Lilium dwelled upon all these things in the silence that followed Braeanor's recounting. She then spoke. "Could you make a map or a compass for the Abyss? My father had these when we fled. You could use these to guide you."

"No," Braeanor responded bluntly.

Lilium crossed her arms and shivered. "Is that something the Divines could do? To make something to guide you?"

Braeanor began to shoot out another blunt "no" but stopped just as soon as he started, for the simple truth hit him. The Divines could perhaps do so. The Divines would often bless them with angelician silver for forging as a reward for completing a quest. It was feasible. It was possible. He could ask for that reward if they grace him with a quest. He could not imagine how such a compass or map or way to speak with the Divines from the Abyss would function, but the Divines could. He need not understand such things.

"What you say may be right. It is possible to pray, and perhaps the Divines may bless me with such a way of navigating the Abyss."

"What is next then?" she asked, relieved that things may be about to get interesting.

He brought a hand to his chin and rubbed it. "We pray."

Even when faint, hope is both a guiding light and a mighty tailwind.

CHAPTER THREE

THE QUEST

. . . Therefore, the faithful must champion the Divines, for they are a bulwark and an everlasting fortress against the tides of the Abyss. Though the sea rage and sky fall and Abyss consume, they shall endure. For the paladin is the hope of mankind, the true sword of the Divines, and it is in him they must trust . . .

1

Braeanor and Lilium walked back inside. Lilium sat on her stool and began wondering what might come next and what part she might play. She understood she was not a paladin and likely could not go on any quest—assuming the Divines even granted one. Nevertheless, she saw that Braeanor's spirits were lifted, and she felt optimistic.

Lilium rubbed her left arm and scratched at it through her shirt sleeve. She realized it had become uncomfortable, and she was unsure why. Braeanor had grabbed her other arm, and it still hurt. She watched Braeanor throw some more wood into the fireplace and set some kindling amongst it. He worked at starting the fire with a piece of flint and iron. She moved closer to the hearth.

"So, what's next," she inquired. "Will we pray here?"

"I'll get us some dry clothes, and we will warm up. I think it would be good to get a bit of rest and eat and get our minds right. Praying for a quest is not your everyday prayer."

Lilium shivered and scooted even closer to the hearth. "How so?"

Braeanor did not answer her immediately as he focused on the fire. He nearly lit the fire half a dozen times, but it resisted his efforts. He gently blew air over the kindling as he worked.

"Praying for a quest is a serious matter. While all prayers are communication with the Divines, and all people, especially paladins, are subject to the providences of the Divines, quest prayer is the very enlistment of a paladin's life in service to a special task of the Divines' choosing." Braeanor stopped speaking to tend the small growing flames.

He finally got the fire going. He tended it briefly and put more kindling on it to ensure it would keep. He added a dried brick of peat to it as well. He then sat and faced Lilium, who continued to scratch at her left arm.

He continued, "Praying for a quest includes a petition for a particular quest reward, which, if reasonable and the Divines find appropriate–will grant. When seeking a quest, self-serving purposes have no place in a paladin's heart. It must fit the will of the Divines."

"So, the prayer is both submission to the Divines' will and a petition?" Lilium asked as she tried to put the idea into her own words.

"Yes. And this is not so unusual for prayer. Supplication and submission are the very heart of genuine prayer. The Divines are mighty and able to grant to paladins without measure, and they long to hear from their faithful. We are blessed to have such benevolence in Bright Haven, but . . ." Braeanor paused. His eyes cut left, and he frowned. "As you know, the Divines are not obligated to answer prayers, including quest prayers. We may struggle with their purposes or that they know what is best."

"Yes, but I have prayed many times before and received an answer in some way, though not always as I expected," Lilium spoke with the confidence of her personal experiences.

The fire was going strong now, casting its light and warmth upon Braeanor and Lilium. Lilium was beginning to sweat.

"Then all we have to do is . . ." Lilium's voice trailed off. She rubbed her face with a hand and swallowed hard. Her throat was dry, and she was not feeling well. "Pray. We must to just pray then and they will. They are kind."

Braeanor noticed the sweat on her forehead and how her speech had become jumbled. "Are you okay, Lilium?"

She closed her eyes and continued scratching her arm. The room was slowly spinning, and dark figures filled her blurred vision. Voices from an unseen place began whispering to her, and she could feel the presence of their unseen malevolence drawing closer. Her head nodded as if she was falling asleep, and she leaned to her left until, finally, she slumped into the floor.

"Lilium!" Braeanor hurried to her side and began looking her over as she lay squirming on the floor. She occasionally jerked as though reeling back from something. Her face was pale and sweaty. He noticed redness on the left side of her neck and, upon carefully pulling back her collar to reveal more of her shoulder, confirmed his fear.

He shot to his feet with clenched fists and drew tight his jaw, nearly biting his tongue. He grabbed the stool Lilium had been sitting on, spun, and hurled it at the wall with a shout. "Pox Contagion!" It splintered and broke apart.

He pulled out his dagger and carefully cut Lilium's left sleeve open to expose as much of the infection as possible. He needed to locate the source of it, the most infected area. He carefully picked and laid the flaps apart as he cut her long sleeve in half to ensure he did not touch her skin.

Once the sleeve was cut in half, he noticed that the side of her arm just above her elbow appeared to be the worst. Her infected skin had pustules of varying sizes. Her skin was red and inflamed, and the small, infected pustules contained an orangish fluid. Some of them wept. The blackish-red skin at the center was likely the spot of exposure to the pox fiend.

Lilium began convulsing.

He moved to her other side, away from the pox-covered arm, and knelt. He carefully pulled her onto his thighs and cradled her head and body, letting her infected arm fall limp toward the floor and away from him. Her convulsions did not make it easy to hold her tightly.

Braeanor closed his eyes and bowed his head.

"Divines, hear my prayer. Please heal Lilium—do not let this take her."

He opened his eyes to see how she was doing. He could still feel her small convulsions, and there was no diminishing of infection. An answered prayer of healing from the Divines did not always work immediately, but it was very quick when curing pox contagion. Because of its deadly nature, it was always purged decisively, and she was not healed.

He looked up at the ceiling, yelled, and began to rock back and forth as hot tears formed in the corners of his eyes. He held her tighter as she continued to convulse in his lap.

"Did you save her for this? Was it not enough to let her family be taken? I was perfectly miserable alone, and you sent her to die in my arms! To remind me that I am accursed? I hadn't forgotten! Haven't enough died in my arms! Have I not lost enough? She doesn't deserve this! Do you mock me? Do you hate me? Do you want the Abyss to prevail? Take my life instead. Please. I'm ready."

Lilium was mumbling incoherently, spittle flung from her mouth, and her eyes had rolled back in her head.

No, no, no, he realized in a flash of insight. *This is not how a paladin prays.*

Braeanor steeled himself and began focusing on regaining his composure. He was acting in a way unbecoming of a paladin. He was praying from a place of fear and doubt—a place in which the Divines did not have the power to answer him. He needed to engage in bold, sincere prayer and could not let his emotions control his supplication. Yes, he was angry and had every reason to be so. However, he should be righteously angry at the Abyss, not the Divines. They did not cause this. Faith was a paladin's weapon, and he must wield it as he did in days of old.

He cleared his throat and looked at Lilium. "Please forgive me, Divines." He knew well that the most effective way for a paladin's prayer to heal was through laying hands on the ill, and the closer to the injury or illness, the better. He pulled her closer and tucked his left hand underneath her body, and reaching over with his right hand, he grabbed her left hand and pulled the infected arm onto her body. He then placed his right hand over the source of the infection, ensuring that he would now be exposed to the pox.

"Divines, from Bright Haven, you rule. You look upon us with compassion, and now, in our hour of need, I pray you pity us. Grace us with your healing touch. Cleanse us wholly of this contagion, and purge her memory of it, for you are able, and be glorified, for you are worthy. May it be so."

He continued to repeat this prayer over the course of the next hour, never ceasing. His eyes stayed closed, and he focused through every discomfort he experienced. His knees were in pain from the stone floor. His back was aching from holding himself upright. His chest and arms were tired from the constant exertion of embracing her tightly. The warm, oily oozing of the pus underneath his right hand made it so that he constantly had to readjust his slipping grip. Nevertheless, he persisted in prayer, undeterred by the delay in the Divines answering him.

Lilium coughed and heaved. She shook more intensely, and then her entire body went limp. She stopped breathing.

He opened his eyes and looked at her face. She was so youthful, but she was much stronger than what many might think at first glance. That would serve her well. "Thank you, Divines," he said as he gently rolled her onto her left side.

She let out a loud, raspy gasp and began retching before finally vomiting onto the floor. Braeanor held her close but leaned her over to ensure she got everything out and could breathe. She began to spit and wipe her mouth with a trembling hand while trying to sit up.

"Easy now, easy. You're okay." He helped get her upright and pulled a kerchief from his back pocket. He handed it to her.

She was confused, and her eyes scanned around to reorient herself as she wiped her mouth more. "What—what happened? I feel awful."

"You were exposed to contagion from the pox fiend, and it decided to emerge."

"Am I going to die?"

"You would have, but the Divines heard my prayers and saw fit to heal you. Do you remember anything of it?"

Lilium looked around as if trying to find a memory of it. "The last thing I remember is walking back inside. Will it come back?"

He inspected her left arm and visually verified that there was no remnant, and he did the same for his right hand as well. Every trace of it was gone, even that which had wept onto the floor.

"No, you are cured. Do not worry."

Lilium said, "You said nobody around could cure contagion."

"I believed it to be true. I assumed the Divines would not answer my prayers."

Braeanor looked at the floor and shook his head. He felt shame for how long he dwelt in his misery, but he was blessedly relieved to see the Divines working through his faith again. He felt a renewed sense of purpose.

They stepped outside again, and Lilium sipped water to rinse her mouth. Her stomach was in knots, but the fresh air was helping. Soon enough, her nausea subsided so she could drink some water.

They returned to the fireplace, and Braeanor cleaned the floor while Lilium rested. They relaxed for a time, ate a decent meal, and then headed for the prayer room without further delay.

¶¶

Once they had both ascended the upstairs ladder to reach the topmost room of the tower, Lilium took in her surroundings. The room had a much shorter ceiling height than other rooms in the tower. There were also no decorations of any sort, but there was a small, ornate chest. Its silvered metal was of an ornate floral pattern that wrapped the entire chest and overlaid blue velvet. The chest was no greater than a foot long by half a foot wide and deep. It sat on a raised pedestal with candles on each side. He lit those candles before explaining what the chest was.

"This is a Quest Chest. Catchy name, eh?" He winked at Lilium.

Lilium smiled and nodded. She supposed everything needed a name, but she wondered how much effort sometimes went into naming things. "I'm just wondering how you repair the roof from here."

Braeanor scrunched his eyes and recalled his words about where the ladder led. "Sorry for that." He said with a hint of embarrassment.

She smiled back at him. "I forgive you."

"This chest is yet another doing of paladin faith. It is a depository for a paladin's quest, if they successfully have one granted. A paladin seeking a quest, typically alone, comes here and prays fervently. We pray just in the middle of the floor across from this chest. Sometimes for days without stopping. Eventually, we get a sense of whether we have been granted a quest. We then check the chest to see if there is a small scroll.

"The scroll is the manifestation of the quest–its written embodiment– signifying that the paladin's quest has begun. The paladin has already accepted the quest as their prayers make it clear they intend to fulfill whatever the Divines see fit to give them. The necessary task or challenge is listed on that quest scroll, as well as anything of dire importance. Upon reading the quest scroll, the quest is impressed upon the paladin's heart so there can be no forgetting of what is required."

Lilium interjected questions while running her fingers across the ornate features of the chest. "But do paladins determine what they will do for the quest? Or do the Divines?"

"The Divines do. A paladin does not know what their quest will be, which is why a paladin should not undertake a quest lightheartedly. Paladins must complete the given quest to be granted the request of their prayer—the quest reward. This could be a blessing of some particular kind for armor or weapons. It could even be receiving actual Angelician ore to make new weapons and armor.

"So, paladins can request anything as a reward?" Lilium asked.

"Well, no, not anything. As the paladin prays, they make their desire known to the Divines. The Divines will determine whether it is something they are willing to grant. Because of this, a paladin can be confident that if they have received a quest, then their desired reward will be granted, even though the quest scroll does not mention the reward.

"Once the quest is complete, the paladin may return to this chest to retrieve the physical object if such were the petition of their prayer. Blessings are bestowed on simple scrolls to be read over the item to be blessed, and many paladins would conduct their own personal ceremony when blessing something."

"So then, if you pray and ask for some way to navigate the Abyss, if you are granted a quest, we will know you will get it once it is complete?" Lilium asked, looking for reassurance that she understood how it all worked.

Braeanor nodded.

"How do we begin?" she asked.

"We?" he responded.

"Yes, I'd like to pray too," she replied emphatically.

"Very well." Braeanor nodded. "You find a spot over there and make yourself comfortable, and I will be here. And then we pray sincerely until it is done. I would ask that you specifically pray the Divines would grant me a quest."

Lilium nodded and sat where Braeanor had indicated.

Braeanor made himself comfortable in a kneeling position. He closed his eyes. He began praying silently for guidance. He prayed for discernment. He prayed the Divines would bless him and that they would answer his prayers. He wanted to be called back to service. He had not forsaken his paladin oath, but he had lost his way. He confessed his weakness, his failure, and his insecurities. He cried silently. He thought through his years of strife and heartache. He felt a stirring of passion which he hadn't felt for far too long. He was now ready to do whatever was required.

Lilium prayed diligently. She was accustomed to prayer and had prayed daily and often throughout her life, but she was not used to such lengths of prayer. She found herself increasingly fighting distracting thoughts as she prayed. It was proving to be more difficult than she first imagined.

Morning gave way to noon, and afternoon and evening also came and went.

In the dark hours of the night, when strange things tend to catch our attention and bid us to fear, Braeanor felt an unfamiliar sense of peace. His prayer had been answered much sooner than anticipated.

He opened his eyes slowly. His knees ached, and his eyes had to readjust to the room. He wiped his eyes and looked around to get his bearings. He had been so entranced in prayer it was as though he had been transported elsewhere. He was back now and needed to reorient to his surroundings. He stood cautiously to ensure he did not lose balance, and he stretched his arms outward and shook his legs a bit to get blood flowing again.

Lilium had fallen asleep behind him. He let out a cough, and she stirred and awoke, realizing Braeanor was doing something. She sat upright and rubbed the sleep from her eyes. "What is it?"

Braeanor walked over to the Quest Chest without answering her. He stood there staring intently at it. He was confident that his prayer had been answered, but what if it had not? He recalled the numerous times in his life he had been here before. He wondered whether he had ever taken opening the chest for granted in the past. He would come forward and open it without hesitation. It had been so long—too long, and it had become a weird ritual he was rediscovering.

Without further hesitation, he opened it. There was a scroll smaller than the size of the palm of his hand inside. He took it, quickly broke the wax seal which bore the initial of his name, unrolled it, and began reading. His hands began to tremble, and he then rolled it up and placed it into a pocket. He exhaled deeply. He turned to see Lilium looking expectantly.

"What is it?" she inquired.

Braeanor looked at her. His eyes lacked all enthusiasm, and his tone was somber. "The Divines have granted me a quest."

"Well, what is the quest?" she asked excitedly.

"I am to judge Malcreus," he said bluntly.

Lilium raised her eyebrows in curiosity, and she detected the disappointment in his voice. "Who is that?"

"The paladin driven to madness, the apostate," he replied.

"The one who had survived the Abyss with you?" Lilium asked.

"Yes, the same."

"Oh." Lilium's words were the last spoken for several moments, and as they hung in the air, she realized she did not want to be left behind or cast aside. "When do we leave?"

Braeanor's eyes locked onto hers as if to verify that she was the one who had spoken and was serious about what she said. "We? Are you so sure?"

"Yes, I do not want to be left here alone. I will help however I can. I will not get in your way." Lilium bit the inside of her lip. She was bracing for him to deny her.

"So, you would join me? This quest will require sacrifice. No telling what dangers we will face, but dangers are certain. I would not make you go, but according to this scroll, you are to accompany me. I would have the decision be yours."

"It says so?" she asked.

"Yes, but you must understand that this will require everything of us. This is no child's play or simple task. The Divines do not ever promise that a quest will be successful. That falls to the paladin."

"Yes." Lilium nodded with confidence. "I am ready to go and do my part, no matter what that requires of me."

Braeanor, with his emotionless face, nodded. He was sure she was speaking from the heart. He could not tell her the fullness of the likely outcome of the quest. If he did, he was sure she would not go, and the Divines ordained that she must go. His mind raced. In the end, concealing things would not protect her.

Still, what the quest scroll read did not make complete sense to him. He would need to meditate upon it, but he could not burden her with knowing what it spoke. The simplest and most obvious fact was that he was to judge Malcreus. That was enough for now; he would entrust the remainder to faithful obedience.

ⅢⅢ

Braeanor packed several bags for the quest. Lilium had asked to help, but he politely declined. She was very eager to help in some way. As she had no belongings whatsoever to pack, she was entirely dependent upon Braeanor packing supplies for her as well. She was at least grateful that he had managed to find a change of clothes for her. They were not flattering and perhaps a bit boyish, but they were clean.

They ate a hearty meal, and Braeanor did a final inspection of what he had packed. Lilium stood nearby and watched as he rummaged through the half-dozen bags.

"Those bags look empty," she remarked.

"Yes, they look that way."

"Are they?" she asked quickly.

He paused and looked at her. "No." He then resumed rummaging through them to ensure everything was accounted for.

"Shouldn't you have your sword and armor on?"

He shook his head but did not look at her, "No."

"Can I look through the bags?"

"No."

"Can you only say 'no?'"

He grinned at her. "No. I know it doesn't seem like it, but these bags hold much more than it appears, and thankfully, they will not feel like it. And it looks like everything is in order. Do you have any last questions before we get going?"

"No," she said emphatically with a smirk. She took advantage of her chance to use the word back at him.

"Good," he smirked. He then bundled the bags together and fastened them to easily carry them on his back as one large pack.

As they exited the tower, Braeanor grabbed the shovel, which had been leaning against the wall near the door. Braeanor shut the door with a hard pull. He then pushed on it in an effort to open it. It would not budge.

"What's the shovel for?" Lilium inquired.

"I will need to attend to some unfinished business inside Haverstead. I should have tended to the pox fiend and the cultist rather than leaving them unburied in the city."

"They do not deserve a proper burial," Lilium shot back, eyes glaring.

"You are right. They deserve to be purged with fire and removed from the town in accordance with the Oracles. Do you remember what I am referring to?" Braeanor eyed Lilium as she thought.

She shrugged. "I don't think so."

"And they shall be as burnt offerings of purification unto the Divines. For the

horror of their bodies should not corrupt the sight of the faithful nor the ground upon which they tread and labor. Therefore by burning they shall be cleansed and by burning shall they be removed. Thereafter, the ashes shall be brought into a heap and carefully removed with—"

"Oh," Lilium interjected. "I recall now. I don't know how I could have forgotten

with how exciting that passage was."

"Yes, well. Regardless, the passage is important and serves the faithful well. Pay attention, and you will see it in practice."

Braeanor and Lilium walked to where the pox fiend and cultist still lay. The pox fiend was more putrid in appearance but had not decayed as much as might be expected. Scavengers had partially consumed the cultist. Thankfully, neither body smelled as bad as anticipated. The ground around them had turned black.

Braeanor placed thatch, dried brush, and pieces of wood on the ground and built a sizeable pallet before pulling the cultist onto it. He searched a nearby house and returned with a small blanket, which he used to wrap the pox fiend's ankles with so that he did not have to touch it. He then pulled it onto the pallet as well. He tossed several small, wooden pieces of furniture on top and then ignited it all with a piece of flint and his dagger.

While the fire blazed, they moved upwind and outside the town. Braeanor dug a decent-sized hole and searched until he found a wheelbarrow. After the fire had died out, he shoveled the ashes into the wheelbarrow, along with the dirt just underneath. He then dumped this into the hole. After making several trips doing such, he covered the hole with some of the clean dirt nearby. He tamped it and then laid his hands on it. He prayed for the Divines to purify the ground and the town.

He then oriented himself to the south, adjusted the straps of the bags now on his back, and began walking with Lilium toward Glenmore.

"So, all our quest requires is that we judge Malcreus? And can I assume that means kill him?" Lilium inquired.

Braeanor looked over at her. He was surprised to see her assume some agency and investment in the quest as if it was just as much hers as his.

"At the heart of the quest, yes, that is all, but if he genuinely repents, I will not have to kill him. And you must understand that a paladin's quest is usually much more than a singular task. Quests are often filled with many providences, for the Divines ordain much which must come to pass. And we do not know what those things are—nor why. There may also be trials of virtue."

"Providences? Are those like coincidences?"

"To those without discernment, they would appear so, but they are things which are intended. While the Abyss will try at every opportunity to stop our quest, the Divines will be using us to set many things in motion and to counter the works of the Abyss, and sometimes, it isn't clear why these things are so. We must keep our eyes and hearts open to opportunities to serve the will of the Divines in the coming days. With time, you will come to understand."

Lilium nodded. "And trials of virtue?"

Braeanor looked over at Lilium. "Have you not heard such in reference to any of the faithful?"

Lilium looked at Braeanor. "I have heard that there may be tests, yes. These are opportunities to prove who we are. That we are living as those who trust in the Divines and not the Old Ones."

"Yes, you have it right. Paladins refer to these as trials of virtue, though these are not usually elaborate or difficult ordeals. You may pass or fail a trial of virtue without ever knowing it was one. This makes them all the more difficult. Therefore, a paladin must be on guard in all they do and say, and much like with providences, be ready to respond to situations in a way that would serve the Divines. These trials involve the tarnishing influences and vices which correspond with the Old Ones."

"So, for example, we might have to act with humility rather than pride in some situation?"

"Yes, and so on with all the virtues."

They continued onward, and after only two days, Lilium was already weary from traveling. She had not been used to crossing such distances on foot. While the distance was not as great as she first thought, she underestimated the emotional toll and inconveniences. She longed for a bath somewhere–anywhere–and some pleasant distractions. Walking, a small meal, more walking, and uncomfortable sleep were her new schedule.

However, there were some things Lilium appreciated. The scenery was becoming less dreary, and the weather was becoming brighter and more pleasant. On more than one occasion, she had spotted a hawk overhead and a bounding fox. Several deer had been grazing ahead, and when they spotted the pair heading their way, they dashed west towards Parnassus Hills. She enjoyed seeing the Craighorn Mountains in the distance. As they walked south, the mountains slowly drew closer on the eastern horizon, reminding her of home.

Braeanor was eager to find a suitable horse to aid them on their quest. He understood that this quest was going to be demanding. Lilium needed to endure it, and it was obvious to him that she was already exhausted from this much walking on foot. Besides this, it was proper for a paladin to have a steed.

Lilium and Braeanor's conversations were generally casual and shallow as they moved towards Glenmore. While they occasionally talked, Lilium felt Braeanor was preoccupied with other thoughts. Nevertheless, important changes required attention.

"Braeanor," Lilium spoke hesitantly. Her cheeks were red with embarrassment. "I . . . I am bleeding."

Braeanor's eyes widened with concern. "Where are you hurt?" He quickly looked her over to find the source. "What's happened?"

"No," she said while holding her hands upright to motion for Braeanor to stop. "I am coming of age, I think."

Braeanor furrowed his brows and looked at her with puzzlement. "I am not sure I understand."

She looked at the ground and regretted how things had been made more awkward by Braeanor's apparent cluelessness on the matter. She mumbled, "Becoming a woman."

Braeanor's eyes widened even more, and he felt himself shrink back. He was not equipped to handle this. He saw that she seemed ashamed, and moreover, it was not lost on him that she did not have her mother to help her navigate this.

"Oh, well. Yes, I see. Well." He cleared his throat. "Becoming a woman is nothing to be ashamed about."

Braeanor rummaged through one of the packs and found a square of cloth, which he folded. He handed it to her. "I must be honest that I am unsure how to best help. One of the innkeepers in Glenmore, Kellina, is an acquaintance of mine and a good woman. She will put us up for the night and can help. I also plan to get a horse while we are there."

Lilium's eyes lit up, and she was immediately distracted by the notion of getting a horse. She loved horses and missed riding them. Though the memory was bittersweet, she recalled fondly riding with her father.

"Really? That's great!" she said with beaming eyes.

As they continued walking south, Lilium found herself increasingly bored and curious. Braeanor appeared perfectly content to walk silently, staring at the ground or looking around.

"How did you become a paladin?" Lilium inquired.

Braeanor rubbed his chin several times. He had not thought about it for so long. He could not forget the story, but the passage of time and the onset of innumerable burdens made it distant and foreign.

"I was around your age actually, which, thinking about it, would have been more than two hundred or so years ago. I–"

"What!" she exclaimed.

"Yes, paladins do not age like others. Our faith draws us much closer to the very source of life, the Divines, much like it was in the beginning, and they bless us—or perhaps burden us—with many extra years of service here."

"You are an old man," Lilium remarked decisively.

"Well . . ." He furrowed his eyebrows as he looked over at her. "Yes, I've been around for a while, for better and worse.

"As I was saying, I lived in Midwich, a small town southwest of Haverstead or northeast of the Evinwald—whichever is easier for you as a point of reference. It had a chapel devoted to the Divines. There was a group of Sisters there who cared for orphans such as myself, and their matron had taken me in years ago when I was an infant. I had become a precocious boy who was as good at getting into trouble as getting out of it. Generally, I was a waste of youth. I would hardly try at any task given me if it did not interest me, and I was perfectly content doing nothing but playing.

"I had become quite smitten over a girl named Hartrice. She was a beautiful girl with an infectious laugh. I can't tell you how often I would do anything and everything I could to impress that girl."

Lilium giggled. It seemed unbelievable to her that Braeanor could have such feelings for another, which made it that much more adorable.

"It was a beautiful day. I remember walking around looking for her. I didn't know where she had run off to. Next thing I knew, she came running as fast as she could across the main path leading into the village. An abyssian, a spawn of Borantulid the Volatile, was chasing her."

"Borantulid the Wrathful?" Lilium asked.

"Yes, the same one. His spawn had three legs. Its gait was an uneven lurch because one of its legs was shorter than the others. One of its arms ended with a single sharp claw the size of a small sword. It was taller than a grown man, with three eyes on its head, no nose, and a small mouth with many small teeth. Its other arm looked normal like a man's—only its fingernails were more like claws. Something black wept from pores all over its body, leaving a dark, oily sheen on its leathery hide."

Lilium contorted her face in disgust at the thought of the abyssian.

"I was terrified at the sight. I instantly shared Hartrice's horror. I looked over to the village watchman standing nearby. He was just standing there, frozen in terror, too. Now, I felt the same thing, but I immediately resented him. This was not what he was supposed to do. He was supposed to protect us.

"I didn't want to fight that thing. I couldn't. I was sure it would kill me. But I was even more sure that I did not want Hartrice to be killed by it, and I was not going to stand there and watch it catch her.

"So, I grabbed the sword from the watchman's scabbard and charged it. I don't even remember seeing Hartrice as I ran past her. I jumped upward and stabbed that sword into the creature's throat.

"It grabbed and threw me. I held onto the sword, and the creature fell over onto the ground. I ran back and positioned myself so I could chop at its neck without being slashed by it. I hacked and hacked until its head came free.

"I stared into those horrid eyes and watched its life, if you would call it that, leave it. After staring for some time, I realized that others from the village had gathered and were standing and staring at the creature, too. I took the sword and stabbed it into the creature's chest, and as I began to walk off, I grew faint.

"I woke up days later. A man had entered the apothecary's hut where I lay. He was wearing bright silver armor. He began speaking without an introduction, and I can remember the conversation plain as day despite how poorly I had felt.

"'They say it was foolish of you, doing what you did. You could have died,' Meliador said. 'Better to have died a fool than doing nothing,' I said back.

'Well spoken. You have familiar eyes, friend. Have we met before?'

'No,' I replied to him."

"Now, Lilium, he was the one who brought me to Midwich years ago, but neither of us realized this at the time."

Lilium began to ask about that story, but she stopped herself, knowing that it would surely be a story about his parents being killed. She resolved to let it go as Braeanor continued telling the present story.

"'Were you not afraid?' he asked me.

'Yes. I've heard stories of monsters, but I had never seen one. Once I saw that thing, I knew they were true, and it means there's more out there.'

'How did that make you feel?'

'More afraid. And angry. Angry in a good way—if that makes sense. I realized how much I hated those evil things, and I knew I should kill it. I knew I had to try.'

'So now what, boy?'

'What do you mean?'

'You killed an abyssian. Few can claim to have done that single-handedly. What is next for you?'

'I don't know. I have never been good for anything, but I want to kill those things. I want to be good at that. So that girls like Hartrice do not have to live in fear.'

'What is stopping you from doing that?'

'The apothecary says I am sick. The creature scratched me, and something is spreading throughout my body. I heard him tell the matron I may die.'"

"He lifted the bandage from my wound, inspected it, and said, 'There is no infection from that creature. You have only been touched by the Abyss. You will recover if you choose to. Do you know who I am?'

'A paladin?' I asked.

'Yes, Meliador of the Evinwald. Do you believe in the Divines?'

'Of course.'

'Do you trust them?' he asked me.

'Yes, I think so.'

'Would you dare to become a paladin, a chosen warrior of faith, champion of all that is good, and devote yourself in service to the Divines through the consecration of our lands and annihilation of these aberrations?'

'Yes, but I am not sure what all that means.'"

Braeanor cracked a big smile while looking at Lilium. She smiled back.

"Meliador laughed. He said, 'Then get up and follow me.'"

Braeanor paused and looked around. He then turned his eyes back toward Lilium.

"There was compassion and strength in his voice. He was a man who knew who he was. He knew what he was about. I didn't know what would be next for me, but I knew if I stayed, I would die. So, I got up and followed him out of our village. And wouldn't you know? I found what I was great at."

"Were you able to say goodbye to Hartrice?" Lilium asked.

"No, not then. I had a chance meeting with her many years later. I explained how I had become a paladin, and she introduced me to her wonderful family."

"That is nice. I am glad to hear that she was doing well."

"Yes. Yes, it was nice." Braeanor's eyes scanned the ground as his mind sifted through the pleasant thoughts of the good things that had happened in her life, thanks to a boy put in a situation beyond his control and his decision to act. She had died peacefully in old age surrounded by those she loved many years ago, a rare reward for the faithful, but as he did not want to spoil the moment, he did not mention this.

Lilium cleared her throat and asked, "Is it true that some paladins have wings? My grandmother told me a story of one who did. She said that some are actually angels, creatures sent by the Divines."

"Angels? That is an old term. One that simply means 'messenger.' In that sense, yes, all paladins can be said to be messengers of the Divines. And the Divines have never sent some creature or person into the world."

"But do some paladins have wings?" she asked again, undaunted.

"I know of only two such accounts, only one of which could be properly verified. Both paladins died in battle."

"My grandmother said she met him when she was a little girl in Tuldanlough."

"Ah, that would be the incident Pythaganor and I investigated after receiving his call for aid. Your grandmother must have spoken of Haptistrian."

"I do not recall his name," Lilium replied sheepishly back. She was embarrassed not to recall something that now seemed quite significant.

"His was a very difficult situation. What did you hear?" Braeanor asked of Lilium.

Lilium shrugged. "Only that he protected her town, even flying her to safety. She said that telling much else would be too scary for me. Grandmother passed away years ago, when I was younger. But she said he saved many people."

"Yes, he saved many. He may have had wings, but neither his body nor his steed's could be found following the battle. Only a quest scroll, which the Divines may have purposefully left, was found of his remains, and it was located in the outline of his body in the snow. And it did appear that he would have had wings, which was reported by many witnesses."

"My grandmother said he was taken to Bright Haven, body and

all." Lilium watched Braeanor carefully as he spoke.

Braeanor nodded. "We could not be sure, but we considered that possibility."

"Did he not have wings before?" Lilium asked pointedly.

"No." He shook his head for emphasis.

"And no paladin does, none that you have ever known?" she asked incredulously. She needed to understand. It was exciting to get confirmation of her grandmother's story, but there were answers outside her grasp. She needed to lay hold of these and wrap her mind around every facet of what took place.

Braeanor looked over at her. "No," he said emphatically.

"Then why would he suddenly have wings?" Lilium asked, demanding to know why. Her curiosity was getting the better of her.

"We never figured that out. We have assumed the Divines blessed him in his hour of need. And if so, it must have been really important that he have wings."

Lilium nodded. It made sense in a simple kind of way. "Hmm. And you've never had wings?"

Braeanor looked at her with furrowed eyebrows. He was losing patience and could not understand why she could not grasp these things.

"Okay, okay," she said quickly and shrugged. "Just making sure. Cause I would be pretty mad walking all the way to Glenmore when we could have flown." She grinned as she looked up at him.

Braeanor shook his head while turning away and rolling his eyes. He did not want her to see his smile as it might encourage her, but it was useless. She noticed, laughed aloud, and counted it as a small victory over the grumpy old paladin.

CHAPTER FOUR

GLENMORE

. . . The paladin's path is one of righteousness and they herald compassion and protection for the faithful, and they walk as the Divines among man. Healing and peace and comfort follow in their wake, and the Abyss shudders at their handiwork . . .

1

They woke early and gathered their bedding and supplies, bundling them together into the tightest, most compact manner possible. Braeanor fastened them together and slipped them into a bag. As soon as the bundles slipped into the bag, it was as though they had disappeared, and the bag was no bigger than it was before they were placed inside. He bundled and strapped the half-dozen bags to his back. They then continued southward.

They were already awake and moving toward their destination by the time the sun peeked over the world's edge and cast its first gaze. There had been very few trees in Edjramor. Most were young or stunted-growth trees, which offered no actual concealment or other benefits associated with healthy stands of woods or forest. Lilium was pleased to see an ever-increasing number of trees around, and she fixated upon the beauty of her surroundings.

Gorgeous leaves bedecked autumn's trees and jeweled drops of dew on blades of grass below basked in the new day's light. Lilium's heart stirred. The vibrant reds, yellows, oranges blended with the greens and browns to color memories of home. Fall came to the south later than back home. The cool, crisp air was refreshing and lacked the harsh chill of not-so-far-off winter. Every fall, her mother would tell her it was her favorite season; perhaps that's why it was Lilium's, too.

She always thought it was a bit peculiar to like fall so much. It signaled a decline in life and a return to the ground. Perhaps it was because it also signaled a coming rebirth—if only they could endure the dreariness and dreadful bite of winter.

Braeanor continued onward, oblivious to fall's emergence. His eyes continually searched their surroundings for the slightest sign of danger. They focused far and then near, scanning the ground in front of him as he walked. Every blade of grass, bare spot of dirt, mud puddle, flipped rock, and broken twig told a story. The story was the presence or absence of something and its effect on the world.

Braeanor was skilled at tracking, and the first and most basic profound truth of tracking is that no one and no thing moves through this world without leaving its mark. Some sign was always left behind. He did not want to miss an opportunity to discover clues in advance that something dangerous may have gone before them, and his diligence paid off.

"Stop, do not move," Braeanor said calmly but assertively.

Lilium stopped moving and looked at him, awaiting an explanation.

Braeanor stooped and began to inspect a hoof print. It was located in a dry spot of ground, and it was easy to see. The hoof looked twice as large as any hoof Lilium had ever seen. Braeanor used his fingers to measure out the size of it. Lilium took a step closer to get a better look.

"Stay where you are," he instructed sharply.

Braeanor parted the grass on either side of it to identify any other features of the sign. He then worked his way out in a small circle in small steps, looking for another hoof print. He found it just southeast of the first, and he could not locate another between the two. They were at least spread out the distance of a grown man, and there was no other set of prints running parallel in the same direction. He determined the creature was bipedal.

He went further southeast and found another barely visible impression. The grass was bent downward around it in a south-easterly direction as well. He compared the shapes of the three prints and was confident that the creature had certainly been headed south-easterly; moreover, given the stride distance, it must have been running. He then questioned his thinking.

Perhaps it was just really tall and heavy, he wondered to himself.

He inspected the first print again. The mud was dry. He picked at it until he pulled a flat piece of mud from within the print and exposed some wetness. The creature had been through there when it was still wet. He picked more at the print and saw that it was much deeper toward the back of the hoof, indicating that significant force had been used to move it forward. He now felt much more confident that the creature was moving quickly, but given the ground was wet when it first moved through, the depth of the print might be exaggerating just how quickly it was actually moving.

He saw no other sign around, so he did not believe that something was chasing the creature or being chased by it. This was certainly pleasant news. He was not keen on the brief thought that something bigger than this creature might be lurking about. This large creature was more than enough concern on its own.

Where was it headed in a hurry? he wondered.

He began running through his mental checklist of all the abyssians he could remember. There were many to consider, but he could only recall one, which was hoofed, bipedal, and large. Its stride distance would seem to match the circumstances.

"Goruphant. I think a goruphant has been through here. It is headed in the same direction as us, but it has about a one to two-day start on us. It was in a hurry, too. It is not likely we will easily catch up to it, assuming it does not hang around somewhere for a while or double back."

"A goruphant?" Lilium inquired. "It isn't a nice one, by chance?" she asked lightheartedly.

"It's like a huge man with hoofed feet. It has an arm that ends in a vicious crab-like claw, which is just as sharp on its inside edge as it is on its outside. Its other arm is a powerful tentacle capable of grabbing and crushing a man in the blink of an eye. Its human-like face is covered with smaller tentacles which drape downward like a beard, concealing its mouth from view."

"Sounds awful," she replied.

"It is, but while it is a very intimidating sight to behold, there are many things which look much worse. A goruphant will easily kill the unprepared in single combat. All things have weaknesses, though. Come along, now. We have no reason to delay any longer. I doubt we will see it, but we will keep our eyes open nonetheless."

With that, autumn's glory subdued, and they continued onward. Lilium had some difficulty matching Braeanor's pace, but she managed.

Glenmore was situated idyllically near the mountains in a fertile river basin. The fields extended for miles around, and the local farmers could expect consistently good harvests. Though located amid such incredible scenery, it was primarily a place of visitation for those simply traveling through, typically back and forth between the mountains and the southern waterways.

The mountains were just days away to the north and east, so those going to and from the mines often came to Glenmore to find respite, resupply, and entertainment. Miners were known to be a rough-and-tumble group. They had to be able to take care of themselves and endure unpleasant conditions and significant toil to find anything of worth. When they did, though, a single quality vein of ore could mean a lifetime's worth of income for themselves—and perhaps their family should they actually return home to share the wealth.

The larger port city of Bevereign is farther south and is the usual destination for the miners' precious finds. The Istrid River runs south along the southern outskirt of Glenmore and connects it to Bevereign before emptying into the Great Ocean. Riverboats make frequent trips back and forth between the two, but it is in Bevereign where traders can quickly load larger sea-capable ships to make their way across the Great Ocean, typically westward, to sell the same wares.

Glenmore profited off those constantly passing through, which is the only reason the town's actual residents tolerated the less desirable things stemming from the miners. These men, generally speaking, were not the pleasant and soft men found in cities of wealth. These men knew a life of securing a living through blood, sweat, and tears, leading them to view those around them as opportunities or dangers. They were not to be trusted. They often had appetites that would make it difficult for any place to have a good reputation, and Glenmore lived under this shadow.

Glenmore came into view, and they made for a path between farm fields. The path they followed soon had noticeable wear from wagons and foot traffic, and there was an increasing number of laborers in the fields tending to crops. The path took them between fields of wheat and others of various vegetables. The heads of grain waved at them as they passed.

"Lilium, it is important that you do not stray from me once we are in Glenmore. Most of the townsfolk are of a generally kind temperament, as best I can recall, but they are used to dealing with unsavory characters, so they do not trust others easily. Any men who appear dirty, rough around the edges, and perhaps who you feel may not be trustworthy . . . well, frankly, you should assume them so."

Lilium nodded. "I understand. I will stay near."

"First, we will secure a horse and then go to Kellina's. We will plan to stay at her inn for the night before continuing east." Braeanor looked around at the laborers. Most did not pay the pair any attention.

Their path became well-worn as they got closer to town. Farther ahead of them was a wagon carrying villagers, but it had come to a stop. A young boy sat with his feet dangling off the end, and he looked exhausted. His face was dirty, and his clothes were disheveled. A man had stepped off the wagon and was inquiring about work with one of the men in the fields.

While some outlying buildings were simple wooden structures with thatched roofs, the buildings comprising the town's interior were of more elaborate construction. Buildings of robust wooden beams and sturdy stone walls, many of which had more stone in their construction than wood, were common. The roofs were tiled, and some buildings had chimneys.

As they neared the northern edge of the town, Braeanor spotted a large stable with a fenced yard on the northwestern side. A prominent wooden placard with a horse painted on it hung on a post near the path leading to the stable.

"I don't recall Glenmore being quite this big last time I was here," Braeanor said.

"When were you here last?" Lilium asked.

Braeanor thought for a moment. "Just five years ago, give or take. I think."

"Just," Lilium said with a bit of smart retort.

Braeanor looked over at her, but he didn't say anything in response to her comment. He wasn't sure what to say, and if it was a bit of her natural wit continuing to come out, he was glad to see it.

"At any rate, I don't recall that horse stable the last time I was here. I was expecting to have to strike a deal with a farmer or a desperate miner. Let's head over."

Lilium nodded. "I can't wait! Horses are the best. They are so pure and majestic."

Braeanor hummed in agreement. "They are that and much more."

As they made their way to the stable, they observed a group of well-armed men walking the outskirts of the city. They were moving in Braeanor and Lilium's direction, but they did not appear to be focused on them. Braeanor counted thirteen men. Eight were armed with spears and swords and simple leather armor, and there were four armed with crossbows. The last man wore chainmail, but he only had a sword. A horn hung at his side. In light of the crest fastened to the cloak drawn over his shoulder and that only he rode a horse, the man was presumably the leader of the group. Braeanor figured he was a captain of the city guard.

Braeanor also noticed a section of wall built on the city outskirts in the distance near the southwest corner, and there were men actively working on constructing a new section.

"They are building a wall too?" Braeanor asked aloud, despite knowing it was readily apparent and that Lilium had never been to Glenmore before.

"I wonder if it will be as big as Munrobeinn's?" Lilium asked.

Braeanor shook his head. "The keep's walls are impressive, but these do not appear to be of that scale."

"No, I am talking about the walls around the city. Not the keep." Lilium spoke matter-of-factly and looked at Braeanor, a bit confused.

Braeanor looked at her and noticed the look in her eyes. "There are no walls around Munrobeinn."

"There have been as long as I have known. They were still standing when I left. But what do I know?" Lilium shrugged as she finished making her point.

Braeanor was having a hard time with this new information. "Around the city?" he asked.

"Yes. My dad helped organize the effort to get them built. That was before I was born and before he led the city council. He wanted others to experience the safety of those behind the keep's walls."

Braeanor shifted and adjusted the bags on his back. "Hmm. I hadn't been there in decades . . . things change with time, I suppose."

"Yes. He said other cities have begun doing so too," she said with a pause before finishing, "since the paladins went away."

He looked away from her and nodded. He did not like the reason for the walls, but he supposed they were for the best.

Braeanor and Lilium finished making their way to the stables. The stable itself looked well-kept and impressive upon approach. The gabled horse barn had ornamental features and woodworking inside and outside. Moreover, a large field was closed in with a fence that connected to the stables, so it was obvious they provided both horses and prospective customers the opportunity to run and ride. Large piles of hay sat just inside the center alley between each side of stalls.

Braeanor pointed over to a spot near the stable fencing. "Please wait here. I need to be the one to get our horse. I'll try to not take long."

Lilium began to protest. "What? I'd like to—"

Braeanor scowled at her, and she was quick to relent.

"Fine," Lilium replied with a frown. She hung her head and sat next to the fence which encircled the stable yard. She picked a tall piece of grass and began to twirl it in her fingers. Braeanor would easily be able to see her from within the stable.

Near the stable alley entrance, a man sat on a stool, twiddling a piece of straw between his fingers. The man was of a unique appearance, to be sure. His face was pudgier than was fit for most of his body, and his body was overall quite lean—save for his stomach. The man ate plenty, and his appearance suggested the food never left his stomach. Every bit of nutrient sat right there, unwilling to grace any extremity but his face. He had a sniveling nose, which had developed a bit of a leak, and he had a habit of rubbing his face. He was allergic to hay, but he loved making money.

"Looking for horses, are you good sir?" the man shouted out with eagerness as he hopped to his feet and approached Braeanor. "My name is Swinmer. I'd be pleased to show you our lot and answer any questions which may ease your mind about purchasing one of our fine horses." He rested his left hand on his hip and motioned with his right hand toward the barn, inviting Braeanor inside.

"Well, Swinmer, I am Braeanor, and I *am* in need of a fine horse. By chance, do you have any with four legs and that run fast?" he queried with obvious jest.

"Why sir, indeed we do, indeed we do. Fact I think I have a barn full of them if that is all you require this fine day!"

"Good! Good! I must warn you though . . ." Braeanor paused and shot a serious look at Swinmer for added effect. Swinmer hesitated, unsure what would be said next. "I am going on a perilous journey, and I am unsure whether I or the horse will survive."

Braeanor let the comment pause in the air for a moment. Swinmer's face began to crack a smile, and Braeanor began to smile, too.

Swinmer let out a laugh, "Ha! Well, I don't do any kind of borrowing or credit so I'll be alright. Best of luck to you, though!"

They both laughed and moved into the covered alley of the barn. There were eight stalls on each side of the barn. The horses had moved to the aisle and poked their heads over their stall gates as if to get a better look at their potential future owner.

"Well, they have different colorations, as you can plainly see. On account of selling one recently and two being with foal, I have a current selection of thirteen fine horses which I can offer you today." As he spoke, he pointed out the empty stall and the two pregnant horses.

Braeanor noticed there was one stall that had not been indicated, and no horse was seen at the stall gate. He only counted twelve horses. "Tell me about these horses, Swinmer, if you would please, sir."

"What is not to tell, good sir? These are all mighty fine horses. Each one a prime specimen of speed and endurance. Seeing you are on a most perilous journey or whatnot—" Swinmer paused and flashed a grin. "I might recommend this one here."

They moved to a stall in the center on the left. The stallion was impressive. He stood tall with sleek hair. Sharp, clean eyes swept the barn and stared deeply into Braeanor and then at Swinmer. Braeanor peered into the stall and checked the horse's legs. Thick and muscular, he could tell the horse was valued and taken care of quite well. He was likely of good stock.

As if reading Braeanor's mind, Swinmer continued his sales pitch. "This one is of good stock here, this one is. Yes sir. He'd do quite well for ya, no doubt. But seeing his quality and fine nature, you must understand he is the most expensive one here. As a matter of fact, he is highly sought after as well. A nobleman had eyed him this morning and expressed great interest. Yes, he did. Now, I didn't commit to the man, seeing he hadn't brought his money—and I don't do no credit—asin' you know."

Braeanor had a slight admiration for the man's gift of selling. He was determined to make a profit on these animals, each and every one. He had obviously spent much of his life fine-tuning his ability to turn a profit. Even though the man emanated a certain repulsive quality, Braeanor had a soft spot for those who perfected their trade. There is value in doing something well, but he was also confident that any nobleman would be an unlikely visitor to Glenmore.

"Hmm. This one is very impressive. If I were a horse, I might wish I had his appearance and vigor!" Braeanor remarked. He was still thinking about that stall with the unaccounted-for horse. "Say Swinmer, is that stall empty there?" Braeanor pointed at the stall in question.

Swinmer slowly turned his head and looked to where Braeanor pointed.

"Ah, yes, that stall—well, no, it isn't empty. But I need be honest with you." Swinmer held a hand to his heart as he followed Braeanor over to the stall. "That one isn't our finest one here. Truth be told, he is worthless."

"Ah, Swinmer, but when I walked up, you said all your horses might be a good fit for me."

"Well, something like that, yes, you are right. Just not this one. Seems like this one is about given up. He just mopes about. I'm about ready to sell it for its meat. Iffin' I'm being honest with you." Swinmer gave a genuine frown. He didn't particularly like horse meat, and he would much rather turn a handsome profit off the beast.

Swinmer's accent was increasingly showing through. His comfort around Braeanor was getting the best of him, and he was getting lazy keeping up his somewhat polished act.

"Hmm." Braeanor sharply hummed as he looked into the stall.

The horse's deep gray coat did not have the gloss of the others—especially of the prized stallion. The horse was kneeling against the edge of the stall. Its legs looked capable enough, and its frame was sufficient. However, its head hung low, and its eyes barely raised to greet Braeanor's curiosity.

"Is it lame or sick?" Braeanor asked.

"Nah, seems healthy as best I can tell, but he won't show it. He lays around and barely trots in the field. It's like he's waiting to die. Again, truth be told, I've debated selling him to a butcher so I might recoup what I put into him." Swinmer leaned forward a bit and began scratching his lower back while wincing.

Braeanor stooped and put his head against the stall gate slats to look the horse more in the eye. He began to whisper and reached his hand through, allowing the horse to see his hand before stroking his head.

"Boy, what's got you down?" Braeanor spoke gently as he stroked the horse's head slowly. "You don't have to talk if you don't want to."

The horse looked at him.

"Yes, actually, I can. Go on now. I'd feel much better talking to you standing, though, if you don't mind."

The horse struggled, but he rose.

"There you are. Can you come closer?"

The horse stepped to the gate and put his head over so that Braeanor could rub his neck.

"I understand. You don't have to tell me anything," Braeanor spoke with a calm, reassuring voice.

Swinmer's eyes got large seeing the horse apparently responding to Braeanor. "Now I can see you like horses a lot, and he has a nice temperament. I just can't in all good conscience sell him to a fine customer like you. I might get a reputation which drives me outa' business if I sell a worthless horse," Swinmer spoke as if he was genuinely concerned for Braeanor's best interest.

"We need not pay attention to such things. No, you are not. Would you tell me why you feel this way?" Braeanor paused.

The horse let out a gentle huff.

Braeanor leaned close and whispered so that Swinmer could not easily hear him. "I've lost loved ones too. I know. I understand. Mine's broken, too. Not a day goes by when I don't think about them. Can I tell you a secret?" Braeanor then whispered right into one of the horse's ears.

The horse lifted its head and nickered. Swinmer stared dubiously at the exchange between Braeanor and the horse, but he was willing to entertain his customer's fancy for a moment.

"No, I am not lying. You have heard the stories, am I right?" Braeanor asked.

The horse nodded.

"That little girl over there, see her?" Braeanor pointed to where Lilium sat. "Just the other morning, she told me that the strongest are sometimes the most beaten down. The ones who have made it through the worst but kept going. I am not done yet, but I need help. I can't make you help me. What I am about to do is dangerous. You have heard the stories yourself. The one thing I can guarantee you is my loyalty. If you will pledge me the same in return, I assure you, my friend, you will find your place among the tales of your kind."

The horse looked him in the eyes and snorted while giving a single firm nod.

"Sir," Swinmer drew in close to Braeanor while scratching his head. "I'm not sure what you are playing at here. If you are intending to just get a pet for that girl of yours and hope it won't keep for long—for convenience's sake—then he might be a good pick. Otherwise, I'd love to show you the others and let you take a ride on whichever pleases ya."

The horse snorted again, followed by a more vigorous neighing.

"Pay no mind, pay no mind. We know you have more to give yet. Let me ask you. Do you believe in the ones who bring the rain? Who bless with the gift of foals and open fields? Of companionship and nobility? If so, come with me then. I'll make you strong for our quest."

The horse whinnied and gave another single, sharp nod.

"How much, Swinmer?" Braeanor inquired with a determined tone.

Swinmer's mouth was agape with surprise. "Sir, I really think that–"

"I understand. But if it is as you say, I'd suppose you would be happy that you recoup what you spent." Braeanor raised his eyebrows and tilted his head as he appealed to Swinmer's weakness for money.

"Five gold pieces would do it," Swinmer said while looking as if one of his feet had just slipped ankle-deep in a cesspool.

Braeanor reached into a pouch at his waist and produced a handful of coins. "Let's make it fifteen gold and throw in a saddle, a couple saddle bags, some sweet feed, and reigns, and on account that he is worth far more than you credit."

Swinmer's eyes got as big as dinner plates. "Done! And I'm not big on credit, but I get your meanin'!"

Swinmer hurried off with pep, and he brought out the supplies and helped Braeanor get the horse saddled and situated. During this, the horse and Braeanor quietly talked. Braeanor learned about how Swinmer obtained many of his horses, and he learned how they all hated him. He had an especially gross habit of petting them after rubbing his snotty nose. They often talked about how they wanted to give him a good kick. By the end of it, Braeanor personally wanted to do more than kick Swinmer.

"There it is, Braeanor!" Swinmer grinned, rubbed his face, and then patted the horse on its head.

The horse jerked its head away in disgust.

"Hey now, he's already done with me it seems," Swinmer retorted.

"Yes, I suppose he is," Braeanor responded. "Some words of advice, Swinmer. Find another source for any future horses. And the horses don't like you rubbing your face and then touching them. They'd appreciate it if you stopped that. I'd hate to see you get kicked, especially by that prize one you got there."

Braeanor winked at the prized stallion as he finished talking, and it snorted in response.

"I'll be honest, sir. You are a peculiar one. Buyin' this horse then seemin' to be talking to them. Wish you the best findin' whatever you lost when you go a'journeyin'." Swinmer then looked around the stall, his eyes nervously darting to and from the horses, each of which were staring at him.

Braeanor walked the horse over to Lilium. She stood from where she rested against the fence and skipped over to meet them. "He looks great!"

"You think so, huh?" Braeanor ran a hand down the side of his neck.

"Yes. He will make our quest much better. I'm sure of it." Lilium petted him and took a close look at him. "He is such a handsome horse."

"Well, I think you are right," Braeanor replied.

"Is it true that horses and paladins have special bonds?" Lilium asked.

Braeanor nodded. "They are creatures specially made by the

Divines to help us."

"Oh, really? Did you have a horse before?" Lilium lowered her eyes and regretted the question. She realized immediately that the answer was obvious.

Braeanor went silent and gently rubbed his new steed's neck. His eyes focused intently on his hand as it moved across the horse's coat. "I did . . . but that is a story for some other time."

He fully turned toward the horse and looked him in the eye. "What is your name, boy?"

The horse neighed gently.

"Aerion, you say? Well, we didn't quite have a good introduction in there, but I am Braeanor. This is my traveling companion, Lilium. It will just be us three on this quest."

Aerion huffed playfully and lowered his head to nuzzle Lilium. His face tickled hers, and she smiled greatly and giggled while rubbing his face back. "Wait, can you actually understand Aerion?" Lilium looked at Braeanor mid-giggle.

"Yes, paladins and horses have retained their connection through the Divines. Though we don't speak the same language, we can understand each other, just like you and I can understand each other. The Abyss has corrupted man over the ages so that only paladins can understand horses, but horses can almost always understand man. Isn't that right, Aerion?"

Aerion nodded and neighed.

Lilium marveled and smiled wide-eyed.

"So, Aerion," Braeanor spoke, "are you sure you are up for this quest or what?"

Aerion whinnied.

"Good to hear it, boy. Now, we need to head over to an inn. We plan to rest there for the night and set out in the morning. We will need to make sure you get plenty of food, too. Speaking of which." Braeanor reached into one of his bags and pulled an apple out. Braeanor then fed Aerion the apple as they walked to the inn.

11

Braeanor, Lilium, and Aerion found their way through the town until they arrived at Kellina's place, The Wild Mountain Goat Inn. As they approached where horses could be hitched out front, the inn's double doors swung wide open.

A man trying to stay on his feet hurtled out and fell down the steps onto his face. A woman escorted another man out with one of his arms painfully twisted behind his back. She then pushed him forward and kicked him to join his friend.

Her fair skin seemed out of place on such a strong frame, and yet, it all the more her beauty accentuated. Her brown boots and tan pants were snug on legs which looked accustomed to kicking every man who walked near her. Her hips, though they might lead a man to think she would make quite a good mother of their children, were not enough to keep one from noticing the formidable hands resting upon them. Her arms were finely crafted from years of tossing both kegs and men around, but these led up to her most beguiling features, that of her neck, face, and dark hair. She was disarmingly stunning—not in the way that some artists may render with ample amounts of flattery and favorable lighting. No, she was a plain kind of beauty, a beauty which would still cause any man to gaze and ponder philosophically about how such could exist, up until she knocked his mugging eyes off her. She was a woman through and through. Few trifled with her, and those that did regret it.

"If you ever come back here, I'll give you a rest you won't wake up from!" She then wiped her hands together as if dusting off any remnants of their filth and then rested her hands on her hips.

Lilium was taken aback by this scene, and she looked over at Braeanor to see what he might do. A smile had crept across his face, and he looked upon the woman with pride.

The woman felt Braeanor's gaze and instinctively looked over at him. Her eyes lit up. "Braeanor!" she called out with delight.

"Kellina!" he called back with a laugh.

She hurried down the steps and gave him a big hug. "It's been so long! And look at this. Just when I think I know you, you've got a girl and a horse following you around!"

Braeanor smiled. "Strange times indeed!"

"Well come along then. No need to stand around out here. Let's get inside, and you all make yourselves comfortable." She motioned toward the doors and turned to ascend the steps.

Lilium followed right behind Kellina. Braeanor hung back momentarily as he saw the two men finally getting up.

"Well, what you looking at!" one of the men huffed at Braeanor.

Braeanor remained silent as the two men, off balance from either the whooping they received or the alcohol they had consumed, made their way closer to him. Their eyes also fixated on Aerion and the bags on his back.

Braeanor looked at the men and made sure he had their attention. He then turned toward Aerion and began speaking. "Aerion, stay here. If these men mess with you or our bags, break them and then call for me. I will finish them off."

Braeanor dropped the reins and did not tie him off, and he did so in such a manner as to ensure the men noticed. As the men stepped closer to cause more trouble, Aerion neighed and lifted one of his hind legs with a jolt as if to kick.

The men jumped back. Aerion took a step backward and did so again. This time, the men lost their balance and fell into each other before hitting the ground.

Braeanor patted Aerion. "That's the idea, boy. Stay here. I'm not sure how long we will be, but I will return shortly to get you more food. I can't stress enough how much we need to get your strength up. We must pray together."

Aerion neighed, and Braeanor then entered the inn.

The inn was full of an assortment of patrons. Men gathered around tables, some playing dice, and each was dirty. Tools, bags, and sundry things lay on the floor near them. The men were catching up on the comforts of this world: drink and play. In such places as these, men were full of suspicions of all the other men, yet they were still drawn to their company. Men knew the risks of dice, daggers, and drams, but the rewards were worth it.

"You are a sight for sore eyes, Braeanor. How long has it been? Five years or so?" Kellina positioned herself behind the bar and grabbed a pitcher of boiled herb water. She filled two mugs, one for Braeanor and the other for Lilium. "And who is this little lady?"

"She is Lilium, a friend I made recently." He smiled politely at Lilium, who was having a touch of difficulty getting up into one of the tall stools.

"Lilium, is it? Nice to meet you." Kellina extended her hand to Lilium.

"Pleased to meet you as well," Lilium smiled as she shook hands. She then looked up at Braeanor with a glint in her eyes, and she unconsciously leaned closer to him. She liked the thought of having a friend.

"There is a story there, and I'm dying to know it." Kellina wore a giant smile and glanced between the two of them eagerly, waiting for someone to speak up.

"Ah, yes," Braeanor said. He didn't know where to start. Well, he knew how it started, but it was not a story with a good beginning. It was not a story that either wished to tell. Before he began explaining, another man stepped behind the bar and approached Kellina.

"Are those men dealt with? Are you okay?" the man inquired.

Braeanor quickly assessed the man. He was tall and appeared fit. He had moved right next to Kellina, and his hand upon her lower back let Braeanor know that he was someone special. He had a leather apron, a groomed beard, and kind eyes.

"Oh yeah, no issues at all. I tossed them right out. I knew you were tending to things in the back. All is well! Farlan, I'd like you to meet Braeanor. Braeanor, meet Farlan."

Braeanor stood from his stool and stretched his hand out, and they each gave a proper handshake. "Nice to meet you, Farlan."

"Likewise, I've heard much about you!" Farlan said with a cheery demeanor.

"Ah, well, I suppose I am at a disadvantage then. Kellina, I suppose there is a story here as well," Braeanor remarked with curiosity. He hoped that expressing some interest might buy him some time before telling Lilium's story.

"Yes, yes, I suppose so! It started with 'em needing a room yet having no way to pay for it. He offered to perform music for the evening as payment. I gave 'em the chance to play me something, and the rest is history. Seems I haven't been able to get 'em out of here since then. For all his love of roaming the mountains and countryside, he found being here with me much more enticing."

"I discovered she gives me much more to sing about!" Farlan added. "I'd be a fool leaving what I had been searching for." He took Kellina's hand and kissed it dramatically while winking at Kellina. She rolled her eyes playfully before looking back into his.

Lilium sheepishly grinned. She watched as Kellina's eyes stared deeply into Farlan's and his back into hers.

"Forgive me for daring to ask the obvious, but you are together?" Braeanor glanced back and forth between them.

Farlan looked at her while feigning anxiety at what her response might be. "Yes, I'd claim him most days," Kellina laughed.

Farlan clenched a fist and pumped his arm as if he just won something. He then winked at Lilium. She giggled.

"Well, good for you," Braeanor responded. "This is quite the establishment you have now. I was confident you would get it up and going, but it has surpassed even what I imagined. I am glad you are not running it alone, and I am happy for both of you."

"It has been good to have an extra set of hands. Though I could use some part-time help too. It stays swamped. I couldn't do it all by myself. I mostly just serve drinks and keep things in order. He helps cook and plays music. We have a good thing—"

"The Abyss take you!" shouted a man in the back playing a game of dice with other men.

"Hey!" Kellina shouted out to get the man's attention. "We don't talk like that in here! Do it again!" She pointed at him in such a way that it seemed she managed to reach out and poke him in his chest. Her threat, like a dart, hit its mark.

"Yes, ma'am," said the man as he sunk into his chair.

"Sorry, Braeanor. Where were we?" Kellina asked as she got their conversation back on track.

Braeanor smiled at her. "It's fine. I was just saying I am genuinely glad for both of you and your success. Seems this whole city has been doing well. It is bigger than I remember, and there is more protection. These are good changes for everyone. Have they finally built a chapel or perhaps even a temple?"

"Thank you. As far as the city, something is constantly being built around here. Things have been more peaceful here over the last couple of years, actually. People continue leaving villages and their homes from all over to find protection in the bigger towns. The Glenmore council funds two full-time watches—one for the day and one for the night. There is talk of making those bigger. And they have started construction of a wall. The guilds support the growth of the city.

"The abyssian attacks are fewer and further apart. I think it has actually been around two, maybe even three months since an actual attack. We still see them around occasionally, and when they are seen, they ring the bells. Everyone locks up inside until they hear three blasts of the captain's horn. Mostly, they seem to bypass the city headed east. The increased safety has helped Glenmore pick up its pace and grow a little faster.

"As far as any kind of chapel or temple, the council hasn't shown any support for that, so no. But before I keep prattling on, I'm still dying to know. How did you meet?" Kellina tried to switch the subject, knowing Braeanor would not be thrilled about the lackluster religious efforts in the city.

"No places of worship? No clergy or Sisters?" Braeanor inquired of Kellina.

"No," she replied with a hint of disappointment. "Occasionally, a sister from Midwich will visit to see if there are any orphans in need of care."

Braeanor shook his head repeatedly. "There are guilds, mercenaries— or guards for hire—more people trusting in themselves and others if the price is right."

Farlan said, "Braeanor, the world is always changing. The stories of how things once were are not enough. People are trying to find a way forward."

Braeanor met Farlan's eyes and nodded. "Yes, I guess we all are." He took a sip of his drink and cleared his throat.

Other abyssians headed east? he pondered to himself before answering Kellina's question about how he met Lilium.

"Well," Braeanor said, "her family was traveling west from the Eastern Reaches. They had to pass through Edjramor to avoid other dangers pursuing them, and they passed through Haverstead one night. A cultist and an abyssian attacked them. She alone survived."

Lilium's eyes hung low, staring through the bar counter. She leaned forward to rest her elbows on the bar top, and her hands covered her ears.

Kellina's countenance fell, and she leaned forward onto the bar, placing a hand on Lilium. "Sweet child, I am so sorry."

Lilium did not look up, but she nodded. Tears were on the verge of forming, but she forced herself to maintain composure. "I must believe there was a reason. Braeanor rescued me, and we are now on a quest that will help others. We are headed east."

Braeanor was surprised to hear her speak so quickly about practicalities. Practicalities were a good way of changing the focus to things that can or should be done. Nevertheless, he felt uneasy about their quest being made public. It would have been nothing unusual for a paladin to tell others they were questing, but it had been so long since he had been set to such a task.

Farlan asked, "East? Why did you come here then? Are you not headed back to the Eastern Reaches?"

Lilium spoke with confidence. "There is nothing and no one for me back there. We are headed over the mountains, beyond the Obsidian Peaks."

"And you are going too, Lilium?" Kellina shot a look at Braeanor. She was surprised and hoping she misunderstood.

"Yes, she is. We are going together. It must be so," Braeanor responded.

"Okay. If it must be, I won't question it then. If there is anyone who can keep her safe, it is you." Kellina nodded at Braeanor as if giving her consent.

Braeanor nodded in appreciation.

Farlan ran a hand across his mouth and then stroked his beard several times quickly. He did not have Kellina's confidence about the matter. After clearing his throat, he began to speak, "Braeanor, which way do you plan to go? By what pass?"

"The most direct one. We make for Viper's Ascent."

"Viper's Ascent? And not Lowland Glen?" Farlan raised his eyebrows with curiosity.

"It must be so," Braeanor responded.

Farlan stroked his beard thoughtfully before speaking. "Are you sure? The other day, a group who had returned from there came through here. They had been out searching for obsidian powder. Ash vipers have already been spotted there."

"Already? They don't go there until the winter spawning." Braeanor looked back at Farlan incredulously.

"Yes, and something has them riled up. They are there early. I take it you are familiar with them?" Farlan's eyes moved from Braeanor over to Lilium, revealing his real intention was to ensure Lilium knew about them.

Braeanor's jaw tightened, and he furrowed his brows. He had not told Lilium specifically about the pass or the creatures yet.

"Yes. Are you Farlan?" he asked pointedly.

"I am not," Lilium interjected.

Farlan immediately and eagerly dove into an explanation. "Yes, I am very familiar. I might know much more than most. I had a chance meeting with a man who called himself a 'purveyor of oddities.' He liked to explore and search for all manner of things for his research and to collect. He was peculiar, but he was wealthy.

"He wanted to learn more about the ash vipers. I joined a group of men recruited for this purpose. We spent more than a month in that pass leading up to winter. Two of our group were killed in their sleep. Several more were bitten but not fed upon."

"Fed upon?" Lilium asked wide-eyed, though her tone suggested she was just as intrigued as perturbed by the thought.

"Yes. You see, ash vipers are not your typical serpents. They not only ambush, they actively hunt and even chase their prey. Their first strike injects a toxin, which weakens and immobilizes their victim. Once they are incapacitated, which doesn't take long, they then latch on and inject a second substance, usually into the unfortunate victim's chest or stomach.

"That substance dissolves the insides quickly and draws the body's fluids into the wound area. The extremities will even dry and shrivel. They drink up the person's insides through their hollow fangs. It is an agonizing death as the person is alive for a brief time while they are being . . . well drunk alive."

Lilium scrunched her nose and leaned back in her seat. Meanwhile, Braeanor found it difficult to stop his foot from tapping. He had brought a hand up to the side of his face, and his jaw was clenched.

Farlan continued. "The man I ventured with dissected several Ash vipers we managed to kill, as well as the two men killed in their sleep. The fangs of these creatures are not just large, but they are remarkable. They connect to two different venom sacs and have a large hollow space for consuming their victims—like the inside of a reed straw.

"The first time you see one of these things moving beneath the obsidian ashes and launching themselves in the air—it is a terrifying sight."

Braeanor tapped the bar top several times. "I will credit that you know what you are talking about. What you say is true. Nonetheless, it is the path we must take. The quest requires it. I don't know why. But this won't be the first time I have contended with them. We will be fine."

Lilium looked at Braeanor and then back at Farlan. "Yes, this is the path we must follow. And we have faced worse—a pox fiend, in fact. Thank you for your concern, Farlan."

Braeanor was pleasantly surprised. He had worried Lilium might balk and have a change of heart. Despite what she had already experienced, she was stalwart. Farlan simply held his hands up in front of himself as if no more needed to be said, and he nodded.

Kellina slapped the bar top. "Well, Lilium, you are a girl after my own heart. I like your attitude about it. I think those ash vipers better stay out of your way!"

Lilium looked at Kellina and beamed, and they each exchanged a warm smile. Farlan rolled his eyes at Kellina's remark, but he did not let her catch him doing so.

"Kellina, can I ask a favor of you?" Braeanor changed subjects.

"You can ask as many as you want." Kellina looked at Braeanor eagerly, wanting to know how she could be of service.

"Well, I think I need to go for a walk. Lilium may need to ask you for some personal guidance regarding matters of which I am of little use."

"Take your walk, old friend. She and I will get acquainted." Kellina looked over at Lilium, whose cheeks were rosy, hinting at her embarrassment. She extended one of her hands, beckoning Lilium to take it and walk with her.

"Come along, little lady. Let's get to know each other a bit."

Lilium hopped from her stool and took Kellina's hand. Kellina paused and looked back at Farlan. "Floor's all yours. I'll be in the back."

"Got it!" Farlan responded with enthusiasm.

As Lilium and Kellina disappeared through a door into the back, Farlan turned back to Braeanor, who was already on his feet and turning to walk to the inn's front door. "Braeanor, one second, please."

Braeanor stopped, slowly turned back toward Farlan, and looked at him. He didn't *not* like him, but he did feel a sense of frustration bordering on that at the moment. He knew it was better to walk and clear his mind, and he needed to bond with Aerion. "Yes, Farlan?"

"I apologize if I came across pushy or presumptuous or–"

"—some other P-word?" Braeanor interrupted flatly.

"Yes, perhaps!" he let out a nervous chuckle. "First of all, I want to thank you for what you did for Kellina years ago. I didn't know her yet, but it means the world to me now."

"I was glad to be there when I was," Braeanor replied.

Farlan then jumped back into expressing his concerns. "Listen, at the risk of over-extending myself. I think you should know that I've also heard other things over the last several weeks."

"You do operate an inn. I should think you hear many a strange or concerning tale," Braeanor replied.

"Yes, yes, of course, but these are consistent. Miners have been disappearing. Only their tools are being discovered left behind. They are disappearing from the northern ridges as well as the eastern. Even the walled camp in Lowland Glen is vacant because of these happenings. The truth is, I don't know that anywhere east of here is safe, regardless of which pass you take."

Braeanor studied the features of Farlan's face and could see genuine concern. He realized this may somehow be relevant to his quest. "Any guess as to what is happening to the miners?"

Farlan shook his head and shrugged. "Not really. There are no obvious signs of a struggle or being attacked by an abyssian. No one knows. Even ores and gems are being left behind."

"Hmm, it is peculiar. I suppose no one has been sent to conduct a proper investigation?"

"No, the city council is content to collect money from the miners traveling through rather than risk trained men to keep them safe elsewhere. Also, as Kellina mentioned, many have reported seeing abyssians moving east, and no one wants to contend with those things."

"Yes, I came across an abyssian's tracks on the way here. From what I could tell, it was headed south-easterly in a hurry."

"So even you can confirm that." Farlan leaned across the bar counter to add to the conviction of his coming plea.

"I urge you to reconsider going, especially taking Lilium with you. The truth is, to go east, no matter which route, is to run headlong into danger."

Braeanor paused and looked downward while he thought of what to say next. If what Farlan said was true, and it might be, it would not change the fact that a clear quest had been given to him. Whatever lay between him and its completion would have to be dealt with, and Farlan had never met a paladin on a quest.

"Farlan, thank you for your concerns. There is wisdom in sincerity, and you've spoken sincerely. But you must understand something. I am a paladin on a quest, and that quest requires me to travel east through Viper's Ascent. Therefore, I will do so. It is as simple as that. Please excuse me. I am going for a walk."

Braeanor and Farlan nodded at each other. Braeanor turned and walked out of the inn. Farlan stared at him as he walked off. He did not know whether to admire him or think him crazy. Farlan shook his head, pulled out a rag, and began wiping the bar top.

111

Braeanor exited the inn and walked over to Aerion. Aerion huffed gently at him.

"No, boy, not quite yet. We will be spending the night here. In the meantime, though, I think I'd like to take a walk around here. What do you say?"

Aerion huffed again and nodded.

"Good to hear. I think it will be good to get those legs moving and start building up their strength. We have a long road ahead of us."

Braeanor inspected the saddle and other items to ensure that everything was still in its proper place and nothing was missing.

"I assume you had no trouble out of those two men?"

Aerion shook his head.

"Aerion, before we go, we should be bound. This involves a paladin and their steed pledging themselves to one another in service to the Divines. Normally, there is more ceremony to it, but it is simply a prayer and a heartfelt commitment to stand together against the Abyss. What do you say?"

Aerion nodded.

Braeanor put his right hand over Aerion's left side, where his heart was.

"Divines, bless and strengthen us, so that we may journey together, through valley and hill, against all dangers, of the Abyss or Kadath, bound until death or you part us. May it be so."

Aerion whinnied.

Braeanor patted Aerion on his side several times, and he then got his left foot into a stirrup and quickly lifted himself onto Aerion.

Aerion huffed.

"No idea where I am headed, boy. Tell you what, let's just make our way around the city, even if we end up walking in circles."

Aerion turned away from the inn and began walking the dirt street. They maintained a relaxed pace and took their time to take in all the sights, sounds, and smells.

One street was lined with food stalls on one side. There were stalls for grains, beans, onions, garlic, other various vegetables, and even spices. Braeanor noticed South Shore pepper among the offerings. He couldn't help but notice the crudely painted sign for the pepper's price. A unit of it was selling for a copper. He could remember when that same amount would cost a gold piece. That was many years ago, and the ability to cultivate the pepper in large amounts changed its value significantly. Once a luxury item, it was now a common household ingredient.

Braeanor turned up the next street, and there were stalls here, too, but this street opened up to a spacious plaza with stalls all over it. Clothes, leather items, knives, cheap jewelry, and other odds and ends were being sold there. Many things had changed in Glenmore, and it appeared that the city was indeed becoming prosperous. Braeanor was glad for everyone.

After leaving the market district, Braeanor continued to the city's southern side, closer to the river docks. He could see the river boats and workers loading and unloading goods in the distance. Just before the docks was a residential district. He saw that many of these buildings were lower quality and dilapidated. Despite the city's growing wealth, there were still people in poverty.

Braeanor saw children running about, as well as women tending to the children. These streets were dirtier, dustier, dingier. Braeanor regretted this for the people. Children, many half-clothed and skinny, ran around and played. They smiled, jumped, and frolicked–oblivious to the value of things–for they had friends and were loved.

As he made his way between a row of houses, he saw a young boy bent over and heaving. He was not even four yet. He had no shirt on, and a tattered cloth served as a covering for his lower half. He looked pale, his hair was patchy, and he did not seem to be vomiting anything.

Behind him was his slightly older sister trying to encourage him, "It okay, brudda. It okay." She patted him on his back.

Their mother stood behind them both. A stained dress, presumably once a clean white, draped on her slight frame. She cupped an elbow in one hand while the other shielded her face. Behind that hand, Braeanor saw a mother's love buried in despair. Her eyes were dim with exhaustion, and she had cried beyond her body's ability to cry anymore.

"Aerion, stop here."

Aerion quietly stopped and instinctively looked over at the family while Braeanor dismounted. Braeanor reached into a bag and pocketed some coins.

"Ma'am," Braeanor softly called out to the mother while slowly walking over.

"Sir, I–I am not looking for work right now. Come back later," she whispered back. She had moved her hand lower on her face to get a better look at him.

"No, ma'am, I am not looking for any such thing. My name is Braeanor. I only wished to inquire of your son's health. I mean no ill will."

"Right, I am sure you don't." She rolled her eyes and turned her shoulder to him.

Braeanor was now only a few feet from her and the children. The daughter had turned to look up at him, but the boy was still bent over, occasionally heaving. Braeanor also noticed that the mother had bruises on her arms and the side of her neck.

"I can only imagine what you have been through, and I see that your son is not well. You have no reason to trust me, but I am a . . ." Braeanor's voice trailed off. He had started to speak out of an old habit, but he was apprehensive to return to the way things had once been.

"You're a what?" she asked, unwilling to entertain the slightest pause as it would prolong the interaction.

"I am a paladin."

She scoffed. "Oh, are you. There's lots more running around here than I thought. I met one of your paladin friends the other week. Wasn't very pious if you ask me."

Braeanor spoke with a subdued confidence. "No doubt many men have claimed such in pursuit of vanity. Such men take. True paladins give, for out of a paladin blessings flow."

With that, Braeanor extended his hand and turned his palm skyward, opening his hand to reveal several gold coins. These coins were years' worth of wages for her.

"These are for you, and I ask for nothing in return other than for you to spend it wisely."

She dropped the hand which had been covering her face to her side and, with eyes wide, stared. She briefly made eye contact with him and then looked at the coins. "Ya going to hit me when I reach for 'em?"

Braeanor's eyes shot wide at the implication. "Ma'am, I would never do such a thing. I am sorry that so many men have been abysmal to you. You never deserved a word of it; a single strike; a moment of fear or pain. Please take, and may the Divines bless you and your family."

She eyed the coins, looked at Braeanor's eyes again, and then back at the coins. She reached over with one hand while she kept the other close to her face, instinctively bracing to be struck by Braeanor's other hand. Her hand trembled as it came close to Braeanor's. Her fingers were frail, and most of her nails were chipped and worn; the few which were not clung to the dirt beneath them. Gingerly, she attempted to pick up each coin, one at a time, so she did not touch Braeanor's hand the slightest bit. She struggled with the last coin, but after several labored attempts, she picked it up without touching his hand. She withdrew her hand quickly and held it with the enclosed coins close to her chest. She stared back at him, waiting for whatever bad thing was to come next.

"I . . . thank you, sir." Her eyes stared into Braeanor's for a moment before averting. She could not make sense of him. He did not look wealthy. He looked nothing special. No man did such a thing.

"You are welcome, ma'am. May I pray with your son before I leave? I would ask that I be able to place a hand on him while I do so. I will then be on my way."

She looked at her son. He had stopped heaving at the moment. He was standing upright and was looking at Braeanor. His lips were chapped and dry, except for a drop of spittle, and tufts of his hair were missing.

"Yes," she replied. "The apothecary says what he has cannae be cured." If she had tears left, she would have cried right then.

Braeanor nodded, took a step closer to the boy, kneeled, and gently called the boy over. The boy stepped forward to him and then began coughing. He then bent over and began to heave once more.

"The Divines can do what the apothecaries cannot," Braeanor said confidently. Braeanor reached up with a hand and placed it around the boy so that a palm lay flat against his back. He could feel each rib flex as his body struggled with each breath and with each spasm of his stomach. His skin was cold to the touch and clammy.

"Divines, by the power of words spoken in faith, I enter your throne room, asking that you hear my prayer. For I know you are enthroned upon the glories of your creation, and there is nothing beyond your ability. I pray now not for me but for this little one. I remember, in faith, in the early days of this world and the glory you bestowed it, that no man, woman, or child knew such sickness. Divines, I ask now, that you bestow this upon the boy. Heal his body of what ails him. Give back to him what the Abyss would take. Restore the vitality of his youth and add to the number of his years to his walk upon this world. Glorify yourself, that all may know faith is not in vain, that we are not alone, for you are worthy of all praises. May it be so."

The boy was still heaving and struggling to catch his breath. Braeanor gently patted his back. When the boy looked up at him, Braeanor whispered something while looking into his eyes with a gentle smile. In of himself, there was nothing he could do for the boy, so he would have to trust the Divines.

As Braeanor stood, the little girl tugged on his shirt tail. "Is brudda be okay now?"

Her deep blue eyes stared into his. A runny nose sat between two rosy cheeks, and her hair, despite being dirty, was tied up in a short, cute ponytail.

"What do you think, little one?"

"Yes. You said beautiful words. He be okay."

"Yes, little one, I think so too." Braeanor smiled at her and then looked at the mother. "If you need help, please go to the Wild Mountain Goat Inn and speak with Kellina. Tell her Braeanor, or the paladin, sent you. She may need a helping hand and have work."

She was silent but nodded. Her hand still clutched the coins near her chest while she stared at her son with a frown.

Braeanor walked back to Aerion and mounted him again.

"Thank you, sir," the mother said, surprising herself with the sudden volume of her voice.

"You are welcome. My life is in service to the Divines. May peace be upon you and your family." Braeanor quickly patted Aerion's neck twice, and Aerion began walking again. The mother watched as the so-called paladin went towards the docks.

IV

Meanwhile, Kellina and Lilium had made their way to another smaller room, which had a basin with water and a mirror on a small table. A brush, a bottle of perfumed ointment, some makeup, and cloths lay next to the basin.

"Well, Lilium, I will spare you telling me anything you don't feel comfortable telling me, but I am a woman who hasn't shied away from playing a losing hand. So, I'll venture a guess. Have you, by chance, started experiencing your monthly?"

"Yes," Lilium replied while staring at the floor.

"Congratulations, though it is terribly inconvenient." Kellina smiled warmly at her. "It is perfectly normal and will be a part of your life for many years to come." Kellina then took the time to graciously explain the reality of managing it well while ensuring she felt no shame for it.

Afterwards, Kellina changed subjects. "So deary, this aside, how are you doing?" Eager to hear Lilium's response, Kellina's face radiated a soothing warmth, which seemed out of character for her tough exterior.

"I am fine, I guess. It doesn't seem real sometimes. I never asked for any of this. It doesn't seem fair."

Kellina frowned. "No, it doesn't seem fair, does it? I'm sorry."

Lilium nodded. "I have to hope that something good, somehow, will come of it. I don't know how. It can't have been for nothing."

"The Divines can work things for good, even against all the evil worked by the Abyss. It doesn't always make sense, but they can." Kellina ran a hand through her hair.

Lilium looked up at her. "You believe in the Divines? I mean, really believe?"

Kellina leaned against a wall. "Yes, I do. My parents were faithful. Though I admit, I have had my fair share of struggles. Braeanor helped restore my faith."

Lilium sat up. "How so?"

"I suppose it is a story of awful things being worked for good." Kellina winked at Lilium. Kellina faintly smiled as her mind drifted back to all that had transpired.

"It was around five years or so ago. I had been quite fortunate mining in the mountains. My mother would always call me her 'wild mountain goat.' I saved up money and had this inn built. There was something magical in the thought that I would run an inn. I would meet all kinds of people and help 'em on their way. It was a different kind of adventure, I suppose.

"Little did I know that within a couple months, I would be the target of the only other inn in the city at that time. They didn't want the competition, especially not from a woman. I began receiving subtle threats and suggestions that I needed to leave town. Things got worse. Now, I am stubborn and can hold my own. I've learned that about myself from an early age, and I think it nearly killed my parents." Kellina laughed at herself.

Lilium giggled, too.

"At any rate, one night, it was closing time. Seven men were hanging around who didn't seem in a hurry to leave despite me having told 'em more than once that it was time to. None of 'em had rooms for the night. In fact, no one had booked a room that night.

"Finally, one of the men got up and made his way to the door. I assumed he was leaving and was thankful that at least one man had come to his senses. The man barred the door and pulled a chair up against it. The next thing I knew, all the men were standing and looking at me.

"'Shoulda left when you had the chance,' one of 'em said to me. With no other words, they all rushed me. I fought like a fiend, but let's be honest. Those are tough odds for anyone. I yelled and called out for help but was no use. Others in town knew of the plan.

"The men had me pinned . . . to put it nicely, deary, those men intended to make me their wife that night.

"Before that could happen, I remember hearing a loud slam from behind the bar but I couldn't see anything. 'Seems you forgot to secure the back door,' is all I hear from the man I can't see. One of the others yells for him to get out, or they will do him worse.

"'Seems I need a room for the night,' he shouts back at them. 'Seems you best leave now. I get grumpy when I'm tired.' The men shouted at him more and finally one of them went over to the man.

"Next thing I knew the man was reeling backwards holding his throat gagging. The other men jumped up to get the man behind the bar. I sprung up and backed into a corner to see what I should do next." Kellina paused as she replayed the events over in her mind, seeing each moment.

"All I had to do was watch. The men shoulda left. Braeanor told them more than once during the fight to leave. They would not. They were mad with their wrath and lust. An abysmal lot, if there ever was one. We ended up burying all seven in unmarked graves just outside the city, west of here. That is how I met him."

"Whoa," Lilium remarked. "Why did he come to the inn?"

"He said he was just out for a walk and was further from home than expected. He needed somewhere to stay for the night."

Lilium's eyes lit up. "After he found me, when I thanked him for rescuing me, he said he had only been out for a walk."

"Hmm. Well, he stayed here for the week following that, and I got to know him a bit. I became convinced he won't let on easily. He is burdened with things he won't speak. As much as I can tell, especially after learning that he lived in Haverstead and would have had to decide to go for a walk days ago, it was simply his way of saying he was sent to me without really knowing why. The Divines must have tugged on his heart or something to make him come all this way.

"So, that is why I believe that even bad things can be used for good. Those were bad men hired to kill me, and I am sure they would have gone on to do the same to others. I suffered for a moment so others would be spared, and I think in some strange way, Braeanor needed that. He was of some use for good, but when he left, he still seemed haunted by things he wouldn't share." Kellina tucked some of her hair behind an ear.

Lilium briefly smiled. "It gives me hope, though I am sorry you had to go through that."

"Thank you, dear. Though you have suffered much worse than me." Kellina reached over and patted Lilium's back.

"And you are right. He has lost people he loved. He is the last paladin." Lilium looked at the floor and then back up at Kellina. "This is why I have to travel with him. I don't know why, but he needs me. Though I cannot help him fight, I can pray. I can be there for him."

Kellina rubbed Lilium's back gently. "And he must need that in some way beyond my understanding. I don't like the thought of you being in danger, but I trust that the Divines must intend to make the most of you two coming together."

"I hope so." Lilium nodded and then looked up at Kellina. "Have you had any more troubles since that day?"

"Braeanor paid a visit to the other inn, and they left me alone from that day onward. There are always other men who drink too much or devise evil, but Braeanor taught me a few things before he left."

Kellina suddenly held a dagger, which Lilium missed being pulled out from somewhere among her clothes. She twirled, slashed, stabbed, and swung it like an extension of her hand. "There are several more unmarked graves now, but they each forced my hand and deserved it. I much prefer just throwing the men out when I have to, but some get violent, even when unprovoked. So be it." She grinned and returned the dagger to a sheath tucked in her waist and concealed by her shirt, which hung loosely.

Lilium admired her skill and how undaunted she was. Kellina

was brave and had every reason to give in and shrink back from the dangers she experienced, but she had a cheery demeanor, unfazed by it all. "Is Farlan a good man," she asked.

"I'd say so. He believes in the Divines, too. Moreover, he is capable of putting up with my stubbornness. I think he actually likes it. He even tries to make me a bit angry once in a while cause 'he likes the fire in my eyes,' and I'm 'so cute when mad,'" Kellina giggled.

Lilium giggled, too. "Does your mother live here?"

"No, she is east of here, about a day's travel. In fact, you should stop by there. It's on the way."

"Really?" Lilium asked.

"She is a very sweet woman. She lives alone now that my father passed away."

"I'm sorry to hear about your father." Lilium frowned.

"Thank you, dear. It was just a couple years ago. He thankfully passed peacefully in his sleep. Couldn't think of a better way. Yes, she would enjoy your company, and she is very faithful to the Divines. It would bless her heart to meet Braeanor. She speaks of the paladins differently than the rest of us. She was born before the crusade."

Lilium nodded and smiled. "Then we will just have to get Braeanor to do so."

Kellina smiled back but then looked away. Her countenance fell. "Saying this makes me realize I have not seen her since my father's passing."

"You should pay her a visit then. Perhaps you can accompany us to her house?" Lilium asked with hope in her voice.

"Oh, I would like to. I have much to tell her." Kellina's eyes had a glimmer of something special as she became thoughtful for a moment, and her hands eased to her tummy, where they rested. "Yes, I need to, but I would need some time to ensure things are in order here. I will encourage Braeanor to pay her a visit before continuing on. It would be good for everyone."

"I do hope you don't delay in seeing your mother. I am sure she misses you very much. We should not take our mothers for granted." Warmth rushed to Lilium's face, and tears began flowing before she even knew what was happening. She began crying.

"Oh, my little lady, come here."

Kellina pulled Lilium into her bosom and held her tightly. She also began to cry softly. She held Lilium until they both settled back down. It had been a long time since she had a good cry.

Braeanor arrived at the docks. They were only large enough for a couple of mid-size river boats to dock, but given the simple hoists, crates, and barrels that lay about, they stayed busy. A couple of boys sat on the edge of the dock fishing. A jet-black cat sat nearby relaxing in the sun, and it stared at Braeanor with its uncanny green eyes before gently closing them to nap.

Braeanor dismounted Aerion. After spying who he believed to be the harbormaster supervising a boat being loaded, he walked over to strike up a conversation. Docks were always good for information. Typically, paladins were very direct when seeking information, but he decided he would try his hand at playing a part.

"Any work 'round here for a man down on 'is luck?" Braeanor inquired.

The harbormaster wore simple pants and a loose-fitting shirt with an anchor pin fastened to it. His dark hair was partially hidden beneath a wide-brimmed straw hat that rested over a face that had seen too much sun.

"Nah, reckon not. 'Less you really down on your luck?" He cut his eyes at Braeanor and sized him up.

Braeanor shrugged. "Might be. Any crews needing an extra hand?" He pointed over at the boat.

"Nah, reckon not. Might try back tomorrow. Should be a couple more shipments arriving. Never can tell."

Braeanor looked over at what was being loaded, and he spotted what appeared to be a large block of dark green stone beneath a canvas tarp.

"Is soapstone worth much these days?" Braeanor inquired.

"You find some up in the mountains?" the harbormaster shot back with piqued interest.

"I gotta lead. I didn't know if it was worth the trouble, is all." Braeanor feigned disinterest.

"You serious? There's a group–" The harbormaster stopped mid-sentence and stepped close to Braeanor while looking around to see if they were being watched, as if he did not even want his words to be seen. "You know the kind, the ones that makes you nervous-like and dabbles with things they shouldn't—hey are paying a fortune for it."

"Oh, don't say," Braeanor softly replied. "What they needin' it for that makes it so worthwhile?"

"Who knows, but—" his eyes glanced around again before continuing, "heard a sailor talk of an island being built out at sea, way out at sea. He said it's a spooky place in the Deep Tides, real hard to navigate."

"Out in the middle of the ocean?" Braeanor asked with genuine interest.

"Yes, they say the so-called man-in-yellow oversees its building. Course I hadn't seen that sailor in a couple months to ask further. Makes me wonder."

Braeanor scratched his chin. "Hmm. Well, if I find some, I'll be sure to bring it back."

The harbormaster turned his head and spit off the dock. "Good luck with that. They pay more for bigger blocks of it, so don't smash it up if you can help it. But they say there is little left in the surrounding mountains anymore. Been mined up already."

"Yes, well, I guess we'll see. Good day then." Braeanor nodded in appreciation of the harbormaster's time.

The harbormaster nodded and turned back to overseeing the ship being loaded.

Braeanor turned and began walking back toward Aerion. Up ahead, he saw the black cat now sitting rather regally upright in the middle of the pier. He stared up at Braeanor.

He walked up to the cat, who did not budge. He knelt and looked into its green eyes. "You need something friend? This something I should attend to, sooner than later?"

The cat blinked very slowly back at Braeanor, stood, and then walked over to the nearby edge of the pier. He turned, faced where he had just been sitting, and resumed his regal posture after wrapping his tail around his front paws. Braeanor was now permitted to pass.

Braeanor stood and turned toward the cat. "Good day then," he said to the cat with a nod. He then walked over to Aerion.

VI

Braeanor left the docks and continued around the city, making his way to the southwestern quarter. The streets became cobbled and less crowded, and all the buildings had finer woodworking. He saw emblems on signs outside buildings, and he knew they represented the guilds of the city. The last time he had been here, there were just three guilds—the miners, jewelers, and blacksmiths. All were tied to the ongoing labor in the mountains or the fruits thereof. Now, he saw signs for masons, other artisans, and farmers.

He was most surprised by the farmer guild. It appeared the farmers grew smart and realized they could leverage some influence rather than eke out a grueling living underfoot. Everyone needed to eat, but few people around a city truly wanted to tend the fields.

Further up the cobblestone path was a larger building with stone columns and ornate bronze doors. The building was the town hall, where the business of the city was dispensed with, and all who were or hoped to be someone came and spoke self-importantly. Aerion brought Braeanor closer to the steps leading up to the door, and he began to look at the ornate features of the double set of bronze doors.

Ding, ding, ding, ding, ding, ding, ding rang out a bell from the city watchtower. Its high-pitched, hollow, metallic screaming announced danger. The sounds of shouting, scrambling people, and of doors and shutters slamming followed.

Aerion neighed and demanded Braeanor's attention over to the buildings across from them. A shadow steadily crept across the front of the buildings. Instinctively, he looked up to see what was casting the shadow. Something flew up above, hidden in the glare of the sun. It began descending toward the ground, somewhere farther into the city.

"Go, Aerion. That thing is landing in the city!" Braeanor shouted.

Aerion hurried back down the street and turned to his left. Off in the distance, men could be faintly heard shouting. Loud chittering and hissing could be heard, too. Instinctively, turn after turn and street after street, Aerion closed in on the source of the commotion, and the sounds grew louder.

Braeanor was back at the market plaza, and the city watch was spread out trying to fight an abyssian with which he was regrettably familiar. It was a ripper locust. These creatures were created to hunt and kill horses, especially paladin steeds. It had already killed the captain of the guard and his horse. Pieces of each were strewn across the plaza.

The ripper locust was a large creature standing taller than a horse. It had a body similar to a locust, with six spider-like legs and two smaller forelegs with talons on the ends used for stabbing or pinning victims. The greatest source of danger was its unique mouth, which consisted of two sets of independently movable vertical pincers, or chelicerae. Their mouth could grip a victim in two separate points and simultaneously slice while pulling apart. The victims would either be lacerated beyond help or, even worse, ripped apart as the sets of pincers pulled in opposite directions.

A thick carapace covered the majority of its body, and its limbs were well protected, too. Very strong blows from sharp weapons may be enough to cut a leg off. Most often, though, the blade would simply glance off. Arrows and bolts were of no use unless it was flying. Only its underside and a small gap on its back between its head and thorax were vulnerable. The only soft spot on its head was its eyes, but these were set deep among protruding carapace. These creatures were not ones to sit still, and only exceptional marksmen would have a chance.

The ripper locust's mouth vibrated to let out a chittering hiss, which sent chills down the spines of all the watch. Its feet constantly shuffled as if the ground were on fire, and it could not sit still. Occasionally, it fluttered its wings before tucking them back into slits in its carapace.

The men of the watch stabbed at it with their spears, and Braeanor could tell they had never encountered one. Each stab and slash of their spears glanced off its carapace in vain, and the men were too afraid to make any bold attempt to search out a weakness. Several guards shot bolts at it with their crossbows from a safe distance, but not a single one had managed to penetrate the thick carapace. Braeanor knew he needed to help quickly, or it would kill all of them.

The creature dashed forward and knocked several men down with sweeps of its forelegs. It then stabbed out with its right foreleg and stabbed a guard in his gut. It pulled him across the ground closer to its mouth while he screamed in pain and terror. It began to lift him to its mouth, but another guard managed an excellent blow and cut that foreleg off.

Without a moment missed, the ripper locust leaned forward, turned its head, and snatched that defiant guard. It then lifted its head while backing away from the other guards. The screaming guard was gripped across his chest and waist. It forcefully closed its pincers and pulled them apart while shaking its head from side to side. The silenced guard was torn into three pieces, each piece being cast aside.

Several of the guards yelled in defiance; one vomited immediately and began backing away from the fray, and another ran off altogether, tossing his crossbow as he fled. The guard impaled in his gut was trying to crawl away while part of the ripper locust's foreleg remained inside him.

Braeanor began looking around for a height advantage. Without his armor on, it would be far too risky to attempt to slide under it and exploit its underside. However, he could strike from above at the gap in the carapace where its head flexed. He eyed a large wooden stall back to his right.

"Aerion, this way." Braeanor tugged and led Aerion to the stall. He placed his hands on the saddle, leaned forward as if laying upon his hands, lifted his feet out of the stirrups, and then pushed himself upward with enough force to be able to bring his feet under him and stand on the saddle. He then hopped on top of the stall.

"Listen carefully, boy. I need you to do exactly as I say, and we can kill this thing. It absolutely hates horses. I need you to run up and get its attention, but you must run back this way and come right along this stall with it chasing behind you. I will be able to jump onto its back. You must not hesitate, and you must keep running even after I am on its back. You understand?"

Aerion huffed. His heart was already beating fast, but this task put it into a full sprint. He was nervous but nodded back at Braeanor and turned in the direction of the ripper locust. It was about fifty yards away on the other side of several stalls. He plotted his course. He would run to his left and circle in front of it, easing for just a moment to catch its attention, and then he'd continue onto the last half of the circle, which would bring him right alongside Braeanor.

After taking a deep breath, Aerion began running. The men were continuing to struggle against the ripper locust. Another man was pierced in his left leg by the remaining foreleg, and it was starting to pull him closer to its mouth. Aerion ran between and among stalls to hide from view until he came from behind the group of men. Shooting out between two of the crossbowmen, he stopped, reared his forelegs, and neighed loudly.

The ripper locust let out a loud hiss as it pulled its foreleg out of the man, tossing him against a building in the process. It began skittering forward so fast that its feet lost traction momentarily. Aerion sprinted off toward Braeanor.

The ripper locust found traction and began keeping pace with Aerion, but Aerion had a sufficient head start. Aerion passed right by the stall where Braeanor maintained a shallow profile to hide himself from view. He held his trusty dagger firmly in his mouth, his teeth gripping it tightly. The ripper locust passed right next to him, and though Braeanor did not have as much of a height advantage as he had hoped, it was enough for him to be able to jump and mount the creature.

The creature hissed again and turned in circles several times before backing into a set of stalls. Braeanor held tight. He knew he would need to wait a few moments before sinking his dagger into it. His legs gripped each side of the ripper locust's body, and his hands held the edges of the carapace at the weak spot in the neck.

The ripper locust then extended its wings from their hiding places, the right one of which caught Braeanor's right leg with enough force to nearly pull him off that side. His grip was sure, though, and he was able to pull himself back into position just as it took flight. Its wings slapped the air rapidly and with a deep, humming beat, which hurt Braeanor's ears.

As the creature ascended, Braeanor knew his opportunity had arrived. Moving his right hand up to his mouth, he grabbed the dagger's handle, and without a moment or motion wasted, he sunk it into the gap and into the vulnerable neck tissue. He pulled it across from one side to the other, severing vitals.

The creature hissed loudly and lurched downward in the air as dark purple blood spurted out. Braeanor was about ten feet higher than the closest building's roof. The ripper locust began to tilt to its right, and its wings fluttered more slowly. He shifted his body so his feet straddled the left wing, and he began sliding off it on his stomach. He then stabbed the wing, and he held the handle with both of his hands. It then tilted to its left as it began to descend.

The dagger efficiently sliced through the wing, and this was enough to slow his initial speed as he came off the ripper locust. As the dagger freed itself from the wing, he focused on the roof below. He was positioned to hit an angled side of the roof, and this allowed him to land in such a way as to go right into a roll. After one complete roll, he planted a foot and leaned against the roof to slide the rest of the way down to its edge. He came off the roof and made the twelve-foot drop without issue, letting go of the knife midfall. As he landed on the ground, he rolled forward and up into a standing position.

He hurried and picked up his dagger. Braeanor watched as the ripper locust continued its descent. It was not able to clear the building in front of it, and it smashed head-first into its stonework. It then fell, twisting midair, and landed on its backside in a defeated heap. With one final spasm and hiss of its jaws, it died.

He was pleased with himself. He did not expect it to go so smoothly. He felt more optimistic about the journey ahead; he hadn't completely lost his touch. Aerion trotted back up to him and nuzzled him briefly.

"Yeah, I'm good, boy. And you did great. Thank you for trusting me and doing what I said. I couldn't have done this without you."

Aerion huffed modestly, but he was basking in the moment. He felt a sense of pride which he had not experienced in some time.

The remaining guards came over to Braeanor; each one exasperated by what they had experienced but very thankful to be alive. After several gruff and out-of-breath "thanks" exchanged with Braeanor, they hurried up to the corpse of the ripper locust to inspect it and ensure it was indeed dead. After further inspection, which involved poking at it while keeping a shield raised, they decided they could blow the horn to let everyone know that it was now safe.

Braeanor stood watching the men while rubbing Aerion's neck. One of the guards walked past them and began looking around. He walked over to where part of the day captain of the guard's body lay, and he began to retrieve his horn. As soon as he picked it up, he realized it was too covered and filled with blood to be of use.

"Something's happening!" shouted one of the guards near the ripper locust's body.

After-death! Braeanor recalled with disappointment in himself. He had forgotten about that parasite which often inhabited certain abyssians.

The ripper locust's softer underside shifted and moved as something stirred. Crunching, squishing noises began to emanate from the body.

"Get back, stand back—" Braeanor shouted as he began running towards them.

Two guards readied themselves near the body of the ripper locust, but they did not move back. The ripper locust's underside exploded, spewing a mix of purple blood and stomach contents onto one of the guards. His face was now covered in the vile mixture, causing him to immediately begin retching.

A mass of tentacles attached to a fleshly, round orb shot out. It spun around and hurled itself onto a guard, each tentacle wrapping around a limb and his neck. A tooth-lined maw in the middle of the ball bit into the man's inner thigh, tearing a chunk free from his femoral artery. Blood spurted out, and the man frantically tried to knock it free with his spear while screaming in horror.

The guard covered in the ripper locust viscera swiped at his eyes repeatedly with the palm of his hand in an effort to see better, but he was panicked. He was so distraught by what little he could actually see that he began wildly swinging at the creature. Though he severed some tentacles, he was also slicing his fellow guard open.

The after-death moved and spun around onto the guard's upper back, where it took out a chunk of the man's neck. The guard began spinning in circles while trying to grab the creature to pull it free, but he could not.

The panicked guard, still barely able to see, struck out at the thing repeatedly. He managed to strike it, but in the process, he nearly decapitated his fellow guard. Both the mortally wounded guard and the creature fell to the ground. He continued to hack at the after-death, unwilling to believe that it was dead given how its tentacles continued to spasm.

Braeanor was now standing near them, having been unable to intervene in the chaotic episode. He turned as he heard another commotion coming across the plaza. It was the night watch who had risen from their sleep to aid in the fight. Though the fight was over, Braeanor was surprised they had arrived rather quickly, all things considered. The men even had their armor on.

The guard who had retrieved the blood-filled horn stared at the after-death and yet another guard killed. He dropped the horn and waved at the captain of the night guard as they came up. "It's down!" he yelled as best he could while still catching his breath.

The night guard eased up, and each guardsman began to take in the gruesome scene all around them. The night captain came up to the day guardsman and began to speak, "It was one bloody fight by the looks of it." While looking over at the now-deceased day captain, he continued, "Real shame, too. He was a good man. Let's have a look at this creature."

They all walked past Braeanor without a word spoken. Braeanor backed away and returned to Aerion, and he watched as the group inspected the ripper locust and after-death. The men then began to motion in Braeanor's direction, and their hand gestures made him realize that they were likely discussing his involvement in killing the ripper locust. The night captain nodded, and he and several of his men walked toward Braeanor.

"Good man, I am Jovar, the night watch captain. May I ask your name?" Jovar carried himself with an air of superiority, and he studied Braeanor as if unsure of the man standing before him.

"I am Braeanor." He nodded respectfully at Jovar.

"Likewise. Guardsmen are saying you killed the big creature." Jovar tilted his head with doubt. "Is that true?"

"Yes, I did. With the help of my horse Aerion, of course." He turned toward Aerion and patted his neck for emphasis.

"I see. Well, sir, we owe you a debt of gratitude, as well as some drinks and a celebration." He patted Braeanor on his shoulder solidly.

Braeanor sighed to himself. "It won't be necessary, sir, though I appreciate the thought."

"Oh, nonsense. Don't be so modest. You've saved guardsmen's lives."

As Braeanor searched for words to protest further, the night captain had already raised his horn to his lips. He blew three loud blasts to let the people of Glenmore know it was safe.

The sounds of shutters and doors flying open filled the air, and immediately afterward, crowds of chattering people scurried through the streets. Citizens scoured the city in a frenzy to find where the fighting had been and to see what had taken place, and it did not take long for everyone to learn where the creature lay slain. They were drawn to the aftermath.

Among the growing ruckus, the night guard sent one of his men to fetch the undertaker and notify the city council of what had taken place. Other members of the guard were tending to the unpleasant task of gathering the bodies of the dead guardsmen. Unfortunately, the guards whom the ripper locust's forelegs had pierced had already succumbed to their grievous wounds.

Braeanor patted Aerion on his neck. "Come on, boy, let's walk back to Kellina's."

The night captain overheard Braeanor.

'Ah, Kellina. She runs a fine inn and has plenty to drink. I will catch up to you there, Braeanor." Jovar pointed at Braeanor as he finished talking.

Braeanor nodded at him and waved as he walked off. He had no interest in being the center of attention for killing one abyssian. When he was a younger paladin, he would have proudly been championed by the locals. He regretted how it had once been his habit to quickly indulge in others' adoration, and for a paladin, killing a single abyssian was nothing special. Self-loathing welled up within him.

Pride was the very champion urging the paladin order to enter the Abyss and end the war once and for all without additional preparations. He should be dead and all the others alive. Similarly, had he remembered about the possibility of the after-death, he might have been in a position to save one more life. He was rusty, and it cost someone dearly. He shook his head and walked, resolving to set aside his feelings upon arriving at the inn so that others would not bear the brunt of his resurgent angst.

VII

The Wild Mountain Goat Inn was already filling up when Braeanor arrived. There were men from the guilds, dressed recognizably for their respective trades; there were a few guardsmen; and there were other various denizens of the city. Lilium sat at a small table in the corner closest to the bar. Her eyes lit up when she saw him enter, and she waved eagerly at him. He smiled back at her and walked over.

"There he is! That's the man who killed it!" shouted a man from somewhere in the room.

People began clapping and cheering, and several men nearby gave Braeanor a good-hearted slap on the back or shoulder as he walked by.

Braeanor clenched his jaw tight, and his nostrils flared as he took a deep breath. He would have been glad to be a nobody. He wanted no attention, no thanks, no anything except to be left alone at the moment. His mind was already too flooded with feelings to be thrust into a situation with a roomful of others gawking at him. Word spread too fast in this city. He managed to politely smile, nevertheless.

"A round of drinks on me!" shouted Tremont, the Jeweler's Guild-Father. The rotund man wore expensive-looking clothes that were adorned with frills, wild patches of sequins, and colorful seams, and his fingers, wrists, neck, and ears could have stocked a whole merchant's cart with his gaudy jewelry.

Braeanor shook his head then abruptly said, "Everyone, thank you, but I do not drink—moreover—"

"Ah, today you must! We must celebrate. We have every reason to be thankful!" responded Tremont. He was squeezing between other patrons, which mostly involved pushing them out of the way with his mass as he made his way toward Braeanor. After doing so, he looked at his clothing to double-check that all his tackiness remained intact.

Braeanor saw the night captain, Jovar, enter the inn out of the corner of his eye. He scanned the room and saw dozens of eyes staring at him.

Tremont neared Braeanor and whispered, "And I've brought a selection you may choose from to celebrate." The man pointed to three seductively dressed women who sat in a far corner while playfully nudging Braeanor with his other elbow. Armed men stood on each side of the women.

A fire was lit within Braeanor, and he could not restrain his urge to put others in their proper place. "You say to be thankful! To be thankful for what? Would you pray to the Divines with such gratitude? Never. You eat and drink to the god of your gut. You revel and encourage the wrongdoer in each other, saying, 'let us eat and drink today for tomorrow the Abyss takes us.'"

The inn had become much quieter now as others were listening closely to him. Dismayed, Tremont recoiled and backed away from

Braeanor; he could not comprehend Braeanor's rejection. Kellina and Farlan then emerged from the back room carrying a keg, which they sat on the bar top.

"Five men and a horse died fighting that ripper locust, and has anyone thought about them or their families?" Braeanor looked around the room. "Hmm?"

Jovar raised his voice and spoke matter-of-factly, "The city council makes all such arrangements, and those very things will be tended to. And on that note, any men wanting to apply to the watch may see me. We actually have six openings. A silver piece bounty has been placed on Linum Oldham for fleeing the fight, and he is to be hanged."

"A ripper locust? Is that what that thing is called?" a man shouted from a back corner.

"How do you know that? How did you kill that thing? Tell us!" shouted another man from somewhere else in the crowd. Several others cheered and slapped the tables in approval of what the man said.

Braeanor paused and glanced around, searching for the origin of those spoken inquiries. His eyebrows were furrowed, and his jaw jutted forward. He was on edge. The fools were undaunted by all that Braeanor had just said. They wanted what they wanted, and that was it.

"He is a paladin," Lilium said loudly and confidently.

Braeanor felt her words as a blow to his stomach, and he closed his eyes as his shoulders sank. She was too young to understand the situation or read the room. Too naive.

"A paladin, says the little girl," a gruff-looking miner exclaimed with a guffaw. "Looks like a paladin to me!" The man turned to the others at his table, who laughed along with his jest.

"Yes, he is a paladin," Lilium sheepishly restated, unsure why those men were laughing like they were.

"There haven't been any paladins for many years," Jovar said. "Not real ones, at least. The only word of paladins you hear is the old wives' tales and drunken stories of the supposed useless gray paladin who lives in Edjramor. I don't suppose we have been graced with his presence, have we?"

"Nothing good comes out of Edjramor, that's what they say," another man shouted out. "Been that way since the crusade my pappy said."

Braeanor turned and walked over toward Lilium. "Say what you will. Celebrate how you want without me. It does not matter."

Another miner shouted out at Braeanor, "If you is a paladin, then you is a failure. I says it to your face, I do. You couldn't protect ya'selves, and look at our lands today. Decent folk flees to the cities to know any peace. Even here we ain't safe. You should be out killing those things all the time, not celebratin'!"

Braeanor turned toward the man with clenched fists, and his lips were pursed as he actively restrained himself from saying much worse than, "Is that what you think!"

Another man shouted out, "My granddad said where paladins went, those creatures followed. Paladins don't bring nothing good! It's why there's so many in Edjramor! It came here cause of you! Paladins just as much in leagues with them Old Ones as the cult be!"

Several voices shouted out in agreement and slapped tables again.

"That's enough," Kellina yelled out while stabbing her dagger into the bar top. "This is my inn, and I won't have it full of men who disrespect Braeanor."

She began pointing at the miner who called Braeanor a failure. "You, Taymin, should I remind you of your contribution to that scheme years ago? By rights, you should be buried outside the city, and I'd suppose your mom would thank me for hiding her shame. It was Braeanor who came to my aid, and it is mercy and forgiveness which permits me to stomach seeing you in my place as a paying customer."

Taymin shrunk into his chair and stared into his drink. Had Taymin's chair not been so sturdy, it might have collapsed under the weight of Kellina's words bearing down upon him.

"There are other men here who are unworthy, and you know damn well who you are–and I'm saying it to your face! Now I continue to choose to live in a city that would reward the unworthy with positions of power–" and with that, she stared at the night captain with eyes that might even pierce a ripper locust, "yet such is how things are. But inside my inn, I run things the way I want.

"Everyone is free to leave or stay, but you better not run that mouth off about paladins. That much is done. Braeanor is blood of my blood as far as I'm concerned."

Kellina looked across the room, her gaze meeting the eyes of any man who wasn't so put to shame that they stared into their mug as well.

"This is how the Abyss wins," Lilium spoke gently. "When men are so focused on fighting each other, it needs only watch and wait." With those words spoken, she stood from her table, walked behind the bar, and entered the back room.

Braeanor nodded and grimaced. She was right. He had come close to walking over and knocking a miner out and only for words spoken. He followed behind Lilium.

"Well," Farlan spoke loudly while clearing his throat and dispensing some drink from the barrel's tap into his mug.

"Seems like someone said a round of drinks was on him!" Farlan drank his full mug in two large gulps and raised it high. "My thanks to the Jeweler's Guild-father! Feel free to walk up and fill your mug while I play a song or two!" Farlan slammed his mug and picked up his vielle from behind the bar.

Several men let out less-than-enthusiastic cheers and walked up to get a drink. Several quietly got up and exited the inn, and the captain of the watch was one of them. Farlan began to strum his instrument to warm up, and Kellina placed a hand on the small of his back while looking him in the eyes. He looked knowingly back and nodded. They made a good team.

"Anyone know the song, *Wench or Witch*?" Farlan shouted aloud with a tone of joviality.

Men cheered, and several slapped their tables several times with great enthusiasm, but Kellina rolled her eyes as she stepped into the back room. She could not stand that song, but it would be good for changing the mood of the room.

Farlan played a few notes on his vielle and cleared his throat before getting into the upbeat song, and men joined in at the chorus:

> From South Shore to Bevereign, I'd like to sail the sea
> But I haven't got a boat to sail, no sir'ee!
> From the docks I spotted one nearby the shore
> To the harbormaster I go for which to implore
> How much for yonder boat set against deep blue sea
> He said if you take my daughter sir, for you it's free
>
> I exclaimed, free! Free? But I asked
> Will she sink or will she float? (will she float?)
> Aye, she will float (she will float)
> Will she float? (will she float?)
> Aye, she will float (she will float)
>
> So out at sea the lady and me are having a good ol' time
> Waves are crashing and birds are singing pretty rhymes
> Now the sails needed stitch'n and deck boards a cleanin'
> And my sea gal was good in a pinch, made things a cinch
> But the storms and creatures of the sea gave us a right ol' fright
> We nearly died a dozen times when she turned to me one night
>
> Will she sink or will she float? (will she float?)
> Aye, she will float (she will float)
> Will she float? (will she float?)
> Aye, she will float (she will float)

A fortnight passed when soon my lass began passing gas
Beyond the smell I must tell her voice became a siren song
And the deck wasn't kept clean and she got real mean
And I couldn't find peace nowhere above or below deck
That sea gal of mine nagged till I wanted to ring that neck
Was this sea maiden a wench or witch, I should check

And I began to wonder. Now I really wondered, men. Do you
know what I wondered? (Will she sink or will she float!)
Will she sink or will she float? (will she float?)
Aye, she will float (she will float)
Will she float? (will she float?)
Aye, she will float (she will float)

Another week went by and her voice was a hue and cry
For everything became a trifle and a pain with her
I'd rather a board of wood for a friend than hear her voice again
So I decided it was high time on the high seas for that test
For I was sure she was a witch and would not sink
So I tossed her in and watched with a grin and drink

And you know what I asked myself men?
(Will she sink or will she float!) That's right!
And you know what! (what!)
Aye, she don't float! (she don't float!)
Oh no! She don't! (no she don't!)
She don't float! (she don't float!)
Oh no! She don't! (no she don't!)

So listen again men to what I have to say
If a man gives his daughter away just say, no way!

Better to sink in the sea than sail away with her

Better yet, stay on dry land with a drink in hand, yes sir!

Men laughed, raised their mugs, punched each other on the shoulder, and chatted amongst themselves. Soon enough, the inn was full of noise, laughter, and just the right amount of rowdiness.

As Kellina walked past Braeanor and Lilium, she offered an apology. "I'm sorry, Braeanor."

"Nah, don't worry about it. I appreciate what you said, though. It means a lot." His eyes met hers, and she could see the weight of his words reflected in his eyes. He did not really need anyone to come to his defense, but a part of him needed to know that there was someone who would.

Crestfallen, Lilium asked, "Should I have not spoken?"

Braeanor shook his head one time and drew a deep breath before answering her. "Well, you will learn there is a time to speak and a time to be silent, and those around you are a big part of that decision. Not everyone shares your faith or your appreciation of paladins is all. I know you did not mean for any of that to happen. Sometimes, things are just complicated. Try to read the room first."

Lilium nodded.

"But there was truth in what you said, that when men fight amongst themselves, the Abyss wins. *You were right.* My pride got in the way in there, and I almost struck a man because of it." Braeanor added some emphasis to bring a measure of reassurance to Lilium. She had discerned something he had lost sight of in the moment, and it kept him from doing something which would have impugned his reputation as a paladin.

Lilium sat up tall, lifted her eyes from the floor, and nodded after Braeanor's encouraging remark.

Braeanor turned toward Kellina. "I think we will take our rooms for the night and perhaps turn in early. We have a long road ahead of us."

Lilium brought a hand to her mouth and cleared her throat suggestively while looking at Kellina. Her eyes shot from Kellina over to Braeanor.

Kellina's eyes lit up as she remembered what they had discussed. "Braeanor, were you by chance going to follow the river east a-ways before crossing?"

"Yes, why is that?"

"Well, my mother, Elspeth, actually lives out that way. There is a large stone between the river and a path which turns north. She lives just a few miles up. Altogether, she is about a day's ride from here. I was wondering if you might be interested or even willing to stop by there. I am sure she would put you up for the night. She would like your company."

"Oh, I don't want to inconvenience her. I would hate to impose, especially not knowing her personally."

She stepped closer to Braeanor and rested a hand on his shoulder, and she looked him in his eyes. "I understand, but I think even Lilium was interested. I plan to make arrangements here so that I can visit her too. I've realized it has been too long since I've checked on her. It would mean a lot to me if you would stop by her place."

Braeanor rubbed his chin. "You sure she wouldn't mind the company? It would put us just a little closer and give us another night of shelter."

Kellina rubbed his shoulder. "I'm confident she would be glad to see a kind face. I think you will find her quite hospitable."

"Sounds like a plan, then. We will do that," Braeanor smiled softly.

Kellina and Lilium looked at each other with large smiles, and they both scrunched their heads and shoulders forward as if projecting excitement at each other. Kellina reached into a pocket and pulled out several keys, and after finding two keys to rooms adjacent to one another, she handed them to Braeanor. "Make yourselves at home, and we will bring up supper after a bit. Let us know if you need anything."

"Thank you, Kellina," Braeanor replied.

"You are welcome. And should you need to up and leave without notice," she tilted her head and raised her eyebrows while pointing a finger, "then just leave the keys on your beds. But I will say I tend to wake early nowadays, regardless of when I turn in for the evening."

Braeanor held up the keys and smiled, "I will say goodbye this time."

They turned in for the evening. After supper, Braeanor washed up and then got into bed without delay. The bed was comfortable, and he was tired. After a quick prayer, he fell asleep easily.

Lilium had a different experience. She washed up as well, but her mind was full of racing thoughts. Images of things she had witnessed mixed with those of things she had not personally seen, but her imagination could. She had heard men talking about what the ripper locust and tentacled creature did to the guardsmen and horse. She had seen what the pox fiend did to her family.

She wondered if she was really ready to go on this quest. On the one hand, she felt increasingly confident in Braeanor. After all, he had defeated two abyssians using nothing more than a dagger.

But were there worse abyssians ahead of them? Could she be the one putting Braeanor in danger by going on this quest? If she couldn't discern when to speak or be silent, could she do what was needed when the time came?

She prayed, and she felt better, though the thoughts did not stop. Eventually, after her mind had exhausted itself, she grew weary. Somewhere between a dream and a nightmare, she drifted off.

VIII

Lilium awoke to Braeanor knocking on her door and calling out to her.

"Are you up?"

"Uhm. I am now," she responded.

"I'll be downstairs."

"Ok." She rubbed her eyes. Some days, mornings were the worst.

Braeanor walked downstairs, and Kellina and Farlan were already up. Braeanor could hear food being fried in a pan in the back room, and its aroma filled the air. Farlan was sitting at the bar, looking groggy. "Good morning, Farlan."

"Mornin'," Farlan replied unenthusiastically. "She really didn't want you to slip out without a farewell, and she made me wake way too early—no offense."

"Ah, none taken." The whole situation amused Braeanor.

Farlan turned toward Braeanor. "Listen, we will be praying for you daily. While I am unsure about this whole quest thing, I am going to trust that it has to be this way."

Braeanor gave a single nod to Farlan. "Thank you, Farlan. Sincere prayers of the faithful work mightily. Do not belittle the workings of faith." He realized what he spoke, and he was suddenly uncomfortable. Those sounded like words, old habits of speech, which belonged to a different man.

"Yes, I agree," Farlan responded matter-of-factly.

As Lilium came down the stairs, Kellina walked out carrying two loaded plates of eggs and strips of pork with large dollops of thick grits on the side. She sat the plates in front of Braeanor and Lilium, and after quickly giving thanks, they heartily ate.

Farlan looked at Kellina with open hands and gestured to the empty bar in front of him. He looked genuinely disappointed. She laughed and rolled her eyes before walking into the back. She returned with two more plates, one for each of them.

"So, you can cook? I could get used to this," Farlan jested.

"I wouldn't," she retorted with a wink. "But say the word, Braeanor, and I will make more."

After finishing his mouthful, he said, "This is more than enough.

Any more would be unbecoming of me. Thank you, though."

After breakfast, they talked for a while, and once other guests roused, they all said their goodbyes. Kellina and Lilium hugged while Braeanor and Farlan shook hands. Kellina then walked up to Braeanor and gave him a large hug, and though he hesitated just for a moment, he returned it in kind.

"You sure I can't convince you to hang around another night? Kellina asked.

"With your hospitality, it is tempting, but idleness feeds the Abyss. It is time to move on," he replied.

"Well, take care of yourself and this little lady of yours," Kellina said.

"By the Divines, I will. Could I ask you a final favor?"

"Sure, what do you need?" Kellina asked in turn.

"Could you see about having the abyssians disposed of in accordance with the Oracles? I don't trust the city to do so."

"I will see what I can do," she assured him.

Braeanor and Lilium walked out of the inn. Braeanor took hold of Aerion and fed him some sweet feed. He then fed him an apple as they walked. Aerion's coat looked sleeker than it did the day before, and his legs looked fuller as well. The three of them turned south toward the river. He would let Aerion's food settle just a bit before riding him.

Before they reached the town center, Braeanor saw Swinmer easing alongside a building, using it for support. His face was contorted, and the arm he wasn't using to steady himself against the building was wrapped around his stomach. Swinmer was mumbling something through labored breaths while he walked doubled over. The signage of the building was for an apothecary.

Swinmer looked up and caught Braeanor eyeing him. Braeanor smiled and nodded politely, but Swinmer only shook his head and began cursing through labored breaths as he made his way up to the apothecary's door. He attempted to enter, but it was still closed, so he furiously banged on it to no avail.

Aerion neighed.

"Yeah, I guess so, boy. I tried to warn him."

"What?" Lilium asked.

"Oh, nothing. Just something Aerion said," Braeanor responded.

As the trio passed through the town center, they saw the ripper locust hoisted and strung up from a large post with the after-death hung next to it. The city had put everything on display. If Braeanor's instinct was correct, in due time, it would be carved up for souvenirs or trophies for those willing to pay more than it was worth, even though such things ought to be only purged from the world by fire. On the other side of the post, a man was hanged.

Lilium stopped and stared. She was amazed by the ripper locust's size and its dreadful dual set of chelicerae. She realized that there was no exaggeration when she heard that guardsmen had been torn in three. She was in awe that Braeanor had jumped on that creature's back and killed it. She assumed who the man was. His body gently rotated back and forth with the breeze. A chill ran down her spine, which lingered as she gazed.

She shook her head and then hurried to catch up to Braeanor and Aerion, who had not slowed their pace. "Doesn't seem right to hang him for running away. You couldn't blame anyone for doing so," Lilium said.

"Honor and dishonor are exacting in what they demand, and he took an oath," Braeanor responded. "Though oaths taken for a wage mean nothing when it comes time to fulfill with one's blood."

When they neared the docks and slums, they turned left to head east. As they turned, movement out of the corner of Braeanor's eyes caught his attention. He slowed and stopped.

He saw the mother from the day before running between two houses. His heart quickened, and he focused to see what she was doing and why she was running. She stopped and jumped back. Her son and daughter popped out from around the corner. They let out playful screeches and giggles before turning to run away from her. She chased after them. They were up early.

They were playing a game. They were smiling. They were happy, and they all had nicer clothes. In the midst of this, the mother instinctively felt Braeanor's eyes upon her and looked over at him. She stood upright and gave a polite wave, and with a grateful smile, she mouthed "thank you" before resuming the chase.

Braeanor flashed a large smile, waved back, and then moved to catch up to Lilium and Aerion, who had walked ahead, unaware that he had fallen behind. They made their way out of the city and headed east.

CHAPTER FIVE

ELSPETH

. . . The faithful are sent help in their hour of need. Their homes are places of healing and rest and wisdom, for their days are ordered according to virtue. These are the people of Bright Haven, whose faith is a guarantor of their citizenship . . .

1

They made their way along the riverside. The gentle flowing of the river was music to their ears, and Lilium appreciated the various plants and flowers that grew along the banks. As Glenmore disappeared behind them, it was possible to become lost in the beauty of creation once more. Lilium did so, but Braeanor focused on practical matters, like looking for tracks. Aerion was just tickled to death to be carrying both of them. Lilium sat in front of Braeanor as they rode.

"So, is this about how quests normally go?" Lilium inquired.

"What do you mean?" Braeanor asked back.

"Well, you made it sound like quests can be full of surprises–"

"Providences–" he quickly corrected.

"Yes, providences," she said.

"I suppose. You never can tell. A paladin must simply endeavor to walk by faith, trusting that they will be directed where they are needed, precisely when they are needed."

"Does that ever worry you?"

Braeanor shrugged. "Worry? No, I don't suppose so. It does raise my awareness of what is going on around me. I assume things are happening which may require me to act, even if they are a bit inconveniencing."

"That seems stressful," she said.

"It could be. Eventually, you learn that some things are beyond your control, and if you try to control those things, well, you would be very stressed indeed and probably go mad. So, instead, you must let go and relax. Entrust the Divines to direct your steps. It is much better that way."

Lilium contemplated what he said. She stared out across the river, enjoying the sights and sounds.

"It's pretty, isn't it?"

Braeanor nodded. "Yes, brings back memories."

"Good or bad ones?"

"Ah, you and your questions, girl," he said with a bit of a laugh to take the edge off how her questions were actually irksome at times.

"What?" she insisted.

"Oh, it's nothing. I suppose both. Good and bad."

"Would you tell me a good one?" she asked.

"Me? You first." Braeanor responded.

"Okay," she giggled. She already had one in mind. "I remember the first time my father took me fishing. We went to a stream much smaller than this river. I finally caught something. He made it seem like it was so huge, but even I knew it was a small fish.

"He took it off the hook and handed it to me. I don't know why, but it felt slimy, and it moved. It surprised me. I screamed and tossed it in the air, but I immediately felt bad that I might hurt the fish if it dropped onto a rock, so I caught it. It moved again, and I screamed and tossed it up again. Again, I tried catching it so it wouldn't land on the rocks. It bounced between my hands. When I caught it once again, I tossed it back into the river while screaming and stomping around.

"I looked over, and my father was laughing so hard. His face was so red, and he had fallen over into the water. He said he almost passed out. I loved seeing him so happy. He was often under such stress being on the city council." She paused as she remembered he was gone. She shook the thought from her head. "Now you tell one."

Braeanor chuckled and looked out across the river. "Ah, yours was great. I don't know if I can beat that."

"It's not a competition," she replied sharply.

"Well, I remember camping along a small river northwest of the Evinwald, closer to the Western Heights. There was a group of us paladins investigating reports of cult activity out that way.

"We had been traveling for several days, so we finally decided to take a proper rest. Vesuvimorian wanted to bathe in the river, so he moved further away from our group and found a section with some overgrowth for privacy.

"Now, I don't believe I've told you about him. He was a jolly paladin who may have been among the largest to ever live. His size alone could strike fear into any sane man, but his deep voice and size hid the most cheerful man alive. It did not take much for him to get laughing. He liked to tell a good joke and to hear one. When he laughed, everyone knew. His laugh was like a siege engine, and we all swore on more than one occasion he would collapse one of our towers with us in it."

Lilium smiled at the thought of him.

"We later heard a commotion coming downstream from where he was. We hurried because it sounded like fighting. When we got there, we saw a naked Vesuvimorian on top of an abyssian—a pummeler, to be precise—and he was beating its head into the ground.

"Now pummelers are human-like and bigger than most men, and they use their bony fists to smash people. But this one picked the wrong person. Vesuvimorian would often just punch abyssians to pieces with his massive gauntlets—he claimed it was satisfying—vindicating—and even without them on, he was a force to be reckoned with.

"Vesuvimorian just kept punching, punching, punching. He was locked in and hadn't noticed the rest of us. So finally, I speak up and get his attention by saying, 'Hey, I thought you were supposed to be taking a bath, not making jam?' It was a stupid joke, really. But his face softened, and he looked at the pummeler's head and then his fists and just laughed.

"He grimaced in pain from a broken rib but continued laughing nonetheless. We were all glad he was okay, and his laughter seemed to have that effect on all of us. That everything was going to be okay.

"When we got back to the campfire together, he explained through tears what had happened. He was struggling on the riverbank. He kept seeing memories, things he would like to forget. Things he had been struggling with for years—the cruelty and violence of the Abyss towards innocent women and children.

"He considered killing himself and was in absolute despair. That's when he saw a dark flash on the far bank. That's when he saw the pummeler, and he realized it had just somehow portaled into our world alone. It crossed the river, and he fought and killed it with his bare hands. With every blow, he saw the face of someone who died too young, and each strike was for them, though he knew it couldn't bring them back.

"For the longest time, we had believed there was a connection between such despair and melancholy and the ability of the Abyss to portal into our world nearby. Cultists and rituals made sense because this provided something to the Old Ones in exchange for the abyssians. However, his experience confirmed that other ways were possible, that they could draw some power from us to send unbound abyssians throughout the world."

"Unbound?" Lilium asked.

"Yes. Abyssians given to cultists as a result of a ritual are bound to a cultist. If the cultist they are bound to dies, they die as well. This ensures the creature won't simply turn and kill its master.

"Anyway, we comforted Vesuvimorian. He was our brother. We would have never guessed that he struggled like he did. The truth is we all had similar struggles. He said it felt good to confess that to us, and among the Order, there is no shame in genuine confession. We embraced him."

Braeanor stopped talking for a moment and took a deep breath before resuming. "I sometimes miss genuine brotherly confession."

There was a brief and awkward silence following Braeanor's story.

"So, was that a good memory or a bad one?" Lilium inquired with a jesting tone to soften the somber nature of his memory.

"Bittersweet?" Braeanor responded.

"Is it common, then, that people have a hard time with such things as Vesuvimorian did?"

"Yes. Too common, but we all like to pretend that it's not the case."

Lilium took this to heart.

"Lilium," Braeanor addressed her with a forthright tone.

"Yes?" she asked.

"I'm sorry. I'm sorry I wasn't kinder when we first met, that I wasn't more compassionate in your time of need. I was too absorbed in what I was experiencing to truly be there for you when you needed it. If it were somehow possible, I would have wished that your family was still alive and well, and you shouldn't have had to experience that. I'm sorry I wasn't the kind of person you needed. I'm sorry."

Lilium nodded and bit her lip as a teardrop fell. "Thank you," she whispered. "And I forgive you."

11

They found the large stone and the path, just as Kellina said, and continued north. Around late afternoon, they came upon Elspeth's small farm situated amid a small cluster of trees with fields in each direction, some of which were fenced. The small cottage house had a thatch roof, and its walls were made with logs and dried clay. It sat on a firm foundation of large stones, and it had a large wooden front door, as well as a pane-less window frame with burnt orange shutters. The house was surrounded with flower beds in which all manner of flowering plants grew.

A covered porch ran the length of the front of the house, and an assortment of tools rested on it. A watering can and unmarked canvas bags sat near the door. There were two simple, sturdy-looking rocking chairs in between two posts, and a small bench rested against the wall just beneath the window.

As they neared the front door, they heard a commotion from inside, and they soon heard intermittent yelling. They listened intently before approaching closer. There was clanging and animals bleating, followed by the sound of hooves stomping around.

"I know! I know! I'm worried about your kids too! Well, I don't know what to do."

There was a loud crash, which sounded like pottery breaking.

"Shoot! Look now. Listen, I'm upset, too. But I'm trying to think about what to do. I don't know where they are, or I would go get them! And yes, you have to sleep inside tonight! I'm not risking anyone else being taken."

Braeanor and Lilium only heard the voice of a single, older woman, as well as the sound of what surely was multiple animals running around inside. "I think I'll knock loudly and give her plenty of time to get to the door," Braeanor spoke to Lilium.

He knocked three times loudly. The clamor inside the house continued without any indication that he was heard. Braeanor knocked again, this time louder and five times. The commotion somewhat calmed, but this was followed immediately by the door yanking open.

A verklempt, older woman opened the door. Gray hair gracefully adorned her head, but the soft features of her face showed clear concern. She was of modest stature, but she possessed the vigor of someone many years less seasoned.

"Divines greet you." The woman's voice was pleasant, though it was apparent she was actively trying to regain her composure.

Braeanor cleared his throat and then said, "Divines greet you, ma'am. I am Braeanor, and this is Lilium. We are just passing through and do not mean to be a burden to you. Kellina thought that you might provide us lodging for—"

"Kellina! Well, I wish she would visit me herself." She huffed and looked over her shoulder, then turned back with a smile. "But it is a nice change to have some company. I'm Elspeth, please—"

Just then, a goat shot out from beside Elspeth's leg, and it darted right between Braeanor and Lilium before either one knew what was happening. The goat was in a full sprint south towards the river.

"Ah! Billy! Get Billy!" Elspeth shouted.

Braeanor and Lilium both took a few quick steps and hopped off the porch stairs, grasping after it, but they were too slow to catch the goat. Braeanor picked up speed, but the goat was in full sprint. Aerion was already trotting over knowing he would be needed. Braeanor hopped on quickly, and Aerion took off after the goat knowing the target of their joint effort.

Braeanor reached into one of the bags and pulled out a rope, which he tied into a loop. Raising an arm over his head and twirling the rope around twice, he threw the rope and snared the goat. He pulled and brought it down. Braeanor hopped off Aerion and bound the goat's legs. The whole escapade ended without further incident. He looked up at Elspeth and raised his hands, motioning for her to let him know where she wanted Billy.

Elspeth called out, "Put him inside that fence for now. He will need to come back inside tonight, but he will be fine there for now."

Braeanor set Billy free in the enclosure, and Aerion hung around the gate. Braeanor then walked back up to the porch. "Well, I don't mean to intrude, but I am curious as to why you have goats inside the house?"

Elspeth looked concerned, and she waved Braeanor and Lilium inside. She quickly closed the door behind them. The house was a mess. There were broken pottery and dishes. Some of the furniture appeared to have been chewed on. The goats were a spectacle. One stood on the kitchen table, and another stood on the small table in the common area. Some were running about, and others were chewing on things. Lilium counted about a dozen goats and two kids.

Elspeth said, "Something is taking my kids, and I'm afraid that the rest of my goats will be next. I've lost a kid each night over the last two days. I don't know what it is. I don't see any signs of them being preyed on here. Anytime my goats have gotten outside their enclosure, they don't wander far. I usually just find them eating flowers out of my garden. So, I decided to keep them inside till I figured it out. I've been praying for help because I don't know what it is."

"You find any signs whatsoever?" Braeanor asked.

Elspeth shook her head. "The gate is unlatched and cracked. That's it. If it were thieves, I probably wouldn't have any of them left. I suspect it is something smart enough to open that gate and lead them away."

Braeanor tilted his head as he contemplated the possibilities. "Is there any kind of scat or fur left behind?"

Elspeth brought a hand to her cheek, thought about it, and then lifted her hand away in befuddlement. "No, nothing."

Braeanor crossed his arms and looked up as he ran through a mental checklist. "Hmm. . . well. We know it's not an abyssian. They would just kill them all and either eat them or leave them there for you to find. Serpents and flying things would not need to unlatch the gate. With no scat or fur left behind, it leaves me to think that it is not something typical. The rest of the goats probably would have gotten rowdy had the kids been taken violently. I assume you would have woken up hearing it."

"Yeah, that seems about right. So, we know much of what it isn't. Doesn't help us with what it is?" Elspeth ran a hand through her hair and held the other on her hip. She was distressed. No one wants their animals taken, and no one wants to live with them, either.

Elspeth then sharply tilted her head and, with furrowed brows, followed up with another question to Braeanor. "Do I know you?"

Braeanor shook his head. "I don't think so. I don't believe we have met."

"Oh, yes. I am sure we have not met, but I think I know you. Are you not a paladin?"

He hesitated before responding. The question caught him off guard, and he could not wrap his mind around how she would discern that.

In Braeanor's hesitation, Lilium said, "Yes, yes, he is. His name is Braeanor. I am Lilium." She extended a hand to shake Elspeth's. Braeanor shot her a glance. "I read the room," she said in response to his glance while giving him a playful nudge of her elbow.

Braeanor shook his head but smiled.

Elspeth shook Lilium's outstretched hand but did a double-take at Braeanor. "Ah. Well, pleased to make both your acquaintances, little lady." She smiled at Lilium, who returned it in kind.

"So, paladin, what is it?" Elspeth put both her hands on her hips and gave him a stern look.

Braeanor noticed that Elspeth was studying him carefully. "Well, first of all, it is nice to make your acquaintance as well, Elspeth, and I have a suspicion. There is no easy way of telling unless we catch it in the act. If you are willing to trust me, I'd like to put all the goats and kids back in their enclosure, and my horse, Aerion, will stay with them. He will not allow anymore to be taken, and he will tell me what he sees. That will determine our next steps."

"Your horse talks, huh?" Elspeth asked.

"Well, something like that. We understand each other."

"Hmm. You might just be a paladin. And you are sure he will protect them?" Elspeth asked.

"Yes, I am sure," Braeanor spoke confidently.

Elspeth studied the features of his face. "Okay then, so what do you think is taking them?"

"Some call it a peekaboo beast. They are peculiar creatures that live in groups. It is a small bear-like creature with scaly skin beneath a thin coat of hair. It has retractable claws and a vicious set of teeth, but it hides them until it strikes. The creatures are about as big as an adult goat. But they are sinister.

"At first glance and when not provoked, they are adorable with big eyes and soft purring cat-like sounds which make them seem harmless. They can be playful with their victims, doing so to lure animals and even children off so they can be easily preyed upon. Peekaboos build a nest, usually in some dark, damp, hollow areas with easy access to food and water.

"A mutation will take over one of the peekaboos, which causes them to grow much larger, and they become the queen of the nest. They will lay cocoon-like eggs which hatch other peekaboos. Eventually–if the peekaboos are well fed and nourished and growing into a large population–there will be an uprising. They will turn on the queen and eat her.

"The most vicious among them will then take her place. This will happen cyclically to ensure the strongest of them produce the next generation. If you are lucky, you can find the nest early before there is a large, vicious queen. One of these may have been unlatching the gate and luring your kids away to take them back to a nest."

"Oh my," Elspeth sighed. She was upset by the news, but she tried to seek some comfort in as much as she might now know what was happening to her animals. She did not want any more of them to go missing. She wanted the threat to stop. "Okay, paladin. I will trust you. They will stay outside with your horse tonight as long as you pledge to help rid the peekaboo infestation if there is one."

Braeanor nodded. "If you are willing to host us as your guests, madam, I would be glad to do this for you."

They both looked over to see Lilium surrounded by the goats. She was sitting on the common area table, and the goats were pressing in on her. They had not even noticed she had managed to draw them to her. Lilium was giggling while she petted them.

"Lilium, you think you can get them to follow you out to their enclosure?" Braeanor asked.

She looked at him with a large smile and nodded. He opened the door and headed out to the gate, which he opened in turn. Lilium had a difficult time pressing through the goats, but she managed. They followed her right into the fenced enclosure. Braeanor closed the gate, and Lilium walked over to it. He opened it just enough to let her slip out without a goat getting out, too.

Braeanor walked over to Aerion and explained the possible peekaboo problem. He unburdened Aerion from the packs and saddle so he could rest for the night. Aerion was confident he would see such a creature sneaking up, and he assured Braeanor that he would alert him if there was any trouble. He fed him some sweet feed and an apple, and they prayed together.

Braeanor, Lilium, and Elspeth then went inside, and Elspeth surprised them with some vegetable stew that she had already put on to cook hours ago.

"How is Kellina?" Elspeth inquired.

"She is well. She has made a name for herself. She actually put us up for a night before we came here. In my estimation, she has the most successful inn in all of Glenmore. She has done well for herself," Braeanor assured her.

"That is good, though I would not complain if she would visit me. She knows I won't go to town. It would be nice to hear these things from her mouth." There was disappointment and a touch of hurt in her voice.

Braeanor made an effort to assuage her, "Kellina did mention that she intended to visit you when opportunity permitted. She regrets that it is hard to find individuals who can reliably run the inn in her absence. Nevertheless, I think my coming here has made her realize she needs to visit."

Elspeth smiled politely. "We will see. I was hopeful she would do well, but that town has some untrustworthy folk—always has. There's no telling how many nights I've prayed for that girl, fearing something bad was about to befall her. I tell you, in those first months of her setting that place up—" She paused and shook her head just thinking back to that period. "I just dreaded it."

"The Divines have kept watch over her," Lilium said while looking upon Braeanor with pride in her eyes. "And I think you will like Farlan. He seems very nice, and he plays music and can sing too."

"Oh, is that so? I didn't know she had met a man. You know, her father played and sang, too. Of course, if I were to point that out to her, she's liable to leave the man on account of me suggesting she had her mother's taste!" Elspeth winked at Lilium as she finished.

Lilium laughed. "So, you live here all alone?"

Elspeth nodded.

"Are you not scared? You are so far from town."

"Well, deary," Elspeth paused to reflect. "I sometimes feel so. When I do, I pray for the Divines to protect and guide me. If there be some terror in the night come to take me away, then I know where I am going. I entrust myself to their light. If there is no terror, then it is only my mind. Either way, I am okay. And I have not always been alone. I had my husband, Hamish, for the longest."

Lilium admired her bravery and faith, but in the back of her mind, she had to set aside the truth that she now knew, that those killed by abyssians were claimed by the Abyss and did not ascend to Bright Haven. She quickly returned her focus to the conversation and away from that unpleasant thought.

"May I ask how long ago he passed?" Lilium inquired.

Elspeth finished her spoonful of stew before answering. "Yes, child. It has been almost three years now. Seems much less to be honest. He was a good man. He loved me dearly. I don't know why, but he did."

Lilium tilted her head. "You don't know why?"

Braeanor watched the two talking with interest. He was glad to see Lilium talking. Braeanor could not provide Lilium with everything she needed. There was something mystical in the exchange of wisdom and life between an older woman and a girl. Whether such conversations were profound or not did not matter, for even the simplest of worldly matters were given significant weight shared between generations.

Elspeth took a sip of her drink. "Not entirely. I mean, I know we shared so much, but love is a strange thing when you stop to think about it. Divines know there are plenty of things about me which are not lovable. Nevertheless, he loved me more than any man should love another. Now, I know he wasn't perfect either, but he lived in such a way as to ensure he took care of me above all things. I never deserved that."

"A blessing of the Divines then," Lilium cheerily quipped.

Elspeth looked intently at Lilium. "Yes, I would say so. It is a shame that some girls grow up expecting this as if it were to be taken for granted. That is a concern I have with girls these days—not that I make it out to town much nowadays—but I fear some are entitled, and in their search for a perfect man, they pass by the one who would love her perfectly. It's a pity they pass gold in search of copper."

Elspeth then changed the subject abruptly. "Paladin deary, want more?"

Braeanor looked at his empty bowl and then over at the pot. He softly tapped the table with his fingers several times while he considered her question. "May I?" he inquired while lifting his bowl.

"My treat!" Elspeth took the bowl, stood, and went to fill it. "Shh!

Ouch," Elspeth shook her hand.

"Are you okay?" Lilium asked while turning towards her.

Elspeth filled the bowl and brought it to Braeanor. "I'm fine, deary. Managed to burn myself is all. You'd think after all these years I'd stop doing that." Elspeth reached over and patted the back of one of Lilium's hands as if to comfort her. "Labors of love are often accompanied by pain, but wonderful things are born from it," she added with a wink.

"May I see your hand?" Braeanor asked while extending his hand toward Elspeth.

"Oh, it's fine, really," Elspeth modestly assured, but she extended her hand toward Braeanor nonetheless.

Even Lilium could see the blister forming on Elspeth's palm just before Braeanor laid his hand on hers. He bowed his head and prayed quietly, and both Elspeth and Lilium watched intently. He prayed for little more than a minute before opening his eyes and smiling with a nod at Elspeth.

She looked at her hand. "Well, I'll be. All better. Like it never happened." She showed her hand to Lilium, who smiled upon seeing no blister. "Thank you, paladin."

She sliced another piece of bread and handed it to Braeanor.

"Thank you, Elspeth."

"My pleasure," she replied.

After supper, Elspeth, Lilium, and Braeanor checked on the goats and Aerion to ensure all things were in order. Elspeth spared no hospitality in making her guests comfortable for the night.

III

The sun had not yet raised its head over the horizon when Braeanor heard Aerion let out a short, high-pitched squeal. He woke, rose quickly, and hurried outside barefoot with his sword in hand. Aerion was near the gate and was standing firmly, looking over the gate south toward the river.

Braeanor jogged over, and Aerion informed him that it was just as he thought. A small creature fitting the description of a peekaboo skulked up to the gate and began to unlatch it. Aerion scared it off, and it sprinted off toward the river.

"Good job, boy. We will make ready and track it to its nest."

Braeanor returned inside, put his boots on, and hurriedly ate some breakfast. Elspeth and Lilium were awoken by the commotion, too, and they joined him at the table.

Braeanor looked up from his breakfast. "It is as I suspected. We are dealing with a peekaboo. I will set out with Aerion soon and track it. After I have dealt with them, I will return. I do not intend to be a greater burden upon you, Elspeth, but this may extend our stay another day or so."

"It is no burden, paladin. I am honored to have you as my guest. Lilium and I will find something to do." Elspeth smiled at Braeanor and Lilium both. Focusing on Lilium, she asked, "You've never had my sweet cake. How about you help me cook up a batch?"

"Sounds wonderful!" Lilium excitedly responded. A bright silver glint from Braeanor's double-fullered arming sword caught her eye as he stood from the table.

Braeanor bid them farewell and walked over to Aerion. He fed Aerion an apple and some sweet feed before saddling him. "We will take an easy pace until your breakfast has digested. We will need to keep our eyes open for the peekaboos and look for any sign along the way. Let me know if you smell anything as well."

Aerion snorted and walked toward the river. Most of the terrain was flat with various grasses, some tall and others in thick clumps. Aerion hadn't remembered seeing so many flowers on the way up to Elspeth's, but they now caught his attention. There were all types. Some were brightly colored blues, yellows, and pinks, and others were white with large bell-shaped blooms. The land around

Elspeth's was pretty, and it obviously provided for her. Autumn had not yet touched her place the same way it had the rest of the land.

Around midmorning, Braeanor and Aerion could see the river. They approached its banks, and Braeanor dismounted. Aerion walked over to it and drank. As he did so, he jerked his head back and snorted.

"What is it, Aerion?"

Aerion explained the problem and fixed his eyes eastward upstream of the river. That was the likely direction of the peekaboo nest.

Braeanor lowered his face to the river and inhaled deeply. "I'm getting nothing, but I'll trust your nose." He walked around and carefully searched for any peekaboo sign. He found some.

There was a small paw print on the river's shore. As best as he could recall, it matched that of a peekaboo. Several steps upstream from there was a small rock kicked up and rolled over. It was still moist where the rock had been. This was recent. Further up from there was a clump of moss on a rock, which was scuffed and torn off. This was enough to confirm the direction of travel as east and upstream of the Istrid River.

Braeanor mounted Aerion, and they picked up their pace in the direction the sign traveled. "It is likely that the nest is in a cave, though it is possible it could be in a large thicket. They like the comfort and protection of the dark, though. They are usually nocturnal creatures, so we may be fortunate and get them all in one fell swoop. They don't tend to travel far from their nest unless they are thriving and need to expand their territory."

Aerion huffed to acknowledge Braeanor.

"Have you heard many stories of other paladin steeds?" Braeanor inquired of Aerion. He realized this could be a good opportunity for them to bond further.

Aerion shook his head. He had heard bits of stories here and there, but he was not sure what was true. His father had told him stories before he had been killed, and while he dearly believed these stories, he also had come to realize that horses tend to exaggerate many things, like who was the fastest. However, he knew without a doubt that horses and paladins shared a bond bestowed upon them by the Divines.

"Well, I am sure some of what you heard is true, at least. When our world was created, it is said the Divines foresaw the need for paladins to fend off the growing dangers of the Abyss. They foremost saw the threat as one of the Abyss corrupting men's hearts.

"Our bond was to serve several purposes. First, it was to provide men with a sense of awe so as to fix our eyes away from the temptations and madness of the Abyss. We were to be transfixed with an honorable loyalty in our bonds as common travelers of this world. Our hearts and minds are susceptible to wandering, but in our wandering together, we are less likely to take the wrong path.

"Secondly, the Divines foresaw the need for paladins to quickly move about Kadath to aid others. Men of power are apt to do things that harm both our kinds, and good men would need to be able to quickly get to a ruler's side to provide wise counsel. We would also need to quickly take messages and respond to those in need.

"Thirdly, you noble steeds were gifted with a unique understanding of the Divines, and you have an innate capacity for faith. Because of this, we can strengthen each other's faith during trials. We can endure the dangers of man and the Abyss alike. We are stronger together.

"The type of communication between man and steed that we share is said to be limited to those of noble intent and—" Braeanor's speech faltered. After pausing, he continued. "To those of noble intent and sincere faith. It is believed that in the beginning, all men could talk with horses, but for ages now, only paladins have been able. The legends of old, which suggested everyone was able to talk to horses, are now understood by most to only refer to paladins, but paladins have not always existed."

Aerion nodded and huffed.

"How did paladins come about? Oh, that is a complicated story. For now, it shall suffice to say that we came about primarily through men of faith who advised rulers and later had to become warriors, too. The first paladin was Hezraniah. The Divines gifted him the courage to stand against the abyssian threatening his people. His faith and courage inspired others. But he became a lightning rod for the Abyss, and sadly, he fell."

Aerion nodded and huffed again.

"Are there any famous paladin steeds? Of course. All have passed on, unfortunately. Have you heard of . . . Ildradath's crusade into the Abyss?"

Aerion nodded.

"Well, I was a part of that. Good paladins and steeds—" Once again, Braeanor stopped talking to collect himself as emotions threatened to surface. After taking a moment, he resumed. "Good paladins and their steeds died as a result of that crusade. When I returned from the Abyss, abyssians spilled into this world through the portal we had created, right on our heels, in numbers never before seen. There were so many we could not manage to close the portal back. Waves upon waves of them, and they just kept coming. We wondered if the Dread One had risen.

"So, paladins who were standing guard nearby tried to close the portal while word was sent for the few paladins who were not near. They learned that all the other paladins had been killed and that their immediate aid was needed to close the gate, or Kadath would be doomed. All would be lost. Word was sent to the Western Heights, Eastern Reaches, and the Evinwald. Only the Evinwald sent warriors.

"Now, the fallen paladins' steeds had been stabled together. They had not been taken into the Abyss due to the particularly treacherous, unpredictable nature of the land there. In keeping with paladin tradition, those horses had their armor removed. Any who wished to remain and commit themselves to further service in the Order could do so. Otherwise, they had faithfully served and could go free, discharged honorably.

"Now, I think there were around a hundred. All were quite distraught at the news. All of their paladin-riders had been killed, and even if they had all stayed, there was no guarantee that any of them could re-enter service with a paladin in their lifetime. Generations worth of paladins had just died.

"So most scattered to the four winds. Now Gargantry remained. He was Vesuvimorian's steed. Vesuvimorian—if you recall—was a man of great stature. With one hand, he could crush a man's head if he desired. He stood well above me and was a muscle-bound man. His laughter was like an earthquake, and his strike like that of a falling star."

Braeanor smiled as he continued recalling things. Aerion huffed; he remembered the story of Vesuvimorian.

"Oh, how we used to compete to see how long we could keep Vesuvimorian laughing. His steed, Gargantry, was his equine equal. Gargantry was filled with zeal and a desire to avenge his paladin. Moreover, he desired an honorable death. He roused the passions of the others who had remained with him. They all scattered to the four winds as well, and in a matter of several days, they had rounded up all their fellow steeds and brought them back for one final glorious ride.

"They returned to the large stable and were refitted with their armor. The remaining paladins were locked in a mortal struggle with the abyssians a field's length from the portal. More paladins had fallen, and the prospect of closing the portal had grown unlikely.

"In the midst of all the fighting, I saw the storm cloud on the horizon. I can still see it clear as day. A mighty tempest rose and cast skyward. There was the sight of a thousand lightning flashes in their eyes, the sound of a thousand thunderous peals of righteous hooves hammering the ground and shaking even the tainted hearts of the abyssians to terror."

Braeanor raised both his open hands, palms down and fingers spread, and shook them for dramatic emphasis as he recalled how the ground shook. He smiled, and sad, proud tears filled his eyes. His voice cracked.

"At the tip of their wedge formation was Gargantry. He and all the others had never looked more glorious, fuller of power. When they hit the abyssians, you would swear the Divines had struck them with a comet. They leveled the field before us and routed the abyssians. They fought with a zeal and fury that shall never depart from the annals of this world's most glorious tales. I can still see them chasing foul creatures—stomping, kicking, knocking down, biting, beckoning paladins to mount them to continue the fight—whatever it took. They did it all and more.

"They turned the tide of darkness threatening to sweep across our world. We were able to fight the rest of the way to the portal and close it. After we had done so, there were only a handful of paladins and steeds left, all grievously wounded. I am the only one to survive."

Braeanor stopped speaking. Aerion let out a quiet snort, and tears filled his eyes. They rode silently for a while, reflecting both on the deep wounds inflicted by the Abyss and in awe of what noble man and steed can accomplish together.

IV

A little after noon, Braeanor and Aerion finally neared a large stretch of woods where the Istrid River formed from its three tributaries. This would complicate things. Moreover, he realized he had traveled much further than would be expected for most peekaboos. Because of this, he was likely dealing with a thriving nest. This would be a most unpleasant side quest.

Braeanor dismounted in order to search for more sign. He figured the creatures would not have swum across the larger river, but the smaller streams were more manageable. He would need to find some sign and follow it until it disappeared. That would likely tell him where the creatures crossed. Peekaboos, like most creatures, would take the easiest path available. Because of this, they likely crossed the stream at the most convenient point possible. Hopefully, this would make his crossing easier, too.

He found more sign where the streams became one, and he followed this upstream along the northernmost, exterior stream. Following kicked-up rocks, partial footprints, and castings, he found a section of shallower stream with rocks easily visible just below the surface. The sign stopped there, so he was confident this was the place they used to cross. Braeanor called Aerion over. He mounted Aerion and began crossing.

"Halt, boy, before we step onto the shore. I want to look first."

Braeanor's eyes scanned the shore below, and he saw signs of frequent activity. It was likely that other creatures, or several peekaboos, used this shoreline to cross. The ground looked softer, and this meant it preserved signs of activity better than the other shoreline.

"How does this stream smell, Aerion?"

Aerion lowered his head and smelled. He took a cautious drink, and he then took several drinks.

"Well, if this one is fine, then it must not take us close enough to their nest. We will walk ahead and have you smell the next stream."

Braeanor was on the inside edge of the woods, and just as he started making his way through them towards the next stream, a burnt-orange leaf gracefully floated and twirled near his face. It caught him by surprise, causing him to jerk his head backward to avoid it touching his face. He watched as it landed softly on the ground. He then looked up and saw many more leaves gently carried along in the tender arms of the breeze.

He had been so focused on the ground and tracking sign that he had not stopped to appreciate the beauty around him. Large trees ascended, some of which were handsomely decorated with swatches of brightly colored mosses. There was a fallen tree that housed innumerable large mushrooms of various types growing from it.

These woods were not especially dense. They had nice spacing, which allowed Braeanor to see further off into the distance than is typical. The tree canopy was thick, but scattered rays of light illuminated the world below. There was an increasing number of leaves on the ground, and they formed a carpet of autumnal majesty. He always liked the woods. They were serene and comforting, and though inhabited by dangers unseen, they were environs harkening to live in wonder.

Just in the distance, he saw a rare sight: a lone Dancing Mother's Oak. Her many branches split out from the main trunk and reached out a considerable distance before turning outward and up towards the sky. Her branches swayed in the breeze, like a mother embracing and dancing with all of nature's children around her, and her golden leaves gently floated away from her grasp to beautify the world below.

However, Braeanor realized that he was not hearing or seeing any animal life. The only sounds in the air were that of the breeze and the rustling of leaves and branches. There were no singing birds, scurrying squirrels, dashing deer, or other creatures bounding about.

"Have you seen or heard any other animal yet?" Braeanor asked with worry in his voice.

Aerion shook his head and huffed.

"We may have our hands full with this one, boy. Better get on with it."

Braeanor and Aerion reached the middle stream, and Aerion quickly detected a much more pungent, foul odor being carried by the stream. His head recoiled from it. Aerion also smelled fear, and he believed this was from the stolen kids.

"Well, boy. If that is so, that may mean we are in time to save them. Perhaps they have not been made food for their hatchlings. This stream will probably take us to the nest. Now, once we find the nest, presuming it is inside some cave, I will need you to stand guard at the entrance. If any peekaboo attempts to flee past you, do what you can to stop them however you can. We must destroy all of these creatures, or they will return and reproduce. None can escape."

Aerion snorted loudly.

They followed the contours of the water's banks and moved upstream. As they entered deeper into the forest, the canopy thickened and blotted out more of the light. They finally saw a large cave entrance from which the Istrid River's middle tributary flowed.

The grass and trees leading up to the cave entrance were dead. A blackness wept from the trees, and the grass appeared burnt and wilted. There were a multitude of various animal bones picked clean around the entrance. Braeanor dismounted and drew his sword. He looked at Aerion, and Aerion nodded back and stomped a hoof.

Braeanor entered the cave. There was ample ground between the cave wall and the stream. As Braeanor continued inward, it became darker and more cavernous. The walls were also covered in a dark green ichor, and a stench rose all around him. The ground, too, lost its loose, pebble, and rock texture and became soft. A dried, thick ooze coated the ground.

He held out his left hand, palm upward, and quietly prayed for the light of the Divines to show the path ahead. A small glowing light began to form in his palm, and it grew to the size of a melon. It was brilliant but not blinding. He then tossed it ahead, and the light floated forward and upward where it hung near the cave ceiling.

Just ahead, near the stream, were the two kids. They were penned inside a makeshift stone and tree-branch cage. They bleated when they saw the light. He noticed cocoon sacks hanging from the ceiling. There must have been at least two dozen cocoons. With this many, the queen must surely be large. He saw shadowy movement ahead and figured he would soon find out.

He heard many feet shuffling towards him and then saw several dozen large, round eyes staring at him from the edge of the light. The creatures were unnervingly cute. They would soon be violent creatures bent on biting and clawing him to death.

Braeanor's eyes then caught sight of a much larger set of eyes peering at him from higher above and behind the others. Its eyes were not cute. Rather than the bulbous, round, and full eyes of the small peekaboos, which made them cute, the queen's serpentine pupils were menacing.

Human-like words rumbled out from the queen with a threatening tone. "We want live. Please let go."

Braeanor had forgotten that peekaboos, especially an older queen, could learn limited amounts of speech. Braeanor spoke loudly and forthrightly, "Yes, I suppose that is the way of all living things. But you devour without mercy, and your gluttony spares nothing. You foul the land so that it becomes desolate and tainted. You know no boundaries and defile without regard. For these reasons, and more yet, I cannot let you live."

He held his sword before him and readied himself for combat. The queen roared and hissed. The others repeatedly called out a coughing, barking sound followed by hissing. One after another, the small peekaboos charged him.

Braeanor shouted and struck out into the darkness with his sword. One, two, three peekaboos were cleaved, but there were many more to go. Several had climbed the cave wall in order to come at him from the ceiling, agilely swinging from stalactites or cocoons to get a drop on him.

He jumped back and took another wide swing, cleaving another three of the creatures in half. The others on the ground began to split up and surround him so they could come at him from different angles. The queen was lumbering towards him, too.

One of the peekaboos jumped from the cave ceiling towards him, but Braeanor was able to bring his sword upward in time to skewer the creature. He slashed downward to cast it off his sword. One of them leapt onto his back and bit his shoulder. He winced in pain while drawing his dagger with his left hand. He struck behind his head, piercing its skull. It fell lifeless.

Keeping the dagger in his left hand and sword in his right, he began slashing, dodging, and stabbing to kill the other peekaboos as they leapt toward him. He continued to step backward toward the cave entrance as he fought. The large queen continued menacingly marching towards him, but it was a bloated, sluggish beast.

Braeanor had thinned the number of peekaboos to six, plus the queen. The queen grunted and screeched. The other peekaboos backed off of him but remained encircled. The queen was moving in to kill him herself.

Braeanor sheathed his dagger and gripped his sword well. She was a nasty thing at least twice his size. She was a monstrosity compared to the others. It was hard to believe that peekaboos would dare turn on such a beast in order to take its place as queen. Weirder yet was how they mutated to become such bloated horrors.

Screeching, the creature slashed out with its talon-like clawed hands. Slash, slash, slash, it swung at Braeanor. He jumped back with the first two swings and swung his sword across the path of the third strike in order to cleave the queen's left hand from its arm. The hand fell to the ground, and she screeched even louder. He took several more steps back and readied himself.

She then barreled forward. She was bent on throwing her mass at him, pinning him, and devouring him alive. Braeanor took several quick steps toward her as she sped forward and leapt. He slid himself onto the ground and used his momentum to carry him forward on the putrid cave floor. As he slid under, he stabbed upward and gutted her from chest to waist.

She landed on the ground behind Braeanor and stood up quickly, realizing she had missed him altogether. She turned to face him, and as she did so, she realized that she had been seriously hurt. Her intestines were spilling out of the wound and onto the ground. She held them with her remaining hand and whimpered while falling forward to her knees.

Four of the peekaboos charged at Braeanor while two others bolted for the nearby cave entrance. Braeanor spun around to pierce one, then spun back to get another, then stabbed backward to catch another leaping up toward his back, and then finally swung downward to cleave the last one in half.

"Aerion, get those two!" Braeanor shouted out to get his steed into the fight as well.

Aerion was on them as soon as they emerged from the cave. He ran up to the first one, anticipating it would simply go around him. As it did so, he turned so his hind legs were lined up. He then kicked backward with a hoof, and it caught the peekaboo in the head, sending it flying against a tree. The other peekaboo was sprinting like mad to get away. Aerion gave chase.

Inside, Braeanor maneuvered around the peekaboo queen so that he was behind it. She had not moved since she had been gravely wounded. He moved forward, and upon Braeanor bringing his sword up, the queen spun around and caught his chest with her remaining clawed hand.

He cut across its neck, deftly decapitating the foul thing. He immediately grimaced and reeled in pain. He reached up and gingerly felt each claw-inflicted tear in his flesh. To his pleasant surprise, he could not feel bone. He resolved to finish scanning the cave for any peekaboos that he may have missed before tending to his wounds.

Back outside, the fleeing peekaboo was fast, but not as fast as Aerion. Realizing it could not outrun the horse, it leaped onto a tree and was going to make for higher ground. Aerion was too close behind, and he bit the nape of its neck. He pulled it off the tree, shook his head, and then slammed it to the ground. He quickly shifted over and stomped it repeatedly until he was sure that it was crushed beyond hope. Aerion then hurried back to the cave entrance, ready for more.

Braeanor walked toward the back of the cave until the ceiling sloped to the ground, and only the stream could continue under and through the rock. He was confident there were no more peekaboos alive, and there was nowhere else for them to hide. He was optimistic that, given the time of day it was, all had been inside the nest as well.

As he walked back toward the cave entrance, he scanned the ceiling for the peekaboo cocoons. He went from cocoon to cocoon, slicing each apart to ensure that the growing creature inside could not emerge. The contents of each seemed to be well-developed and likely would have hatched in the coming days. Each released a fetid stench and gory mass. Strings of the gore clung to his sword with each swing. Once he was finally done with these, he walked over to the kids.

The two kids were still in the cage made by the peekaboos. It was unnerving to see that kind of intelligence from the peekaboos. It was another reminder that they were devious creatures who could always be expected to innovate ways to further their territory and corrupting influence. The kids were bleating loudly.

Braeanor smiled at them. "Looks like you guys get to go home."

He walked out and retrieved some rope from a bag on Aerion and, before returning inside, assured a worried Aerion that it was not as bad as it looked. Aerion remarked that was good because it looked really bad. Braeanor tethered the kids so that they were bound together with just enough slack and tied the other end off on Aerion.

He rinsed his wound with clean water and placed a clean cloth on it while he prayed. Aerion joined him in prayer. After half an hour of prayer, he pulled the cloth off and felt the wounds. They had stopped bleeding, and the wound channels felt shallower.

Braeanor reached into another bag and pulled out four apples, and he fed three to the kids and Aerion. Braeanor then mounted Aerion and began the trek back to Elspeth's while enjoying the fourth. On the way back, Braeanor decided he needed to tell Aerion about who he really was.

While the peekaboo problem was being handled, Lilium and Elspeth were enjoying each other's company. They were in her kitchen gathering the ingredients they would need for baking.

"Deary, how did you come into the company of the paladin?" Elspeth asked.

"My family had left in a small caravan from Munrobeinn. My father had been helping run the city and was head of the council, but people were threatening our family, not just mom and I. He decided we had to just leave. He planned to take us to the Western Heights. He had friends there.

"We couldn't cross Craighorn Pass to come south through Glenmore or take a ship through the North Sea. A man still loyal to my father had caught up to us and told us assassins would be lying in wait there. So, my father decided to head for the Western Heights across Edjramor. He knew it was dangerous, but he was hopeful.

"We were attacked by a pox fiend while going through Haverstead. Only I survived, and I ran off and hid in a collapsed windmill. I prayed all night for the Gray Paladin of Edjramor to come save me, and Braeanor showed up that morning. He took me back to his tower. We later went to bury my family, and he ended up fighting and killing a cultist and the pox fiend that killed my family.

"I became miserable there. Truth is, Braeanor was just as miserable and maybe even more so. As he and I talked, I learned more about the Abyss, and eventually, he decided to pray for a quest from the Divines. They gave him one. The quest requires that I go with him. We are headed to judge a former paladin, Malcreus, who turned to the ways of the Old Ones. He lives in the mountains far east. So that is kinda it." Lilium finished her explanation with strength left in her voice.

There was a pause as Elspeth finished moving what she needed about on the table. She then turned toward Lilium. She was taken aback. "Oh deary, that is so much more than I would have ever guessed. I don't even know what to say. I am so sorry." Elspeth placed a hand on Lilium's shoulder.

Lilium nodded. It was becoming easier to talk about it. "It's been hard to not think about them and what happened. Sometimes it doesn't seem real."

Elspeth patted Lilium's shoulder. "I can understand. When my Hamish died, this place didn't quite seem like home anymore. I constantly expected him to pop around the corner or open the door and come back in from working in the field. I had to remind myself that he was gone, but I didn't want to do that. I wanted to believe it was just a bad dream and that I'd wake and he'd be there. And I'm a grown woman, deary. Losing those we love is never easy."

Lilium nodded and wiped a tear from the corner of her eye. It was nice that someone could understand how she felt. "This is nice though. My mom and I would sometimes bake together. She was so good at it."

"Oh, that's splendid. So, you should be a big help then." Elspeth gave her a big smile, and Lilium tried to smile back.

"You know, Kellina used to help me bake, too. I miss it. How I wish she was here to make a mess and make a hundred little mistakes for me to help her through."

Lilium nodded. "My mom would never get upset when I made a mistake or mess. She was so patient with me, even when I didn't deserve it."

Elspeth gently nudged Lilium. "Mistakes are memories, deary."

Lilium's voice faltered, and with tear-filled eyes, she sniffled as she said, "I wish I could tell her how thankful I am for all she did for me. For who she was. And I'd tell her I was sorry for any mean words ever spoken . . ."

"Oh, sweet child." Elspeth wrapped her arms around Lilium and held her close. "I assure you, little one, that your mother would forgive you a thousand times over for anything and everything and that she knows you are thankful. It's not easy growing up or being a mother. Ideas of perfection are madness. We must embrace each other, warts and all, and only by doing this can any love be sincere, and the only wise thing to do in life is to be sincere in all we do. Wisely if sincerely, deary. I am confident your mother and you loved each other sincerely, and that surpasses all the riches of this world."

Lilium nodded her head and slowly pulled away while wiping her eyes.

"Ready to bake us up something sweet?" Elspeth asked.

"Always. And I think we should make extra for when Kellina visits," Lilium suggested.

"For when she visits?" Elspeth asked as if she doubted what Lilium said.

Lilium looked over all the things Elspeth had set out and thought carefully before answering. "Yes, I know she will. And Farlan, too."

"That would certainly be nice. Double batch it is!" Elspeth clapped her hands together a single time.

Elspeth walked Lilium through her time-tested, family-proven recipe. Ingredient by ingredient; what to do and not do; and the reasons. Before mixing, she paused. "Now, there is one final ingredient, a secret one, but I will share it with you."

Lilium looked at her inquisitively, eager to be let in on it.

Elspeth covered her heart with both of her hands and closed her eyes.

"Divines, may those who eat this feel my love!"

She then brought both hands to her mouth, kissed her fingertips, and softly blew out as if sending love into the bowl.

Although Lilium found it to be a tad silly, it was too endearing not to feel a sense of warmth just witnessing her gesture of love.

Once they finished mixing it, they put it in a glazed dish and placed it inside a small oven, which was built into the hearth. Elspeth added a few pieces of wood to ensure it would have the heat needed to bake properly.

"Deary, I'm due for a good hair wash, and if you don't mind me saying so, I think you may be due one as well."

Elspeth's gentle smile and wink in her eye more than softened the suggestion that Lilium's hair was a dirty mess.

"That would be nice," Lilium replied.

Beneath the chirping song and tweets of birds that were due to fly away to warmer skies any day now, Elspeth drew a couple of pails of water from her well and filled a nearby basin outside. She washed Lilium's hair first. She took her time soaking Lilium's hair, running her fingers through it, and working the water through every strand. She then rinsed her hair with a fresh pail of water. When it was Elspeth's turn, Lilium returned the favor in kind. They gently wrung their hair out with their hands and patted them dry.

"Now for my favorite part," Elspeth remarked while motioning for Lilium to follow her back inside.

Elspeth retrieved a glass flask containing pressed lavender, mint, and rosemary in oil. They took turns working the oil into each other's hair.

"It smells wonderful," Lilium remarked as she took deep breaths.

Elspeth then retrieved a brush and began brushing Lilium's hair. "Yes, it's my favorite. I always grow plenty of lavender and rosemary every year to ensure I never run out of it, and there is no shortage of mint around here. Deary, would you mind if I burn a bit of smoking leaf?"

"Oh, do you smoke it?" Lilium tilted her head some as Elspeth worked the brush through her hair.

"No, but my Hamish did. I like to burn a bit once in a while. It reminds me of him and our evenings together." Elspeth held Lilium's hair firmly enough to brush out tangles.

"I would like it. My father smoked it. Especially when he had a bad day. On those days, he would always have Mom and I sit with him just after he finished. He said it made everything better." Lilium enjoyed how it felt to have someone else brushing her hair again.

Elspeth grabbed a dish and placed some embers from the fireplace on it. She then placed a large pinch of smoking leaf on it and sat it nearby. "Hamish would often smoke while rocking in his chair on the porch. Such sweet memories, child. They take us to the past long enough to give us the strength to keep moving forward."

Elspeth took a deep breath. "Smells like home," she said.

Lilium nodded. "I didn't know I missed this smell."

"You know, Kellina and I used to brush each other's hair all the time. Things were simple back then. How I long for days gone by."

"It was the same for mom and I," Lilium quickly agreed.

Elspeth had nearly gotten Lilium's hair brushed to perfection. "It takes much effort to do this, and I encourage you not to neglect this as you grow older. You will recall memories with each pass of the brush, most good, some bad. Others will just see your beauty. They won't know what you've been through. And they don't have to. But you will have just that much more confidence when holding your head up high. This is a tough world, and it isn't easy to be beautiful in a place where so much works to tear it apart and foul it up. The fact that beauty exists, despite all the reasons for it not to, tells you something about the Divines, deary."

"Would you brush mine?" Elspeth requested while holding the brush forward for Lilium to take.

They swapped places, and Lilium brushed Elspeth's hair. "I sometimes worry that I am already forgetting what my parents looked like and what they sounded like."

Elspeth frowned. "Was there anything they used to say to you regularly?"

Lilium thought for a moment. "Yes."

"Would you tell me?" Elspeth asked.

"My mom would tuck me in at night. She would place her hands on the sides of my face, look into my eyes, and tell me, 'I love you.' And she would sometimes sing me a lullaby."

Elspeth tilted her head forward as she felt Lilium brushing more toward the base of her head. "That's sweet, deary. Your father?"

Lilium paused mid-brush stroke as she thought. "He would always say 'I'm so proud of you' and squeeze me tight." She resumed brushing.

"That's very nice. Those are the very memories you need to think of every day. You do that, and I assure you, you will not forget what they look like or sound like." Elspeth changed the subject after a pause in their conversation. "So, this paladin is from Haverstead?"

As Lilium brushed, she suddenly realized she had not come across a single tangle in Elspeth's hair. She hummed affirmatively before adding, "He has a tower there."

"And he says his name is Braeanor?"

"Yes, why?"

"For generations, my family has devoutly prayed to the Divines, and we have kept the Oracles of Faith and the many stories of the paladins close to our hearts. I say that deary because it was my understanding that following the crusade, only Ildradath survived, and I've never heard of a paladin by the name of Braeanor."

Lilium stopped brushing. "Are you saying you don't think he is a paladin?"

Elspeth shook her head. "I think he is just not telling people who he really is because he blames himself for everything that happened."

"I don't think he would lie about that." Lilium resumed brushing, attentively running the brush through in long strokes.

"Oh deary, his name may have once been Braeanor, but all paladins take a new name once they become a paladin. It is like a rite of passage, going from their old life to the fullness of their new one. I don't say this to cause you concern. I say this to help you understand how important it is for you to help him return to being who he really is. Because of how he surely feels about this, I would recommend you not bring this up until it is the right time. When that is, I have no idea. It is certainly a sensitive subject, and because of that, it deserves attention in prayer."

Lilium once again paused brushing Elspeth's hair as she thought about it. "I understand. But I still trust him, regardless of his name. I have seen too much to doubt that he is a true paladin. And I am going to continue with him, even if I will probably die. Too many others depend on it. I don't want others to suffer like I have."

Elspeth drew her elbows and hands in tight to her body and tensed up. "Why do you think you might die, deary?"

Lilium turned her head and blankly stared at the floor. "Because it is only going to become more dangerous as we go. And after he read the quest scroll, he said this would require sacrifice. He also said the quest requires that I go. He is a paladin. I am not. I cannot protect myself. It just makes sense."

Elspeth took a long, deep breath and let the aroma of the smoke fill her. "I see. And you still plan to go with him despite this?"

Lilium resumed brushing Elspeth's hair. "Yes. I have made peace with death, I think, though I am anxious about what horrors we may encounter that should cause it. This is what the Divines require, so I will go."

Elspeth turned to her right, reached backward, and gave a gentle pat and squeeze of Lilium's thigh. "You are courageous, deary, and as long as you walk by faith, this will serve you well."

Lilium then said, "I do worry about what I may see. And I worry that it might make me doubt or lose faith. It is difficult not knowing what will happen."

"My deary, faith is sometimes the same as knowing, but many times it is not. Have you ever loved and trusted someone so deeply that nothing could be more sure and true in all the world, and then something happened that caused you to question that?"

"Yes," Lilium said.

Elspeth continued. "It can turn your whole world upside down. Everything you knew is called into question. Even your memories. Choosing to trust and believe in what you have known to be true, even in the face of reasons to doubt, is an act of faith, deary. There are always reasons to doubt what we know and hold to be true, and even those who witness a miracle may choose to disbelieve. That is why paladins are such a wonder. They fight face to face with all of man's fears and enemies and reasons to doubt, and they do it not even for themselves but for others—not just once but for their whole lives.

"Faith requires the resolve to live in accordance with the will of the Divines, no matter the consequence, and the conviction to see it through to the end, no matter how uncertain the future may be. We cannot be deterred by the presence of evil or the absence of light. We cannot be swayed by what others claim or what they will think of us. We hold true and stand fast, knowing that only tests, trials, and tribulations await. Faith is everything to those who have it, and it is nothing to those without it. A paladin, in all he does and is, is faith. Faith and nothing more.

"Deary, if you ever feel the temptation to doubt the Divines in any way or for any reason, remember what they have done and turn toward them, not away. Trust them, and let them exceed your expectations."

"I shall do so," Lilium replied.

After finishing brushing their hair, they took out the cake and set it aside to cool. Elspeth put some food into a pot for supper. They then went outside and rocked together on the porch while awaiting Ildradath's return.

In due time, they were not disappointed. With kids in tow, he appeared in the distance.

The kids were returned to their enclosure, wherein they bleated happily to be back with their family. Elspeth and Lilium made no little scene upon seeing Ildradath's chest. His shirt was torn open and soaked through in now-dried blood. They were both dreadfully concerned and then quickly amazed, given how it was already healed, though scarring remained.

Aerion was unburdened and fed, which was accompanied by prayer. Ildradath cleaned up and changed clothes. Elspeth served supper to everyone, and this was followed by a portion of the cake, which they all thoroughly enjoyed. They then stepped outside to enjoy the sunset. Elspeth and Ildradath remained on the porch, but Lilium went over to the goats and Aerion.

Aerion watched as Lilium went over and played with the goats for a while, but she quickly turned her attention to him as he relaxed outside the enclosure. She climbed up the wooden fencing and sat on the top rail carefully. She called over to him, and he trotted over.

"Hey, Lilium," he nickered.

"Aerion, do you ever just—I'm scared. I just needed to tell someone. Each passing day it feels worse. I am worried about what is going to happen. Sometimes, I think I'm fine with it. Sometimes, I'm scared." Lilium tapped her fingers on the top railing as she held it to steady herself.

"I understand, but don't be afraid," he huffed as he shook his head. "Ildradath is a great fighter, and I'm pretty good too. You should have seen it. When those peekaboos came out, I totally kicked one in the face.

"I was like, 'take that,' and then the other one thought he could outrun me," he huffed again. "But I caught him, and then I threw him to the ground and 'bam, bam, bam'—not today, friend! Not today!"

He stomped a front hoof into the ground as he finished.

He nodded his head one time and softly nickered, "But when Ildradath came out, and he was bleeding, yeah, I guess I was scared. But then I saw he had those kids, and they were safe, and he seemed so calm. It reminded me of my dad and how sometimes when it was storming badly, he would just be so calm, and it made me feel like everything was going to be fine."

Lilium reached up with a hand and ran it across the side of Aerion's neck. "Aerion, do you miss your family? I miss mine so much. I think about them every day."

"Oh, Lilium. I wish you could understand me. I miss mine so much. My dad was amazing and so much fun . . . but I'm the reason why—why he—" Aerion snorted before continuing. "My mom was the best. She was so sweet. Ildradath has given me a chance to make them proud."

Lilium looked into Aerion's eyes and rubbed his mane. "I'm trying to think of you all as my new family. You, Elspeth, Kellina, and Braeanor. Well, Braeanor is actually Ildradath, according to Elspeth. I don't know why he lied."

Aerion huffed and shook his head. "Oh. He hadn't told you yet? Well, I'd be glad to have you as family. You're so sweet."

She sniffled and rubbed her nose. "I feel this fear just sitting in my chest. Like something really bad is going to happen, and there is nothing I can do about it. And I wish I could understand you. That would be so great. I still feel so lonely."

Lilium began to softly sing:

There on yonder mountain peak
From eagles' wings to the deep
My love I sing to thee

From first I laid eyes on you

Blessed child of my womb
My love I gave to you

Hush, and don't you cry
For this too will pass us by
My love in you abides

Tomorrow is a brand-new day
To guard your heart, I pray
My love in you shall stay

"Forever and—and . . . Oh, Aerion. I don't remember the rest of the words." Lilium hung her head.

Aerion nickered, "Forever beneath sun and moon. In Bright Haven one day soon. Our love will be made anew. At least, that is what my mother would sing."

Lilium wiped tears from her cheeks.

Aerion shook his head again and neighed, "Oh no, no, no. I can't have that. My sister can't be sad." He nuzzled the side of her face and tickled her ear, and she giggled in response. "Come on, hop on, let's go for a ride. We can play a game called 'Catch the Sun.' We run at the sun and stare at it, then turn and run away from it and chase all the spots we see. Come on! Come on!"

Aerion trotted over a bit and neighed loudly at Ildradath. "Hey, can we go for a quick ride?"

Ildradath looked up and, after a momentary delay, called out to Lilium, "You want to go for a ride, Lilium? It's okay if you do. Just don't go too far."

Aerion trotted back over to Lilium and positioned his left side so she could easily step from the fence onto his back. "Alright, hop on!"

A smile graced Lilium's red face. "We going for a ride? Okay."

He whinnied, "I won't go too fast, but hold tight!"

Aerion headed due west, straight toward the setting sun—into which he stared without so much a blink. He then made a wide turn. He let out a loud, joyful whinny, "There's so many of them!"

As he chased the spots in his eyes, Lilium clung tight and laughed. And each time Aerion charged the sun, turned, and shook his head while running in circles, she laughed more. She didn't know what he was doing, but it was silly, and she loved every moment of it.

While Lilium and Aerion were spending time together, so were Elspeth and Ildradath. Out of hospitality, Elspeth pointed out that she had smoking leaf and a pipe, and after he mentioned how he used to occasionally take some after supper, she insisted. He gratefully accepted.

He leaned against a wooden porch post as he smoked and looked out toward the sunset, and Elspeth made herself comfortable in one of the rocking chairs.

Elspeth felt joy welling inside her as she took in her surroundings. It was nice to have company and to be able to enjoy the sunset with them. She looked over at Ildradath and studied him for a moment. "The night before my husband died, he looked out to that horizon with the same look. I think a part of him knew it was his last night here. I think he wanted to tell me, but how do you tell someone that without sounding crazy?

"A part of me knew. I wanted to ask him. I think the longer you are with someone you truly love, the less you have to say certain things. You both can know it and know the other knows it, and you can both want to say it . . . and yet you don't. It is a magical thing to be that way.

"He always said he hoped to die before me. Not because he wanted to leave me alone," she said with a light-hearted laugh, "but because he knew I could make it without him. He would say he couldn't make it without me. Hamish is gone now, but when the wind blows and his old rocking chair rocks, I can still see him sitting there. I can see him toiling in the garden or with the animals. Everywhere I look here, I see memories of the man who loved me more than life itself. I miss him."

"Sounds like you both had something special," he interjected.

"Hmm, yes. I remember his prayer when we went to bed that night. He prayed to the Divines that I would live to see the return of the paladins. I have looked for that sign every day, that it might tell me my journey was near its end. I do not look sorrowfully but with hope for all those who come after me. I may not see the peace brought by the paladins, but I will rest well knowing that others will." Elspeth silently rocked for a few moments before continuing. "You never know what the rivers of life may bring, so I wonder now if the return of the paladins has found me, Ildradath?"

He sharply turned his gaze from the horizon and stared back into her eyes. He did not know what to say. He turned his eyes away from hers and looked intently back out toward Lilium while taking a long draw of the pipe. "Perhaps Elspeth, but I am not sure what the return of the paladins means. Things cannot go back to the way they were, not for a very long time. And how did you know who I am?"

Elspeth gently rocked back and forth, and her hands were gracefully folded in her lap. "My parents and grandparents would tell me stories about the paladins. They spoke often of one called Ildradath. You fit the description, and it is said only you survived the crusade. Many believed you were the chosen of the Divines—that you would be the one to break the yoke of the Abyss and free us from their bondage."

Aerion neighed loudly, and it took a moment for Ildradath to realize Aerion was talking to him. He cleared his throat before speaking. "You want to go for a ride, Lilium? It's okay if you do. Just don't go too far."

Aerion trotted over to Lilium, who stepped off the fence and onto him. They ran toward the setting sun.

Ildradath had tears in his eyes. He shook his head and looked toward the ground, then back up at the sky while trying to suppress the surfacing anguish. "I might be more of the reason why that won't come to pass. It seems I'm the one who doesn't believe in myself, I suppose. Stories about me were once nice, and I assure you, they were a certain comfort at times. However, they seem now to speak of someone I could never return to being. They are now more salt in a wound than an encouragement, no offense meant to your goodwill. Whatever was good of me back then, I question daily and see only now as inadequate. And if the man I was back then was not up to the task, then how can the man I am today be."

The wind blew, and the empty chair rocked in tempo with Elspeth's. They both watched for several moments until the wind subsided, and it came to rest. Lilium was still riding through the field and playing with Aerion. She wore a large smile and was having a tremendous amount of fun as the sun descended deeper on the horizon. Elspeth and Ildradath could hear her laughter. A passerby would never have known all she had endured and the horrors ahead.

"Ildradath, you are the man you were back then with added wisdom. You've hurt and lost more than any man should by rights. Yet, here you stand. If you believe like I do that the Divines guide things to a purposed end, to a day of renewal, then you know you must not be done yet. They have entrusted your hands with work of a cosmic magnitude. You know that the Divines still have more for you, and that means, in some strange way, that they still believe in you. They still need you. I believe in you. I've prayed for you by name for years now. But I'd say most of all, that little girl out there believes in you."

"Is that so?" Ildradath asked.

"She told me she knows she may die on this quest. She knows you will do everything you can to protect her, and she believes you can. She believes it like it is something she has already seen. She has hope that this quest of yours will be a success and that it will save families and little girls like her all over this world from the Abyss. She is not naive, Ildradath. She believes. And I believe that the Divines have big plans for her. I can feel it in these old bones."

Ildradath took another long draw of the pipe, let the flavor fill his mouth, and then exhaled slowly. "Even if this quest is successful, there is much more ahead that must be done. I want to believe as well that there will be much good to come from this and that I can do what is needed. I have moments of it. I do not doubt the Divines the way I once did. I spent years in that tower, tossed to and fro by waves of doubt and faith. Now, I only doubt my ability to be of service and to have the faith to do what is required of me when the time comes, and I worry what all of this means for her."

"Faith without action is worthless, but here you are. Faith has gotten you this far. If I had to guess, it will get you over the river tomorrow and onward to your journey's end. And worrying is like rocking in one of these chairs. No matter how much you do it, it never gets you anywhere. Let the Divines do the worrying. You just keep those eyes open, steady that sword of yours, and beat back the Abyss." Elspeth finished speaking with a solid tap of her palms on each chair arm for emphasis.

Ildradath tipped his pipe up and outward as if offering a toast to Elspeth. "I tell you what. Based on what your daughter said, I expected hospitality. I've found much more here than I expected, and I think it should help me through the days ahead."

Elspeth beamed with gratitude at his remark. The thought of being a blessing to a paladin blessed her heart in a way she had never experienced. She turned her eyes from Ildradath to look at Lilium and Aerion. She felt as though she had more blessings than she could count. "It is a blessed thing to be able to look at the future."

Elspeth and Ildradath continued watching Lilium as she rode with Aerion and played beneath the setting sun.

CHAPTER SIX

VIPER'S ASCENT

. . . And Hezraniah, the first of his kind, heard the voice of the Old Ones whispering to him "folly" and "futility" and "madness." His world was torn asunder, and he knew things which he had not, and he forgot that which he knew, for even he could no longer discern the voice of the Divines. And so he fell from their grace and into the maw of the Abyss . . .

1

They rose with the morning sun and readied to leave. While Lilium enjoyed a piece of cake, Elspeth wrapped several more pieces securely in a cloth bundle for the trip ahead.

Ildradath spoke with Aerion as he prepared him for the next leg of the journey. "Listen, boy. Things will only get more dangerous from here on out. Please do as I say when I say it. We have difficult days ahead of us. If anything should happen to me, give me your word that you will bring Lilium back here to Elspeth."

Aerion huffed and nodded.

"Good boy."

Lilium joined Ildradath, and she squinted her eyes while tilting her head upon seeing Aerion. "Braeanor, does Aerion look bigger to you?"

Ildradath looked at Elspeth momentarily to gauge her reaction to Lilium addressing him as Braeanor. She simply looked back at him with raised eyebrows, which suggested he should tell her sooner rather than later.

Ildradath turned his attention to Lilium. "Mayhaps. He has been eating well, and the prayers of the faithful work mightily. Could you feed him this apple?" He handed an apple to her, and she gladly took it over to feed Aerion.

Ildradath walked over to Elspeth and eased her out of earshot of Lilium. "Can Lilium return here afterward?"

Elspeth patted the side of his arm reassuringly. "Of course. Divines willing, I would welcome you both back, deary."

"Divines willing, thank you," Ildradath replied.

Elspeth placed her hands on each of Ildradath's arms and looked him in the eyes. Her kind eyes shone into his. "Thank you. Thank you for all you've done and for what you are about to do." She embraced Ildradath, and he wrapped his arms around her in response.

"My life is in service to the Divines," he said.

Elspeth walked over and embraced Lilium, and they exchanged their final heartfelt goodbyes. Elspeth made it plainly known to all that they were always welcome back. She sat in a rocking chair and watched as they departed. The chair next to her rocked in the breeze as well.

Aerion carried the others along the now familiar path to the river. He followed the riverbank back toward where he had crossed the stream to get to the peekaboo nest. He made his way across the other two streams and then continued south.

The green fields became sparser and more patched. The dirt became increasingly dark. It was not due to the richness of the soil and abundant nutrients that might nourish plants; rather, it was from the blasted remnants of the long-dormant volcanic mountain range known as the Obsidian Peaks. He was heading for the closest traversable pass, Viper's Ascent.

The only visible living trees were well behind them, and the pass was only a half-day's journey ahead. They continued to chat as they made their way closer. Lilium sat in front of Ildradath on Aerion.

"Do you expect much trouble making it through the pass?" Lilium inquired of Ildradath.

"Hmm. It's certainly a possibility. Although Farlan has heard reports of the ash vipers returning to the pass early, they typically don't for another month or two. Usually, it takes colder weather to drive them to the warmth of the pass and the surrounding mountains. I am hopeful that the reports are exaggerated, as with most things spoken at inns."

Lilium felt a knot in her throat. She was not particularly afraid of snakes. She was fine seeing them, though she would never willingly get close to one. What Farlan described was beyond anything she ever wanted to see. "What if they are right?" she asked.

"The plan is to keep moving forward. I expect Aerion to move as quickly and safely as he can. I will handle any ash vipers that come after us. We must stay together at all costs. The pass takes several turns, and there are points at which it would be easy to slide off. The rocky slopes break and give way easily, so we must be mindful. If need be, we will back into an outcrop, and I will take care of any which come at us."

Lilium did not like needing a plan to deal with serpents coming after them. "Sounds like a plan. What do they look like? Are they easy to spot?"

Ildradath drew a long breath. He supposed it might be better if he provided an explanation than let her imagination run wild. Then again, maybe not. "Their scales are typically mottled dark gray and black. They burrow just under the black obsidian sands and ash heaps, and if any part of them remains uncovered and exposed, it will look remarkably similar to the sands and rocks. There will be no mistaking them if they strike. Their thick bodies will flatten out as they launch themselves upward, and they are able to glide for some distance as they attempt to strike. They almost always go for your torso when they strike. They will certainly startle you the first time you see them."

"Just the first time?" Lilium asked with a nervous laugh.

"Well, maybe every time," he laughed.

Aerion huffed and shook his head from side to side.

"Yes, Aerion. You can kick and stomp them if you are quick, but I'd prefer you to get us out of the pass quickly rather than fight. These things will be just as content to have you for a meal."

Aerion whinnied softly with a slight nod to affirm he understood.

"Once we get into the pass, we must not talk unless necessary. The less sound, the better." Ildradath leaned over a bit to scan the ground ahead.

"So, you have been through the pass before?" Lilium asked.

"Yes, I have, but it – whoa, Aerion, halt."

Aerion stopped.

"What is it?" Lilium inquired, her voice cracking with concern.

"Tracks. I'm hopping off, but you stay for now." Ildradath hopped off Aerion and began looking among the sparse grass and dark ground to their left. He knelt and studied the ground intently for a few moments. "Hmm. Looks like our friend, the goruphant, traveled this way. Probably a few days ago. Or more. Hard to tell. All of the ground is so dry here."

Lilium watched as he began scanning the ground ahead, stopping every few paces to inspect more sign.

Ildradath pointed along the path of the sign until his finger aimed ahead of them. "Yes, he came this way. I'd say he headed through the pass."

Lilium looked around nervously. "Do you think he is close by?"

Ildradath saw Lilium's apprehension. "No, not likely. You can relax. It looks like he is not moving as quickly as when we first crossed his path, but given our delays in Glenmore and Elspeth's, I am confident he is well ahead of us. It doesn't mean we let our guard down, just that I don't expect to see him anytime soon."

"Where do you think he is going? There is no city on the other side of this pass, is there? There is nothing, right?" Lilium asked.

"You are correct for the most part. But it leads to the flats, which is the way toward Malcreus."

Lilium tilted her head. "Do you think it is going after him too?"

Ildradath shook his head while returning his focus to the sign. "Not likely."

She reached forward and stroked Aerion's neck. "Why? If he was once a paladin, wouldn't it want to kill him too?"

Ildradath stared at one of the hoofprints longer, stood, and then placed his hands on his hips while studying the path further ahead. He collected his thoughts before continuing. "Unfortunately, he is an apostate now."

She scrunched her nose. "So, does this mean he no longer believes in the Divines? Like at all? After all he has seen and done?"

"Well," Ildradath said while looking around for a way to explain it in simple terms. "For paladins, it goes beyond that. He knows the Divines are real, but he serves the Abyss now. He believes their power is greater, that in a strange way, they are even more real."

She shrugged her shoulders. "So, he is a cultist?"

"In a way, but certainly the worst kind. The Abyss promises power to those who forsake the Divines. Sometimes, it grants it, too. And a fallen paladin is a trophy for the Abyss and foe to the Order. They do not simply abandon the Order. They hate it." Ildradath found himself clenching his jaw at the thought of such betrayal.

Lilium brought a hand to her jawline as she shook her head in confusion. "But why? If he had the blessings and gifts of the Divines in fighting the Abyss, how could he turn away?"

"We spent several years fighting together in the Abyss, and we were the only two who made it out alive. The things we saw—the things we experienced affected us. It–" Ildradath paused again. Scenes of those days flashed before his eyes. Sounds of clanging weapons, screeching creatures, and screaming men filled his ears.

"It what?" Lilium inquired, uncomfortable with the minute of silence which had passed.

He shook his head and regained his bearing. "I'm sorry. Sometimes, I still see and hear things from back then." He brought one of his palms to his forehead and wiped downward as if to clear those memories away before continuing his explanation. "In the end, after everything, only he and I survived our physical wounds. His spiritual wounds were too much. After closing the portal, we tended to the injured. He suddenly stripped naked and walked off without any further words."

"He went mad?" she asked.

He tilted his head to the side. "Mad? A crisis of faith? They are closely intertwined, to be honest. I fought it for nearly half a century. I'm not proud of it."

"You shouldn't be ashamed of it, though," she replied emphatically.

"Oh," Ildradath turned towards her and raised his eyebrows. "How so?"

Lilium scratched the back of Aerion's neck as she spoke. "Well, my father used to tell me on his bad days, 'Girl, we keep faith. We keep it like it is something a robber is waiting nearby to steal. On the days we struggle, we must fight to keep it.' You have fought."

Ildradath softly smiled. "Yes. Yes, I guess you are right. And faith is worth keeping. Faith is a paladin's reward."

He walked back to Aerion and remounted. He reached around Lilium and grabbed the reins. With a quick snicker, Ildradath signaled Aerion to carry on.

"Was he a good paladin," Lilium inquired.

Ildradath shook his head. "You have no shortage of questions."

"Is that a bad thing?" she asked with a serious tone. She genuinely wanted to know if having such curiosity about things was bad.

"No, I suppose not. Those unwilling or unable to investigate matters more deeply often fall victim to preventable events. And the Abyss loves to work in the dark and behind closed doors—among whispers and signs others miss." He drew a deep breath.

"And to answer your question, yes, he was. He had been with the Order for some time before I became a paladin. He was a fantastic swordsman, and he was one of my instructors. Few could match him. Unfortunately, he had a habit of acting like it too, but I suppose great skill can make even a paladin insufferable at times."

"Could you match him?" Lilium asked.

"Once. Just once. The look on his face was priceless, too. He called me a dishonorable cheater. Haha. I was willing to see the bigger picture in situations. Sometimes that is needed, even in combat."

Lilium did not voice it, but she was uneasy at the thought that he only matched him once. Nevertheless, she remained confident in him and trusted that the Divines gave the quest, knowing he was up to the task.

Ildradath continued to recall more about the paladin who became Malcreus. "Truth be told, he was quite the encourager. I can think of numerous times when he would pray with another brother, and he would lift the spirits of those around him. He was a good listener, attentive to the burdens of others, and quick to offer words that provided comfort or quickened men to take action in times of doubt. Ultimately, his burden was too great and prevailed against him. Even now, I try to remember the good days, the man he was, not what he has become or the path he has taken."

Lilium interjected. "What was his paladin name?"

Ildradath hummed disapprovingly. "This is another reason why the Abyss is so vile. I strain to remember him as he was, a dear brother whose paladin name I cannot even speak unless he finds repentance. So I go now to judge him as he is. Malcreus is not our great enemy, however. He is but a symptom of the Abyss—the Old Ones—the Dread One. All one and the same, really."

"What do you think he has been doing all these years, then?" she asked.

"I am not sure. But you must understand that we are dealing with an evil that festers in dark places. It grows, malignant and cancerous, until it is ready to spill out and lay waste. Whatever he has been doing, it is not good," Ildradath said.

There was no longer any greenery or sign of living vegetation. Viper's Ascent lay just in the distance. It was a simple, sloped path which ascended between rocky outcrops. The dark rocks, black sand, and cloudy sky enveloped the path, making ominous the portal to their destination.

"It is not far from sunset. We will camp here for the night. The pass is far more perilous at night," Ildradath asserted.

Lilium was pleasantly surprised by this suggestion. She was not eager to enter the pass, and the closer she got to it, the more dreadful it felt. It was putting off the inevitable, but she was fine with that for now.

Ildradath made a small fire for warmth and light, but they ate a simple meal of some dried meat and apples. Aerion stood nearby and dozed off and on.

"You brought plenty of apples along, huh?" she asked with a mouthful of apple.

"Always," he quipped back.

Lilium finished her mouthful before speaking again. "So, I was wondering. Why did the Order never tell others about people's souls being trapped in the Abyss when they are killed by it?"

"Because the Abyss and especially the Dread One is empowered by despair and fear, which would have multiplied with such news. It would not have helped anything. We hoped that destroying the artifact would stop souls being pulled into and trapped in the Abyss."

"Is that also why you didn't tell anyone about the artifact?" she asked.

Ildradath raised an eyebrow. "I suppose so."

"But what exactly does the artifact do?" Lilium inquired.

Ildradath raised a hand and pointed repeatedly toward her. "That is precisely the kind of question we wanted to avoid answering."

She was undeterred by his pointing. "But it doesn't change the fact that the artifact does something. What does it do?"

He sat up and then looked into the fire. "Do you know the oracle concerning the Dread One waking?"

She crossed her arms tightly against herself. "Yes, but it has been some time since I read it."

Ildradath's face went expressionless as he stared deeply into the fire. The flames danced in the reflection of his eyes. "It is written:

The Dread One did speak his name unto them, and his name was the first spoken among the Old Ones. His name is a name of power and authority, one who does not abide the will of others. And to this day his name is not spoken among the faithful of man, for it is a curse and an omen and a summons. For he sleeps only to awake again, and in that day, there will be tribulation like never before seen among all peoples. It will be a day of great lamentation, of smoke and fire, of raging tempests and sundered land, of broken bone and rent flesh, of madness and despair. Woe unto those with child and who nurse, for they shall be laid open, and the born and unborn shall be worse than orphans. In that day the sun will retreat behind darkened sky, but man will have nowhere to flee, and he will tread among and over man, and cities and all of creation shall be cast down, for there is no weapon of man which may pierce his form.

"The artifact is to be used to lead a chorus of the Old Ones in singing the praises of the Dread One's name, and through this, the very power of the countless souls trapped in the Abyss will be siphoned into him to replace the power he spent in creating the Abyss and setting things in motion to overthrow our world. On that day, he will awaken from his slumber. And then that oracle would come to pass, and our world would come to an end. This is obviously why the Order fixated upon the artifact's destruction."

Lilium shuddered.

Ildradath continued. "That Oracle is why—"

"But isn't there more to that oracle?" Lilium interrupted. "*And man's only hope will be to throw themselves into his service and to worship him and to speak his name?*"

Ildradath shot a look at Lilium, which pierced her to her core. "Where did you hear that!"

Aerion woke at the sound of Ildradath's raised voice and looked on at Lilium and Ildradath's exchange.

"What!" she exclaimed defensively.

"What you said is not part of the oracle," he shot back.

She held her hands up as if to stop him. "It is what is taught in the temple of Munrobeinn."

"Then the city has already fallen into the hands of the Abyss! That is a line from the so-called lost teachings of Hezraniah. Those are the words of an apostate, of heresy—of blasphemy!"

"I—I didn't know. I'm sorry!"

"Have you heard the whole book recited?" he demanded to know.

"No, I don't think—"

"Have you heard his name spoken?" he stammered the question in follow-up.

"Who?" Lilium asked back.

"The Dread One. Have you heard his name!" he demanded again.

"No!" she shouted back. She lowered her head and folded her arms.

Ildradath shook his head and stared into the fire. Neither he nor

Lilium disturbed the silence for some time.

Finally, Ildradath said, "It's not your fault. I understand that you didn't know. You know now. Those teachings can damn a genuine believer. It blends the truth with tainted words. They corrupt saving faith. He wrote those words before repenting and being pulled free from the grasp of the Old Ones. But it was too late. The things he wrote were already out there, and try as we might, the Order has never been able to destroy them."

Ildradath buried his face into his palms and then looked up to the sky. He was disappointed, mostly at himself. He felt responsible. Perhaps had he spent many of the last years actively serving the Divines, he could have caught that heresy before it took root, but his time in the tower was a complicated matter in itself. Now, the blossoming heresy would be immensely more difficult, and if his quest was successful, he would not be here to ensure it was done. This, along with the possible cult activity he learned about at Glenmore's docks, did not bode well.

Lilium cleared her throat and still had more questions to ask. "Is it true he would hear if you speak his name? And if it is so bad to say the Dread One's name, why do some openly say the names of the other Old Ones?"

Ildradath looked over at Lilium with a glum countenance. "It is because his name is connected with the oracle, not the others, and no one knows if he can hear you speak his name. Even so, it is best not to risk drawing his attention."

"But he's asleep, right? So, he can't hear us." Lilium spoke with confidence as what she said made perfect sense.

"He is not like us, Lilium. Nothing about the Old Ones is like us."

Lilium held her palms out toward the fire to feel its warmth and stared into the flames. "Including the Dread One, there are eight of them, right? Orph the Acedious. Evodia the Flooded, or is it lice-something?"

"Licentious," Ildradath replied as he turned to the fire. "Yes, she and the others have been called different things throughout history, but it is easiest to associate them with their particular corrupting influence."

"And the others?" she asked.

Ildradath's eyes left the flames and looked at Lilium momentarily before returning to the fire. "Well, Borantulid the Wrathful. Pormikiun the Gluttonous. Gordast the Avaricious. Yrdnyarl the Vain. Deicharon the Envious—though the Blackest suits him well, too."

Lilium tucked her warm hands against her body as she folded her arms. "And it's true that they have children?"

"There are children, unfortunately. All born of Evodia. For example, Ripculleron the Flesh Weaver is the son of Yrdnyarl. And I pray you never meet one of his creations. Contrary to what some have believed, the many abyssians are not their children. These aberrations are, however, sometimes the result of two of the Old Ones' twisted minds dreaming up new terrors with which to torment us."

"Will we have to fight any more abyssians?" she asked.

"Most assuredly," Ildradath responded matter-of-factly.

Lilium bit her lip before she asked her next question. "Are there ones worse than the pox fiend?"

"Lilium." Ildradath looked straight at her and paused until she looked at him.

"What?" she asked with a shrug of her shoulders.

"I understand your curiosity, and for some things, it is better to be knowledgeable. But I don't think discussing this further is helpful at the moment."

Lilium slumped and stared into the fire.

Ildradath decided to change the subject to learn more about Lilium and the state of affairs in the Eastern Reaches. "You said your father was on the city council of Munrobeinn, right?"

"Yes, for much of his life. When we fled, he was the presiding regent, the head of the council."

"Did he discuss city affairs with you?" Ildradath asked as he leaned closer to the fire.

"Often. Mostly to complain about the stupid ideas people had and all of their unreasonable complaints. Sometimes, he was bothered by others on the council."

"I imagine he had a difficult time with it. It isn't easy to bear such responsibility for the administration of a city, especially one with such historical importance. No other city can boast of casting off a monarchy—though that was before your father's time."

Lilium nodded. "Though he said he often wondered whether it would be better to have a single king ruling—one who devoutly worshiped the Divines, of course."

Ildradath leaned forward more and used a stick to poke at the fire. "Hmm. Yes. Probably. Did your father tell you much about those who conspired against him and your family?"

"Only that other council members were involved. Two other council members were found murdered. Word came to him that our family was next. On his way home after getting that message, he felt eyes watching him everywhere he went. We left in the middle of the night. It happened so fast." Lilium frowned. "Father never wanted to go through Edjramor."

Ildradath frowned, too, upon seeing Lilium's expression. "And you stayed within the keep?"

"Since I can remember. All council members' families did. It was good mostly, though I didn't see much of the rest of the city. Usually only did when we went to temple services or for a ride. My tutors came to me."

"Well, I am glad that you were able to escape. And that despite all the circumstances, your faith has held. I am concerned that Munrobeinn, all of the Eastern Reaches even, will eventually fall into the hands of the Abyss cult if it hasn't already. I can tell from you, that your dad was a man of genuine faith. This may have been a reason for the threat against your family. He may have learned of things which the cult did not want made known.

"If those conspiring against your father only needed to secure political power, forcing him to flee was sufficient. He abandoned his position and did not stand to inherit a throne. The Abyss cult, however, would maintain their pursuit of him. They would persist as long as he lived. And so, I am worried about the future of the Eastern Reaches and what this means for you after this quest."

"Well, I don't know," she quickly responded while staring into the fire. "I may not have anything to worry about after this quest." Lilium abruptly leaned over, turned her back to Ildradath, and covered herself. "But I do know that I am going to get some rest. Goodnight, *Braeanor*," she said with a snide emphasis on the name.

Ildradath was unsure whether her added emphasis was her revealing she knew who he was or just her temperament at the moment. He wanted to explain things to her, but he understood she was done talking. Something was bothering her, and he needed to let it be for the moment.

"Goodnight, Lilium," he responded. "And goodnight, Aerion." He huffed softly back.

11

With the morning light, they woke and set out on the next leg of their quest. Aerion carried them toward the mouth of the pass. The surrounding land had darkened and withered, and the ground was now covered with dark, coarse sand. It became thicker as he approached the initial slope, and he did not like the feel of it shifting beneath his hooves. He was looking forward to being safe on the other side.

"Aerion and Lilium, it is best we refrain from speaking this point forward," Ildradath said.

They neither nodded nor uttered a sound. Everyone was anxious to get through the pass uneventfully, and as if to increase their odds of success, their breathing became more shallow and quiet. Their eyes scanned their surroundings dutifully.

Step by step, Aerion led them higher until the path leveled out. Each cluster of rock, mound of dark sand, and curved line became suspicious. They looked for the slightest movement with such terrible fixation that they believed they observed movement when there was none on more than one occasion. Aerion halted momentarily each time he believed he had, and no words were exchanged. After tense moments of observation, he resumed walking after he convinced himself that his eyes were playing tricks.

After a short while, they made it through a sharp bend in the pass and saw that something lay across the path ahead. Aerion slowed, and Ildradath shared his concern, too.

"Quietly," Ildradath whispered, "Closer, slowly."

At first, it appeared to be some kind of large branch or part of a tree, but once they got within twenty feet of it Ildradath recognized that it was the goruphant.

Ildradath tugged the reins gently, and Aerion stopped.

"Stay alert," he said with a whisper.

He slowly and methodically slid off Aerion. He reached into a bag and grabbed his heater shield. It was dingy, but there were spots which shone its metallic brilliance. A beautiful flower symbol was centered on the shield. He unsheathed his sword from his waist. With these at the ready, he moved forward to inspect the goruphant.

The goruphant's large frame lay flat on its back. Its whole body, including its clawed arm and tentacled appendage, were withered and desiccated. The torso had multiple sets of large puncture wounds and clear signs of multiple ash vipers feasting upon it. Further on the other side of it, he observed at least two ash vipers torn to pieces. He knelt and inspected the wounds closely. Some of the wounds in the torso appeared to be gouges, not just clean punctures.

Ildradath looked around at the sand and saw unmistakable signs of a struggle. The sand was kicked up in various places, and trails indicated that the ash vipers had slithered off further after feasting. Presumably, the goruphant was attacked simultaneously by multiple ash vipers. As they bit, he tore several off and snapped them apart. In the end, their venom was too much, even for its large body. It eventually grew weak, unable to fend any others off, and then they feasted on him.

This was not a good discovery. The ash vipers had indeed returned early to the pass. He hoped, if there was any silver lining to be found, that perhaps the goruphant had been enough to satiate them. Perhaps they would be full, lethargic, and uninterested in their group as they passed through. There was no shortcut or way to circumnavigate the path ahead. If they turned back, they would lose more than a week, and to do so would be to disregard the fact that he was supposed to take this pass.

He decided that they would continue ahead, treading carefully. He walked back to Aerion and Lilium. "We continue on, slowly and quietly," he whispered. He put his shield back in a bag and sheathed his sword before mounting Aerion.

Aerion immediately began walking forward. When he reached the desiccated corpse of the goruphant, he stepped over it, and he picked a path forward that avoided having to step on or over the dead ash vipers' heads. Their open eyes were startling, and he worried that they might still somehow manage to bite him.

They continued onward and around the next bend to a more open stretch of the pass, which fell away on the northwest side. It led to a valley covered in a dense haze. Aerion stuck to the middle of the path, and everyone was vigilant. Ahead and to their right, several small rocks tumbled from the top of the pass onto the ground. Aerion stopped. Everyone carefully surveyed the ground and then scanned the rock faces on both sides of the path.

This stretch was particularly soft with loose sand and ash, and each hoof sunk just below the surface. Each step took extra effort, and this made Aerion uneasy. If he needed to sprint off, it would be that much more difficult to pick up speed. Aerion took a deep, slow breath and then proceeded forward.

After several more steps, Aerion reflexively reared when he stepped onto a burrowed ash viper, which hissed and struck out at him. Had Aerion's hoof not been stepping on part of its body when it lashed out, he would have been bitten. Lilium and Ildradath were thrown off.

Lilium had just enough grip on the reigns to keep her from going straight back, but it pulled her off Aerion's left side. She still hit the ground hard, and she gasped as the fall knocked the wind out of her. Ildradath exclaimed in pain from landing flat on his back, but he had braced himself for the impact. He was quick to get to his feet and draw his sword.

Aerion stomped furiously around and crushed the ash viper to death beneath his hooves. He snorted and began trying to calm himself.

"No need to apologize," Ildradath replied.

Ildradath helped Lilium to her feet and quietly assured her she was okay. She was able to catch her breath. Just a stone's throw ahead, Ildradath and Aerion spotted movement beneath the surface. Multiple lines began tracing their path toward the group.

Aerion squealed.

"I see 'em, boy!" Ildradath shouted out.

Ildradath ran forward, held his sword at the ready, and readied himself to step to the side and swing. Two ash vipers shot out from the surface. Their coiled bodies unfurled and lay flat so that their momentum would glide them right toward their targets. One went straight for Ildradath, the other for Aerion.

Ildradath jumped to his left while swinging downward, and the ash viper was split in two. Both halves writhed, and its jaw opened and closed repeatedly in a final futile effort to bite him, though it was not close enough to do so. Its eyes stared up at him.

Aerion had already begun turning to present his hind legs toward the burrowed ash vipers heading their way. When the one launched itself at him, he barely missed kicking its head, but his kick made contact and diverted its path. It went spinning towards Lilium.

Lilium shrieked and jumped back as it landed on the ground just feet from her. The ash viper quickly righted itself and struck out at her, but she was just out of its striking range. She jumped back again, lost her balance, fell to her side, and began slipping off the side of the pass.

Aerion hurried forward and stomped that ash viper's head with his front hooves. He was dismayed to see Lilium slipping off the side. He squealed loudly and sprinted to Ildradath, who had just dodged another ash viper and cut it in half. His mind was fixed on those which remained beneath the surface and had not revealed themselves yet.

Aerion neighed loudly, and Ildradath looked at him with eyes wide. He then turned to look where Lilium had been. She was nowhere to be seen.

Lilium was sliding down the side of the rock face. Its slope was gradual, but its crumbly, loose composition made it impossible to stop her descent. She groped and reached out desperately for anything that might provide her a firm hold. Despite her efforts, she only picked up momentum.

As she disappeared into the fog below, she screamed out, "Help!".

Ildradath could tell where her voice came from and knew there would be no way for her to get back up on her own. The hissing of one of the ash vipers preparing to lash out at him snatched his attention right back. He slashed it as Aerion sprinted away from another one, then abruptly stopped and managed a good hind kick at its pursuing face.

As another ash viper struck at Ildradath, he swiftly sliced its head in half lengthways with his sword. "Aerion! Run to the end of the pass, do not stop for anything, then turn north and head for the three large boulders stacked at the edge of the fog. Do not enter the fog! I will meet you there!"

Aerion squealed and then took off in a sprint with another ash viper hot on his tail. Ildradath sliced at another one that had just emerged near his feet. He turned back to where Lilium's voice had come from and ran over.

He stopped at the edge of the rock face and realized their danger was about to multiply. He looked back and ensured that Aerion was making his way off into the distance before sheathing his sword, stepping off, and leaning onto his right side to make the best of the bumpy ride to Dead Man's Valley.

CHAPTER SEVEN

DEAD MAN'S VALLEY

. . . The hand of the Divines is at work in both the seen and the unseen, guiding the many providences of the world so that even evil may be worked for good. And like a master of war, they turn the Old Ones' plans against them . . .

1

Ildradath reached the bottom and found himself immersed in the fog of Dead Man's Valley. The haze was thick and worrisomely palpable, tinged with an acrid odor of rotten eggs and decay. The ground was carpeted in a spongy, fibrous fungus. The valley was littered with ponds of various sizes, all of which should never be drunk from or disturbed in the slightest. Though the surrounding mountains had not been active for many generations, they were still deeply affected by its volcanic history. Noxious, poisonous gas clouds could be burped from the ponds at any given moment. This was not a place to linger.

"Lilium! Where are you?" Ildradath shouted. He eagerly awaited a response, but there was nothing. He grimaced upon experiencing how the air tasted worse than it smelled.

He looked around, and there was nothing visible beyond twenty feet. He stepped along the edge of the rock slope and looked for any sign of her. He became worried that she may have chosen to run along, looking for another way to climb back up. While that normally might be a good idea, the visibility was so poor there was no telling what she might rush into.

"Lilium! Lilium!" he called out into the fog.

He continued along the rock slope and increased his pace. The smell of sulfur became increasingly noticeable, and he said a silent prayer for the Divines to protect them from any ill effects of the valley. He heard a faint voice in the distance. He strained his ears to listen, but his heart was racing and making it difficult to hear over its beating.

Somewhat closer now, he heard Lilium's voice calling out again, "Braeanor! Help!"

He felt a rush of excitement to know that Lilium was somewhere nearby. He continued along the slope and called out several more times. "Lilium! Lilium! Where are you?"

"Braeanor, I hear you!"

"Stay where you are. I will come to you!" He continued in the direction he last heard her voice. "Where are you!"

"I am here!"

Ildradath heard the voice behind him. He must have passed her in the fog, so he turned back and moved away from the rock slope so he would cover new ground. "Where are you!" he shouted again.

"I am over here!"

This time, he heard her voice closer to the slope, so he turned back and headed straight towards it, looking up with anticipation that she may have somehow ascended the slope partway.

"Lilium, where are you!" he called out once more.

"I found you!"

Lilium's voice was so sudden and unexpectedly close behind him that he was taken aback. He turned around to see her standing there. She immediately wrapped her arms around him and buried her face against his shirt.

"Thank the Divines. Are you okay?" he asked. He placed a hand across her back, pulled her tight, and patted her reassuringly. A wave of relief washed over him, and he let their embrace linger.

She let go and took a step back. "Yes, I am fine. Thank you for coming. I was so worried you wouldn't."

"Of course, I would come for you. Take my hand. We need to make our way east. Starting from these slopes, we need to continue in this direction." He motioned ahead. "Aerion will meet us on the other side."

Lilium gripped his right hand tightly. "Let's hurry. I don't want to be here anymore. This place gives me a bad feeling."

"It is dangerous. Stay close, and we will move quickly. Do not go near any of the water. All of it is not fit for drinking, and dangerous fumes may emerge without notice. We are in Dead Man's Valley, and I'd like us not to be counted among its victims."

They moved eastward, but Ildradath felt the difficulty of navigating in such dense fog. He could not see that sky, and he could not see into the distance. He was trusting that he was not deviating from the initial heading he had set, but he had not traveled far before hearing something surprising.

"Braeanor, where are you!" cried another voice in the distance.

He immediately looked over at Lilium. "Did you hear that?"

"Yes, I did. It was a girl's voice. She was also calling your name. How could that be?" Lilium tugged at his hand as if to keep him from proceeding.

Ildradath looked at her with alarm in his eyes, and she looked back eagerly, awaiting what he was going to say or do.

"We shouldn't check it out. It could be a trap," Lilium stated.

"Yes, it could be a trap, but our shouting could have been overheard by someone else here. They may need our help." He squeezed her hand briefly to let her know that it would be okay.

"Help me! Where are you?" the girl's voice repeatedly cried out.

Ildradath, frustrated by how the fog seemed to even distort sounds, followed the sound of the voice as best he could, and it sounded closer to the rock slope up ahead. He began to see the shape of someone emerge in the fog. Once the figure was in view, he was alarmed to discover it was Lilium. He looked next to himself and saw Lilium. He looked back at the other one, and she was still there. There were two Liliums.

"Braeanor—who is, is that—" The second Lilium was visibly shaken and pointed at the other Lilium with a trembling finger.

"She is some trick of the Abyss! Do not listen to her," the first Lilium pleaded.

Ildradath looked back and forth between the two of them. He became very nervous and even alarmed that he may be suffering from some side effects caused by the fumes in the valley. "Which of you is the real Lilium?" Ildradath asked.

"I am," they both responded. They each looked at the other and then back at Ildradath. "She is not the real me!" they shouted in unison.

While he could not entirely be sure that he wasn't hallucinating or losing his mind, he presumed that he and Lilium were now beset by some other thing imitating her. If so, he was sure it would be a nyarlan.

Thankfully, he had a way of handling this situation decisively. Merely asking questions and interrogating them would be of little use. The ability of nyarlans to psychically leech the knowledge, behaviors, and desires of their mimicked victims would make that futile.

"Would the real Lilium trust me?" he asked.

Both Liliums responded, "Yes, I would."

Ildradath unsheathed his sword and held it in front of himself. With his right hand gripping the sword handle, he rested the tip of the blade on the palm of his left hand. The sword was between himself and the two Liliums, supported in the air as if he might be ready to hand it over to one of them.

"Lilium, please grab my sword, but do not worry. I will not cut you," he spoke reassuringly.

The Lilium on his left was quicker to grab the sword than the one on his right. He watched how they gripped the blade. Their fingers shifted uneasily on the cold metal.

Ildradath looked into the eyes of the Lilium on his left.

"Are you Lilium?" he asked.

"Yes," she responded quickly. "It is me. I have been with you since Edjramor. I can tell you more to—"

"Shh, it is not necessary," he responded politely.

Ildradath looked to the Lilium on his right.

"Are you Lilium?" he asked.

"Yes," she responded even more quickly. "You know it is me. We had recently come from Elspeth's—"

"Shh. Not necessary. I think I have an idea of who the real Lilium is," he said bluntly. He looked back and forth between them.

He decisively yanked the sword to his right and upward, forcefully enough to sever all of the fingers of both Liliums. However, only the fingers of the Lilium on his right were cut off. Blood spurted out, and her digits changed appearance as they fell to the ground. She screeched; her eyes turned black, and sharp teeth now filled her mouth.

Ildradath flourished his sword once and brought it underneath its jaw and into its skull. The nyarlan could only let out a single guttural shriek as its head was impaled.

Her flesh immediately went murky, and the texture began changing.

"No more lies!" Ildradath shouted. Ildradath ripped the sword out through the side of its head. Its lifeless body slumped to the ground. Over the course of the next moments, the creature transformed from looking like Lilium into a pile of numerous small grayish tentacles. A thicker, more bulbous tentacle, which was its anatomical equivalent to a head, was torn open, and yellowish blood poured out of it.

The real Lilium had not even moved from where she was as

everything had transpired so quickly. She looked at her hand, and it was fine. There was not even a scratch. She trembled. "How did you—" she began to ask and then stopped. She struggled to finish the sentence. She was not sure if it was the sheer violence, the shock of it happening so close to her, or her disbelief that her hand was not injured despite the imposter's hand being cut apart.

Ildradath took a cloth out from a pocket and wiped his sword as he began to speak. "My sword has a blessing of adjudgment. In situations, such as the one we just found ourselves, it will only cut the liar. It has been quite useful in settling important matters over the years or extracting information. So yes, Lilium, I knew what I was doing and spoke truthfully. I knew it would not cut you. I was just not sure which *you* was actually *you*."

He looked at her as he sheathed his sword, and she looked at the blob of smooth, interwoven tentacles.

"What is that?" she asked.

"It is a nyarlan. One of the most dangerous abyssians if you ask me. It is not very effective in open combat, but it is quite the assassin. It is good at imitating people, even having ways of learning the memories of those they mimic. These things can sow such mischief and confusion that a garrison of men can be turned against themselves, making them much more vulnerable to subsequent attacks from other abyssians. One of these was responsible for the end of King Urtaman's reign and cost a paladin his life. They are creatures of deception."

"They change appearances so well," she replied. "It was even wearing my clothes. I thought I was losing my mind when I saw myself. I was terrified when she was with you, like I had been replaced or I was the one who was not real."

"Hmm. Had it been able, it would have likely killed you so that I would have had no opportunity to discover it. It then would have killed me when it got a chance."

She grimaced as she looked at the nyarlan's corpse. "What a terrible creature. It really does look disgusting."

"Yes. Throughout my years, Lilium, I have found that to be the case with those who live by deception." He patted her on the back. "You, okay?" he asked.

She nodded, but her eyes shifted about as she scanned their surroundings. "Let's get out of here."

11

They spent a few more hours making their way east. The haze discernibly lessened, but it still clung to the features of the landscape. The improving visibility and decreased stench brought some relief, but a sinister scene that came into view dashed their growing comfort upon the rocks.

There were stone structures on a larger, elongated stone foundation ahead. Steps were built into every side. A larger chapel-like structure sat at the far end of the foundation, and two parallel rows of a dozen or more stone columns with chiseled eldritch symbols ran out from this structure toward the other end. Here in this open space among the columns, men in crimson robes were walking around, and several men wearing nothing more than tattered clothes were being chained in a circle.

Ildradath and Lilium crouched behind a large stone and watched. Ildradath understood what he was seeing. This was a group of cultists preparing to offer sacrifices to the Abyss. There among the structures were multiple cages, and he could see that some still contained others to be sacrificed.

On the near side of the sacrificial altar, a likichurpkin lumbered to the steps. The large abyssian had a narrow frame despite being the size of a small cottage, and it had copper-patina-colored, leathery skin. It walked on all fours and had short hind legs; its long arms, which ended in dexterous, clawed hands, were used for walking until it needed to stand itself upright. They had unusually small, featureless heads sitting atop very long necks, and they had a long mouth slit which ran the length of their necks. Its back was covered in a sticky mass of goo and prehensile tendrils.

Of all the abyssians, they were perhaps the most docile, but they were still a menace in their own right. They possessed three long tongues within their mouth slit, which could be shot out bundled together or independent of one another, and they could reach quite a long distance. The tongues were covered in numerous barbs, which imbed into their victims, making it very painful and difficult for someone to pull free.

Likichurpkins pull their victims in and then hoist them over their backs, where they unfurl their tongues and drop them. Their sticky backs and tendrils keep them held in place. It is impossible for someone to free themselves once entrapped. They were the ideal abyssians for transporting the living sacrifices needed for rituals.

Three men trapped upon its back were crying out, begging for help. Their hoarse voices did not carry very far. The likichurpkin lay on its side, and three cultists began the process of pulling and prying each man free from its back. The thick, tar-like goo did not release them easily. The cultists each grasped one limb at a time to pull a man free, and a cultist would forcefully hold and pull on each prisoner to ensure he did not plop back into the sticky substance that imprisoned them.

Once the three cultists freed a man, another two would escort him over to the stone structure, up the steps, and then into a cage. Anytime a prisoner feebly attempted to pull away or resist, they promptly shoved him to the ground and beat him until he stopped. They then forced him back on his feet and resumed pushing them along into a cage.

Ildradath spotted the lead cultist, a priest of the Old Ones. The priest's crimson robe had a golden embroidered edge. Even from this distance, he recognized the large medallion hanging around the priest's neck. It depicted the typical symbol for the Abyss cult: a mass of intertwining tentacles wrapping around a single eye in the center. He stood on the platform and silently watched as the other cultists finished their tasks. The priest was older than the rest, and his pointed nose and weasel eyes made him look like some kind of creature himself.

Once the likichurpkin no longer bore any prisoner, it stood and meandered about. A dozen other cultists emerged from the other side of the platform. Ildradath and Lilium had not seen them until that moment. Although the fog had lessened and was not as dense as it had been, they still had difficulty making out everything they were seeing. This heightened the danger they were in. While they could use it to their advantage to hide more effectively, it also meant the cultists and abyssians could, too.

Ildradath was thinking carefully about what to do next. He should disrupt and end this cult activity while he had the chance, but it would risk himself and, most importantly, Lilium. If he did not do something, this would continue. These cultists would continue summoning and binding abyssians to themselves for lifelong servitude. While Ildradath did not immediately see any other abyssians around, he assumed there were more wandering about, and this explained the nyarlan they had encountered earlier.

Cultists unlocked two of the cages and bound two more men in shackles. The men were led to where they were positioned in the circle alongside the other men. Each was fastened with chains to large metal rings that were anchored deeply in the stone foundation. No matter how the men pulled and tried to free themselves, the bonds were too strong. Some of the men screamed and begged to be let go, but others simply stood in petrified terror or resignation.

The priest moved behind a stone podium, which also bore eldritch symbols. A gold chalice and book rested on it. He placed his arm over the chalice, pulled the sleeve back, and then cut into his forearm with a knife. The blood dripped steadily into the chalice. Two other cultists stepped forward and quickly wrapped a bandage around the priest's wound. He then pulled his sleeve forward and carried the chalice into the center of the circle. The two other cultists scurried away to join the others, who were now forming a larger circle just behind and outside of the sacrificial victims. The cultists began chanting rhythmically.

Ildradath knew he was out of time. They were already starting their ritual, and soon enough, a portal to the Abyss would open in the middle of the prisoners. The men would be torn from this world, and the Abyss would send forth an abyssian commensurate with the quality of the sacrifice made.

A gleeful screech emanated from behind Lilium and Ildradath. They turned quickly to see something charging towards them from out of the haze.

Lilium stood, began backpedaling, and screamed, "Pox—" Her scream was cut short as she tripped backward and fell beyond the stone where they had been hiding. However, her scream was enough to alert the cultists and the likichurpkin.

Ildradath held his sword to his right side, both hands grasping the handle to deliver a decisive cut. The pox fiend bound towards him and leapt for his face. He swept the sword across his body while stepping to the right and spinning around a full circle. The pox fiend's arms and head were severed, and the creature hit the ground lifeless.

"Ildradath!" Lilium shouted out.

Shocked to hear Lilium shout his paladin name, he turned with a jolt. He saw that the likichurpkin had her already wrapped in its tongues and was pulling her toward itself while it reared onto its hind legs. Without hesitation, he sprinted forward, but the creature's tongue was retracting faster than he could run.

A spark of righteous intention and faith shot forth from his spirit. Guided by old instincts, his left hand raised and pointed at the likichurpkin's throat. An illuminated bolt tethered to a golden chain shot forth like a ray of light and pierced the creature. It screeched. Ildradath grabbed the chain with his left hand and held it tight as he willed it to retract and pull him forward like a streak of lightning.

As he passed Lilium in the air, he swung and severed the tongue to free her, and he continued forcefully toward the likichurpkin, piercing it with his sword. It bellowed and reached for him with its clawed hands. He let go of the chain, and it dissipated into wisps of light. He held his sword firm with both hands and yanked it downward, slicing the creature from its throat to its waist. As he hit the ground, he rolled to the side to avoid the creature's insides, which were beginning to spill out. The likichurpkin swayed and fell over.

Cultists already surrounded Lilium. The priest stood behind her with a hand to her throat, his blade already piercing the skin of her neck and drawing droplets of blood. She was still wrapped in the likichurpkin's severed tongues.

"Do anything but yield paladin, and I kill her," he said with a nasally, condescending tone.

Ildradath paused. He could see the blood dripping out of the wound, and he believed the priest. He also knew they believed he would kill them the first chance he got, and that was absolutely true. However, they had the advantage, and he did not want to risk Lilium by acting impulsively. Yielding at this moment might provide an opportunity he could exploit to save them both. He needed to choose his moves carefully.

Ildradath would pretend to be righteously naive. "Give me your word that you will let her go, and I will yield."

"You have my word," the priest said with a smile.

He tossed his sword in front of him. One of the cultists ran forward and grabbed the sword by its handle to carry it out of reach of Ildradath.

"Ahhh! Ssshh!" the cultist exclaimed as he dropped the sword and fell to his knees, gripping his right wrist with his left hand. He winced as he stared at his right palm. The sword had instantly seared it.

"Fool. It's a paladin's sword. Leave it be," the priest stated, showing no regard for the other's wound. "Bind him and add him to the circle. This shall be a special sacrifice. I will surely be blessed with something of great power this time."

"You and your fellow cultists will all be dead soon," Ildradath spoke matter-of-factly.

The priest smirked. "Oh, not today, paladin."

Four cultists approached him and bound his hands with metal shackles. They pushed him along toward the stairs. Ildradath overheard the priest speaking to another cultist. "I have claimed the last paladin. Malcreus, the fool, will be jealous. Ha! Chosen champion of the—"

"Malcreus!" Ildradath shouted out. "What business do you have with him?"

"None! I will be glad to be rid of him, and with your help, I will be one step closer. You know, he was preparing to come for you in that tower of yours."

Ildradath turned his head so he could look at the priest out of the corner of his eye. "Is that so? I planned to pay him a visit."

"Well, it would not have ended any better for you there." He and several cultists laughed. "At least here you will do more than simply die. Thanks to you, the Abyss will surely honor me as their new champion."

Ildradath let out a hearty, mocking laugh. "Look at you, a champion!"

The priest still held Lilium as he ascended the stairs behind Ildradath, but his blade was now held at his side. "Laugh, go ahead, paladin. This girl of yours will watch as the Abyss consumes you, and then, we will do as we please with her."

Ildradath feigned disbelief as he said, "You gave me your word that you would let her go."

"Oh, all of you paladins are the same. So blissfully naive. If you understood anything about real power, you would not waste your time on empty promises and faith." He pushed Lilium along because he could tell she was slowing her pace.

While Ildradath never believed they would actually spare her, he liked to hear liars admit their falsity aloud. It made passing judgment more cathartic.

"Gag him," the priest shouted while motioning at another standing nearby. "He's grown tiresome. Don't need him praying during the ritual either."

A cultist scurried around, looking at the ground until he found a blood-stained shirt. He picked this up, shook several unidentifiable sticky globs off it, tore a long strip, and then hurried over to Ildradath. He raised it to tie around Ildradath's mouth, but he jerked away.

Ildradath shouted out, "Do not listen to their words, Lilium. Do not—"

The cultists escorting Ildradath kicked the back of his knees so that he fell forward, and one of them struck him on the side of the head, causing him to see stars for a brief moment. They held him tight as the other forcefully secured the vile strip around his head. It was tight enough that Ildradath could not avoid touching it with his tongue, and it tasted of dried blood and death. He began to retch, but he brought his senses under control to regain his composure.

"You are interfering with a paladin on a quest. You are a dead man walking. You don't have to do this," Lilium stated emphatically. "It's not too late to—"

The priest spun her around midsentence and backhanded her across her face. Lilium faltered but managed to stay on her feet. Her mouth hung open as she stared back at the priest with fire in her eyes.

"But we can, and we want to. We are earning favor for the day of his awakening. Be thankful that you will not witness that day." The priest then spun her back around and pushed her onward toward a cage.

Ildradath was led over to the circle where the others were bound.

They placed him in between two of the other prisoners and began connecting his shackles to a chain anchored into the ground.

Now that he stood close, he could plainly see the mutilated body of a man in the center of the circle. His body was severed at each major joint: ankles, knees, hips, wrists, elbows, shoulders, and then neck. His body was arranged in an x-shape with a space between each piece, and his torso was split and splayed open with the entrails placed next to it. The priest's blood chalice rested inside the cavity of the torso.

Once the cultists finished connecting the shackles and had walked off, Ildradath twisted his wrists and tugged on the chain. They were too tight for him to slip his hands out. Their heavy cast iron construction was rusted, but the dark red coloration was owed to more than rust. Dried, caked-on blood covered them as well.

He understood that the ritual would begin once again. Without outside assistance, it would conclude successfully. Each of the bound men, including himself, would be snatched into the maw of the Abyss—whether whole or in pieces. Their hands would be torn out of the shackles or torn off. It did not matter to the Abyss. Once summoned for a sacrificial meal, it would take the offering as violently as it pleased.

The maw would form first around the chalice. He looked left and right at the other men held prisoner, and then he thought of Lilium. Many had already met their end here.

Should they be any different? Did they deserve better? he asked himself.

Many cultists wrongly believed that paladins must pray aloud to be heard by the Divines; Ildradath began praying silently. His face was stern, his eyes partially closed, and his jaw was tight. He asked the Divines to help them escape. He asked them to unlock their shackles and free them. He did not pray from a place of fear. He prayed from a place of reverence and in awe of what was about to take place. The Divines had a purpose, and though it was difficult to discern how they planned it to unfold, he submitted to it.

The cultists resumed their places surrounding the circle of prisoners, and the priest threw Lilium in a cage and locked it. She slowly and painfully began to unwrap the slimy tongues which still clung around her body. Each barb was like a large thorn, and she found it challenging to grasp the tongues anywhere without poking her hand or fingers. She winced as she worked them free. She began praying for the Divines to intercede and save them.

The priest then took his place behind the podium just outside of the circle of cultists. He turned the book to a specific page and prepared to read a passage.

"Brothers, let us begin!" he shouted. He then raised his hands in praise as he prayed. "Old Ones, hear our prayer! We come to you! We are nothing, but you are great. We are small, but you are mighty! Each of you deserving of an eternity of praises! For you are unrivaled in being! Hear my words!

"It is written, 'From old, you have purposed to make known your power. The First Born of the Old Ones shall awaken, he who was, and is, and is to come. Then shall the Divines know the futility of their ways. Then shall he rend the heavens and tear the Divines from their throne!'

"This is our prayer! It is to this end we sacrifice now. Accept this offering. Grant unto me a creature worthy of this offering, bound in servitude, that we may continue your work to hasten that day! Show your power!"

The others then began chanting in unison, saying strange words and uttering strange sounds. Ildradath could comprehend what they were saying, for this was not the first time he had heard such a ritual, and he had studied their ways. Lilium, on the other hand, could not discern the words. This was for the best. Nevertheless, Ildradath focused intently to drown out their words, for they spoke things that mortal man should not.

The cultists moved clockwise just outside the sacrificial circle, stopped and swayed, then moved counter-clockwise. They repeated this continuously. A purplish, dark light emitted from the inside of the flayed torso. It grew larger and larger until the chalice fell inside the growing hole. The torso began to cave in and sink.

As the hole continued growing larger, sinister sounds became audible; screeching, snarling, and gurgling noises rose in a chorus of the coming terror. The hole began to swirl rhythmically, and a wind ruptured forth from it, filling the air with noxious odors. A deep fog spilled upward and crawled across the ground. A portal to the Abyss was opened, and as it grew, more pieces of the mutilated body fell inside.

A series of loud whinnies emanated from somewhere out in the haze of Dead Man's Valley. Aerion shot up the far side of the stairs and let out a very high-pitched, lengthy, loud squeal as he charged the priest, who was only able to turn in time to see Aerion's chest plowing him aside.

The cultists scattered in a frenzy, incompetent with how to deal with a furious horse on the offensive. Aerion kicked a cultist and drew satisfaction from the crunch made by the man's chest. He bit another cultist's hair, yanked him off the ground, and then dropped him. Aerion then stomped him repeatedly.

Amid this scene, Ildradath's shackles suddenly fell to the ground. He ran for his sword, punching a cultist in the side of the head when he dared run near him. The cultist had no idea what hit him as he was too fixated on the mad horse, and he hit the ground unconscious.

After jumping off the stairs, Ildradath grabbed his sword and quickly reascended. Several cultists had pulled out daggers and were readying to stab Aerion, who was now encircled. Aerion was rearing at them in order to keep them back.

Ildradath sprinted to Aerion.

"Hey!" Ildradath shouted out to catch the attention of the nearby cultists.

The closest cultists turned to see Ildradath charging them, and they were woefully unprepared to deal with an armed paladin. A series of quick swings and thrusts left them missing limbs and bleeding to death.

Aerion seized this opportunity and took off in another direction to run a cultist into the ground. The cultist was able to slash Aerion with his dagger before being crushed underfoot.

Ildradath ran over to the sacrificial circle. The portal had grown to the point it was just feet from the prisoners. He ran around the circle, mightily swinging his sword to cut the chains, and the sword sliced through them with ease.

"Run north! Run north to Lowland Glen!" Ildradath shouted to the men. He knew they had a long road ahead of them, and he was unsure whether they would even be able to tell which way was north. The prisoners shouted their expressions of gratitude and "Divines bless you" while fleeing the sight of the portal.

It was a chaotic scene. Prisoners, cultists, and Aerion ran about, each with different purposes in mind, but this was just the calm before the storm.

A tentacle emerged from the portal. It was like a kraken's, covered with suckers, but the end possessed a mouth turned along its length. Off-set, jagged teeth like bony mismatched icicles lined it.

This single, slow-moving tentacle slithered into the air, easing into the unfamiliar territory. It then smacked and grasped around the portal in search of the offerings. It checked each side and then traced the rim of the portal as if licking its lips. There was no one. There were no sacrifices nearby. It had been summoned for nothing. This was unacceptable.

Several more tentacles erupted out of the portal and twisted high into the air with echoey screeches. Each of these had the addition of a bulbous eye protruding along its side, and a black, oddly shaped pupil peered out from its purple iris. One of these tentacles shot out and grabbed a cultist by his face. A muffled scream emerged from the tentacle's mouth as it retracted with the resisting victim in tow. Kicking and screaming, the cultist was dragged across the platform and into the Abyss.

The other tentacles each flung out looking for any living thing to grasp. Its summoning would not be in vain, and it would take everyone it pleased as punishment to those who dared inconvenience it the least bit.

"Aerion, follow me!" Ildradath called out while he ran to the far side where Lilium was imprisoned in a cage.

He struck the lock with his sword, and Lilium hurried out. She had freed herself from the tongues, but she was on the verge of shock. Her eyes were wide, and she stared off into the distance at the maw of the Abyss. Ildradath spotted three nearby cages that held captives, and he quickly struck those locks.

"Flee, men! Go! Go North!" he shouted at the men who fled without so much a word spoken.

Aerion let out a whinny and stopped nearby. Ildradath helped Lilium up. Several cultists armed with a mace, knives, and a short sword charged Ildradath before he could mount Aerion.

Ildradath spun and stabbed out with his sword so that it pierced a cultist through the face. As he pulled his sword out, he kicked a nearby cultist backward in the direction of a tentacle. It wrapped around him, and as it pulled him toward the portal, another tentacle snapped repeatedly at his head but narrowly missed each time.

Another cultist swung his mace downward in an effort to smash Ildradath's head, but he turned his body into the cultist and brought his sword upright in front of himself. The cultist's strike only caught empty air, but Ildradath turned and pressed the edge of his sword into the man's throat and then slashed outward to cut another cultist's hand free from his body as he slashed at Ildradath with his knife.

The first cultist, while holding his bleeding throat, had his legs wrapped by a tentacle and pulled out from underneath him. The force of being snatched caused his head to smash violently into the stone platform while being yanked to the Abyss. The second cultist fell onto his back screaming while holding his profusely bleeding arm, but another tentacle flung out and latched onto the man's chest and dragged him screaming across the platform to join the others in the Abyss.

The other nearby cultists had enough. Between the paladin and the tentacles, they realized they stood no chance. They turned and fled, but this did not deter the tentacles from seeking them out. Tentacles lashed out and coiled around them, one by one, flailing around with them in their grasp before pulling them to their eldritch doom.

Ildradath hurried back over to Aerion and began to mount him. Undeterred by having to reach out over fifty feet away, a tentacle flung out to latch onto Aerion. Ildradath spotted it, partially turned, and cut its mouth in half. Screeching emanated from the wounded tentacle as it retracted into the portal. At that same moment, the Abyss priest grabbed Ildradath from behind and began to pull him down while raising his dagger to stab him.

Three tentacles raced across the platform towards them, but they landed upon the priest standing between Ildradath and the portal. One latched onto his left leg, one on his raised right arm, which held the dagger, and the third onto his left shoulder and neck. They each snatched him back towards the portal, but they pulled and tugged in different directions, each vying to be the one to pull the victim into the Abyss.

The priest frantically screamed as their tussle became more violent. Finally, his arm and leg were torn off, and the third tentacle had the pleasure of pulling the majority of him into the Abyss.

Ildradath had wasted no time in finishing mounting Aerion. "Aerion, get us out of here!"

Aerion did exactly as Ildradath instructed and ran east as fast as he could off the platform and disappeared into the fog. They left the screams of the remaining cultists in the distance.

Lilium clutched Aerion's neck as tight as she could and squeezed her eyelids closed. She trembled. The sights and sounds were too much.

"I thought I told you to wait for us?" Ildradath addressed Aerion with a sarcastic tone.

Aerion sharply nickered, and Ildradath laughed aloud.

"Yes, Aerion, I saw you. Just like Gargantry, my boy. You were just like him."

CHAPTER EIGHT

HOPE IN THE DESERT

. . . And even creation strikes out against the Abyss. For it does not suffer its corruption quietly. The rocks cry out and beat their chests and the stallion is quick on the chase and in battle. Creation yearns to be and to be free, and this is the spirit of defiance against the Abyss . . .

1

Aerion ran until he reached the black sand of the Obsidian Flats. The salt flats were mostly barren lands. Petrified trees, some of which even had a branch or two, were a rare sight that might serve as a useful landmark, and an occasional large stone or boulder dotted the landscape. Life was scarce here, but it existed. Most life in the flats found shelter in burrows or underground caverns, and it was rare to see it moving about on the surface. Swaths of the flats were covered in honeycombed patterns of ground, but the remainder was a blanket of coarse black sand as far as the eye could see. A subtle odor of sulfur and iron filled the air.

"That's good enough, boy. Let's stop here," Ildradath said.

Aerion came to a stop, and Ildradath dismounted. He helped ease Lilium down. Her eyes appeared heavy, and she was quiet. She had been the entire time since fleeing the maw of the Abyss.

"Are you okay, Lilium?" he asked.

She nodded.

Ildradath looked her over and saw many small wounds with dried trickles of blood. He remembered that the likichurpkin had grabbed her. "Could you eat a bite?"

She partially nodded and shrugged her shoulders.

Ildradath understood that to be a *maybe*. Ildradath reached into a bag and grabbed several apples as well as a large bladder of water. He handed an apple to Lilium, held one for himself, and fed another to Aerion while keeping the bladder tucked under an arm. "Lilium, won't you take a seat for a bit? I'll lay hands on you in a moment and ensure those wounds are healed."

She did nothing to acknowledge him other than taking a seat on the sandy ground. Ildradath became concerned. He recognized how affected she seemed following the encounter with the nyarlan. Since then, she only had more reasons to be disquieted in her spirit.

He leaned in close to Aerion, who had gently neighed after finishing his apple. "Oh, your chest?" Ildradath leaned forward and began inspecting Aerion's chest. He found a gash. He placed a hand on it and silently prayed for several minutes.

Afterward, he said, "I'll check on it later. Divines willing, you will be right in no time. Did the Divines tell you to come to our aid?"

Aerion whinnied.

"Just a feeling? Please understand there are difficult times ahead, and I would ask that you honor what I tell you. By all means, if the Divines lead you to do otherwise, I won't object. But I don't want to lose you, too, because you act on a whim. I am proud of you, though. And to think you've had no real training. You were very brave. We certainly needed you back there. Thank you."

Aerion nodded.

Ildradath reached over to a large bag, which he unlaced. He reached inside and pulled a metal basin out. He sat this in front of Aerion. He then pulled the cap off the water bladder and began pouring.

Lilium watched as Ildradath filled the basin. The bladder continued to pour out until, finally, the basin overflowed. It took several minutes. She shook her head. The bladder was a tenth the size of the basin. Aerion drank eagerly.

Ildradath knelt next to Lilium and offered the bladder to her. She took it and drank, though not as much as Ildradath would have liked.

He then partook and placed the bladder next to Lilium. "May I lay hands on you?"

She nodded.

He laid a hand on one of her arms and another on her back. He prayed silently for several minutes. He then stood and retrieved a clean cloth from a bag, poured some water on it from the bladder, and gently wiped her wounds, some of which disappeared as he wiped.

"Divines be good," he whispered to himself.

She nodded.

Ildradath sat next to her and looked at the expanse of the flats ahead of them. "Ever seen anything like these flats?"

She rubbed her hands on the ground in front of her, scooped a handful of the coarse grains, slowly turned her cupped hand on its edge, and watched as the grains tumbled back down. "No," she whispered.

"Lilium, it would be wrong of me not to worry about how you are doing. So, I am going to ask you. But you don't have to talk right now if you don't want to. Are you okay?"

She shrugged. "I . . . it's just a lot. I don't know how I feel."

"I'd say it's probably been overwhelming," Ildradath added.

"Yeah," she replied as her fingers traced lines in the sand.

"Well, if there is something specific you want to share, you can. You've done well. Few people would have made it this far, and nobody could without being affected by it. There is always one thing you can do in situations like this."

"What?" she asked.

"Pray. Even if you don't feel like it. Even if you don't know what to say or how to say it. Silently or aloud. Even if it doesn't feel right, or you just cry, or you feel that the Divines should already know—pray all the more."

With that, he gently patted her back and stood. He walked away and faced east, resting his hands on his hips. He was glad they made it this far. It was more eventful than he had hoped it would be, but they made it. The expanse of the flats looked innocuous, but he knew they were only drawing closer to other dangers.

After spending some time in solitude and quiet prayer, he walked back over to Lilium, who was still tracing lines in the sand. He realized he owed her an explanation as to his name. He knelt on a single knee next to her and rested his hands on his raised thigh.

"Lilium, I need to apologize. I . . . I was going to tell you at some point, but I wasn't ready. You see, I had prayed for a week straight, asking for a quest for the Order to enter the Abyss for the crusade. Eventually, I understood the Divines' answer was 'no.' When I came out from praying, many brothers were gathered praying, too, and they looked up at me expectantly.

"I can still, uh," Ildradath spoke and abruptly paused to take a quick, shallow breath. "I can still see the look in their eyes. I knew what they wanted, but it wasn't what the Divines wanted. There was no quest. A good leader must be willing to tell their people the hard answers. But what did I do? I told them to make ready, we march.

"Vesuvimorian had that glint in his eye he would often get when he's happy. He said when he saw the Dread One, he would punch him right in the mouth. It was finally time to strike back at the Abyss on their territory—to go on the offensive. We held a large feast before our crusade began. We knew we would lose some men, and we wanted to commemorate what we were about to do.

"Afterwards, there was only me. I had failed the Order. It wasn't long before I simply couldn't bear the name of a paladin any longer. A paladin's name is their identity. I was the reason for the fall of the

Order. So, I returned to my orphan name. Every day I woke became penance. I didn't deserve Bright Haven. I didn't deserve the safety of the tower. I didn't deserve—"

Lilium reached over and placed a hand on his, causing him to stop talking. "It's okay," she said. "I can now begin to imagine all the things you have seen. The Abyss, the more I see it, the more I—the more I—" She shook her head. "All of the paladins wanted to make the world safer for us. The Order did everything for us. Mother used to say, 'Even the best isn't always perfect.' So, thank you."

Ildradath nodded. "You're welcome. My life is in service to the Divines."

He made camp for the night, including a small fire with wood and peat bricks from one of his many empty-looking bags; the flats were rather cold at night. He cooked some vegetables in a small pan and served it with some dried meat. He took the first watch, so Lilium and Aerion could rest. Aerion would take the second watch.

¶¶

Lilium awoke with a jolt and sat up immediately. As she turned to the fire, Aerion snorted gently, inquiring if she was alright.

"I'm fine. Just a bad dream is all," she said.

Lilium crossed her legs and wrapped her arms around herself while staring at the few embers that remained of last night's fire. The dream rattled her. She only remembered seeing her hands covered in blood, and she was in pain. She turned, looking for help. Ildradath was riding off into the distance on Aerion, and a voice, an ominous whisper, spoke saying, "Soon." She assured herself that it meant nothing and stood to spend time with Aerion.

The morning sun came and ushered in the day with its blanket of warmth. With its rays, they continued on the next leg of their quest, enjoying the pleasant, though dry, breeze. Bleak Top Ridge stood in the far distance, waiting for them.

After three uneventful days and nights of traveling, they discovered something extraordinary.

"What is that?" Lilium pointed across the blackened ground toward something shimmering.

Ildradath said nothing as he stared at the thing some stone's throw away. Cautiously, Aerion walked over to it.

"It's some type of rose," Lilium proposed.

Ildradath shook his head as his eyes grew wide. "No, this is a myth. In all my years, I have never seen one. I truly believed it was only a story. Here it is. A madrigaia."

The madrigaia blooms were comprised of white rose-like petals which spiraled around a tight bundle of delicate yellow-capped stamen, and six larger elongated red-spotted, white petals tenderly cradled this in its lily-shaped caress. Multiple blooms gracefully rested upon the tops of tender stems, which descended into a small diaphanous shrub, and the stems were bedecked with heart-shaped green gossamer leaves. The madrigaia radiated a faintly pulsing bluish-white aura, and a gentle, dulcet, nearly mellifluous tone floated in its air. Its atmosphere was an aromatic tapestry of honied apples, vanilla, and lemon interwoven with fragrant petrichor, forming a sublime Elysian bouquet.

Ildradath nearly fell over as he dismounted Aerion while staring at the madrigaia. Lilium then dismounted, eyes transfixed as well, but Ildradath assisted her, somehow managing to do so without turning his gaze from the flower.

"A what?" Lilium asked in a hushed voice.

Ildradath placed a hand onto Aerion and felt around until he finally found the bag he was seeking, and he reached inside, pulling out his shield. He held it up to show her the flower symbol on it. "It is a madrigaia. It is said to be the first flower created by the Divines— the most beautiful flower, too. Like a parent to the rose and the lily, believed to have died out a millennia ago. No paladin I have ever known has laid eyes on one."

Lilium did not turn her eyes to look at his shield, and Ildradath did not notice either. "Oh. Yes. I have seen these in paintings." Lilium tilted her head and walked forward with a hand reaching out. "But they didn't look like this."

"Yes, not like this," he said as he also tilted his head. He let his shield drop to the ground and walked towards it slowly as well. "These were believed to have died out because people coveted them, how they looked, and how they made them feel. They would pluck them up and do as they pleased, but these never seemed to fare well confined to pots and gardens or cared for by selfish hands. They belong to the course of creation, to be loved for what they are and not defiled. They are pure. Untarnished.

"This has surely survived because so few people would dare venture here. And yet it grows here, in this harsh land, resilient, able to weather the ravages, even time itself. It is a testament that endurance and strength need not be flaunted in a proportionate frame."

"Amazing," Lilium responded. "Who would ever believe us?"

Once they reached it, they stood staring and breathed in its wondrous bouquet.

"No one would believe us without seeing it in our possession," Ildradath said, "for they are said to be irresistible." Ildradath knelt and leaned towards it.

Lilium looked longingly at it, but she soon became aware of Ildradath, who was motionless and locked in on the madrigaia, too. She then realized how captivated she had just been. "What is it, Ildradath?" Lilium asked.

He looked up at her and shook his head just once while searching for words. "These flowers are a symbol of the Divines' power through acts of love, a promise that life, despite all the powers of the Abyss, will prevail. That the Divines will preserve the faithful. I believe this is a good sign for our quest." Ildradath slowly reached forward to touch the madrigaia.

"Ildradath, wait." She placed a hand on his shoulder. "Let's leave. Before we do something."

He stopped and looked at her. He pulled his hand back and glanced around in a daze momentarily as if to reorient himself, closed his eyes, and then shook his head. "You are right. It is better to have admired from afar. To not spoil it."

Ildradath stored his shield, and they remounted Aerion. They resumed their trek east. After several hours, Ildradath could see a small dark dust storm building to the south of them. He knew it would blow northerly at some point. They continued east as the dust storm marched closer.

Ildradath pointed ahead. "We will stop among those rock formations. They will offer some protection until the storm passes. We will bundle up there and wait it out."

The winds increased and steadily blew northward, and it dispersed sand everywhere as it moved through. Ildradath, Lilium, and Aerion leaned against the largest mound of rocks on the leeward side to reduce their exposure to the blasting sand. Ildradath covered Aerion's head with a blanket, and he and Lilium covered their faces with their shirts. After about thirty minutes, the winds subsided, and sand no longer filled the air. They shook the sand out of wherever they could and drank some water.

"Nightfall is upon us. We might as well make camp here where we have some protection from being out in the open," Ildradath spoke.

Lilium sighed. "Fine by me. I could use some rest. I almost fell asleep during that dust storm."

Aerion huffed in agreement.

Lilium patted Aerion's neck. "You alright? Sand gets everywhere, doesn't it?" she asked him.

He neighed, and Ildradath immediately laughed.

"What?" Lilium asked with a smirk.

"He says he has it in places he didn't even know he had."

Lilium laughed and rubbed his neck.

As they began to get out the other items needed to make camp, something caught Lilium's eye. One of the smaller rock formations had shifted. She walked away from Aerion and Ildradath to take a closer look. She noticed the formation looked just like all the others, but it was much smaller. The dark rock was partially obscured by the sand collected in its nooks and crannies, but it had a glassy sheen to it. "What kind of rocks are these, Ildradath? They look quite strange."

She bent over and rubbed the rock, and began knocking sand off it.

"Hmm, it is unique, isn't it," Ildradath responded as he took a moment to inspect the large outcrop in front of him. He paused. He now felt danger. Something he had forgotten was now returning to his mind.

Lilium began gripping parts of the rock to see if there were any loose pieces or chunks, "I wonder if I could take some with—"

The small rock formation emanated a rapid series of hollow-sounding shrills.

"Get back, move away!" Ildradath shouted. Aerion followed Ildradath as he ran toward Lilium. He swept her off her feet as he pulled her back from the center of the formations while shouting, "Obsidian golems!"

Each rock formation groaned and bellowed deeply as they shook free from their positions. The ground vibrated and rumbled as the creatures stood upright on all fours, their limbs shifting into new positions, and the sand that had settled upon them flowed off to return to the ground. Their concealment as rock formations lifted. There were now six black obsidian golems of various sizes, with the largest standing facing Ildradath.

It was fifteen feet tall and covered in dark obsidian, though glimpses of other minerals and metals could be spotted within its frame. Some sections of its body were smooth, but others were rough and angular, as if pieces of its hard exterior had fractured off. It had short, thick back legs and long arms, which also assisted with walking, but it could support itself on its legs without issue. Small, blue crystal eyes set inside the crooks of an obsidian armor-plated mound on top of its bulky torso stared down at Ildradath. The living rock creatures faced the trio.

The smallest golem had moved behind the largest one. Its quieter and somewhat higher-pitched crying continued.

"Did I hurt it?" Lilium shouted out to Ildradath.

"Kneel, Lilium and Aerion. Kneel so that only I am standing," Ildradath commanded in a loud voice.

They kneeled, and Ildradath reached into a bag and pulled out his shield, followed by his one-handed war hammer.

"You are going to fight it!" Lilium shouted out in disbelief. "Shouldn't we say we are sorry and just ride away?"

Ildradath fixed his eyes on the largest golem. "I'll explain later. Just stay out of our way. Do not move, and when the time comes, do exactly as I say—both of you—understand?"

"Yes," Lilium quickly replied, and Aerion huffed.

Ildradath approached the largest obsidian golem, smashed his war hammer against his shield once, struck the ground four times, and then shouted.

The golem struck its chest once, then smashed the ground four times and bellowed. The other golems lowered themselves to the ground.

Ildradath charged it, and it lurched towards him. He raised his war hammer and struck one of its arms. It pulled its other arm backward and swept it forward at him. He blocked it with his shield, and keeping his stance firm, he was knocked back several feet, leaving two lines traced in the ground where his feet skidded; he managed to stay upright.

The blow was as mighty as he thought it might be, and it was unpleasant. He shook his arms as if it might help dissipate the force which reverberated within his bones. He shook his head. He did not want to drag this out for any longer than he needed, but he had to put on a worthy show.

He charged forward, shouting again, and he leapt in the air, striking it in the chest. As he landed back on the ground, he rolled to his right and avoided a downward slam of its other arm.

He was on his feet and moving. Spinning, he swung the hammer into the side of one of its legs. It spun, too, not nearly as quickly as Ildradath, but it had the clear power advantage. The arm barely caught Ildradath's shield, and its momentum knocked him away and to the ground.

Ildradath rolled onto his back in time to raise his shield as both of its hands descended to smash him. With his will in tune with the blessing of his shield, the shield repulsed the blow and sent all the force back into the golem. The reverberation of the blow sundered the air with a crack and surprised the golem. Tiny obsidian fragments shot into the air, and the golem reeled backward momentarily. It let out a deep bellow.

That should do, he thought to himself.

Ildradath ascended to his feet and quickly backed away from the golem while it regained its composure from the surprise of the force it experienced. Ildradath positioned himself in front of Lilium and Aerion.

He hit his shield again with his war hammer, struck the ground three times, and shouted. He then knelt.

"Stay kneeling, Lilium and Aerion. Bow your heads. Do not move!"

The golem moved closer, hit its chest, and then smashed the ground right in front of Ildradath three times. Ildradath did not make eye contact with it. He then slammed his war hammer twice into the ground and did not shout. The golem paused, inched closer, and then struck the ground right next to Ildradath three times. Any closer and Ildradath would be crushed to death.

Ildradath paused for a moment. He then struck the ground one time, this time with much less force. The golem struck the ground two times quickly. It then lowered its head toward him and waited.

Ildradath did not move a muscle or look at him. He felt its intense gaze inspecting him, Lilium, and Aerion. For nearly a minute, all three remained motionless. It then let out a very long, deep bellow. The other golems came and stood in line with the largest one. It bellowed again and struck the ground three times.

"Lilium and Aerion hit the ground three times!"

Though their timing was askew, Ildradath, Lilium, and Aerion hit the ground three times, as all the other golems did. The largest golem let out a quieter but longer moaning bellow before turning away and walking off. The others turned and followed it.

"Up Lilium and Aerion. We have to go with them for now," Ildradath said.

"What do you mean?" Lilium asked. She threw her hands wide in confusion.

Ildradath looked at her and, with raised eyebrows, said, "Move, do it now. We should remain silent for a while."

They all stood and followed after the golems.

¶¶¶

The six obsidian golems marched southeasterly. The largest led the single file line, and the second largest was last. Ildradath, Lilium, and Aerion found themselves walking ahead of the last golem, and the baby golem was just in front of them.

Night had come, and the air was cold. Ildradath retrieved two warmer cloaks from a bag so that he and Lilium would have some extra warmth. "Aerion, you warm enough?" he asked.

He huffed agreeably in response.

"Just checking, boy," Ildradath responded.

"So, we can talk now? What is happening? What was all that?"

Lilium pressed.

Ildradath tossed a cloak to Lilium. "We are now a part of this obsidian golem herd. They have a ritual of sorts, which they use to determine who will lead or join a herd. I had to convince the biggest golem, the alpha, that I was the leader of our group and that I thought I was powerful enough to be worthy of leading his. I then submitted to his strength and showed him that we would recognize him as alpha of ours. He saw us worthy enough to join his herd."

She placed her hands on her head in disbelief. "So, what is the ritual for getting out of the herd?"

Ildradath grinned at her. "There isn't one that I know of."

Lilium took a deep breath and then turned her head partially away from Ildradath. "That's great. We are obsidian golems for life. What I always wanted."

Ildradath leaned forward a bit and peered at her face. To his surprise, she had a smirk on her face. She was making the best of the situation. "We will be patient and look for an opportunity, but for now, let us take advantage of their company. They are formidable allies, and they are headed in the same direction as us."

"It will be nice to have some friends, I suppose," Lilium added. "So, we will trust it's providence."

"Yes, I think so." Ildradath gave her a gentle pat on the back.

"How do you know their ritual anyway? And why do you think they are going east?"

"Everything I know about the obsidian golems is from reading the works of Irwinnor. He was consumed with a curiosity for the creatures of this world, and he had a gift for studying them. He would travel the world, learning and making notes. Instead of serving alongside a ruler or aiding a kingdom of man, he claimed he served creation itself. It was under assault by the Old Ones, too.

"He was convinced that any malign attributes of the creatures were an effect of the Abyss and that some, for example, the peekaboos, had once been markedly different and docile creatures. Peekaboos are believed to have been playful creatures who genuinely posed no danger, not even to children.

"When he first discovered these golems, he fought an alpha for days. Periodically, the alpha would stop and pound his chest and the ground, and then Irwinnor would jump right back at him. Eventually, he discerned the ritual and submitted to the golem. He realized he was in his territory and needed to follow its rules.

"What surprised him was that when he tried to walk off, the golems made sounds, and the alpha would come after him to get him back in the group. Thus, he traveled with them until they reached a mountain where they ascended. The golems soon began pounding the ground in unison until, finally, they cleaved into the ground, partially burying themselves. He was finally able to leave the herd, and he did so in a hurry as the ground beneath him continued to rumble.

"Hours later, he heard a large explosion and turned to see that the mountain had erupted. He waited several days and then cautiously returned to the mountain to see what had befallen the golems. He found them among the ruins, much as they were, though with a slight glow. He surmised that the golems either migrate knowing where there is going to be an eruption, or they actually can cause them. He believed they were sustained and reproduced at those times. He also believed they were the laborers who helped shape Kadath."

Lilium's eyes cut over to Ildradath. "The laborers? Wait. They are headed in the same direction as us!"

"Hmm. Yes." Ildradath replied. "Let us hope our paths diverge before that."

The group followed along with the herd throughout the night without incident. Daylight came, and the herd clustered more closely together to rest for the day. Their forms shifted downward, with their limbs, heads, and torsos being drawn tight against the ground to make them all appear like large rocky outcrops.

Ildradath, Lilium, and Aerion each found some shaded space within the group to rest away from the overbearing sun. Lilium was extra careful to ensure she did not disturb any of the golems as she made herself comfortable. They were all very tired and eager to sleep, and they did so despite their newfound friends resting nearby.

Shortly after noon, the winds increased, and sand began flying through the air. Ildradath, Lilium, and Aerion did not appreciate waking in such a manner, and they were quick to cover their faces from the sandstorm. The winds began to howl, and the sand soon stung their exposed skin. This storm was much fiercer than the first one they experienced.

To add to the group's dismay, the golems woke and began making sounds that were even more alarming than when Lilium upset the baby golem. As they stood, the alpha turned toward the other golems and Ildradath and beat his chest and the ground, repeating a series of sounds. Ildradath had no idea what he was conveying, but he could tell it was some sort of instruction.

The golems all faced outward to form a circle around the baby golem, Ildradath, Lilium, and Aerion. The golems then backed up so that they were trapped inside. The alpha golem began repeatedly, rhythmically, booming out a sound that reverberated through the air with a thunder-like quality. The other golems joined in, save for the smallest.

The baby golem hunkered in their midst, and it vibrated. A low, deep whine occasionally emanated from it.

"They seem scared!" Lilium shouted in an effort to be heard above the noise.

"I suppose so!" Ildradath yelled back.

Even with their faces covered, bits of sand managed to find their way into their mouths as they spoke, causing each to reflexively try to spit the tiny pieces out.

The howling winds shrieked and hissed as their intensity grew.

The voice of some unseen terror was carried in the winds. There was now even more sand in the air, and the group could not peek out from their face covering without immediately getting sand blown into their eyes. The dark sandstorm encircled them.

Ildradath prayed and raised his hand upward, willing that a barrier would form around himself and the golems to keep the sand out. A clear, blueish bubble formed around them, and they finally found some relief from the blasting sand. Upon feeling the cessation of blasting sand, Ildradath and Lilium removed their face covering and looked around.

They could not see much, given the stature of the golems surrounding them. Leaning and peering through the gaps between their bodies and limbs, they could only tell that they were caught in a great sandstorm that appeared to be centered upon them.

The alpha golem then began pounding the ground, alternating arms as he did so. He had a slow rhythm at first, and after all the other golems were pounding the ground in sync with him, the frequency and intensity of his blows against the ground increased.

The shrieking sounds of a creature cried out from the sands swirling about them. Ildradath drew his sword. The sounds came from one side of them, then another, and then moved again.

Aerion neighed, and Lilium shouted, "What is it?"

"I don't know!" he shouted back.

A large, scaly, raptorial limb shot out from the sands above them and attempted to seize the baby golem from their midst. The talons struck Ildradath's barrier. It pressed and clenched tight several times, fighting to get through it. It was big enough to certainly snatch the baby. The taloned limb retracted back into the swirling sand.

"Get down, Lilium!" Ildradath shouted.

Aerion neighed. There was not enough room for him to lie.

Lilium crouched but looked upward. She would have been glad to close her eyes and wake to find it was all a dream, but she knew she must keep her eyes open and face the danger pressing in on them, even if she was not sure what she could do. She leaned on the baby golem and wrapped her arms around it. "Do not be afraid, little one," she shouted. Her reassurances to it were just as much for her.

The shrieking of the unseen creature turned to screeching, followed by a series of trills. The golems increased their intensity, pounding the ground harder and chanting more loudly. The baby golem remained balled up, and it whimpered loudly. Ildradath, Lilium, and Aerion's ears were hurting from the sound and pressure of the golem's blows; they were growing disoriented, too.

Again, the limb erupted from the blasting wall of sand and struck, this time with enough force to break Ildradath's barrier. The talons pressed down in an effort to reach and grab the baby golem. The large talons scraped against the backs of the large golems and caught on their jagged forms. Twisting, tightening, and then plunging again, the talons descended into the center of the group.

Ildradath shouted and drove his sword upward, piercing a taloned digit. It retracted upward quickly with a shrill scream. It plunged again and opened enough to be able to snatch Ildradath, but he swung upward and pressed against a golem to avoid it. He severed one of the talon digits, and it fell to the ground next to Lilium. It was as long as she was tall. Blood spurted from the wound, and the creature withdrew its limb. The creature shrieked more intensely.

Ildradath, Lilium, and Aerion's ears were beginning to bleed from the concussive blows of the golems. It was too much to bear, and their bodies, though they were not being struck directly, were feeling each blow, and without the protective barrier, the blowing of the sand added to their disorientation.

A large, gaping maw descended from overhead. Its snarling mouth opened wide, revealing large, jagged teeth and a black tongue. It gnashed against the group, its teeth scraping the backs of the larger golems. The alpha golem bellowed and reached upward, seizing one of the largest teeth, and he ripped it out effortlessly.

Before the creature could even reel in pain, the alpha had seized another tooth with one hand and the jaw with the other. He mightily twisted and drove his body forward to pull the creature's head close while driving it away from the group, and with this, he disappeared into the sandstorm with the creature. A cacophony of howling shrieks and booming grunts emanated from the swirling torrent of sand.

Ildradath recovered his face and secured it tightly. The blasting sand was unbearable while sheltered among the golems and given how unforgiving that was, stepping out was going to be much worse. He would not be able to see, but if he failed to act now, the alpha might fall victim to that menace in the sandstorm. He certainly did not want to fight it alone.

"Pray, Lilium," Ildradath shouted, but she was already praying, and she clung tighter to the baby golem while doing so.

Ildradath quickly felt his way across Aerion's body to grab his shield. With his sword and shield in hand, he shouted, "Divines guide me," and disappeared into the wall of sand.

Clanging metal and flashes of light joined the chaotic chorus within the roaring sands. The other golems were still pounding the ground and chanting, and Lilium and Aerion prayed fervently.

Several minutes later, the sandstorm began to calm and shift away. The shrieking of the creature had become more of a wail, and it was becoming more distant. As Lilium felt the stillness in the air, she looked through the gap in golems and saw the outline of the alpha golem. The other golems stopped pounding the ground.

She stood and walked through the gap to take a better look, but she did not see Ildradath. The sands had moved off, and the alpha golem was walking back to join the group. She strained her eyes, but he was nowhere to be seen.

"Ildradath?" Lilium called out.

The alpha stopped near Lilium and looked at her.

"Ildradath!" Lilium cried out. He was nowhere in the distance, and he was not answering her.

She looked up at the alpha, who was now making strange hacking sounds. Ildradath's form was now visible overhead. He was on its back.

"Ildradath!" she called out, relieved to see him.

He was holding onto the back of the alpha, and he was trying to cough and spit out some of the sand that had blown into his mouth. The alpha lowered itself enough so that Ildradath could work his way to the ground more easily. His sword was already sheathed, and his shield was hanging from his left hand. He shook his head and then uncovered his face. He squinted to look at Lilium.

"I don't know what—" Ildradath stopped talking as he coughed several times. "Don't know what that was. I don't know how I ended up on the back of the alpha. But I know I never want to do that again."

Lilium ran and wrapped her arms around him and buried her face into his sandblasted shirt. He hugged her firmly back just before he began to cough and spit more. He was perturbed by the grains of sand still sticking to the inside of his mouth and teeth.

"Water, please," he asked Lilium. She retrieved the water bladder quickly, and he rinsed his mouth out before drinking a good bit. Lilium did the same, in turn, and then she helped Aerion as well.

"We will never get all the sand out," Lilium joked.

"Never," he replied with a laugh.

The alpha golem grunted and stared at Ildradath. He looked up at it. The golem struck its chest three times and looked at him expectantly. Ildradath took his shield from his back and drew his sword. He half-heartedly struck the side of his sword against the shield twice and looked at the golem in return.

The golem grunted discontentedly. He struck his chest three times again. Ildradath was puzzled and was not sure what the golem was intending. Ildradath struck his sword and shield three times and looked at the Alpha.

The alpha grunted, turned, and resumed walking to the east. The others followed.

"What was that about?" Lilium asked.

"I don't know," Ildradath replied.

Aerion huffed.

"Gratitude and recognition?" Ildradath asked back. "Whatever it is, I am glad that creature fled. I should hope we never encounter it again, and I will count it a blessing that we faced it with the golems rather than alone."

As they followed the golems, they tended to their bleeding ears and shook the sand out. Prayers were said, and they drank plenty of water and ate some apples and dried meat. The sun was hot, but all of the discomfort was a reminder they were alive.

The baby golem walked next to Lilium, and it would occasionally turn towards her and look up at her face. She was unsure what it was doing, but she thought it was cute. Now and then, she would reach over and rub its head, and it would let out a low vibration that reminded her of a cat purring, which made her smile.

IV

The golems stopped at nightfall this time. Ildradath could only guess they were tired, too, and this was a relief to him. Everyone wanted to rest. He made a proper camp for them, including a fire. The night air had grown cold, and he and Lilium wanted to eat something warm. Such small comforts were essential when exhausted.

After eating, they lay on their pallets, and they both found themselves staring into the night sky. The bright stars and constellations hung over them without a cloud in sight. It was a clear reminder of their cosmic diminutiveness.

"Do you think the Divines are watching?" Lilium asked aloud.

"Hmm," Ildradath mumbled while thinking through her question. "Yes, I am sure of it."

"Do you think they actually care?" she asked.

Ildradath uttered nothing, and the question, like the stars in the sky, loomed over them. The night air carried a chill across their bodies, and sparks and warm wisps of ash swirled upward from the small fire before turning dark and cold as they drifted away.

"I have wondered—and even started to believe on more than one occasion—that perhaps they don't . . . They seem to want to help things, but do they send some creature or warrior from Bright Haven to intercede? No. They purpose to use us instead.

"And it seems at times that the Abyss is better at using man against himself than the Divines are us against the Abyss. The cultists don't need faith. Their rituals and those damned creatures are proof of the Old Ones being ready to intervene in the affairs of this world and their followers. It seems like they care what happens here, but when you understand who the Old Ones really are, you realize they only use man as pawns in their cosmic schemes.

"But are the Divines any better? Because if they were, would the Paladins not fare much better? Would the Order be reduced to a single paladin? Could they not rend the heavens and send us help? I've prayed. I've prayed, I don't know how many times, for those very things. Do they intercede in response to our prayers? Yes—but not always.

"Around 40 years that tower had been my home following the crusade. In the first days, before I began to lose hope, I prayed fervently. But not even the stones of that tower bothered to echo my cries, and if the Divines heard my prayers—Well, they didn't let on.

"Hmm, 40 years. Then, there was the strange occurrence of mind and body, which led me to Kellina. To this day, I don't know what came over me. I felt pulled. *I must needs go to Glenmore* I thought. Why? Prayers of the faithful, I assume. All I know is that to this day, she and many others are grateful it happened that I did go.

"I have looked into the eyes of children; that is where I have seen the purity of their intent, the very face of the Divines looking back at me. I am reminded of what the Divines purposed for us and how the Abyss, that den of thieves, corrupted us and this world as their only contribution.

"And out of this heap, the Divines are content to merely set aside certain people to protect all the others? To bless and heal and sacrifice and wage a holy war . . . and I have seen genuine faith in its full power bring ruination to the Abyss time and time again, and it was always through the hands of men. There was no hand of the Divines reaching from Bright Haven with a sword to slay any monstrosity that stalked these lands.

"It has always been the paladins. I have been reminded time and time and time again that we are their true sword, and so the question, Lilium, is not whether they care—the question is, do we care? For paladins are the face of the Divines, so when man, woman, or child looks back into our eyes, as long as our hearts remain faithful, they shall know the Divines care. The Divines love them. They need not fear. There is a power in that beyond my comprehension.

"This question is not one that you answer once and never again ask. It is a night haunt. It is a shadowy specter that will revisit you all your days, and it will come to lie next to you in the quiet hours of the night. There is a war contained within that question, and I pray that you win every such battle until Bright Haven takes you."

Ildradath rolled over and eased onto his elbow to look straight at Lilium. His gaze was as sure as the ground beneath them.

She saw his movement and turned toward him, studying the features of his face as he spoke.

"Lilium, the Divines care. I'll say it again. The Divines care."

She smiled momentarily and nodded before lying on her back and looking into the starry night sky.

"Then I shall sleep well tonight. Somehow . . . we will beat back the Abyss. We will do it together. Good night, Ildradath. Good night,

Aerion."

Aerion knickered, but Ildradath bit the inside of his lip, frowned, and hesitated before responding.

"Good night, Lilium."

CHAPTER NINE

ADJUDICATION

*. . . A Paladin renders judgment upon the world as the
Divines in Bright Haven—their sentence is one and the
same. They are officials of the most high court, dispensing
wisdom and carrying out the will of the Divines. Their words
are life and death, their sword friend and foe. They do not
abide the Abyss nor those who turn to its ways . . .
The apostate must perish, for they are a living blight who
turn others to folly and madness and everlasting death . . .*

1

They reached their destination and watched as the obsidian golems lumbered up the forlorn slopes of the Bleak Top mountains. Except for the baby golem, the golems were thankfully indifferent that Ildradath and Lilium were no longer following them. They were focused on their ascent.

The gentle slopes ascended gradually but terminated in a lengthy ridge of dramatic, sharp peaks, but interspersed among the peaks were a series of rims that ensconced shallow depressions. It was toward the largest and highest of these rims that the golems appeared to be moving. At that very moment, another massive obsidian golem was already cresting the top of the largest rim in the distance. Even from where the group was, that golem appeared several times larger than the alpha they had accompanied. It did not appear to be a part of any visible herd.

The baby golem approached Lilium, and though she had at first been afraid of it, she was now drawn to it. It had become a most unusual but welcomed companion. She was as curious about it as it appeared to be of her. It struck its chest once gently and then turned to follow the other golems. It stopped when it noticed Lilium was not following.

Lilium recognized that it expected her to follow. "I'm sorry, little guy. I have to go a different way." She struck her chest once and motioned towards the south.

It then walked back to her. It struck its chest several more times and gripped a protrusion of its obsidian armor. There was a sharp crack. It then held its hand out towards her.

She saw a small, oblong chunk of obsidian, and she took it. The fractured underside had a silver liquid coating it. It absorbed into her skin when she touched it.

"For me?" she inquired.

"Yes," it rumbled back.

Her eyes shot wide, and she took a step back. "You understand, you talk? Wait, I can understand—" she stammered.

"Yes," it rumbled once more. "Keep this part of me as a token of my gratitude for what you and your companions have done for us. For as long as the mountains stand, I shall remember."

"Thank you." She clutched the obsidian tight and marveled. "I don't know what to say. I'd like to ask you so much."

Ildradath and Aerion stood off, but they were watching attentively.

"Then you must come with me," it softly bellowed.

Lilium frowned. "I have to go. We are on a quest for the Divines."

"Then you must go your way," it softly reverberated before deeply bellowing, "and I must join the Mountain Smith. It is time for this mountain to give birth, to breathe new life. May the Divines go with you." It turned to begin its ascent.

"Wait, my name is Lilium. What is yours?" she asked.

"Habsjuradan," it bellowed out as it continued walking.

"Divines, go with you," she called out to give her parting blessing.

And with no other words, Habsjuradan hurried to join the others. Lilium turned to Ildradath with her mouth wide open and smiling.

"Now I understand what others must think when they see me talking with Aerion. What was that about?" Ildradath inquired.

"Did you hear it speak?" she asked in response.

"Words? No. Just sounds. But you did?" he asked with a raised brow.

She popped up with a giddy bounce. "I did!"

"What? You could understand?" Ildradath asked in disbelief.

"Yes! It gave me a shard of itself," she said proudly. "Its name is Habsjuradan." She walked over to him and held her hand out to display it.

"Mark that as a first!" Ildradath said with enthusiasm to mark the special occasion.

Lilium turned and watched Habsjuradan continue his ascent. "I want so badly to go talk with him more."

"I can only imagine how many questions you might ask," he said playfully. "Our paths part here, Lilium. Divines willing, perhaps one day you will get a chance." He patted her back.

Lilium nodded and looked at the gift in her hand as she bit the inside of her lip. She then lifted her eyes and stared at Habsjuradan. Those shared words had opened a whole new world.

Turning his attention, Ildradath looked ahead. "Malcreus should be on the southern base of this mountain."

"You have been here before," Lilium stated. She shuffled uneasily after saying this. He had never specifically told her, but she had pieced it together.

They stopped, and Ildradath now knelt, looking the ground over for sign. His eyes were focused on the ground, and he remained silent.

"I've been wanting to ask you. But it seemed like you had," she added.

He nodded, lifted his head, and looked out into the distance. The wind blew gently while her words hung in the air. "Yes. Yes, I have." He rubbed the palm of his left hand as he recalled it. "The last time I came was to bring back a brother, but I, uh—I left alone."

She had felt there was something else in his past that was a part of this quest. She did not want to pick at a wound, but she felt she needed to know. She wanted to understand. She truly wanted to be there for him. "I'm sorry," she said.

He nodded, and his eyes darted to hers. "Me too."

Ildradath stood, and they moved farther south, skirting the base of the mountain as they went. Eventually, Ildradath came across a series of tracks that crisscrossed, but all were headed in the same direction. These, too, moved along the base of the mountain. It did not matter whether they were recent or not. It only mattered that they seemed to be converging, gathering.

Ildradath looked around and felt satisfied with their current position. "Yes, we are very close now. We will rest a moment here and make our final preparations before continuing to the entrance."

Aerion huffed, and Lilium rested against a large stone after inspecting it carefully this time, of course. She faced away from the mountain and looked west out across the salt flats. The sun was moving towards the horizon, and it was concealed behind dark clouds.

Lilium shivered. "I don't . . . I don't know if I can go in there." She drew her legs in and wrapped her arms around her knees. She slowly rocked back and forth.

Ildradath placed two bags on the ground. Though they appeared empty, he did so with care. "Good," Ildradath spoke. He finished moving things around and began feeding Aerion a large apple.

"What do you mean, good? I'm scared. I just. I keep thinking about everything we've seen, and I don't know what is in there, but I know it is worse than what I first imagined. It is so much more awful, and there will be things, things I cannot even think of. I just know it. And I don't want to burden you with me any more than I already have. Since we left, it's been one bad thing followed by another."

Ildradath finished feeding Aerion the apple and did not immediately respond to her. He let her words hang in the air. He needed to speak forthrightly with her and tend to her failing spirit. She was experiencing a genuine test of faith. She had been such an encouragement to him, and she did not understand this. It was time for him to kindle her spirit.

He patted Aerion on the neck and turned around towards Lilium, and he knelt in front of her. Her head now hung low and rested on her crossed arms, which pressed into her knees. Her hands trembled, and her hair hid her face. Tears rolled down her cheeks.

Ildradath gently placed his trembling hand on her crossed arms. The weight of what lay before them was upon him as well.

Tenderly, he said, "I have looked upon all the horrors of the Abyss, times innumerable, and I have likewise seen the blossoms of spring and autumn's pageantry, joyous foal and friends, and hearth and kin, and I stand here now reminded of not just who I am and what I must do, but why.

"It is okay to struggle, to falter and forget, but truths do not change with our circumstances. So, remember. Even when it is impossible. Remember what is true. Keep that ever before you, in your heart, before your eyes, and upon your tongue. The despair will not be so maddening, the dark so deep, and the path forward so uncertain.

"It is good that you feel the weight of what we are about to accomplish together. It is good that you recognize your fear, and if you did not feel it, I might wonder whether you had lost your mind. It is okay to be afraid, but that fear should drive us toward the Divines' love.

"When you came to me, I had been afraid that I was not enough. I was afraid that the Divines had abandoned me. That they had forgotten me. I was afraid I'd never be able to do what was needed. I was alone, and I was sure that was how I would die. But you, Lilium, you were the answer to years of prayers.

"Through you, I have been reminded that the Divines keep watch in accordance with what is best, even when we've made mistakes or failed. When you were snatched in Dead Man's Valley and called out my name, everything became crystal clear again. I regret that was what it took.

"Rest, take comfort in the arms of the Divines. We possess a promise. They will not abandon us. They will not forsake us. I embody their will. I cannot abandon the faithful. I cannot forsake all the people praying and depending upon the Divines to take action.

"I had forgotten so much. But now I remember who I am. I remember where I belong. I remember what I am fighting for. Sometimes, what we see threatens our remembrance of what we have seen. Even when the light is most faint, look back and see all that you have seen. How far you've come is more real than how far you have yet to go.

"I used to question why the Divines would leave scars behind when they granted healing. I understand now. Scars are gifts because the greatest danger is that of forgetting. So, Lilium, remember what the Divines have already done to bring us here and trust them in what comes next.

"You have a simple choice. Turn back or press on. This decision is the only one that determines whether you should be ashamed of your fear."

Her head was still lowered, and quiet tears continued to fall from her eyes. With words unspoken, she moved a hand and rested it on Ildradath's. Her fingers gripped the back of his hand. He could feel her hand trembling along with his.

Ildradath prayed aloud, "Divines, bless us in our hour of need. Give us strength and valor's wings. Give us your grace and power to be vessels of your will. Go before us, abide within us, and safeguard our path. Without you, we cannot do what must be done. We are your children. Bless us so that we may do all that is required, no matter the cost. Bring your deeds to remembrance and add to them. Glorify yourselves. May it be so."

With that, Ildradath squeezed her forearm and rested his other hand on top of hers. He remained there for precious moments, but he needed to resume making preparations. As though recognizing the same, Lilium moved her hand and wiped tears from her eyes. Ildradath gave another gentle squeeze before standing and returning to finish preparations.

He pulled pieces of armor out from one of the bags on the ground. One by one, he laid out his helm, chest plate, gauntlets, greaves, pauldrons, sabatons, and more—every piece and all that was needed to fasten them. He surveyed what he had laid out and accounted for each piece.

Each piece bore grime and dried blood from the crusade so many years ago. The sheen of the metal was dulled and hidden. The blackish-red dried blood was evidence of all that had been sacrificed during those awful days. The greaves and sabatons had red mud-caked bottoms, remnants of a blood-soaked battlefield. Moreover, his armor, especially his chest piece, had nicks, dents, and gouges.

He took out several pieces of cloth from another bag and paused, readying himself. He had put this off for so long. His armor needed repairs and to be cleaned, and he knew he should have done this long ago. All he could do now was clean each piece, and it was right that he did so, even if they were going to be fouled again.

He noticed Lilium and Aerion watching out of the corner of his eye. Lilium had retrieved the last of Elspeth's cake, and she and Aerion were both enjoying it. Her stomach had been in knots, and she had been nauseous. The cake was making her much better. She could feel Elspeth's gentle presence.

Ildradath cleared his throat. "Before this quest, I hadn't touched my armor since the fall of the Order." He began to wipe a piece of armor, then retracted his hand and clenched his fist around the cloth. Images and sounds from those days flashed in his mind. He heard brothers calling out to him. He shook his head to cast those thoughts out. He collected himself.

"It is dirty, but a paladin's armor neither stains nor rusts." Piece by piece, he began cleaning. With each wipe came more memories and scenes from the crusade and those dear to him lost. Occasionally, he would pause to compose himself. Tears gathered in the corners of his eyes. Such good men had been lost, and he missed each one. A strange sense of guilt came over him as though he was wiping away all that remained of them.

Then came a rush of righteous anger. He must honor their sacrifice. Now was an opportunity to strike a blow at the Abyss. Although he was not sure of what would come after this day, he knew the task appointed him. It was time for him to be faithful. That was enough.

Ildradath prayed aloud:

The blood of paladin saints adorns me
The taint of the Abyss clings too
May the blood of the holy sanctify
May the taint of the unclean hone my wrath
For I am called to this sacred task
To right what is wrong
To cleanse the impure
To rend what destroys
To shine in darkness
May it be so

The dried blood and grime were wiped free with ease, like dust being wiped off a table with a damp rag. He did this for each piece. His armor was ready to be free of it all; it would abide the filth no longer.

Once he was finished, each piece was returned to its natural shine. Each piece reflected the setting sun brilliantly. Methodically, he donned his armor, taking time to ensure each piece was carefully in place. After uttering a brief prayer, all the straps and fasteners moved and secured themselves independently and to the degree each was needed. Ildradath especially valued that blessing bestowed upon his armor, for it reduced a tedious, two-person task to a simple, faithful breath of air.

He secured his sword and scabbard on his left hip. He took his war hammer and placed it on his back. It held, secured by a mysterious force, yet again another blessing. It was positioned diagonally across his back, the head near his left hip, and the end of the handle protruding just above his right shoulder. He held his shield in his left hand.

Finished donning his armor and armament, he drew his sword. He knelt and placed his shield against his legs, and he then turned his sword upside-down and rested his clasped hands on its pommel. He bowed his head and began praying softly.

Lilium and Aerion could not discern his words, but they watched him attentively. Both were in awe as they had never seen an armored paladin, but to add to this, a ray of light pierced the dark clouds and illuminated his frame. Lilium had seen paintings, and despite the worn condition of his armor, they could not compare with the image before her.

He finished praying, stood with his shield, sheathed his sword, and then turned to the others. "Are we ready?"

"Yes," Lilium replied confidently.

Aerion whinnied.

"Good. Now, once we get inside, I want both of you to find a safe place near the cavern's entrance to stay hidden. Lilium and Aerion, I covet your prayers during the upcoming battle."

They nodded.

"Furthermore, should I fall in battle, you must both flee. Return to Elspeth. Mark my words. Leave immediately, and do not look back. Aerion, I am trusting you to this. Do not leave without Lilium, and do not hesitate. Do you both understand?"

Lilium and Aerion looked at each other, then back at Ildradath. Aerion was quick to nod. Lilium did so shortly thereafter, but she did not look Ildradath in the eyes.

They continued around the base of the mountain until the large cave entrance stood before them. The last edge of the sun was now dangerously low on the horizon, and a blanket of darkness was descending upon the land. Without any further words or hesitation, they entered the bleak, craggy mouth of the mountain.

¶¶

The entrance led to a large tunnel that descended at a slight angle into the ground, and this straight path took them to a cavernous vault. Evil inhabited this place, and its presence greeted the trio. The air was foul and pungent. The first thing they saw were upside-down torches burning with bright purple and red flames. They were insufficient to actually illuminate the cavern, but they were spaced at regular intervals all around the cavern and provided a sense of space. The cavern's roof was not visible, but chandeliers made of various bones hung with many more upside-down torches. They were at least sixty feet in the air, making the cavern much taller than expected.

In the distance, a sprawling mass of abyssians had gathered. Ildradath was confident he spotted Malcreus on the far side of the mass, standing between two large braziers on a rocky outcrop facing in their direction. He was speaking loudly. His words were difficult to discern, but it was apparent that he was addressing the abyssians who faced him.

Ildradath spotted an outcrop of rocks to his right, and he motioned to Lilium and Aerion. They understood and moved to hide among the rocks while Ildradath passed before them.

As Ildradath drew closer to the abyssians and Malcreus, he was able to see that there were many more abyssians and cultists than he expected. There were no fewer than two hundred, and Malcreus was giving what could only be likened to a speech.

Though it was difficult in the darkness, Ildradath surveyed the gathering. Some of those gathered were ones already encountered on the quest: likichurpkins, pox fiends, goruphants, ripper locusts, nyarlans, and cultists. Others not encountered on the journey were also present: pummelers, corpse worms, a corpse colossus, night scourges, eviscerators, and needle beasts. He had never faced these odds.

The corpse worm was as long as three horses and as tall as one, but its vile body was a fetid, corpulent amalgamation of human remains. It moved like a caterpillar, but it otherwise looked nothing of the like. Its body had decaying human limbs sticking out in all directions, and those that touched the ground, regardless of whether they were an arm or leg, helped to propel the nasty thing forward. The hands that stuck out from its sides and into the air groped around, eager to lay hold of anything nearby. Countless heads protruded among the skin on its sides and back, and these moaned or chattered their teeth as if eager to bite anything that might get close. At the front of the creature, a mouth capable of opening as wide as it was tall bore its sharp teeth, which were formed from a random assortment of the broken bones of its victims, eager to chew or swallow whole anything it could, whether alive or dead.

Nearby human remains would be gathered by spindly, sinewy tendrils, which would creep out to incorporate them into the horrid mass, further growing its size.

Once of sufficient size, a corpse worm's putrid horror only worsened. They eventually make a cocoon within which to transform and become a corpse colossus.

The corpse colossus towered over everything else in the room as it was over twenty feet tall. Its large body was covered in draped portions of human flesh or intact corpses. Its body looked like a flayed man but was covered in countless spiky protrusions, which allowed remains to be tacked on by its long, spindly fingers without trouble. Occasionally, pieces of remains would slough off, especially as they rotted and decayed. The layers of human remains functioned as armor, and it was content to smash and stomp at anything it wanted to add to itself—or it might simply grab someone and tack them on while alive. Only its large, bony head with round, blank eye sockets was not decorated with flesh. Large flat molars used for crushing whatever it ate lined an unnervingly wide mouth.

The night scourges, like large bats the size of a medium dog, had featureless faces lacking eyes, ears, or noses, but their mouths were filled with four opposing, curved fangs that were exceptionally good at slicing open anything they bit. Curved, dagger-like bones protrude from the middle of their wings and their feet to help them cling to their prey. These creatures preferred to swoop onto the backs or heads of their prey, bury their claws deep into flesh so that they cannot be easily pulled free, and then proceed to bite the necks and faces of their victims while stabbing their backs with their spear-tipped tail until their victim dies from blood loss. Even if pulled free by another person, the victim is left with many deep lacerations all over their back and head.

Eviscerators are the aquatic shock troops of the Abyss. These bulbous-eyed marine humanoid creatures prefer the sea and river but are just as capable on land. They have four arms, and each hand and foot are webbed. Dark green, slimy, scaled skin covers their bodies; they have gill slits in their necks, but they also have lungs. Though they are capable of using human weapons, they enjoy using the claws on their webbed hands to tear people open. They are fond of pinning their victims and, while staring into their helpless eyes, use their free pair of hands to tear out organs while the victim is alive.

Needle fiends have a body reminiscent of a scorpion, but it is covered in thick, hollow barbed needles. Its tail is the length of its body and has an orifice capable of plucking barbed needles from anywhere on its body. It can then propel them at its target from a considerable distance. These needles have barbed tips, but it is their hollow nature that is devious. Once inside a victim, blood can flow freely out as through a spout, thus causing rapid blood loss. Grievous wounds are left when pulled free, ensuring its victims have little hope of survival.

Ildradath had never seen such a gathering. Abyssians seldom displayed cohesion or recognized leadership among their kind, but here they were hissing, cackling, grunting, chanting, and many other indescribable sounds in response to Malcreus' words.

Ildradath fully understood now. Malcreus had been drawing abyssians from all over to serve him. The cultist responsible for killing Lilium's family had been keeping an eye on him. They were assembled to slay the last paladin and unleash the greatest of evils.

Malcreus shouted, "Now we march together! We will revel in slaughter! We shall slay him and end the Order! We will wake the Dread One! We will do what all others have failed to do! We are children of the Abyss, and none shall stand before us!"

Ildradath was now close to the backmost row of abyssians. He shouted with righteous defiance, "Here am I!"

Malcreus' hideous smile disappeared in momentary confusion. He strained his twisted eyes and, in disbelief, realized that it was indeed Ildradath standing on the other side of the throng.

The abyssians rapidly turned to face the intruder, and they let out a cacophony of sounds to proclaim their hatred for the man. Before the mass of monsters could move against Ildradath, Malcreus cried out loudly and decisively. "Wait! Do not move until I say! Make way! I said make way!"

Malcreus jumped from his elevated position and hurried forward toward Ildradath. The sea of abyssians parted before Malcreus. Malcreus' disbelief turned to delight upon seeing it really was him.

Malcreus was barely taller than Ildradath. Veins crept across his purple-gray skin, and long, dark, unflowing hair hung from his head. His eyes were bright yellow, and his fingernails were unpleasantly long and unkempt. He wore black armor, and the contours and ridges of each piece were coated in blood as a type of decorative edging to accentuate its design. A sword was strapped to his back between a small pair of folded dark wings, which appeared much like the wings of the small drakes of the Great Archipelago—for appearance rather than function. Malcreus stood about ten feet from Ildradath, and as he talked, Ildradath could see his rough teeth, some of which were broken, were no longer like that of a man.

"And the Old Ones have even granted me this boon, that they would send you here to me. Indeed, I am their champion! I will turn this world over to them and forever claim my place by their sides to rule Kadath for all time." Malcreus chuckled with delight.

"Look at you," Ildradath replied with stone-cold disappointment. "What has become of you?"

"I am clothed in the vestiges of the Abyss, blessed to represent the true cause. Shudder before my assembled power!" Malcreus raised his hands in the air, and as if rehearsed, the throng at his back let out a quick cacophony of confident cheers.

Undaunted, Ildradath shook his head. "Arrogant fool. You stand accused. I am here to judge you."

"Ha! Me the fool? You are the one who still believes their lies. Open your eyes. You're their errand boy. And you have returned to carrying their water. To think I pitied you, wasting your talent locked away in that tower. Time to let it go. Spare yourself." Malcreus rested his hands on his hips. "Join me. There is room at my side. The alternative is oblivion. This is your only chance. The Divines have abandoned the Order. Now be a man of reason."

Ildradath pointed at Malcreus as he said, "Do you not understand that Bright Haven's gates are closed to you unless you repent? Only the Abyss awaits."

"I repented of the Divines a long time ago, and I have only grown in power since then." Malcreus laughed. "We are born into the grave, old friend. The Abyss beckons us to embrace, that we might take the power of death's sting for ourselves, to wield it as anointed champions."

Ildradath pointed to the madrigaia on his shield. "Malcreus, we are born into a promise. The Divines walk by our sides through the door of the grave and into rapturous light. Death's sting has no power, and faith is my crown."

Malcreus growled. "Faith alone will not save you! You will die, and the Abyss will take you, like all the others. We will then take Kadath and serve, with pleasure, the Dread One."

Malcreus stood defiantly where he was, and the unholy mass behind him shifted about excitedly. Fury and hatred of the paladin boiled within each. They shifted, slinked, and swayed where they were as if jockeying for a better position from which to charge the paladin. Each wanted to be the one to kill him.

Ildradath surveyed the mass before him and then stared firmly at Malcreus.

"I am the adjuror of the Order!" he shouted.

"You are alone!" Malcreus shouted back.

"I am faith's vindication!"

"You are a failure!"

"I am a steward of creation!"

"You guard ashes!"

"I am an angel of purgation!"

"You are nothing!"

Ildradath unsheathed his sword, brought his shield up, and then thrust his sword into the air.

"I am Ildradath!" he shouted.

Three rays of light shot from the tip of the sword and encircled each other as they ascended to the ceiling.

"Kill him! Kill him!" Malcreus bellowed as he motioned both arms toward Ildradath.

With that long-awaited order, the mass of abyssians and cultists rushed toward Ildradath, and Malcreus held his ground, content to watch them tear the paladin apart.

The three rays of light coalesced at the cavern roof into one large sun-like orb, which exploded into being with such force that it faltered the charging mass. The entire cavern became brilliantly illuminated. At this same time, Ildradath's armor became bright, giving off its own light, and wings like crystal feathers of bottled lightning flared from his back. As his mind entered the state of continual battle prayer he had honed over a lifetime of service, he never felt more in union with the Divines.

He leapt into the air, and with supranatural instinct, flew into the giant orb of light. The abyssians below were dazed, and they could not pierce the light to discern Ildradath's form.

There, cloaked in light, Ildradath recognized each horror below as a foe he had slain, if not once, a multitude of times. Contempt and righteous indignation swelled within his chest. He scowled beneath his helm.

These aberrations should not exist, he thought.

Like retribution's comet, Ildradath descended into the mass with his war hammer now in hand. He struck the ground, and a shockwave erupted, knocking all the abyssians around him off their feet. With each coming dash or jump, his wings flapped and emitted a hum and flash of light like a visitation of the Divine's glory.

He dashed forward, his wings flapping once to propel him. He brought his war hammer down on a pummeler's head, spun, and then brought it down again upon a needle fiend before either had a chance to stand, killing both instantly.

As others began to stand, he tossed his war hammer behind his back and transitioned flawlessly to his sword. He dashed to and fro, delivering killing blows with each slash. The swarm of night scourges descended upon him. Their dagger-like claws violently tore against his armor, but they were unable to pierce it.

Bringing his shield to his chest and sword upright in front of it, he willed a wave of heat and light to erupt out from himself. The scourges caught fire and were blown back. Some fell to the ground and writhed while others flew around in a futile effort to put the flames out, only fanning the flames hotter. The sudden blast caused nearby abyssians and cultists to stumble backward and hesitate before charging Ildradath again.

The corpse colossus was not daunted, and it was now swinging a hand to smash Ildradath into the ground. He was not caught off guard, however. He quickly sheathed his sword while taking a knee and raising the shield above his head. The corpse colossus' hand crashed upon the shield, but the shield sent the force explosively back into its hand, leaving it in tattered, barely attached pieces. It bellowed in pain.

Ildradath stood and cast a golden-chain tethered bolt out from his sword hand, which anchored into the colossus' face. He drew himself upward while simultaneously propelling himself with his wings. Like an arrow shot into the sky, Ildradath ascended and raised his shield to strike its face. Willing the blessing of the shield once more, he sent another blast of force straight into the colossus' face. Ildradath's momentum carried him right through the channel where much of the colossus' head had just been. The colossus slumped over and fell forward, crushing several abyssians and cultists beneath its corpse.

He flipped in the air and looked for his next target. He spotted a large group of cultists wearing armor and carrying huge swords. He smiled. He shot towards them and landed just in front of the group, and he then charged at the nearest one. The cultist raised his sword to cleave Ildradath in half, from top to bottom, but in a blink of an eye, the cultist was looking up from the ground at the half of his own body standing over him.

Ildradath stepped to the next cultist and parried a strike, following through with a pommel strike, which smashed into the top of the cultist's head. He swung right and caught another's head in the blow and then thrust forward to pierce another through the chest. He raised his shield to block another strike, and the force from his shield shattered the sword and sent the shrapnel flying into several other cultists, who fell mortally wounded. Several abyssians who had been bound to these cultists fell dead.

Out of the corner of his eye, he saw a ripper locust barreling towards him. He charged it and, with a great beat of his wings, accelerated forward while tucking his wings behind and sliding onto his side. With sword upraised, he zipped underneath and returned to his feet on the other side of it. It scampered to turn around quickly as the contents of its abdomen spilled to the ground. It crumpled to the ground, unable to continue after its prey.

He sensed that the mass of abyssians was nearly upon him. He decided to create space. He sheathed his sword and brought out his war hammer once again. Holding it in front of him, he willed it to become three war hammers upon throwing it. He spun in a circle, and with an underhanded side toss, the war hammer spun and encircled him. It spun and revolved around Ildradath's body about fifteen feet away, and it split into three hammers spread equidistant apart which maintained a uniform orbit.

The barreling mass of abyssians had too much momentum to stop before meeting the war hammers violently spinning in midair. A pox fiend was caught mid-jump and had its torso caved inward. A cultist was struck aside his head; two eviscerators charging side by side had their legs broken in half; and a goruphant who believed he could defy Ildradath and seize a war hammer out of the air had his tentacle arm torn off. As the goruphant spun sideways from his attempt, another war hammer struck its back and plowed it aside.

Malcreus stood his ground and watched. He felt great contempt for Ildradath and loathed seeing his success; nevertheless, he was delighted at the prospect that he may have to be the one to kill him. It would surely mean that much more favor from the Old Ones. He knew those pathetic abyssians and cultists would not be missed. As long as Ildradath died, he could still finish the most important part of the Old Ones' plan.

Lilium and Aerion prayed mightily. Lilium's hands were either in intense pain, or they had gone numb; she could not tell. As she squeezed them together, she pressed them against her thighs. For some portion of the time, she would pray with her eyes open. She felt that if she could see what was happening, she could pray for blessings upon his every circumstance—every twist, turn, and strike. Other times, the sights and sounds were too much. She felt both awe and terror.

Aerion's heart pumped. He was torn between running forward and jumping into the fray or praying next to Lilium. He understood his orders, though, and he also would have much preferred a nice set of paladin horse armor before such a charge. These were not just peekaboos and cultists, and he and Ildradath were greatly outnumbered. No, he recognized that his continual prayers were sufficient, and he was confident that both his and Lilium's prayers were being heard. They were helping to empower Ildradath.

Encircled by his war hammers, needle fiends launched barrages at him. The war hammers smashed some needles; others struck his armor and fragmented futilely, and others embedded in unfortunate cultists and abyssians caught in their careless trajectory.

Ildradath decided to strike back at the abyssians from a distance. He willed glowing knives to be cast out with each throwing motion of his hand, and so he struck out at the aberrations beyond the spinning wall of war hammers. Each blade soared to its targets and struck with sufficient velocity to tear holes through them.

An after-death which had just burst from the dead goruphant came twisting and writhing toward Ildradath. He took his sword, held it over his shield, aimed the tip at it, and pulled it backward. As it scraped the top of his shield, he willed the spark to form a blast of fire, and this blast engulfed the after-death. It screeched and spun in place as it burned.

Ildradath willed the hammers to continue to spin where they were and then ascended into the air in an arc, landing behind a corpse worm that was on the exterior of the group. With his back to it, he casually walked away from it. The worm lurched around itself to pursue Ildradath. The many human heads covering its body eerily moaned and screamed as if remembering their horrid deaths. The worm wriggled and propelled itself forward, eager to bite Ildradath.

He willed for his war hammer to reform as one and then to return to his back with alacrity. It did so and flung itself like a ballista bolt. Abyssians and cultists who could dodge it did so, but the corpse worm was ignorant of what came its way. The hammer plowed through it, exiting through its mouth, before securing itself to Ildradath with a mighty thud. He used the momentum of his hammer's return, combined with a flap of his wings, to fly forward and flip in the air to face the abyssians charging after him.

He fixed his eyes upon his foes. He had killed many, but there were many more to go. He was feeling the vigor of battle. He felt confident. He felt the presence of the Divines. He was empowered. He was better than in old times.

And so, he fought throughout the night, smiting foul creature after foul creature, until at last, only he and the apostate remained.

111

The cavern was littered with abyssians and cultists. Malcreus surveyed the scene, laughed, and began slow-clapping as he paced back and forth in front of Ildradath. He then grabbed his large sword and held it firmly with two hands. "But it only means the glory will be all mine!"

Malcreus dashed forward, his wings flapping to help propel him, and brought his sword down to cleave Ildradath, but it was parried aside. Ildradath rushed forward a step and slammed his shield into Malcreus, knocking him off balance. Ildradath was surprised to see that his shield did nothing more than this.

Ildradath slashed out at Malcreus, but even off-balance and facing away from him, Malcreus deftly blocked the sword strike behind his back. He then spun to deliver his own mighty slash at Ildradath, who in turn blocked it with his shield, but Malcreus followed this with a kick, which sent Ildradath reeling backward.

Ildradath willed a blast of heat and light outward to buy himself a moment, but Malcreus instantly responded with a shadowy blast. They were each neutralized, and Malcreus rushed forward through the haze of smoke left behind and struck out at Ildradath. He barely blocked the strike with his shield.

Malcreus summoned a dark mist that enveloped Ildradath, blinding and suffocating him. Ildradath dashed backward and willed this to be purged from him. He regained his senses just in time to deflect another blow.

Ildradath willed for his sword to intensify its power, and it began to glow and cast a bright light. Without missing a beat, Malcreus did the same for his sword, but it darkened and became a shadow. Malcreus then slashed and struck out rapidly while spinning circles and half-circles, moving back and forth with such fluidity that it was difficult for Ildradath to follow the path of his sword.

The brilliant light of Ildradath's sword swirled and was sucked into the darkness of Malcreus' sword like water swirling violently down into a whirlpool. Their swords clashed, parried, and struck out with no clear advantage to either. This continued for a time until they found themselves at a distance from each other, and then they paced in a circle.

Ildradath shouted at Malcreus, "Is this how you would honor the memory of our brothers? The Sisters? The children? Of Matron Ophelia?"

Malcreus pointed his sword at Ildradath. "Silence! You are unworthy to speak Fee's name!"

Ildradath pointed his sword back at Malcreus. "And you would serve those who keep them imprisoned in the Abyss? Those who plan to use their souls as fuel for waking the Dread One?"

Malcreus stabbed downward with his sword several times as he spoke as if demanding Ildradath to recognize the truth of what he said. "They possess a mercy you do not understand! This will allow me to protect others. Once I have finished proving my worth, I will be granted—"

"Do you actually think the Old Ones care?" Ildradath shouted out his interjection. "That they will make things better?"

With sword in hand, Malcreus raised his hands outward, beckoning Ildradath to witness his superiority. "They have the power to. The Divines prevented them from gifting us things in our creation. The Divines are selfish, unworthy of being served."

"You believe lies," Ildradath called out flatly.

"They are powerful. Unlimited power to keep those we love safe," Malcreus replied while letting his arms fall to his sides.

Ildradath scoffed. "Unlimited? The Dread One exhausted himself with his acts of creation. Had he not killed Azathoth and used his corpse as a foundation for the Abyss, he couldn't have even done that. Now he sleeps, unable to do anything and completely dependent on others."

Malcreus laughed. "You greatly simplify things. His power in slumber is mighty enough to keep the Old Ones united and to draw people unto himself."

Ildradath swept his sword outward and said, "You have truly gone mad! Can you not see? Those responsible for all of our pain and loss, for Ophelia—"

"Silence!" Malcreus shouted back as he took a step towards Ildradath.

"Turn back," Ildradath commanded. "Repent and be saved or be judged."

Malcreus jabbed his sword in Ildradath's direction repeatedly. "And do you think I could ever serve alongside the man who brought the Order to its knees? No, I have seen the truth. I will serve those with actual power. Your judgment means nothing."

"So be it," Ildradath said decisively. Ildradath quickly sheathed his sword and willed a golden chain in his hand, which he lashed out and wrapped around Malcreus' ankles. He pulled Malcreus off his feet and yanked him mightily towards him. He then drew his war hammer and prepared to crush Malcreus.

In this same instance, Malcreus gripped the ground with one clawed hand and propelled himself even faster towards Ildradath, catching Ildradath off guard. As Malcreus swung his sword across to cut Ildradath's legs out from underneath him, Ildradath leapt forward.

Malcreus extended an arm and grabbed one of Ildradath's ankles, pulling him down so that he landed on his chest. Malcreus rolled onto his side, and as he reached to stab Ildradath in his back, Ildradath kicked him in the face with his free foot.

They both scrambled back to their feet and, with renewed ferocity, continued combat. Slash, stab, swing—each would occasionally score a hit, but their armor defended against each blow. Ildradath's paladin-forged sword and armor were matched equally by Malcreus' warped sword and armor, and each faith-imbued power was met with another power bestowed upon the Abyss' champion.

They continued exchanging blows for more than another hour. Ildradath wondered how likely it would be for him to best Malcreus.

Malcreus was an Abyss-empowered version of his former self, and he had always been the superior swordsman. Each technique and ability was proving ineffective. He realized that he was straining against all odds to defeat Malcreus. He was playing into his strength. He needed to find a way to exploit a weakness.

He recalled the words of the quest scroll, and he embraced them as the means to defeating Malcreus. He knew his foe well, so he would leverage Malcreus' pride against himself, and this could be used to create an opportunity to strike him down. Ildradath would make himself vulnerable in order to lower Malcreus' guard, and then this would be their ending. For a moment, Ildradath looked over at Aerion and Lilium, and he hoped that he might somehow be able to say goodbye.

Malcreus saw Ildradath doing so and seized the opportunity to taunt him. "I saw them hours ago. Do not worry," he sneered. "I will tend to them once I am finished with you."

Ildradath let the taunt go without a response. He slowed his pacing and apparent skill of parrying and blocking Malcreus' sword strikes. He blocked all strikes, which would have ended him instantly, but he left openings in his defense. Finally, Malcreus swiftly drove his sword forward and exploited an opening. His sword found a dent mid-torso, and it pierced Ildradath through.

Ildradath exclaimed in pain and dropped his sword and shield, and the war hammer fell from his back; his wings dissipated in a flash.

Malcreus smiled, "You have failed everyone, Ildradath, and most of all, the Divines have failed you. But you should be used to that by now."

"I've known forgiveness. I've—" Ildradath grimaced. "I've been faithful. To the end."

Malcreus grabbed Ildradath's shoulder with one hand while the other drove his sword up to its cross-guard.

Ildradath exclaimed again. He was now face to face with Malcreus, who stared intensely into his eyes, eagerly waiting to see his light fade.

Malcreus smirked. "Those are fitting last words for a paladin. Your faith has brought you to this moment."

"Yes. And so my quest fulfilled." Ildradath winced. "You always despised the small things."

Malcreus looked at Ildradath with an amused smile while scrunching his brows in confusion.

"Tell them I'm coming. The Abyss take you." With his left hand, Ildradath quickly swung his secretly unsheathed dagger into Malcreus' ear, killing him instantly.

"Divines, see your judgment passed." Ildradath gasped in pain.

Malcreus fell backward, and Ildradath maintained his grip on his dagger. With his dagger in hand and Malcreus' sword still stuck through him, he turned to see where Lilium and Aerion were. They were already running to him. He fell to his knees, dropping the dagger. The adrenaline was keeping him going for now, but it would soon give way. Pushing through the pain, he removed his helm and tossed it aside.

Lilium and Aerion reached Ildradath. She fell to her knees in front of him. "Divines have mercy!" she cried out.

"You were right," Ildradath spoke quietly. His eyes searched for hers.

"Hold on! We will get you help," Lilium pleaded.

"I didn't go for a walk. Your prayer. Clear as day. Too ashamed. Here." Ildradath reached over, touching Lilium's hand, and he placed the rolled-up quest scroll inside hers. He then coughed up blood and fell over onto his side, wincing in pain.

"What?" She was confused and quickly pocketed the scroll.

"Thank you. For saving me. For redemption." His eyes glanced over at Aerion. "You'll both do well. Keep the faith. Divines bless you." Ildradath coughed more blood and sighed, then went silent and motionless.

Aerion let out a dispirited snort.

"Ildradath! No, Ildradath! Stay with me, please! We will take you—we will get help!" she pleaded.

Ildradath's open eyes stared across the cavern floor. They were now devoid of life and looked beyond, and the Abyss had laid its claim on his soul. A low rumbling emanated from the ground and shook everyone. Ildradath's sword rattled.

Tears streamed down Lilium's face. Aerion came close to her and lowered his head. He huffed, and he nudged her head gently to get her attention. Tears had formed in his eyes.

"Ildradath. I didn't want to be alone, but I am no longer afraid of it. I know I am not, for the Divines keep watch. I know that despite everything, they care. They don't always do what we think they should, nor the way we think they should. But you've shown me that we are the vessels of their power. I've always chosen to believe. I still choose to believe. But this world needs you." She shook his body. "Ildradath!"

Aerion nudged her head again with more force. He snorted this time. Several small rocks and stalactites fell around the cavern. The ground rumbled even more.

Lilium looked at Aerion. "I know what he said. I know you promised him."

Aerion stamped one of his feet repeatedly and neighed loudly.

"I know!" Lilium yelled back at him. "And I don't care what happens to this place! I will hurry."

Lilium rolled Ildradath partially onto his back. She stood and grabbed the handle of Malcreus' sword. The large Abyss-tainted sword scorched her hands as she grabbed it, but she grimaced and pushed through the searing pain and sound of singeing flesh. She held it firm and, placing a foot on Ildradath's chest armor to gain leverage, she pulled the sword out and threw it aside.

Wincing, she knelt back down to Ildradath and placed her burnt palms over his chest armor. The armor soothed the burns, and as she pressed down to get her hands closer to the wound, her blood smeared on his armor. She closed her eyes and began to pray. Focusing her mind to envision the glory of the Divines, she sought to channel their power.

"Divines, I come to you yet again. Ildradath has slain Malcreus. He has done what you commanded. Please, heal this wound. Keep him here. Do not let him die. We need him. This world needs him! Please!" Lilium pleaded.

Lilium opened her eyes expectantly, but Ildradath lay motionless, breathless. His eyes stared indifferently upward to the cavernous ceiling. She reached over and grabbed Ildradath's sword firmly by its grip, and she pulled it onto his chest. "Get up!" she commanded, and with each additional command, she clanged his sword against his chest armor, "Get up! Get up! Get up! We were supposed to finish this together!"

Lilium let go of the sword, looked at her blistered, bleeding hands briefly before wrapping them around her waist, and then doubled over, resting the side of her face against Ildradath's chest. Her heart raced; beads of sweat rolled down the sides of her face to join her tears, and pain shot through her stomach. She began struggling to breathe, and truncated, rapid breaths shot panic through her body as her diaphragm spasmed. "Why does it hurt so bad," she cried.

Her heart ached. Her soul ached. She had lost everyone she loved. She could not accept that Ildradath was dead, even though she lay against his lifeless body. He was there and yet not. She despised death, for it was the greatest of robbers.

Aerion now stamped around her and huffed loudly. More small pieces of the volcanic ceiling were falling, and a smell of sulfur began filling the air.

Mustering all the strength she could, Lilium rose and grabbed Ildradath's sword. With head hung low, she began walking over to Aerion while dragging the sword at her side, fighting for breath with every step; heaving, panting, and sobbing, she moved like her soul remained chained to Ildradath's body.

She grabbed hold of Aerion's saddle and put her left foot in the stirrup. She steadied herself and prepared to heave her sword arm over his back in order to mount him. She paused and looked over her shoulder at Ildradath one last time. She stopped. She turned towards him. She shook her head.

Lilium pulled her foot out of the stirrup and began walking back towards Ildradath with the sword in tow. Once again, Aerion neighed urgently while stamping.

"Aerion, I am not leaving here without him. He is coming with us. I would rather die. Help me pray!" Lilium fell back to her knees at Ildradath's side and let his sword rest across his body.

Aerion stopped stamping, and he lowered his head. He understood her dedication to Ildradath. His heart was breaking, but he did not want to forsake the last commandment of his master. He needed to fulfill his promise, but he resolved to pray with Lilium. He was not sure what good it could do, but she apparently believed it could save Ildradath.

Aerion came close to her, and he nuzzled her head. He gently huffed, and Lilium heard him beginning to pray. She caught her breath and focused.

"Divines," Lilium prayed, "I come to you, seeking your power to work through me. Ildradath is your servant alone. Deny the Abyss. I know you hear me, and I know that you can do this if it be your will. I know you can do far more than I can imagine, that you can even bring him back to life, that you may be glorified and faith rewarded. Please do it. May it be so."

The mountain grumbled, and puffs of smoke began to rise through fissures throughout the cavern. Aerion and Lilium looked upon Ildradath expectantly. Ildradath still lay motionless. There was no sign of life. After several moments, their countenances fell in disappointment.

Lilium laid her head upon Ildradath's chest and wept. She was sure it would work. It did not seem right to her. All the good stories she heard growing up had happy endings, and she hoped that hers might, too. They had made it this far. Ildradath had done all that was commanded of him.

How could he die at the end of it all? she lamented to herself.

Tears ran down Aerion's face. He looked at Ildradath and Lilium, and he hated the evil of the Abyss. He longed for a world where the fields extended beyond sight, where the meadows and pastures were safe for foals. He longed for the reign of nobility. He longed for a world in which the meek wielded power righteously and savagery was tamed for the common good. He longed for a world in which the response to death was not despair but a joyous farewell to greener pastures.

Aerion let out a dispirited huff. He sensed the mountain was going to erupt at any moment. They needed to go, and he recognized that Lilium would not leave. He could not bring himself to abandon her. He would stay and die with them both. The sulfur had grown stronger, and the temperature was rising. Sporadic jets of smoke shot out from fissures now. The end was upon them.

"I thought I told you both to leave me and get out," Ildradath said while coughing and clearing his throat. He let out a groan and moved a hand to his chest where Lilium's head lay.

Lilium's head shot up, revealing a red face with tears streaming down it. "Ildradath!" She wrapped an arm around his neck and hugged him tight.

Aerion let out a joyous and surprised whinny and stood upright, stamping around.

"Alright, alright, girl, you'll pop my head off. I've died enough for one day!" he chuckled. "Yes, I guess I am Aerion!"

Ildradath hurried to his feet with Lilium's help, and he sheathed his sword and dagger, secured his war hammer, and grabbed his shield and helm.

All three instinctively turned their heads to see the new danger emerging. In the distance behind them, a massive dark purple Abyss portal opened on the surface of the cavern wall, and a deep fog gushed out. Tentacles began to emerge. The Abyss, like a spoiled cosmic child denied its plaything, was expending vital energy to get what it wanted back.

"Aerion!" Ildradath shouted.

Aerion needed no instruction. He oriented his head toward the cavern entrance, which was becoming difficult to see through the smoke and falling debris. Ildradath and Lilium both mounted Aerion hurriedly. They did not need to steer him, but they did need to hold tight.

IV

Aerion neighed loudly, and after raising his front legs off the ground in a proud display of power, he stomped them. He wanted the mountain—no, all of creation, the Abyss, everyone and everything to know he was Aerion, and by the power of the Divines, death would be denied twice this day.

Aerion shot forward, placing his faith in the Divines to guide him. The loud peals of splitting ground and fractures opening to reveal molten depths below did not slow him as he leapt from edge to edge. Through billowing smoke and flashes of fire, he ran faster, faster, faster as his hooves strode the turbulent destruction. Large pieces of the cavern fell around them, and only a faint light shone through the smoke of the cavern.

The tentacles shot through the air and strained after the group. Multiple abyssians had now poured out of the portal and were joining the chase, including multiple ripper locusts. Lilium clung to Aerion's neck, and Ildradath leaned tight against her to make their profile small. They knew it could do little to protect them from the dangers all around, but they felt safer pressing close.

Aerion huffed loudly, and he picked up speed. His eyes were fixed upon the morning light shining into the cave entrance. He could see nothing else, not even the ground upon which his hooves trod. He trusted he would find solid ground, but he was having difficulty breathing in the acrid air. His breaths were getting shallower.

Divines guide me. Divines bless my legs to be bolts of lightning that I may tread upon a cloud and hasten us to safety, Aerion prayed.

A loud groaning filled the cavern. The laboring mountain was angry and tired of everything and everyone. It was intent on expelling the group violently and purging the abyssians with fire.

The outside light grew larger and brighter until, finally, Aerion shot out of the fuming mountain's mouth. Aerion exhaled forcefully to clear out the smoke and detritus of the cavern's foul air. He shook his head and then began breathing deeply again. The clean air fueled him. He turned west.

As though struck by a bolt of lightning, Aerion's eyes filled with light and determination. The world was lighter now. He charged forward with a haste never before seen in any noble steed. The wind rushed and whistled past his ears. He had never heard the air move so fast past him.

Ildradath and Lilium still clung closely, unable to move. The air pushed them down and locked them onto Aerion's frame. If they had been able, they would have surely turned to see the volcano's eruption.

Without further warning, the cap of the mountain blew upward. Pitch-black smoke blew skyward in an assault upon the heavens themselves. Dirt, rocks, toxic gasses, ash, and molten material flew upward and outward. The explosion boomed and cracked the air with its deafening cough. Debris shot out in all directions like stones fired from a besieging army of catapults. The cavern, its foul contents, and the pursuing abyssians were violently purged. The growing streams of lava would ensure nothing remained to taint Kadath.

A pyroclastic flow shot down from the top of the mountain. The obsidian golems clung deeply to the mountainside, basking and feeding upon the hot wrath. Carrying along everything spewed out, it also armed itself with every other loose stone or object on the surface of the ground in its path. The pyroclastic flow hurtled with grim momentum toward the group, and it grew in size until it was a large, dark, churning maelstrom chasing them down.

Aerion did not slow down or risk a look to see if they were far enough away. He would keep going until he passed out or died. He would not stop. He would ride until he found the edge and then push beyond it. Rocks whizzed by and struck the ground all around him, blasting dirt into the air as the volcanic siege engine took repeated aim and continued to fire.

The maelstrom began gaining on them, and Aerion sensed this danger growing nearer. He continued his silent prayers, and Ildradath and Lilium each said their own.

The clouds steadily raged closer. They sought to devour everything in their path. Closer, closer, closer still, they licked their lips with anticipation of consuming the group. They chuckled and, with ravenous delight, roared deeply.

Aerion felt the growing heat of the pyroclastic flow behind him. His heart thudded and ached, pressed beyond its limits. His legs burned, and his lungs hurt. He was already exhausted and felt his pace waning. He was slowing.

Unexpected memories shot into his mind. He could see his father running through his childhood meadow. They had such fun together, wild and free. His father was swift and graceful. Aerion had not been; despite this, his father was kind, even when he pushed him beyond his limits. He remembered the games they would play to help him get stronger and faster. He remembered how his dad would nuzzle him and whisper, "You can do it, Aerion. I believe in you."

He remembered the day the men came to capture them. He remembered how he ran as fast as he could, but it was not enough. His father came back to try and fight them off. Had he been faster, his father would still be alive. They would still be running through the fields. A squall roared within him, surging blood through every fiber of his being with renewed force. He refused to lose his new family on account of being too slow.

Though they could barely keep their eyes open, Lilium and Ildradath thought they saw extra legs appear below Aerion's frame as he picked up incredible speed. The rushing of the wind became deafening while the roaring heat of the maelstrom snapped at their backsides.

The dark sand of the Obsidian Flats mixed with the air to form a gray torrent in Aerion's wake, and this blasted backward and clashed with the pursuing pyroclastic wall. Aerion's wake shouted at the screaming wall of death in defiance. The wake grew in size and strength as each hoof strike picked up more ammunition to launch. A clearly defined battle line had formed behind him. Dust and debris swirled violently as the two fronts meleed.

Intense moments passed. The maelstrom slowly became quieter, and its frenetic force began to gasp. It was losing its strength. Aerion began to pull away, and he was able to put significant distance between them and the wanton destruction of the volcano. The maelstrom slowed and dissipated, its gasses rising and clouds of debris settling. It was conceding defeat.

Aerion felt his body losing strength, too, and he was unable to keep his pace. Aerion slowed, but he kept driving forward as best he could. Ildradath turned to see if they were safe.

Ildradath shouted, "Aerion, you can ease up. Ease up, boy. We are safe. You did it!"

Aerion slowed his gait and it took him a while before he could slow to a walk. His body wanted to keep charging forward. It felt unfamiliar to walk again. Aerion was breathing sporadically and trying to catch his breath in uneven gulps.

"Let us get down, Aerion. It will help you catch your breath,"

Lilium said.

Aerion stopped, but his legs were restless. They needed to move. As soon as Lilium and Ildradath had hopped off, Aerion began trotting in a circle around them. His eyes were glassy and troubled. Aerion neighed gently.

Ildradath responded, "Walk it out, boy. Keep moving but slowly. Pace your breathing. Deep breaths in and out."

Aerion continued walking around them briefly before falling over.

"Aerion!" Lilium exclaimed as she ran over to his side. Ildradath followed.

He lay on his side panting. He was having great difficulty. Everything hurt and ached. His lungs were on fire. He could no longer keep his eyes open, and a growing black tunnel was cutting his vision off.

"Rest, boy. Rest. Catch your breath," Ildradath spoke in a reassuring tone. "It'll be okay. You did it! We are safe now."

Aerion's eyes closed.

On the one hand, Lilium felt exposed lying in the open on the Obsidian Flats, but for the first time in a long time, she felt she could actually relax. The deerskin and linen blanket were spoiling comforts, and the warmth of the fire joined the hope kindling within her. She smiled at the thought of how Ildradath seemed to have no shortage of surprises he could pull out of some small bag. After all this time, he still had firewood, dried meat, and plenty of apples.

She looked over at Ildradath. He was soundly asleep. She had not known him for very long, but she had never seen him sleep so deeply. It was very understandable. He had fought for hours, from sunset to sunrise. That would be enough on its own to kill a man, she figured, and he had died. Not even a full day ago, he had a sword through him.

Aerion was sleeping, lying on the ground. As far as she could recall, he had not slept lying down since Elspeth's. Between having exerted himself so greatly that he had nearly died and perhaps sensing that no more dangers were near, he truly rested. He had carried them to safety away from the mountain's eruption, which she now believed, despite all its danger, was a providence using the golems to protect them from the Abyss.

She also could not wrap her mind around the fact that she heard Aerion speak. She could understand him. Initially, she had thought it was grief playing a trick on her, but she actually did understand him. Ildradath only smiled and shrugged at her when she asked him about it. She laughed at herself. Aerion needed to rest well because she had at least twenty questions she could presently think of to ask him tomorrow.

Lilium was exhausted, too, but she was restless. She wondered how long Ildradath would remain before entering the Abyss. Once they returned, he should receive the reward of his quest. She understood that once he did, he would enter the Abyss. She would likely never see him again.

He would be doing so for the opportunity to free the souls of those imprisoned and to hinder the Dread One's plans. This was a noble cause, and she liked the thought of her family ascending to Bright Haven. She did not like the thought of Ildradath leaving forever and not ascending himself. Perhaps, she thought to herself, there may be some way he makes it out of the Abyss alive. She resolved to hope such was possible.

She then remembered that Ildradath had handed her the quest scroll before he died. She reached into a pocket, pulled it out, and unrolled it. She turned her body so that the light of the fire would illuminate the words.

The scroll read:

Go to the apostate in the east

For he must be judged
Through your sacrifice
The Order will be reborn
Lilium must join you
Take Viper's Ascent

She was baffled. She looked over at Ildradath as her mind raced with questions: *He knew he would die? He knew he was not coming back? With his death, how would the Order be reborn? How could he enter the Abyss to free anyone? Even if he survived the quest and had his reward in hand, he would enter the Abyss and not be able to rebuild the Order, right? He was the last paladin, wasn't he? Why did he even give her a choice in joining the quest if he knew she was supposed to go?*

Ildradath left his tower, knowing what awaited. She supposed that he must have wondered some of these things himself, and yet, even with bruised faith and unanswered questions, he chose to trust the Divines.

She traced her fingers across her palms as she looked at them in the fire's light. Some minor scarring remained, but they were healed hours ago following her prayers to the Divines. She rolled over, closed her eyes, treasured all these things in her heart, and pondered them until she fell asleep.

CHAPTER TEN

FAREWELLS

. . . And farewells shall be as greetings for the citizens of Bright Haven, for they have a promise as sure as the love of the Divines, that they will neither be forgotten nor forsaken, for a home has been prepared for them. And as they knew the presence of the Divines all the days of their life, it shall be multiplied unto them for all eternity . . .

1

T he morning light came, and they all roused. After a breakfast of fruit and bread, they continued west. They decided to stop at Elspeth's on the way back, for Lilium was excited to tell her all about the quest.

They rode on Aerion after he repeatedly assured them that he was feeling great and could bear them homeward. They made for Lowland Glen. They did not mind taking the extra time to have an uneventful trip back. They all agreed they never wanted to see another ash viper, Divines willing.

"Ildradath, can I ask you something?" Lilium's voice was direct, but her tone indicated she would understand if he did not want to answer the coming question.

"Sure," he replied. He could not keep himself from feeling very grateful, given recent events, and he rather liked the thought of Lilium barraging him with questions.

"What was it like? Dying?" she asked.

Ildradath did not hesitate to answer. "It's the only thing I have been able to think about. As you might imagine, my body was in pain from being impaled, but it was not as painful as I would have expected. I remember having difficulty thinking and talking to you as I grew weak. It hurt to talk, to breathe. Everything was spinning and growing dark. Then I felt extremely heavy as if being pulled down through the ground, and then I immediately felt as light as a feather.

"I was floating upward through some dark space. I saw a light shining brightly around a set of large gilded doors. I knew it was Bright Haven's gates even as I strained to see through the light. I continued to float toward them, and I felt at peace.

"Then I heard whispering, and out of the darkness, tentacles emerged between me and the gate. It was a mass of them, swirling and writhing as they slowly reached out for me. They began to wrap around my limbs and my neck. I knew that I was to be pulled into the Abyss and denied entrance to Bright Haven. The Abyss had claimed me. I was pulled down deeper than seemed possible. Out of the corner of my eye, I saw the Abyss sky in the far distance.

"But I heard a voice like the sound of a thousand rushing waters, though it was as clear as the waters of Lake Meridian. It was the voice of a multitude speaking in unison, a chorus that boomed. It did not scare me, for it was plain to me that it was the Divines. Had I not realized this, I would have surely been terrified.

"The tentacles immediately screeched and retracted and disappeared as I was bathed in an exploding light of such brilliance—words fail to describe the peace and comfort imparted by it. After that flash of light, I opened my eyes and saw you and Aerion."

Lilium marveled at the thought. "So, you heard the Divines speak? What did they say?" she asked.

He took a deep breath and felt a pleasant frisson at the thought, and a large smile crossed his face. "Ildradath is ours," he replied.

Lilium smiled and felt blessed just to hear him say it.

They continued westward. They did not waste time, but neither did they rush. They appreciated each other's company, especially after all they had experienced together. And even so, the Divines' hand was upon them to ensure their return was uneventful.

11

They set their faces toward Elspeth, and they decided to keep things simple and follow the river around to her home. The gently flowing water would be a welcomed sound and scene after having spent so much time in a parched land. Aerion would greatly appreciate it, and it would not take much effort to maintain their heading.

After another day's travel, they came to the path leading to Elspeth's. Eagerly, they turned north and followed it. The cool, steady midday breeze filled the air. They saw the goats, all of them safely contained in their field. Fall had finally made its way to Elspeth's, and the wonderful flowers that once flaunted their colors were now tired and ready to sleep for the winter. They would need their rest in preparation for their next season of dancing with the wind.

As they approached the house, they observed no other activity save for the motion of the two empty chairs rocking in the breeze. Lilium and Ildradath dismounted Aerion. Ildradath began taking the saddle and bags off him to ease his burden, and while doing so, his eyes scanned for Elspeth.

"She won't believe all that we did," Lilium said with a large smile. She had been looking forward to telling her all about the quest. She had it nearly rehearsed. When she had left Elspeth's, she was anxious. Now, she had returned as a victor over the Abyss. "I know just where to start! I will—"

"Lilium," Ildradath interjected to get her attention before she became carried away. He could see her excitement and sense of pride shining through her eyes.

"Have you seen her yet?" Ildradath asked.

Lilium scanned around and saw nothing, but she did see that the front door was cracked open. "No. She must be inside," Lilium responded with confidence.

"Okay, wait a moment for me. We will go together." Ildradath quickly finished unburdening Aerion and then walked to the house with her. He knocked several times loudly and called out, "Elspeth?"

"Out back," a woman's voice responded from behind the house.

"Was that Kellina?" Lilium inquired.

"I believe so," Ildradath replied.

They walked around to the other side of the house. Kellina stood next to Farlan, and they stood by an elongated mound of dirt next to where Kellina's father had been buried. Farlan was setting a shovel aside.

Lilium stopped cold and momentarily struggled to make sense of what she was seeing. It was the tears in Kellina's eyes and the redness of her face that told her it was so. Lilium brought a hand to her mouth and began crying. She walked straight to Kellina and buried her head against her in a tight embrace. Kellina held her firm and wept with her.

Ildradath walked over to Farlan, gave him a slight pat on his back, and shook his head. Farlan nodded back, affirming the silent condolences. Kellina looked at Ildradath.

"I'm sorry, Kellina," he spoke with tears in his eyes.

She nodded and looked back down as Lilium continued to cry against her chest. Several long minutes passed, and everyone was reluctant to break the silence or interrupt the flowing tears.

Kellina eventually managed to do so, and Lilium stepped back, finally able to look at the others in glances. "We found her this morning. She was in such a good mood yesterday. She was happy. Had been for the last few days, really. Was glad to see me and meet Farlan and learn that—" her voice broke as she held both hands against her tummy. "I'm with child," she finished.

Ildradath and Lilium smiled through tears. They both simultaneously stammered out their congratulations. Ildradath turned to Farlan and shook his hand while looking him in the eyes. Farlan nodded and responded, "Thank you."

Kellina continued. "Sheena, the woman you suggested see me about work, did so. She told me her situation and what you did. I trained her so I could come to see Mom. I'm so glad I did." She fought back more tears.

"I couldn't bear the thought of not having seen her again before she passed, but still, I wished she would be there to meet her grandchild. We had a wonderful time catching up. She spoke about your visit. Told me about the peekaboos and the time spent with Lilium. If she didn't tell me about you both twice, she must have three times. Your visit meant so much to her. She was so happy to host a paladin and spend time with Lilium.

"Lilium, she told me that it was your idea to make a double batch of her cake so that I would have some when I got here. Thank you."

Lilium forced a smile through her frown and nodded.

Kellina shook her head in disbelief. Tears flowed down Kellina's face once again.

"She passed peacefully. She was in such a good mood when she went to bed last night. It's a strange feeling to be here now, to be home, and yet my parents are not. The inn had become my home, but it was never truly 'home,' you know. But now this place is something different. It is home, and it is not." She paused to collect herself and then asked, "Paladin, can we ever truly return home? Is such a thing a lie?"

Ildradath looked back into Kellina's eyes, but he noticed Lilium watching him carefully. "I have found that every pure and true notion we ascribe to home is there to point us to the one we are journeying toward. We must be thankful for everything our Kadathian home was to us while setting our eyes ahead on Bright Haven."

Kellina nodded. "May it be so."

There was a pause in conversation as they stared at Elspeth's body's resting place. Each one treaded a sea of rushing thoughts and sorrow, but Ildradath silently began to draw comfort from the Divines.

Kellina cleared her throat and asked, "Would you say something that she might receive a proper burial? It would mean so much to her."

Ildradath nodded.

Kellina held one hand out to Lilium and the other to Farlan.

Ildradath began collecting his thoughts. He took a few moments to look skyward with closed eyes. "Elspeth was a woman after the Divines' own heart. She lived her faith, not as vanity but as a matter of course. In a world beset by the Abyss, she fought back in her way. She embodied a love for what is right and good. She was proud of you, Kellina, and I know there is more of her in you than you might realize."

Kellina softly smiled.

"Lilium, within a day of knowing you, she looked upon you with such love, and she had great confidence that you would do great things. She believed in you and your role in the quest. You proved her right."

Kellina squeezed Lilium's hand, and she smiled in response.

"Farlan, no doubt you felt her love and hospitality in your short time with her."

"Aye, like a son," Farlan was quick to affirm.

Ildradath continued.

"And I, as well. In my brief time of knowing her, she spoke words that assured me. She encouraged my faith. She spoke what I needed to hear, and the Divines, by their providence, made our paths cross. We are all the better for it.

"Such hospitality, kindness, warmth, and love are hallmarks of the Divines and Bright Haven itself. Some might dismiss such things as quaint and unable to change the course of our world, but when we look around, what do we see? People. People are very much this world. It is a shame that some who aspire to change the world for the better neglect the portion given to them, but this was not her. She had a way of affecting people with her love that made us all better. She believed in the better parts of those around her. She was not selfish with her love, and by it, she has changed us for the better."

Ildradath's voice became more assertive and emphatic. "I have this confidence before the Divines. They have made a home for us with them there, and it is Bright Haven. There is room for all who love what is right, pure, and good, who are selfless. It was made for such people as Elspeth, and I do not doubt that at this moment, she is even more full of love and rejoicing in the fruits of a life well lived. We are sad for our loss, and rightly so. We should be.

"However, let us not shed a single tear for her as if she was now in pain or suffering. She now knows that joy can abound to degrees we presently cannot fathom. She knows the Divines face-to-face while we see them through a mirror dimly. She is with Hamish again. She is with all the godly who have ascended before. And even now, I am sure she speaks of those she loves, each of us, with pride and with a desire that the Divines keep watch over us.

"Your child, Kellina, has an advocate in Bright Haven, a guardian, who will be in continual prayer. What we have lost, Bright Haven has gained, and I am convinced her love will be poured out upon us daily in greater measure than we knew before so that we yet gain more ourselves. Let us take heart and be glad that we had such a gift of Elspeth for a time—even if we would have chosen never to lose her—we lose her to something greater, and in love, we must accept this and let her go to her reward. May we honor her memory by loving as she did.

Ildradath finished by saying, "May she abide in the love of the Divines forever more. May it be so."

"May it be so," repeated Kellina, Lilium, and Farlan in unison.

Kellina walked over to Ildradath and hugged him, and Lilium joined in, too. Farlan walked over and patted Ildradath on his back and rested a hand on Kellina.

Lilium then scoured the surrounding area until she could find a handful of flowers, which still had beautiful blooms intact. If it were possible to plant a madrigaia on Elspeth's grave, she would have, but her gathered bunch was beautiful enough. During this, Farlan grabbed his vielle and looked at Kellina to eye her approval. She nodded.

Farlan cleared his throat as his fingers began to strum the slow, stirring melody of *My Jo*:

No birds sing and trees are now bare
Some may feel that it's not fair
Whether fair or head-covered gray
You've grown young again today
Autumn leaves have become deep
Just a little more then we sleep
Days gone by must stay in the past
Good times go and do not last
But when our time comes along
We will be sure to follow on
From loch to ben, and back again
My jo, we will meet again

Lassie, away, wait for us there
Aye, you took the low road home
This high road is ours to err
But we have some time to go, my jo
Lassie, away, wait for us there
Aye, you took the low road home

This high road will get us there
We'll arrive before you know, my jo

Bonnie look down with no more tear
We've done dried our crying here
You're better than you ever been
You've earned every laugh you ken
Mountain flowers hide today
But winter comes, winter away
Broken hearts are mended sweetly
Above where eyes cannae see
Though we still toil here below
When our work is done we'll follow
From hill to glen, and back again
My jo, we will meet again

They all went inside and took a seat at the dining table. There were some apples at the table, and a pitcher of water, but the nicest surprise was yet another batch of Elspeth's cakes cooked up and waiting. Though Kellina and Lilium did not have much of an appetite, they both instinctively knew how close to Elspeth they would make them feel. They were the first to grab pieces, and Ildradath and Farlan were quick to follow.

"Oh, Lilium," Kellina spoke, recalling something important with an upraised finger. She walked over to a corner table and grabbed a small canvas-wrapped bundle. She returned and placed it in front of Lilium. "Mother prepared this last night as a gift for you."

"For me?" Lilium was surprised.

Lilium untied the twine, which kept the canvas secured around the contents. A hair brush, a pipe with a pouch of leaf, and a small piece of parchment were inside. She picked up the parchment to read:

Lilium my deary, I hope this finds you well. I had a wonderful time when you were here, and I know these things might bring some comfort to you. The brush, because you have to be strong to be beautiful in this world. It is right for you to be beautiful, so be strong—the two are not exclusive. Mothers know this well. The pipe and leaf, because it is good to remember those who sacrificed and loved us more than we deserved. May the smell take you a measure closer to them, for their love is greater than you know. Below is the recipe for my prized cake so that you may enjoy its comfort whenever needed. And do not worry. Say a prayer, and I will send you all of the secret ingredient you need, plus a little extra. Love, Elspeth.

Lilium teared up as she read the parchment, but her face radiated joy. "If anyone ever deserved Bright Haven, it was her," she said.

Kellina beamed at the sight of Lilium's happiness. "When we heard the eruption, we prayed continually. It wasn't until the next day that we saw the great plume of smoke. She constantly prayed that all of you would return safely. She was in such a stern and worried mood for days. But then yesterday, while we rocked on the porch, she just looked at me, smiled, and said, 'They are okay. They are coming back here. All three of them."

"I just smiled back, but how could anyone know? I couldn't share her confidence. She was in such a good mood the rest of the day. She gathered these gifts for you and baked another batch of her cakes. We talked about names for her grandchild. She liked Sareth for a girl and Harlen for a boy. I had hardly thought about what name to choose, but we had a great time, and maybe no little disagreement over names.

"She said there were difficult days ahead but good ones, too. That things were going to be alright. She kissed me goodnight and gave me her final 'I love you' before turning in for the night."

Farlan said, "I cannot help but wonder if she could speak with the

Divines. She carried herself that way, and now, looking back, I think it was the case. Maybe it wasn't with words. Maybe it was. Regardless, you all came back. She was right. I take it your quest was successful?"

"Yes, but before we continue, I need to ask forgiveness first," Ildradath said. He then proceeded to succinctly explain the matter of his paladin name, and Kellina and Farlan were graciously understanding. He then turned to Lilium and, with a wink, asked, "Would you care to fill them in on the details?"

Lilium's eyes lit up. "Oh, would I!" She talked with childlike frenetic energy, zipping from detail to detail, incident to incident, sometimes having to stop and go back to add to something said earlier. Ildradath listened attentively. She told it with much more excitement than he would have, and she made it sound much grander than he recalled. She had endured it all so bravely, and most would not have.

Ildradath enjoyed seeing Kellina and Farlan's eyes go wide with surprise and horror from time to time, and he enjoyed nodding when they looked at him for affirmation that she was telling the truth.

Perhaps it was as grand as she made it out to be, he thought.

After she finished telling the story, they mingled about for a bit, and then they tended to necessary things before turning in for the night. Lilium fed and talked with Aerion while Ildradath watched. Kellina and Farlan tended to the goats.

The next day, Ildradath made it known that he would be returning to the tower outside of Haverstead.

"What am I to do?" Lilium inquired.

"What do you want to do?" Ildradath asked back.

"To go back with you," she said.

Ildradath nodded. "Very well. Come along then."

Kellina interjected, "You may stay with us if you'd like. Or if you go, you are always welcome back."

"Thank you," Lilium responded. "I will remember that. For now, I will go with him."

"And you? What will you do now?" Ildradath asked Kellina.

"Oh, I haven't decided yet. Someone needs to look after mom's place and goats. It could be a nice place to raise a family. I don't know. I don't want to give up the inn, though. Perhaps Sheena and her kids could keep this place for me. I guess I've got some thinking to do."

"Sounds like it," Ildradath responded. "I am sure it will work out, Divines willing."

"Yes, Divines willing," she responded.

Goodbyes were exchanged, and Lilium and Ildradath mounted Aerion. While holding hands and gently rocking on the front porch, Kellina and Farlan watched the trio ride off.

ꕈ

After returning to the tower, Ildradath unburdened Aerion and let him roam. Ildradath opened the tower, and he and Lilium carried the bags inside and placed them against a wall. They each sat to rest. They were worn out. Both of them felt that they could not move for a week and it would be too soon. As they relaxed, the quiet became obnoxious.

"Are we going to just sit around," Lilium inquired with a skeptical tone in her voice.

"Ha, I guess not. Too much to do to get ready. We shouldn't delay. Come along," he said.

They made their way to the top of the tower and ascended into the prayer room. Once there, they walked over to the quest chest. It sat there, just as they had left it.

"How do you know if your quest reward was granted," Lilium asked.

"Well, it's an old paladin secret. But I will share it with you. We carefully approach the chest and place a hand on each side." He motioned with his hands while making his face very stern as he acted out how to open the chest. "After doing so, we open the chest." He then grinned, amused by his attempt at sarcasm.

She stared at him and then giggled.

He stepped forward and actually opened the chest. Inside, there were two scrolls, one bearing Ildradath's name and the other Lilium's on a wax seal. Beneath Ildradath's scroll was the Abyss compass, and beneath Lilium's were multiple ingots of angelician silver. Ildradath took the compass and his scroll out.

A metal chain was attached to the body of the compass, which was a less-than-palm-sized flat silver disc with a sky-blue gem set within. The gem glowed faintly. The backside was engraved with the words, "Pray and Be Shown the Way." While staring into the gem, he heard a faint voice speaking his name, and it was the very voice of the Divines. "Come closer," Ildradath whispered to her.

She stepped forward. "Wow, is that the compass? There's another scroll? And metal?"

Ildradath pointed. "Yes, all of that is yours, and that metal is angelician silver."

She looked into his eyes with shock and then peered at the scroll in the chest. She extended a trembling hand to take it before abruptly stopping. "Can I?" she asked.

"Yes, go ahead," he said encouragingly.

She took it and then paused. "Can I?" she asked again.

"Yes, read it." Ildradath smiled, but he understood she was opening a life of burden. He removed the ingots and closed the chest. They both unfurled their scrolls and quietly read them.

Ildradath's scroll read:

A Paladin's sacrifice is never in vain
Train Lilium and then enter the Abyss
Set the captives free
We go with you

Lilium's scroll read:

Faith is its own reward, paladin
Through you the Order is reborn
We will be with you.

"Is yours the Divines' affirmation that you are a paladin?" Ildradath inquired.

"What?" Lilium was stunned. She stared blankly at him as she tried to understand what was happening.

"May I?" Ildradath asked while reaching out for her scroll. She allowed him to take it. He read it, nodded, and handed it back to her. "Just as I hoped."

"What do you mean?" she asked.

"By your actions, you proved what the Divines had set in motion. That you are a paladin. This scroll is their affirmation, their confirmation that you are a paladin. We need only conduct the Order's ceremony."

Lilium stared at him, then at the scroll, and then over at the chest. She was trying to wrap her mind around it.

Ildradath patted her on the back. "I wish I could be here to set the record straight should someone believe I was the reason for our quest's success."

"What do you mean?" she asked as she continued to stare at the scroll.

"You were there all along, and I could not have done it without you. Without your prayers, without your presence to keep me going—to remind me *why* I must do what has been ordained."

She was dumbfounded, and her head was spinning. She liked the thought of being a paladin, but it was so unexpected. She had not dreamed that such could be possible for her, and she strained to comprehend what all this would mean.

Ildradath pointed over to the ladder. "Come along. Let us go to Aerion."

"Okay?" she responded incredulously.

They made their way back down the ladder and stairs and outside. Aerion was grazing near the tower.

"Aerion, boy. Come here, please," Ildradath called out.

Aerion trotted over.

"Guess what?" Ildradath pressed Aerion.

Aerion softly neighed.

"The Divines have blessed Lilium. They have recognized her to be a paladin. She is to be accepted into the Order."

Aerion whinnied.

Ildradath turned to Lilium.

"Normally, this would be done with more pomp and circumstance, but we are the only three who remain." Ildradath rested a hand on her shoulder and looked her firmly in the eyes. "Lilium, tonight you must bathe and pray. You must confess. You must search your heart and truly wrestle with whether you will join the Order and uphold this calling upon your life. You must also choose a new name in keeping with your new life. If you do these things, we will conduct the ceremony, and you will give your oath."

Lilium looked at Aerion and then Ildradath. She nodded. "I am ready."

Later that evening, Lilium bathed and entered the prayer room, and Ildradath did as well. They took no supper. They prayed together for a time, and he brought a copy of the *Oracles of Faith*, which they took turns reading aloud. Ildradath then left her in solitude to pray and consider her life.

IV

When morning came, Ildradath and Lilium wore simple, white clothes, and a well-brushed Aerion stood close by. The weather was most unusual for Edjramor that morning. The sun's warmth shone upon the group while a cool, gentle breeze blew, which would occasionally and playfully push Lilium's brushed hair across her face. She would gracefully pull it back behind an ear each time without fuss. Wisps of clouds traveled on to some unknown destination, waving gently as they moved, and there was not a drop of rain to be found in the sky. The morning dew was in attendance for the ceremony; it clung happily to blades of grass, eager for the ceremony to begin soon as they had places to go.

Ildradath stood in front of Lilium and pulled out his sword. "Please kneel."

She looked at the sword and then at the grass. She knelt. He placed the sword on her right shoulder.

Ildradath spoke with cogency and sincerity. "You prayed when my faith faltered. You stood by me when I could not stand. You sought answers when I was afraid of the truth. You chose to believe when there were reasons to doubt. You had no sword, yet your words proved true. No shield, but you withstood the trials. No armor, yet you endured. You believed in the impossible, and because of that, I stand before you now.

"Having proved yourself in accordance with the sacred Paladin Order, do you accept the honor and burden of the Paladin Order by faith, to endure all odds and all trials, great and small, and to conquer all doubts and enemies, within and without, by the help of the Divines?"

She reflected upon all that had been said, upon all she had done, upon the horrors of the Abyss. *Wisely if sincerely,* she thought. *Wisely if sincerely.*

"I do," she answered confidently.

"Repeat this oath after me," Ildradath instructed.

Lilium repeated each phrase spoken by Ildradath, just as follows:

I am the true sword of the Divines
I heal the broken and lift the downtrodden
I go where I am called
I pursue the Abyss and the faithless
I speak truth and oppose falsehood
I am a keeper of Bright Haven's gates
Faith is my armor, my weapon, my crown
My reward is faith
My family is the Order
Till my final breath, this is my life
I am a Paladin

With those final words spoken, Ildradath moved his sword over to her left shoulder and continued.

"What shall be your name?" he asked.

Without hesitation, Lilium said, "I shall be the Gray Paladin."

Ildradath pulled his head back, recoiling in surprise. "The Gray Paladin? I wanted to escape that name. Why would you choose that?"

"I'd wear it as a badge of honor and tribute to you. I'll make it a name of redemption. So those who scoff may be put to shame, and those who hope in it be made to rejoice, for there is indeed a Gray Paladin in Edjramor. Their faith will not be in vain."

Ildradath cleared his throat and took a moment to maintain his composure. Her explanation touched him. "Well, your reasoning is flattering, convincing, and selfless. I admit it does not fit convention, but you *are* the first female paladin." His kind eyes looked upon her with admiration.

Lilium gently nodded in determination. "Yes, I will be the Gray Paladin." She then glanced up at Ildradath. "But you may call me Gray."

"Very well," he said with a smile. "I, Paladin Ildradath, in the presence of those gathered and by the will of the Divines, hereby declare you, Gray Paladin, to be a paladin of the Order and welcome you into our midst. May the Abyss shudder and Bright Haven rejoice. Arise, paladin." As he lifted his sword from her shoulder and sheathed it, the Gray Paladin stood, and Aerion nickered proudly.

Ildradath then turned his focus to Aerion. "Now, there is another matter. Aerion, I cannot and will not take you into the Abyss with me. You have been faithful, and it is right that we recognize that here and now. You may be formally bonded to another paladin and are even allowed to take a new name, or you may be released from service."

Aerion nickered his desire for continued service.

"Gray Paladin and Aerion, would you two be bonded?"

The Gray Paladin looked into Aerion's eyes. She loved him, but this brought a new weight to their relationship. "Yes," she replied.

Aerion nodded once.

"Gray, stand on his left side and place your right hand on his body." Ildradath stepped forward and helped position her hand over Aerion's heart.

"Aerion, you have proven yourself faithful to the Divines. You have been courageous in the face of certain death. You have outrun all dangers of this world and the Abyss. You have carried a paladin faithfully on his quest and returned successfully. You have proven you are indeed a paladin steed. Would you accept further service to the Paladin Order alongside the Gray Paladin, or would you be unburdened and set free?"

Aerion snorted.

"Very good. Would you keep your name or choose another?" Ildradath inquired.

Aerion whinnied loudly.

"Aerion the Gray?" Ildradath tilted his head and grinned. "May it be so."

The Gray Paladin smiled at Aerion the Gray.

"Would you, Gray Paladin, and you, Aerion the Gray, journey together, through valley and hill, against all dangers of the Abyss or this world, bound until death or the Divines part you?"

"Yes," the Gray Paladin replied.

Aerion the Gray huffed proudly and excitedly. His heart was already thumping at the thought of his next quest.

"Let us pray. Divines, bless these two, that they may both remain true to this oath, bound in service and in your sight. Strengthen and bless them that they may do all that is required of them. May it be so."

Ildradath walked forward to the Gray Paladin, "Welcome to the Order, sister." He embraced her. He then stepped over to Aerion the Gray, "I rejoice at your continued service to the Order." He hugged him around his neck, "Thank you, Aerion the Gray. You were perfect on our quest. I am proud of you. I know you will serve her well."

Aerion the Gray nuzzled him in return.

Ildradath stepped away from Aerion the Gray and allowed him to resume grazing.

"Come here, Gray Paladin." Ildradath motioned to his position near the tower door.

She walked over and stood next to him. She noticed he was looking at the tower door.

"You see this door?" he asked.

"Yes, several times now," she said.

He just shook his head and smiled. "Open it."

Gray attempted to do so, but it would not budge. She looked over at Ildradath. "It's locked."

Ildradath raised a hand in front of himself. "Now place a hand on the door, state your name, then enter."

She placed her right hand on the door and said, "Gray Paladin."

This time, the door gave way, and she stepped inside. Her mouth dropped wide open. The inside of the tower radiated. The stones were polished marble with gilded edges. Light emitted from every stone so that it was as bright as day inside. Smokeless torches burned at evenly spaced intervals in the lowest room.

"Come here," Ildradath spoke while motioning at the second closet door on the first floor.

Ildradath opened it to reveal a large velvet curtain. A large map that depicted most of the known world was embroidered on its face. Gray's eyes were immediately drawn to the four bright blue tower symbols. There was one in the Western Heights, the Evinwald, Edjramor, and Southshore.

"What? This was a closet, wasn't it?" she asked.

"It appeared so to you, yes. Now you have access to it. It actually contains a map and a door to the other towers Pythaganor built. There is another door on the other side of the curtain. Watch and follow behind me."

He stepped to the curtain, pushed it aside some, and gripped the handle of the door behind the curtain. "Western Heights," he spoke loudly. He then pushed the door open and walked through, and Gray followed behind him.

They stepped into a room that looked almost identical to the one they had left. They were now standing in the tower located in the Western Heights. Gray excitedly looked around and then hurried over to the exterior door.

"No!" Ildradath said quickly. "Not yet, Gray. This tower is on the edge of Hyrapolis, and you would likely be seen stepping out. You should wait."

Gray stopped, but she was disappointed. She was curious to see something of the Western Heights, especially given that her family had intended to find sanctuary there.

"Come along, let's go back through, and you can see the many other secrets of the tower." He motioned back towards the door from which they came.

"More?" she laughed and hurried behind Ildradath.

Once back through, she ran to the staircase, and Ildradath followed quickly. She ascended to the next floor, nearly tripping in the process, and barged into the kitchen. She was so eager to see inside the room that she barely noticed that the kitchen's door was ornate, engraved wood with silver fittings. The inside of the kitchen was as bright as the lower floor.

"Now that you are a paladin, you may access all of the secrets of this tower. Come here to these curtains." Ildradath motioned her over.

Gray stepped forward.

Ildradath said, "Close your eyes, pray for something like an apple, reach in through the curtains, and open your hand. Believe it will be placed in your hand."

Gray did as he said. She reached in, and to her delight, she felt an apple gently fill the palm of her hand. She pulled her hand out, looked at the apple, and then at Ildradath. She giggled with wide eyes. She could hardly believe it. She took a bite, and as she chewed, she covered her mouth with a hand. She shook her head and smiled.

"Another thing created by Pythaganor to bless the Order. Through it, the Divines bless with food and drink of any kind." Ildradath took a nearby mug and reached through the curtain. He quietly prayed, and he pulled the now full mug out."

He took a sip, followed by a longer drink. "Oh, wine," he sighed contentedly. He looked at Gray with a big smile. "It has been too long. In moderation and amongst the Order—remember that," he grinned with a wink. "Come along and let us go to the library—oh, wait."

He turned to the pantry door inside the kitchen and opened it, and he motioned for Gray to step forward into it. She approached the room, and her eyes widened, and with furrowed eyebrows and mouth agape, she shook her head in confusion. She looked at Ildradath and then back into the room. She entered.

Again, what had once appeared to only be a small pantry before now revealed a large dining hall with room to sit at least twenty at the long center table. Smokeless candles lined the center of the table, as well as two large candelabras hanging from the ceiling. There were portraits, weapons on racks, two fireplaces, and cushioned chairs around the edge of the room to recline and relax.

"Wow," she muttered through her mouth full of apple. "How is this in the tower?"

"Pythaganor explained it to me once. It did not help me understand." He looked over at Gray with a serious face and then quickly chuckled. "This, in my opinion, is perhaps the most important of all the rooms in these towers. It is a place full of mirth and companionship. Gray, do not neglect the importance of the bonds and memories you forge with fellow paladins.

"I implore you, bring back the feasts and the celebrations and songs, for it is right and good to laugh and joke and be merry, to enjoy the friendships of those who walk your path. It is another way to strike back at the Abyss." Ildradath nodded as he surveyed the room. "In fact, yes, we shall feast before I depart. Come, let us go to the library now."

They then hurried along to the library. Gray was first to arrive, and she hurtled through the door and into the center of the room. The wall to her right caught her attention. She turned toward it and covered her mouth. Her hands began to tremble.

A multitude of small portraits hung on the wall. Each portrait was that of a paladin, and their names were carved on the bottom of their frame. The features of their faces were lifelike. There were so many portraits. So many faces of the fallen. She looked at Ildradath and frowned before looking back. She held back her tears as she began to understand the time Ildradath spent in this room.

Ildradath moved to her side and put a hand on her shoulder. "We must choose to live with gratitude for their sacrifices. And we must live in a way that honors who they were. This is how we remember them. Before you came, I had forgotten this."

Gray continued surveying the portraits for some time, taking note of names she had heard Ildradath speak before. "I did not realize just how many had fallen," Gray spoke.

"Yes, but this wall includes those who had fallen before the crusade or were taken in old age. But otherwise, yes, many of these men fell during the crusade. The Order was at its largest then."

Gray placed a hand on Ildradath's arm. "I'm sorry, Ildradath."

"Thank you. Understand Gray, that these now are your brothers, just as I am. So, I am sorry for you too. For they are your family, many of whom you may never meet unless we can free their souls from the Abyss so that they may ascend to Bright Haven."

She nodded.

Ildradath motioned to the set of curtains at the back wall. "Come along. This is where books are stored. They may be taken out when you are going to study. Afterwards, you may place them back. As before, you reach in, prayerfully ask for a specific book, and then it will be placed in your hand."

"But how do I know what to ask for?" she asked.

Ildradath reached through the curtain, silently prayed, and pulled out a small book. "This one is the list of all books contained in this library. Most of the paladinariums have copies of the same books, but they are not shared between towers. You may keep this one handy to know which to ask for."

"What do you recommend? Where should I start?" she asked.

"Ah, that is a good question. All are worth reading, but some should absolutely be a priority. Let's see."

Ildradath reached a hand through the curtains and prayed. His arm suddenly dipped under the weight of the stack of books, which he quickly moved his other hand to support before walking over to one of the stands near a chair.

"I would start with these. There is *Prayer and the Dangers of Verisimilitude*, *Virtues of the Chapel*, *Forging and Blessings*, by yours truly, *Chronicles of the Faithful*, and the *Oracles of Faith*."

"You wrote the book on forging?" Gray asked.

"Well, the best one," he replied with a wink. "Truthfully, though, it is the culmination of the labors of earlier paladins."

She smiled back at him and bent over to view the books. Each looked immaculate and was neatly bound.

"Oh, one more!" Ildradath spoke out. Once more, he reached into the curtains, prayed, and withdrew his hand with a book. "*Aberrations of the Abyss*. This book is a compendium of the many abyssians and their variations that come out of the Abyss or serve the Old Ones. It also documents in detail what we know of the Old Ones. When you study this, under no circumstances should you study more than one abyssian or Old One a day, and your study should both be preceded and followed by a reading of the oracles, understand?"

"Yes," she spoke with hesitation and a sly smile. This would be the first book she read. As much as she had been horrified by the sight of the abyssians, studying them would be fascinating and would help her overcome any remaining apprehensions.

Ildradath had begun to turn away when he realized that smile really wasn't setting well with him. "I mean it," he replied with a pointed finger and stern, fixed eyes. "Curiosity will get the better of you, and next thing you know, you are looking at one after another and studying everything about them. It leads down an irksome path. Their other-worldliness becomes overwhelming and draining upon one's sanity and faith. Keep to one a day."

Her smile quickly disappeared. "Understood." She raised her eyebrows and looked away as she noted how that seemed to escalate quickly.

Ildradath walked over to the library's closet door and opened it, and Gray saw a room with a dozen beds. The room looked cozy, and there were nightstands and chests next to each bed. All of the bedding looked cozy, and for a moment, she resented having slept on a pallet inside the tower for those first months.

After looking around, Gray left the room and hurried to the

floor with the forge. She then opened the closet door and barged inside. There were a multitude of weapons and shields around the perimeter of the room. There were stacks of straw, wooden dummies, and hanging targets.

"This is the chapel," Ildradath informed Gray after catching up to her.

"The chapel?" Gray looked back at him in confusion. "This does not look like any chapel I have ever seen."

"Yes, but it is a special place of worship for paladins. When we train, we call it 'holding chapel.' When a paladin fights, they must use their faith above all, and if they train properly, they will be exhausted and demoralized, unable to finish the training sessions without many prayers. Training must be rigorous, for the Abyss seeks to exploit every weakness, and disciplined training cultivates a disciplined spirit which communes with the Divines continually, even in combat, for faith is a paladin's armament."

"And that is how you were able to fight all those abyssians?" she asked.

"Yes. Faith empowers every act and deed of a paladin." Ildradath turned toward Gray. "I want to take some time to make certain preparations before I leave. For one, I could use some extra training and conditioning. Faith moves mightily, but even the Divines frown upon a lazy paladin. Secondly, you must receive years' worth of training in much less time, maybe a few weeks at most, depending on how you progress. The Abyss is always at work, always scheming, so I should not delay more than necessary."

Gray did not like the thought of Ildradath leaving at all, so any delay to this was welcomed news. Moreover, she much liked the thought of being trained. She was not keen on the prospect of being let loose on the world as an untrained paladin. "I will train hard. I will do what it takes."

"It will be needed. With much prayer and reading books in

between sessions, you will advance quickly, but some things take time. Swinging weapons, blocking with shields, and wearing armor are not things you do well overnight."

"I understand," she said. Gray continued to take in her surroundings. "I was wondering. Why have there never been any women paladins before?"

Ildradath looked at her and shrugged. "I don't know. Most men serve in the clergy, teaching and running places of worship, whereas women become Sisters who minister to orphans and the poor. Few are so devout that they serve the Divines in these ways, and it is rare for even a man to become a paladin. Some things are only the way they are because that's the way they have always been. Nothing more."

Gray nodded as she walked the perimeter of the room, taking in all the sights.

Ildradath could see the awe in her eyes. "I was thinking there is no better time than the present to hold chapel. What do you say we eat a light meal and then begin?"

"Yes, I am excited!" she responded.

After eating, they returned to the chapel, but before entering, Ildradath stopped and turned to Gray. "I must warn you before we enter that nothing must be taken personally, as fellow paladins should never intend to truly hurt another during training. Understand?"

"Yes," she responded.

He began to go through the door again but once more stopped. "I want to emphasize that there is much in training a new paladin, which can be unpleasant, but everything has a purpose. Remember this, okay?"

Gray shrugged. "Okay, now may we go inside, or do you have something else you'd like to add."

He paused for reflection, shook his head, and then stepped through the door. As soon as they were both through, he turned and, all in one motion, backhanded her hard enough to knock her to the floor.

She looked at him with daggers in her eyes. She was stunned.

"How does that make you feel?" Ildradath inquired.

"What do you mean, 'how does that make you feel,'" she replied in a mocking tone. "Angry. That was unfair. I wasn't ready."

"First rule of the Chapel. The Abyss does not care how you feel." Ildradath rubbed the back of his hand. "Second rule of the Chapel. The Abyss strikes without provocation."

He extended a hand to help her up, and she reached to accept his assistance. He retracted his hand so that hers grasped the air, and he walked away. "Third rule of the Chapel. In combat, you must avail yourself."

Ildradath went across the room from her and grabbed a practice sword. They would start with only swords, and they would progress to using shields and then other weaponry. He motioned her to retrieve her sword. She did so.

Ildradath bowed while maintaining eye contact with her. "The fourth rule of the Chapel. Mercy and justice assume the capacity for violence."

Gray followed Ildradath's lead and bowed. He stepped forward and stabbed at her. She attempted to parry it, but his sword struck her shoulder solidly.

"Again, but parry with more force." He showed her what he meant, and he exclaimed loudly as he did so. "Sometimes vocalizing helps us put more force into our actions. Do not be afraid to be loud in combat. Let your opponent fear your voice, for your voice is as the presence of the Divines themselves."

He struck at her again, and she shouted as she parried his blow. Ildradath felt his shoulder turn toward her, exposing his side. "Good, much better! Again."

And so, they trained daily over the coming weeks. Ildradath added new techniques each time, introduced other weapons and shields, and taught footwork, spacing, and timing. It was the harnessing of faith as its own implement in combat that most excited Gray.

While in the chapel, Ildradath taught her of the special feats of prayer that paladins are granted. Harnessing faith adds power to their blows; it empowers their armor; it sharpens their senses, and it works wonders against their foes. These wonders are what some call "magic."

"Tower, torches off in the chapel," Ildradath spoke. The chapel went dark. "Gray, hold out the palm of your hand as if you want something to be placed in it."

She did so. "Okay, now what?"

"Pray for the Divines to fill your palm with light," he said.

"With light?" she asked with puzzlement.

"Yes," he said, and then added for clarity, "And believe that an orb of light will fill it."

She did so, and a dim ball of light spontaneously appeared in her hand. "Whoa," she gasped in response.

"Yes, this is perhaps one of the most useful things to know. The Abyss loves the dark, and we must be ready to dispel it. Now, make the light brighter."

She did so, and the light filled the room.

"Brighter," he commanded.

She did so, and the light became nearly blinding.

"Good," he said. "Now, cast the light upward so that it clings to the ceiling."

She tossed it upward, and the light gracefully ascended to the ceiling where it hung.

Ildradath clapped briefly and said, "Very good, Gray. Very good. It took me a month to do that."

"A month? Pfft. That was easy," she laughed.

"Yeah, rub it in. Our faith connects us to the power of the Divines, and our will is able to exercise their power as our own, as long as our intentions are true to theirs. We must neither be prideful nor doubting in our use of faith. When we are in the right place spiritually and mentally, it flows effortlessly from us. Instantly, without speaking a word or even consciously praying, our faith can manifest what we need the moment we need it." He then added for emphasis, "We will it to be. It is mysterious, and it is something you shouldn't overthink."

"Got it," she replied. "Is there something else I can try?" she asked.

"Hmm. Sure. You see that straw target over there? Extend your hand toward it as if throwing a dagger, and in doing so, pray and believe a dagger of light will shoot out towards it," he said.

Gray had never thrown a dagger before, but she had seen it done. She brought her hand to her shoulder and rapidly extended it toward the target. A dagger of light shot forth and struck it. "Haha! Look!" she exclaimed.

"I see," Ildradath said. "But you missed the center of it. You need to aim—"

Gray threw another one; this time, she intentionally threw it towards the wall but willed it to turn and strike the center of the target, and it did.

"Well, I officially hate you now," Ildradath spoke in a deadpan tone.

Gray's eyes beamed. She was ecstatic and barely able to contain herself.

He smiled back at her. "I am glad, Gray. It means less time is needed to get you where you need to be before I leave."

With that comment, Gray's smile fled. She looked at the floor and then back at him. "Yeah, I guess you are right. Take a break?"

"Sure, let's go grab a snack. You've earned it," he replied.

They laid hands on the forge and prayed silently. The forge began to warm. Its heat grew and grew until a fire erupted.

"Keep praying, Gray," Ildradath instructed. "It is not ready."

They continued to pray until the forge roared within its confines. It was louder than Gray expected. The heat was intense, but she could tell that its heat was wondrously restricted. Had this been a normal forge, the room would be an oven.

Ildradath directed Gray's every move over the next three days. She worked the ingots one by one. Heating and then shaping. For hours upon hours, Ildradath led her through each strike of the hammer, each turn on the anvil, every heating in the forge, every quench, every turn of the whetstone, grind, and polish. Blisters developed on her hands, and her forearms were exhausted and barely able to grasp anything. She began her days clean and finished them covered with streaks of black soot and char and drenched in sweat.

During their time forging, Ildradath also repaired his armor, sharpened his sword, and strengthened his war hammer. He also fashioned a small setting on the top of his chest plate for the Divines' compass. He would keep the chain attached to it and around his neck while in the Abyss, and the setting would allow him to easily secure it in between uses. Moreover, it would look nice.

Finally, Gray had made her first sword and set of armor, and she had even managed to make a necklace fitting for Habsjuradan's fragment. Ildradath looked over every piece she had made and gave a final inspection.

While examining her sword, he said, "There is no delaminating, no cracks or warps. Seems sharp, which we shall put to the test soon enough. But it is an inch longer than it should be by our design, the handle is a fingernail width thicker on this side than the other, and the guard has a very slight but noticeable degree of difference in the angle from the center. Oh, and it appears the blade is a hair width thicker in some parts. It does have a rather nice balance, though." He gently swung it through the air as he finished speaking.

Gray bit the inside of her lip. Each critique stung. She had labored intensely, and her heart was poured into every beat of the hammer.

He held her sword out for her to take. "It is a much finer sword than the first one I made. Well done. You are off to a great start."

Her eyes brightened. She did not see that commendation coming. "Thank you. I did have your help, though." She held the sword and carefully took it through a series of motions to feel its weight.

"I am still amazed at how it is so much lighter than it looks," she remarked.

"Yes, a blessing of the material the Divines give us. It will land with the heft of a sword several times its weight, rest assured. And in due time, as you quest, you may ask for blessings to bestow upon it. These can make it all the more deadly or serve purposes beyond combat, like how I would use my sword to learn the truth during disputes or to interrogate cultists.

"You will be able to do so for your armor, too. For example, my chest plate has a blessing of sustainment. While I fight, it nourishes me, so I do not have to eat, drink, or sleep. It allows me to fight without stopping. A little more training, this time with your real arsenal, and you should be ready."

Gray nodded.

VI

Ildradath called for a feast of celebration for the successful quest, for Aerion the Gray's continued service, and that the Gray Paladin was to become the next Adjuror of the Order.

A large portion of honied oats mixed with diced apples, pears, and apricots was prepared for Aerion, and the group reflected with gratitude for all they had accomplished together. Aerion had grown during their journey, not only in his spiritual strength and will, but his body had changed. He was not the smaller, weak horse first found lying in a stall. His coat was sleek, his eyes sharp, and his frame was muscular and taller. He was a paladin's horse, and no man could look upon him without being impressed.

Ildradath and Gray continued the feast in the dining hall. Roasted duck, pig, lamb, and venison lay before them. Bowls and plates filled with stew, roasted and creamed vegetables, fresh fruit, and fresh loaves of bread filled the space between. A pitcher of dark wine and another of water rested next to several goblets. Multiple candles were lit, and the room radiated joy. A blessed lute that had belonged to the paladin Cresinor hung from a wall, and it was playing a song he had written, *The Joy of Days Gone By.*

Ildradath prayed, "Divines, we give thanks for all that you are and all you have done and will do. We celebrate the life you have given us and the people you have placed in our lives, and we ask you to bless this gathering and the food to the wellbeing of our bodies and souls. May it be so."

"May it be so," Gray replied.

Gray and Ildradath heartily partook of all that was set before them. They had not eaten so much—perhaps in their whole lives. They partook of the wine, though with moderation, for it was not that all paladins forsook it. They forsook taking it in the manner and for the baser reasons most would. Its consumption was an act reserved for partaking within the Order, not the world.

Ildradath and Gray told jokes and spoke of their fondest memories. At one point, Gray could not control a loud burp, which had surprised even her. Ildradath, knowing full well such things happen, missed no opportunity to poke fun at her, and she laughed at herself—until Ildradath bested her with his own—at which time she then directed her laughter at him.

Ildradath told great stories of paladins past and humorous moments shared in celebrations. They laughed to the point of tears, and they felt a gratitude and optimism about the future which they had not felt in far too long.

But as with all great celebrations, there comes in a strange hour of the night a sobering silence, an unwelcome visitation of somber realities. The music continued to play, but words no longer filled the air. Each drifted in thought about the splendid time they were having and that it would eventually come to an end. The void in their conversation became another presence in the room.

Ildradath found himself reclined and staring at the table, and Gray did so as well. She stole looks at him occasionally. She had been keenly aware over the last week that, at some point, he would announce when he would be entering the Abyss. She felt a desperate hope that perhaps the silence might linger the rest of the night rather than be broken by those very words.

"I must leave tomorrow," his voice spoke with a strain of disappointment. "If I stay longer, I worry I may become too attached to how things are now or that I may shrink back and grow to fear the very thing I must do next."

Gray only nodded and swirled her goblet around. She watched the watered-down wine lap the inside edges. Her right foot quickly tapped the ground. If there had been a way to stay in their present moment forever, somehow without forsaking what must take place, she would have willed it so.

"Do you think you will ever be able to make it out of the Abyss?" she inquired.

He stared across the banquet table and into the distance and began tapping the edge of the table with his hand, and before speaking, he looked, pursed his lips, and exhaled. "That is not for me to worry about."

"I am. Right now. And I don't see how I'll ever *not* worry about it," Gray insisted.

Ildradath leaned forward as he spoke. "What lies ahead of you will require all of your attention, Gray. What I go to do is certain death, but it is a simple matter. I go to free the captive faithful that they may ascend to their reward. I hope that my presence there will cause the Abyss to expend great energy contending with me and that it may buy you more time to rebuild the Order. I will draw their attention. Every soul freed will further deprive it of energy and hinder the Old

Ones' schemes. Nevertheless, it will eventually lash out with renewed vigor, and it will never stop seeking to awaken the Dread One.

"It is difficult enough to build something, let alone while beset by the Abyss. You must rebuild under the threat of dangers around every corner."

"I will manage," she muttered with defiance.

"You have to contend with more than cultists and abyssians, Gray. You must find those faithful to the Divines. You must wrestle against men with calloused hearts who would rather see you fail than help you. They will despise your youth. You must be slow to take offense and slow to give offense. You must turn foe to friend. You must instill faith in the doubting. The Order is not built on the carrion of the Abyss. It is the body of the Divines, the living faithful."

"Got it," she snapped as she looked away from Ildradath.

"You knew this day was coming before we even set out on our quest," he insisted.

"This day looked differently back then," she quickly replied.

Ildradath nodded. "You are right. I was looking forward to death and wanted nothing more to do with this world. I believed the Order would end with me. I was wrong. I would like to stay here and rebuild. But I must leave that now to someone who I believe, thankfully, is better suited. You will become the de facto Adjuror of the Order. You will rebuild. You have been appointed for it."

These things made sense to Gray, but it did not lessen how conflicted she felt. She permitted herself to feel this way, but she then forced herself to think about practical matters. She did not have much time left with Ildradath. "Do you have any suggestions on how I should begin? What should I do first?"

Gray looked at Ildradath, and he met her gaze.

Ildradath leaned onto the edge of the table. "Firstly, I encourage you to pay attention to events in the Eastern Reaches, for heresy grows there, and the Order must intervene. Secondly, the cultists are doing something in the Deep Tides, and these schemes cannot go unchallenged. Glenmore's harbormaster spoke of someone referred to as 'the man in yellow' who may be at the heart of this activity. They are building something.

"Thirdly, the Evinwald is a fount of the faithful, and their seamanship knows no equal. They will make fervent allies. Nurture this. Moreover, you should never navigate the Crashing Coasts or the Deep Tides without a captain of the Evinwald. Promise me you will always heed this."

Ildradath paused and awaited her response.

"You have my word," she replied.

Ildradath continued. "Fourthly, the emperors of the Western Heights had once been loyal to the Order, but I fear they have grown to love the things of this world. They did not answer the Order's call for aid when we needed it most. See if you can earn their support again. Seek the faithful amongst them and prove your worth.

"Fifthly, following the crusade, many paladins' armor and weapons were stolen by vultures looking to turn a profit. Find these and return them to their rightful place within the Order. Future paladins will benefit greatly, and it is not right that these artifacts have been despoiled and are even used by corrupted men to impersonate paladins. They have added insult to what we have suffered, and as long as such men go about freely, unchallenged, their vile deeds will only make your legitimate claim as paladin contested.

"Sixthly, as the Order grows, you will not be alone in addressing these matters. Seek the Divines' guidance in prayer. They will direct you to the most pressing needs. I have faith that your quests will cause your path to cross with those ordained to become paladins. Keep your eyes open, and be discerning. Many things are not what they seem, so investigate all things carefully. Eldritch signs and powers, as well as the activity of the Abyss, are clever at hiding—even in plain sight. Be vigilant and stand fast against all the trials ahead of you. I believe in you. Keep the faith. The Divines will guide you."

Gray nodded and then returned to staring at the edge of the table. "Well, and here I was worrying that I might get bored."

Ildradath smiled at her remark and leaned forward even more as he grabbed one of the large bunch of grapes from a platter close to Gray. He plucked a couple of grapes and popped one into his mouth.

"Enough of all this. We are breaking an unspoken rule of our feasts," he said as he chewed.

"What is that?" Gray replied glumly.

"We don't discuss the affairs of the Order during a feast." He then reached back and flung a grape at her face.

Gray's mouth dropped wide open, and she looked at him in disbelief. "That stung!"

"Hmm. I wouldn't know," he said coldly. His eyes then traced a line from her eyes to the remaining large bunch of grapes on the platter near her. He then looked back at her eyes and winked.

She lunged for the bunch of grapes, and he jumped from his seat to put some distance between them. Armed with grapes, they ran about, ducked behind chairs, and battled, each hurling their armament with comical purpose. Laughter refilled the dining hall.

VII

The moment had arrived, and they descended through the once-forbidden, rug-covered trap door on the bottommost floor of the tower to reach where the portal device lay. There was a single, well-lit large room, and there was no reason the space should feel ominous other than the single covered object that lay against a wall. Ildradath walked over, took the sheet off the device, and extended the metallic arms, which held various colored crystals clasped along even intervals. The contraption was only half a foot tall, but its arms stretched out to about ten feet. It contained a complex series of gears that connected to a small lever, and this would orient the crystals into the necessary positions to activate the portal.

Ildradath drew close to the Gray Paladin. He was in full armor, save for his helm, which he had not yet donned. The blue jeweled compass swirled gently within its setting on his chest, his war hammer rested on his back, and his left hand held his shield while keeping his helm tucked against his waist. His eyes were illuminated, shining forth a righteous determination, but they gazed downward, knowing that only difficult days were ahead for both of them.

He wished he could say something elegant, something that might make the coming days easier. He knew all too well that rousing words were no real boon when it came to fighting the Abyss. Still, his heart was burdened for her, given all that she needed to do, but at the same time, he was eager to embark on his quest to strike at the Abyss.

The Gray Paladin looked at him. Like him, she had donned her armaments, save for her helm. Beneath the ruins of that old windmill, he was her savior when they first met, and in the end, she had the honor of saving him. Perhaps in another life, he could have been just a mentor, her uncle, or even her father, but he had become much more. He was her paladin brother. Now, they were parting ways to continue their ordeal, to save Kadath. The immensity of that idea was too much to properly comprehend, and it felt preposterous for her to be included within its framework. But such were the times, and such was their destiny.

"Gray, I will miss you. And all your questions, too," Ildradath said with a soft smile, hoping that the modicum of levity might make what was about to happen somehow easier.

Gray nodded. "I will miss you, brother. I will pray continually for you, and I will pray that we will meet again one day. I will rebuild the Order. I will not relent. We will be ready for whatever lies ahead, and we will oppose the Abyss at every turn. I will bring back the feasts and memorials, and we will save you a seat at our table. May the Divines direct your steps and your blade."

She moved forward and wrapped her arms around him as best she could, and he eagerly did so in return. Their armor put an uncomfortable distance between them; still, their embrace was not rushed, as neither wanted to depart the sweetness of the present moment. They would soon be apart, but they were in this together.

Tears quietly crept their way down each other's cheeks, but they were no secret. They were glad for them, for they were appropriate and right and good. They embodied the weight, significance, and sincerity of all they had become together, as well as the righteous concern for what the other must do.

"I love you, sister. Thank you for everything," Ildradath managed to say.

"I love you too, brother, and thank you," the Gray Paladin replied.

After letting go of each other, Ildradath turned around and stepped forward to the metal device on the ground. "As I depress that lever with my foot, I will speak my name, and the portal will open. It takes just a moment to fully open. As soon as I am through, you must push it again as you state your name to close it. It will take a moment to fully close, but you must not delay closing it as soon as I am through. Be ready for anything."

Ildradath donned his helm and lowered his visor, pulled out his sword, and raised his shield.

"Understood," the Gray Paladin replied. She donned her helm and held her sword and shield at the ready.

Ildradath raised his left foot and decisively stepped on the lever while stating his name, and he immediately moved his foot back into fighting stance.

The soft clicking of hidden gears quickly transformed into a low, rumbling hum. Unfurling from the metal frame on the floor, a blackish, purple glowing curtain ascended upward to the ceiling. A stench blew into the room, carried by an odd wind, and horrid sounds emanated from the portal, along with a fog that poured across the floor. The strange, dangerous, eldritch land of the Abyss stretched out into the distance, as far as the eye could see.

Ildradath rushed through the portal without another word spoken, and the Gray Paladin quickly stomped the fog-shrouded lever behind him while shouting her name.

The portal reversed and began closing just as it had opened, the curtain descending back toward the metal frame. She heard snarling noises and Ildradath shouting. The grotesque head of an abyssian flew into the room and onto the floor somewhere just before the curtain of the portal had fully closed. She scanned the room, looking for where it landed, but the fog obscured it. Finally, as the fog dissipated, its form and movement became visible.

The creature had multiple eyes on its face, sharp fangs, and a large distended jaw, and it was covered in dark green, scaly, wart-ridden skin. The decapitated head lay there, all of its eyes moving in unison, searching the room. They fixed on the Gray Paladin in unison. A long, forked tongue unfurled from its mouth. The tongue flicked about until it gained traction on the stone floor so that it could pull itself towards her. Little by little, flick by flick, the head pulled itself closer. It was still making faint hissing, gurgling noises.

The Gray Paladin sheathed her sword, took off her helm, and grimaced in righteous indignation. She stepped towards it and raised her right foot waist-high before defiantly bringing it down to crush the head with a twist of her heel. She felt the crunch and squish beneath her boot.

She smiled wryly while staring at what remained of the crushed foe. "Time to hold chapel."

ABOUT THE AUTHOR

Garet Davidson was born and raised in middle Tennessee. He has attended various colleges and ultimately received his B.S. in Criminal Justice from Bethel University. He served in the Metro Nashville Police Department from 2011 to 2024, taking an early retirement in order to pursue his passion for stories.

His interest in stories and their effect on others may have been kindled after he was introduced to Stephen King at the age of four (4). While running through the house, he sprinted into the living room, whereupon he looked over the couch to see multiple people transforming into werewolves in a dark church. That scene from *Silver Bullet,* the film adaptation of Stephen King's *Cycle of the Werewolf,* is still living rent-free in his head to this day.

Other authors who had an early influence on him include Terry Brooks, J.R.R Tolkien, H.P. Lovecraft, and Edgar Allan Poe. His first name actually comes from the character Garet Jax of Terry Brook's *The Wishsong of Shannara.*

Garet is an eclectic individual who enjoys many things, including strength training, video games, and a good whisk(e)y and cigar or pipe. He is also a co-host and co-creator of the show *IA: The Good, The Bad, The Ugly* which showcases actual stories of police conduct.

He is very thankful for his amazing wife and four wonderful children, and he aspires to make a positive difference in the lives of others.

OTHER WORKS

PALADIN SERIES

Book Two: Chronicles of the Faithful

This book highlights important stories involving other paladins of Kadath. Vesuvimorian, Irwinnor, Haptistrian, Pythaganor, Meliador, and Athanasor are counted among those featured. Readers will learn more about these paladins and Kadath's history.

Book Three: The Dread One

This book follows the return of the Paladin Order. Join the Gray Paladin as she seeks to protect mankind and foil the Dread One's plans. Readers will not be able to unsee what they witness unfolding in this sequel.

Book Four: Rending the Heavens

This book follows the dramatic events of book three, and providing details about it at this time would spoil several important events in book three.

Aberrations of the Abyss

This special book is a collection of mythos, facts, and depictions of the Old Ones, their abyssian creatures, and the Abyss. It is a fun companion book to the narrative of the other books.

FATE WEAVER SAGA

The Men Who Move Mountains

A hulking man barges into a snowed-in hamlet near a city under attack. The surprising guest rests and tells the legend of the rag-tag group of strongmen performers known as the "Men who Move Mountains." Secrets and betrayal put those men in the middle of a battle long in the making, but the storyteller has an important point he traveled a long way to make.

The Brothers Who Break Bonds

This story is told after the events of The Men Who *Move Mountains*. Join the storyteller as he tells a group of young men about Edha and Jahani's beginning and how fate forced them together.

The Women Who Went to War

This story picks up concurrent with the events occurring in real-time as the storyteller relays the story of The Brothers Who *Break Bonds*. It follows historical events to their dramatic conclusion.

The Kraken and the Siren

The storyteller takes the audience back in time to Magnar and Aedriella's unlikely romance. Join them as they fall in love; join Magnar as he seeks revenge with the help of a fate weaver.

THE PLANES WARS

Necromantic

Morrigan is a necromancer. She can't remember much about her first life other than it ended in a fireball cast by a cruel wizard. She does remember she loved a man, and nothing will stop her from bringing him back. But what happens if those you love are locked behind death's wall, forever removed from the cycle of rebirth?

The Second War for the Last Gate Key

There are two weeks left. Two weeks, and then the planes will converge for the first time in 1,000 years. Eleven planes worth of armies will finally be able to descend upon the final free plane in order to seize the last plane gate key. Millions will suddenly appear near the fortress city; the skies will swarm; the seas will teem; the underground will crawl in mass. The heroic and the ordinary people of the last free plane have been preparing for this day, for it was coming. For generations, it was always coming. And its day was upon them.

Join dwarves, sea elves, gnomes, humans, northern and southern orcs, pixies, troglodytes, Morrigan, and more as they defend the gate key. Witness spectacular feats of courage, martial prowess, and magic as the largest war in the history of the twelve planes unfolds in just two short days on land, sea, sky, and the underground.

STAND-ALONE WORKS

A Candle for the Darkness

One of Japan's most cunning and elusive shinobi has gone into hiding following defeat at the hands of Oda Nobunaga. A messenger arrives, desiring to arrange Oda's assassination while promising the necessary help to ensure this revenge will be a success. Learn the story of the Honno-ji incident and the supernatural forces responsible for it.

Songs from the Suffering

Sara, a gifted violinist, grew up hearing her poor neighbor repeatedly abused by her man. Now, she performs music tragically inspired by such victims to raise awareness of this societal ill. With blood dripping down her neck, she wakes one day to a blurry figure pacing back and forth in front of her under the orange glow of the vintage Edison bulbs in her music studio. *How did I get here?* she wonders. Neither Sara nor her soon-to-be killer saw this day coming.

A Collection of Short Stories and Poems

The title really says it all. Really. It's just a collection of short stories and poems. Or is it? Maybe it's a stunning, award-worthy novel with a clever title? Only one way to find out. Well, with social media nowadays, there are probably several. It's really just a collection of short stories and poems, though. I promise.

www.ingramcontent.com/pod-product-compliance
Lightning Source LLC
Chambersburg PA
CBHW022220010726
47493CB00002B/529